DRAGON LAND

MAUREEN REYNOLDS

DRAGON LAND

BLACK & WHITE PUBLISHING

First published 2014
by Black & White Publishing Ltd
29 Ocean Drive, Edinburgh EH6 6JL

1 3 5 7 9 10 8 6 4 2   14 15 16 17

ISBN 978 1 84502 743 8

Typeset by RefineCatch Limited, Bungay, Suffolk
Printed and bound by Grafica Veneta S.p.A

For my grandfather Charles Dwyer, of the Royal Dublin
Fusiliers, who fought at and was gassed at Ypres, 1915

The Somme (Don't Think)

The officer shouted, 'Over the top,'
Pick up your heels, run till you drop,
Don't think about your loving wife,
Or the children who are the light of your life.
Forget the girl who kissed you goodbye,
Who vowed to be true as time went by.
Never mind that your life has been in vain,
That you'll never see your home again.
Don't think about the tears and pain
Or lying dead in the pouring rain.

Maureen Reynolds

ACKNOWLEDGEMENTS

My thanks go to the Archive Department at the University of Dundee for all their help on the Dundee College of Education in the 1920s.

To Bob Thomson for sharing his memories of his Merchant Navy days, when he sailed to the Far East.

A big thank you as usual to my family for all their help with the Internet.

Finally to Karyn for her helpful comments and suggestions, and to all the team at Black & White Publishing.

CONTENTS

I

EASTER 1932

My mother always loved clocks. As far back as I remember there was always the quiet ticking of our old grandfather clock with its deep, sonorous chimes, and the delightful carriage clock, which sat on the mantelpiece and struck the hours with tinkling, melodic sounds. The alarm clock in the bedroom, which had to be wound up every night and sounded like a screeching parrot, always annoyed my father. Mum, however, always said the clocks were the heartbeat of the home, and Dad would smile fondly at her and nod his head.

As I headed down Cotton Road at the end of my time at Ann Street School, I felt sad that the clocks she so loved were ticking away her life. Slowly but surely, bit by bit, *tick, tick, tick, tick.*

The cold wind that had blown in from the east slapped against my face, and my hands were freezing in spite of my thick woollen gloves. Polly, one of my colleagues at school, said the wind had come straight from Siberia and I didn't disagree with her.

I tried to shield the bunch of daffodils that had been my parting gift from my primary three class, but the wind whistled and caught the yellow flower heads, almost pulling them from my grasp. Smoke from the chimneys blew almost horizontally and the rows of houses had a shuttered look, as if no one but myself dared be adrift on such a day. I was crying quietly and hoping that anyone outside on such a bitter day would assume my eyes were watering with the cold. I knew I would miss my teaching job and the schoolchildren very much, but I also knew that I had to look after Mum and be at home to care for her.

I was glad to be almost home, especially as flakes of snow harried by the scouring wind blew straight into my face. If this weather continued, then the Easter holiday would be spent indoors and the children would grow restless, being confined to their houses.

Mum was looking out of the window as I hurried towards 88 Victoria Road. She gave a feeble wave and I smiled up at her. When I entered the sitting room, Mrs Maisie Mulholland, our next-door neighbour, was relaxing by a glowing fire, her head resting on the back of her chair. She was sound asleep. The ball of wool from her knitting had fallen onto the floor and a line of blue wool stretched over the fireside rug. Mum put a finger to her lips, but the draught from the front door had acted as a wake-up call and Mrs Mulholland opened her eyes.

'Oh, I'm sorry, Beth. It must be the heat from the fire.' She quickly gathered up her wool, winding it slowly and pushing it onto the end of her sharp needles.

I made straight for the miniscule scullery, which was only big enough for a sink and the cooker. 'I'll make us some tea and toast.'

Mrs Mulholland said she wouldn't wait, as she had a meeting later at the church hall. I was so grateful to her for coming in most afternoons and sitting with Mum. I said so as she made for the door.

'It's no bother, Lizzie. Beth sleeps most of the afternoon and she's a great patient.'

I put the daffodils in a vase and carried them along with the teapot to the fireside, placing the flowers on the side table beside the bed. Mum smiled as she looked at them.

'They're a present from my class and they all sang a song for me before I left.' I tried not to cry again, but Mum took hold of my hands.

'I wish you hadn't given up your job, Lizzie. I'll be fine once this tiredness passes.'

I turned away so she wouldn't see my face. She didn't know there would be no miracle cure for her, and the clocks, as if in agreement with me, struck five o'clock. *Bong, bong, bong, bong, bong.*

She sipped some tea but didn't eat any toast. She barely ate anything these days except scrambled eggs, which I'm sure she only ate to keep me happy. I had brought her bed into the living room from the bedroom we had shared when we moved in with my late grandmother, as I thought she would enjoy looking out of the window at the pedestrians and traffic.

'I saw a poor horse today, Lizzie. It was pulling a cart with big bales of jute and it looked so downtrodden I almost opened the window and shouted at the driver.'

'Oh, I hope you didn't do that, Mum. You would freeze in this weather.'

She laughed, but even that small gesture tired her out and she lay back on the mound of pillows. 'No, I couldn't open the window and Mrs Mulholland wouldn't help me. She said she had to finish her little jumper for the poor families' fund at the church.'

I had to smile. Mrs Mulholland wouldn't put her knitting before helping Mum with anything, but she knew it was too cold for open windows and she was forthright enough to tell her patient. I suspected that Mum had invented the story of the little jumper.

'Tell me how your last day at school went,' she said, trying to sit up and pulling her blue bed jacket closer round her thin white neck. Her delicate watch hung loosely from her wrist, as did her gold bangle.

I couldn't betray my emotions at her condition so I went to refill my cup and leant against the sink, smiling and trying to keep calm. I found myself stirring my tea over and over and had to make a conscious effort to keep my hands still.

After a few minutes I made my way back to the bedside, a wide smile plastered on my face. Where had I read of someone being described as wearing a smile while her heart was breaking?

3

'The children all said their goodbyes and some of them were crying.' I stopped and laughed. 'At least some of the girls were. The boys were more interested in where I was going.' I didn't mention that Charlie had asked, 'Are ye ga'en tae anither skale, Miss Flint?' and that I had answered, 'No, I'm leaving to look after my mother,' and that Charlie, the class clown, then piped up, 'Meh mither looks efter me and meh three wee sisters. Does your mither no look efter you, Miss?'

I took out the lovely brooch that had been presented to me from the staff. It was a plain circle with a seed pearl in the centre. Mum took the box and gazed at it for ages.

'It's lovely, Lizzie. They must think a lot of you.'

'Yes, we all got on very well, and even though I haven't been there for long it was a happy place to work. Polly and Jane are going hiking during the holiday and plan to stay in the youth hostels, but Polly did say if this cold weather keeps up they might change their plans. The headmaster, Mr Drummond, is hoping to go away with his wife for a week in their caravan to Arbroath.'

'That's the worst of Easter,' said Mum. 'Often it's colder at this time of the year than at Christmas.'

That was true, I thought, and as I pulled the curtains to shut out the darkening skies I saw the snow was lying on the pavements, gleaming white in the light from the street lamps.

After tea, during which she left more food on the plate than she ate, Mum picked up her book, but within ten minutes she had fallen asleep, so I quietly removed her glasses and made sure the fire was well banked up.

I brought the blankets and quilt through from the bedroom and lay down on the couch. I wanted to make sure I would hear her if she woke up during the night. She looked so beautiful and peaceful lying there that I felt a tightness in my throat at the unfairness of her illness and the fact I wouldn't have her for very long.

To take my mind off the worry about the future, I decided to reread one of my childhood books, *Treasure Island*. It had been a favourite of mine and I was soon immersed in the adventures of

Jim Hawkins and Long John Silver. I especially liked the bit about his parrot, Captain Flint, and as a child I had been impressed that our family name was in print, albeit as the name of a bird. I smiled as I recalled my childish dreams of adventure and how I had wanted to be a pirate. It was strange how life turned out.

'What are you smiling at, Lizzie?'

I looked up to see Mum propped against her pillows.

'Oh, I hope I didn't wake you,' I said. 'It's just the memory of this book. Do you remember how I wanted to be a pirate? And Granny almost choked on her tea?'

Mum laughed. 'She wasn't the only one. I got a shock as well, if my memory serves me right.'

I put the book down. 'Anyway, it doesn't matter any more. Now I'm teaching young children to look to the future and immersing myself in their dreams.'

Mum looked keenly at me. 'There's still time for an adventurous life, Lizzie. Once I'm better and back working in the hat shop.'

We both laughed at that and recalled how shocked Granny had been when I called it that. She couldn't imagine anyone calling the millinery department in DM Brown's anything as common as a hat shop.

2

DR BENNETT

The weather didn't get any better. More snow blew in with a bitter northerly wind, and apart from going out to the nearest shop for food, I stayed indoors. Mum became tired looking out at the wintry scene and I got a bit edgy being cooped up in the house.

I would have liked Mum to get out for some fresh air, but it was far too cold. Also there was the difficulty of trying to get her downstairs. Up till a few weeks ago she had been able to negotiate the stairs slowly, but not any more. I realised sadly that her illness was getting worse.

Dr Bennett had been my grandparents' doctor, but Mum and I knew him well. He had a surgery in his house in Constitution Terrace where we would go any time we needed treatment, but now he came every week to see us.

He had been frank with me about the tumour in her breast, but Mum, in her usual mode of denial and general vagueness, had dismissed his diagnosis.

'That's rubbish,' she said, waving her white hands in a fluttery motion that was typical of her attitude to anything unpleasant.

Sadly it wasn't rubbish. I could see her life slowly going downhill and I didn't know how to cope with her denial.

Dr Bennett arrived a few days after I gave up work. He was well wrapped up from the cold. In his early sixties, he was a tall, thin man with a grey beard and a cheery manner. I always thought he looked more like a stage actor than a doctor.

He sat by the side of Mum's bed and opened his black bag. 'How are you today, Mrs Flint?'

Mum denied there was anything wrong with her and asked when she could get up and go back to work.

He jollied her along. 'Not for a wee while.' He looked out of the window. 'Anyway, it's not the kind of weather to be outdoors. No, you mark my words, Mrs Flint, you're better off inside the cosy house than traipsing through the snow.' He closed his bag and refused a cup of tea. 'I've another three patients to see, Lizzie, so I'd better get a move on. There are a lot of influenza cases going about.'

I saw him to the door and he stood on the landing. 'Your mother isn't in any pain at the moment, but when she is I'll be able to give her something to relieve it.' He saw my worried face and he took my hand. 'Just keep her warm and comfortable and I'll be back in a few days to see her.'

My stomach was churning as I went back inside. Just as the clock chimed twelve o'clock, Mum propped herself up on her pillows. 'He says I've got influenza, Lizzie, so it won't be long till I'm on my feet again.'

I had to turn away in case my face betrayed the emotions that were somersaulting through my head, and I went to heat up some soup for our dinner.

Mum barely touched hers, even although I tried hard to spoon more liquid into her mouth. 'I've had enough, Lizzie. I'm not really hungry.' She picked up the book lying on her quilt. 'I've finished this story. Can you go down to the library for another book, Lizzie?'

'Yes, I'll go now and get something for the tea,' I said, picking up the book, which I knew she hadn't read.

I called in at Maisie's house and she went to sit with Mum till I got back.

The snow had turned to a wet slush when I reached the street and it was difficult to keep away from the passing tramcars and carts as they sent sprays of icy water onto the pavement. I was grateful I had put my galoshes over my shoes as I hurried towards the library.

I loved books and always enjoyed being in the quietness of the library. After picking up a romantic-fiction book for Mum, I wandered over to the travel section and spent half an hour looking at travel books about distant countries. I chose two and carried my small bundle to the desk.

The middle-aged woman at the counter stamped them and smiled as she handed them over. 'Isn't it terrible weather for this time of year? What a pity we don't live here,' she said, pointing to one of my travel books – the one entitled *A Journey through China*.

I agreed with her and hurried out onto the windswept pavement. Before going home I decided to make a detour to Keiller's baker's shop to buy some cakes for tea. Mum loved fruitcakes and I smiled as I recalled Dad calling them 'fly cemeteries'. However, he never said it to her face.

Mum was looking out the window as I approached the house, and I waved. Maisie was chatting to her as she knitted another small garment, but when I came into the room, she stood up, gathered up her needles and wool, and placed them in her roomy bag.

'Please stay for a cup of tea, Maisie. I've bought some cakes.'

Mum said, 'I hope they are fruitcakes, Lizzie.'

I laughed. 'Yes, they are.' I was pleased that Mum seemed more alert. Maisie also appeared glad of the opportunity to stay, but I was puzzled by a feeling the two women had changed the subject when I entered the room. But as I made the tea I decided my mind was playing tricks.

However, later Maisie confirmed my suspicion when I went with her to the door.

'Thank you for coming in to sit with Mum, I'm really so grateful.'

'I'm just pleased to be able to help you, Lizzie. I did think Beth was looking a bit better today and she didn't sleep as much as she usually does.' She hesitated. 'There is just one thing. When you were out, Beth was looking out of the window and she said she saw your father walking up the street. When I went to look, she said he had walked past the close.' Maisie's round, homely face looked distressed. 'I hope you don't mind me mentioning it.'

Suddenly my previous feeling of hope vanished, but I didn't want to upset our neighbour. 'Don't worry about it,' I said. 'You know she sometimes gets these strange feelings.'

Maisie looked relieved.

I went back into the living room. Mum was propped up on her pillows with her book, but I knew she wasn't reading it. I sat beside her and took her hand. She laid the book down and sighed.

'I was just saying to Maisie that you're looking a lot better today.'

She waved her hand as if annoyed. 'I'm not ill, Lizzie, it's just a bad bout of influenza.'

I wasn't going to be fobbed off. 'Maisie said you enjoyed looking out of the window.'

Mum nodded, but I could see a flash of evasiveness in her eyes as she turned her head away.

'She said you thought you saw someone you knew walking up the street.'

Suddenly she turned and glared at me. 'Well, I didn't mention it because I know it annoys you. I saw your father, but he passed the close and didn't come in.' She sounded vexed and tearful and I was annoyed with myself for bringing up this painful subject, but before I could go on, she said, 'I know you and Granny always thought I was mad whenever I mentioned that your dad hadn't died in the war so now I don't tell you any more.'

She lay back on the pillows and turned her head away from me. I couldn't bear seeing her so distressed. Although I didn't believe it, I said, 'If Dad's still alive, then he will come back to us.'

Her eyes were bright as she turned to face me. 'Yes, he will, and one day he'll walk back through the door. I think he has amnesia and one day his mind will clear and he'll remember us and come home.'

I stroked her hand. 'Yes, of course he will.'

I hated lying to her, but I couldn't bear to make her face up to the truth about my father. Before she died, my granny had tried to make her accept his death but hadn't succeeded and I knew I couldn't make her see sense.

Later, I lay awake with the glow from the fire making patterns on the wall and I recalled the sadness from the past.

3

THE TELEGRAPH BOY

The telegram arrived on my sixth birthday, in August 1917. I was almost bursting with excitement because Mum had arranged a small party for some of my school friends, so much so that I had received several warnings from her about the noise I was making.

'If you don't behave, Lizzie, I will cancel your party.'

Prophetic words, although we didn't know it then.

I was wearing my new dress, a present from my granny Flint, and a new pair of shoes. I ran to Mum's bedroom to admire myself in the triple mirror of her oak dressing table, looking at myself from three angles before brushing my dark curly hair with her hairbrush. I had my own brush, but I knew she wouldn't mind me using hers because it was my special day.

We lived one stair up at 10 Garland Place, almost next door to Barrack Park, where Mum had promised to take me after my party. I was so happy I felt I would combust with joy.

The doorbell rang. Mum looked a bit annoyed as she looked at the clock. 'I hope it's not one of your small pals arriving early. I haven't finished putting the candles on your cake.'

She went to the door and I followed, eager to see who had arrived, fully expecting to see my friend Emily, who still couldn't tell the time, even though Miss Price, our teacher at Rosebank School, was always trying to drum numbers into our lethargic brains.

But it wasn't Emily. A young telegram boy stood on the doorstep. He looked unhappy as he handed over the telegram. Mum took one look at it and she slumped to the ground with a sound I had never heard before, a cross between a howl of rage and a scream.

Paralysed with fright, I could only stand and stare. The telegram boy ran to help her, while Mrs Murphy from next door came out to investigate the noise.

'Oh dear Mary, Mother of God,' she said as she tried to help my mother into the room that held all the party food on the gateleg table. 'Please sit down, Mrs Flint, please.'

Mum held up the telegram, while the young lad looked sad. 'It's Peter, Mrs Murphy. He's been injured, I know it.'

Although Mrs Murphy tried to placate her, both women knew there were hundreds of households in the city that had received telegrams with bad news from the Western Front. Mum tried to open the flimsy letter, but her hands were shaking so badly that she handed it over to Mrs Murphy. 'Please read it for me.'

Mrs Murphy was uncertain, but she was saved from this awful task by the arrival of my granny Flint, with Emily and her mother, Mrs Whyte, following behind her. My friend was clutching a small box in her hands. Emily's mother quickly took in the situation and came over to my side, as Emily's small voice piped up, 'What's the matter, Mummy?'

Meanwhile, I hadn't moved an inch. I could feel the sharp corner of the hallstand dig painfully into my back

'Come with us, Lizzie,' Mrs Whyte said. 'You can play with Emily in our house.' She glanced at the women and Granny nodded to her.

I was putting my coat on when I heard Mum crying again, huge deep sobs that made me want to run to her and cuddle her, but Mrs Whyte ushered us out through the front door, with Emily still asking what was wrong.

'Is Lizzie not having a birthday party, Mummy?'

Mrs Whyte said no, not today, but maybe it would take place some other time.

Because Emily was hanging back and asking questions, I heard Granny Flint say, '. . . Regret to tell you Private Peter Flint is missing in action.'

I rushed back into the room, almost colliding with the telegram boy, who was making his way out.

Mrs Murphy was crying and Granny Flint was holding a glass of water. My mother had fainted and lay motionless on the floor. I tried to run to her side, but Mrs Whyte quickly took my hand. 'Come with us, Lizzie.'

I let myself be guided down the stairs and out through the close, into the sunshine. The park was busy with people out for a stroll on such a lovely day and I remember thinking that we wouldn't be going to the swings after the party.

Emily lived around the corner from us, on Constitution Road, and normally I loved going to her house, which I often did after school. I liked the cosy, untidy kitchen and Emily's bedroom with her doll's house and the pram with the two dolls, but not today. I felt bewildered and frightened by this unexpected turn of events.

I knew my father had enlisted in the army earlier that year, but I knew little about war or what was being fought for in France and Belgium. When I had asked Mum about it, she said he would be home soon and that we weren't to worry. I had believed her with that childish faith that children have in their parents knowing what is right and wrong.

Mrs Whyte ushered us both into Emily's room. 'Now, go and play with the toys while I make the tea.'

Emily began to arrange the furniture in the doll's house, but I stood beside the door, feeling, for the first time, like a stranger. Suddenly Emily turned.

'Is your daddy dead, Lizzie?'

I burst into tears, loud sobs that soaked my face and the neck of my new frock. Mrs Whyte came in and took her daughter out into the lobby.

'I want you to behave, Emily, and not upset Lizzie. Do you hear me?' She looked angry and Emily nodded. 'If you don't do as I say, you will go to bed without your tea.'

Emily appeared back in the room and, without looking at me, went over to the pram, where she began to sing to the two dolls: 'All Things Bright and Beautiful'. This was one of our favourite hymns, which we sang in the school. Meanwhile, I silently wondered what had happened to my golden day, which had begun with such joy and promise.

Later, we had beans on toast, sitting at the large kitchen table with its bright checked oilskin cover, which Mrs Whyte cheerfully wiped over with a soapy cloth. It was so unlike our white starched cover at home. Still, Mum always placed a large mat in front of me, which meant it didn't matter if I spilled some gravy from my mince or custard from my pudding.

After tea, we sat on the squashy settee and read Emily's books until her father appeared from his work. A tall, well-built man with short hair and a ruddy face, he was the foreman at a boilermaker's factory in Dock Street.

Emily jumped up. 'Daddy, Lizzie . . .'

Mrs Whyte ushered us back into the bedroom. Although still bewildered, I knew I had to find out what had happened. I went back and stood outside the kitchen door.

'Oh, it's terrible news, Albert. Peter Flint is missing in action. Beth got the telegram this afternoon and she's in a terrible state. Lizzie's granny is there, along with Bridget Murphy, and they've sent for the doctor.'

Albert's voice was angry. 'This bloody war, Jean, has a lot to answer for.'

'Don't swear, Albert, the girls will hear you.'

'Well, it is carnage. Look at the hundreds of people in this city alone who have received telegrams about their husbands, sons and brothers. We had eight young lads who worked with me who all joined up at the start of this war and they've all been killed. Then there were a dozen others from the foundry who all perished at Loos.'

Emily's mum began to cry. 'I'm so thankful you were too old to enlist, Albert, but the telegram said missing in action.'

Albert snorted. 'Army lies. No, he'll be dead all right.'

I noticed Emily standing beside me. She took my hand and we both began to cry.

The door opened and her parents both appeared, looking shocked. Mr Whyte took a coin from his overalls. His hands were so large and rough that I couldn't see the coin in his palm until he held out a sixpence.

'Emily, Mum will take you and Lizzie down to the ice-cream shop and buy you both a cone.'

Mrs Whyte hurried forward. 'Yes, that's a good idea.' She took our hands and we had almost reached the front door when Bridget Murphy arrived.

'I have to take Lizzie home. Her granny will be staying in the house to look after Beth, but she wants to thank you for all your help.'

So I walked out of this unreal world, back to our house with Mrs Murphy. I felt relieved that we hadn't gone for an ice cream because I just knew that if I'd eaten it I would have been sick, and Mum had enough to deal with without that.

4

MOVING ON

The first thing I noticed when we reached the street were the families emerging from the park. The sun was still bright in the western sky and the children looked dusty and tired, as if playing on the swings and running about on the grass had worn them all out.

Mrs Murphy remarked as she surveyed the noisy exodus, 'They'll all be sleeping like logs tonight, bless their wee hearts.' She gazed at the sky. 'And it's going to be a lovely sunset, I reckon.'

I looked at her as we walked ever so slowly towards our close. Mum had said that Mrs Murphy had come over from Ireland but had been a widow for years and had brought up six children on her own. Most of them had moved away, but she still had two daughters who regularly came to visit her, which, Mum said, was a blessing because she was getting old. I had no idea of Mrs Murphy's age, but she certainly looked old, with her grey hair pulled back in an untidy bun that seemed to be too heavy for her thin face and wrinkled neck.

I liked meeting her on the stair, especially on a Sunday morning when she was setting off for the chapel. She wore her best dress and hat on those occasions and I knew this because she would tell me. I would also smell the mothball aroma from her black coat as she passed me by.

'I've got on my Sunday best clothes, Lizzie. Do you think I look good enough to go and speak to the Lord?'

I always said she looked wonderful, which seemed to please her.

She gave my hand a squeeze as we reached the close and the second thing I saw was that all the curtains were closed, even the ones in the basement. I didn't want to ask her why this was, so we walked up the stairs. I could hear voices as we approached our door and was surprised to see Mr and Mrs Collins from downstairs and old Mr Willison from the top landing.

Mr Willison was leaning heavily on his stick as he said goodbye to Granny. 'Aye, it's a bad business, Mrs Flint. A bad business.'

When the neighbours saw me, they patted me on the head, but Mrs Collins dropped down on one knee and gave me a tight hug. I could hardly breathe but, minding my manners, I stayed still until she released me. Wiping her eyes with a handkerchief, she hurried away with her husband, back down to her own house.

Granny moved ahead of me and went into the kitchen. To my astonishment and outrage, I saw the table had been cleared of the sandwiches and jelly and my birthday cake. My outrage turned to tears and I cried loudly.

Mrs Murphy said, 'That's right, wee lass, get all your tears out now and you'll feel better in the morning.'

Granny sat down wearily on the chair by the fireside. The grate held a colourful paper fan, which Mum always placed there during the summer months when the fire was unlit. I looked around, but there was no sign of my mother.

Before I could speak, Granny said, 'Now, Lizzie, you must promise to be a very brave girl and let your mother sleep. Will you do that?'

I nodded so hard that I was sure my head would fall from my neck. 'Yes, Granny.'

'I want you to go and get washed and put your nightdress on and I'll make cocoa.'

I moved slowly, as I wasn't sure my legs would hold me up, but I did as I was told. Granny got up from her chair and went to the door with Mrs Murphy.

She spoke quietly and I had to move nearer to hear what she said. 'The doctor has given Beth something to make her sleep. Thank you for all your help.'

Mrs Murphy said she hoped we would all be well, adding, 'I'm off to the chapel to light a candle and say a prayer for poor Mr Flint.'

For some reason, this kindly act of praying to Jesus and the angels comforted me and I fervently hoped that Jesus would answer Mrs Murphy's prayer and send my father home safe and well.

By the time Granny re-entered the room, I was in my nightdress. She quickly made the two cups of cocoa and then, to my delight, she produced a large slice of my birthday cake with one small candle sitting on top of the icing.

'You didn't think I would forget your birthday, Lizzie, did you? Now, blow out your candle and make a wish.'

I screwed up my eyes and wished and wished that my father would be all right and come walking through the door.

I lay in bed and knew I wouldn't sleep, but to my astonishment I awoke next morning with the sun trying to penetrate the closed curtains. I heard someone moving around and hoped it was Mum, but it was Granny. She was stirring a pot of porridge on the stove and the table was set for two.

When she saw me looking at it, she said, 'I'll take some tea and toast to your mother when she wakes up.'

The curtains were still closed and the room looked dim, like it was underwater. I asked if I could go and play with Emily, but Granny shook her head. 'I want you to stay here while I quickly go back to my house. I'll only be an hour.'

Then the door opened and Mum appeared. She looked tired and ill. I made to jump up, but Granny gave me a stern look as she stood up.

'Beth, come and sit here.'

Mum looked around in confusion, almost as if she had found herself in the wrong house with the wrong people, but she let Granny guide her to the chair next to me. Then Mum put her hand over mine and held it tightly. I was on the verge of tears, but I knew Granny would be annoyed if I upset her.

'I'll make you some breakfast', said Granny, bustling over to the stove, but Mum said she didn't want anything.

'Just a cup of tea will be fine, Mary.'

Granny brought it to the table. 'I've told Lizzie I must go back to my house, but I'll just be an hour. Is that all right, Beth?'

Mum nodded listlessly and stirred her tea with the spoon. Granny gathered up her handbag and coat. 'I'll be back soon.' She looked at me. 'Take care of your mum, Lizzie, until I get back.'

I was still nodding my head when she disappeared out through the door.

Mum was still stirring her tea. 'I'm sorry about your birthday party, Lizzie.'

'It doesn't matter, Mum,' I replied, feeling guilty that a few hours earlier I had been outraged and tearful. But now the grim news had penetrated my brain and I knew things would never be the same again – not unless by some miracle my father wasn't missing but on his way home. I screwed my eyes up tight, as I didn't want to burst into a fresh bout of tears.

'I know what we'll do, Lizzie,' she said, standing up and making her way to the display cabinet. This was one of her favourite pieces of furniture and I loved it as well. I had been told that it had belonged to her own mother: a mother who had died when she was a small child, leaving her distraught father to bring her up on his own until in later life he married a widow with a daughter. The bottom two shelves of this cabinet held all the cups and medals my father had won when he was young. Mum gathered them in her arms and carried them to the table.

'Put yesterday's newspaper down, Lizzie, and we'll clean all Dad's trophies.'

She brought out the small tin of silver-cleaning fluid and the cloths. 'I'll put the Silvo on and you can polish it off.' She picked the first trophy up and turned it in her hands. 'You know your dad is a champion swimmer, don't you?'

I nodded. My dad's sporting achievements were well known in our house.

'This was the first cup he ever won, when he was 14. He joined the swimming club at the local baths and he was the champion that year.'

For a few minutes we busied ourselves with our task. Suddenly, Mum said, 'You look so much like him, it's uncanny. You have the same hair and eyes, and you're going to be as tall as he is, and I also think you have the same nature. He loved adventure and doing things with his life. He loved his swimming and tennis, and he spent a year sailing around the British Isles with the Naval Cadets. Of course, that was before I met him.' She picked up an ornate trophy, which had his name engraved on it. '1908, the year he won this tennis cup, was the year I met him. I had gone with a friend to see the championship match.' She stopped. 'I didn't like tennis very much, but my friend loved it. Well, Dad and I met afterwards and both fell in love and that was it. We were married two years later. I never understood what he saw in me, because I don't like sport and I always thought you had to share the same tastes when you got married.'

I knew I resembled my dad very much and Mum would often tease me by telling me I didn't have one single feature inherited from her. She was right, of course. I gazed at her over the table. Her head was bent as she concentrated on cleaning this special cup. Her hair was a soft, glossy brown and her eyes were hazel. She was slim and tiny and had delicate white hands. In fact, she was beautiful, and no wonder my dad had fallen in love with her.

Soon we had polished all the trophies, and Mum placed them gently back into the cabinet, where they gleamed brightly through the glass door. As we gathered up the dirty newspaper, she suddenly sat down again. Wiping tears from her eyes, she said, 'Dad will be home soon, Lizzie. I just know it.'

I fervently hoped this was true.

A few minutes later, Granny arrived back. She must have hurried because she was out of breath.

'There's something I want to say to you, Beth,' she said, glancing at me as she spoke. 'Lizzie, do you want to go and play with Emily?'

I was surprised, as she hadn't let me go earlier, but before I could answer, Mum said, 'I think we should both listen to what you have to say, Mary.'

Granny nodded. 'I want you both to come and stay with me in Victoria Road.'

Mum looked wearily at her. 'What if Peter comes home and we're not here?'

'Well, he knows my address, Beth. I'm not asking you to move to another country, just to another house. I mean, will you have enough money to pay the rent here, and what if you have to get a job, who'll look after Lizzie?'

'I would rather stay here, Mary. What will happen when Peter comes home and we've given up this house? Where will we all live then?'

'Well, let's compromise. Keep this house on for the foreseeable future but come and live with me, just to begin with. After a few weeks, you can return here if that's what you want.'

Mum looked at me. 'Do you want to spend a few weeks at Granny's house?'

I didn't know what to say. I could feel Granny's eyes boring into the back of my head. Mum looked so delicate and weary, and I was worried about her coping on her own. However, I was saved from making this momentous decision by Mum.

'All right then, Mary: we'll come for a few weeks, just until I feel stronger. Lizzie will be back at school soon and then we'll talk about it again.'

Granny looked relieved. 'Well, let's get your packing done.'

We packed our clothes and I was allowed to take some of my toys. Mum brought another suitcase from the lobby press and she carefully wrapped up all Dad's trophies. 'I want to take these with us.'

'Granny, we've polished them so they'll look nice in your display cabinet,' I said.

She smiled. 'So I see.' She got the suitcases together. 'I've arranged for a car to come and collect everything.'

'Mum, have I got time to say goodbye to Emily?'

Granny looked unsure, but Mum said, 'Just a quick visit, Lizzie, and don't forget you'll see her at school soon.'

I ran as quickly as I could. Mrs Whyte opened the door. 'Lizzie, Emily was hoping you would come along. How is your mother?'

'We're going to stay with Granny Flint and I have to say goodbye to Emily, Mrs Whyte.'

Emily came in and her face lit up.

Her mother said, 'Lizzie can't stay long, Emily. She's going to stay with her granny, but you will still see her at school.'

Before Emily could answer, my mum appeared. 'That's the car now, Lizzie. Goodbye, Mrs Whyte and Emily. We're not going to be away for long, just a few weeks, so we'll see you soon.'

Emily and her mum came down with us to the street and they both waved as we set off towards Victoria Road. Mum's face was white and strained-looking, while I had a strange lump in my throat. Still, it was only a few weeks and then we would be home again, hopefully with Dad by our side.

Granny's flat was two stairs up at 88 Victoria Road, in the close nearest Nelson Street. The front windows overlooked the stairs that led down King Street and the road was much busier than Garland Place. It also didn't have the park beside it.

We put our suitcases in the bedroom, which Granny said I would share with Mum. It was a lovely room and had two single beds that had matching colourful patchwork quilts.

For a brief moment I thought Mum would collapse on the bed, but she pulled herself together and began to unpack. She placed our clothes in the large wardrobe and the chest of drawers and put her silver-backed hairbrush on the top along with mine.

She looked around her. 'Well, Lizzie, this will be home for a few weeks.'

I had my box with its collection of postcards in my hands. 'I've brought Aunt Margaret's postcards with me. Will I put them under the bed?'

Mum thought that was a good idea. 'I will have to write to Margaret tomorrow. Oh, I wish she could be here with us, but she's in Rio de Janeiro with Gerald.' She looked tired and there were dark shadows under her eyes.

My aunt was Mum's stepsister. Mum had told me that she was two years old and Margaret was fourteen when her mother had married my grandfather, but they had always got on with each other and I knew how much my mum missed her when she married Gerald Cook, who worked in the Diplomatic Service. Up till that point she had been a headmistress at a private school in Edinburgh, but now she travelled all over the world with her husband and we rarely saw her. Still, I had loads of postcards from various foreign countries and I loved looking at them and imagining I was going to visit them all, just like her.

Before he went off to the army, Dad had also loved rummaging in the box, but unlike me he had been abroad. He had visited Paris and had gone on a skiing holiday to Norway while still at school, but now he was missing somewhere in France. I hoped he would manage to find his way home.

Granny came in and said she had made the tea, so we sat at the table in the window and I watched the people walking quickly in the street and the many carts and horses pulling large bales of jute on their way to one of the many jute mills in the area.

Later, when we went to bed, I heard Mum crying softly, and I lay in my strange new bed and wished we were back at Garland Place and that life would get back to normal.

5

THE HAT SHOP

Although we didn't know it at the time, the few weeks would stretch to five months. Mum kept saying we were going to go back to our own house, but by the winter of 1917 there was no more news about my father, so she had to reluctantly give up the keys to Garland Place.

It was mostly financial. My parents' savings were slowly dwindling away and even with a great deal of help from Granny Flint and Aunt Margaret, Mum had to face reality. Her best pieces of furniture were put into storage and everything that was portable was brought to Victoria Road. The rest of the things Mum didn't want to keep were sold.

I know she was deeply unhappy with the situation and I missed our own house very much, but Mum said there was no choice. I was still able to go to Rosebank School, which was one small blessing for me, although it meant a longer walk every morning and afternoon.

To begin with, Mum would walk with me up Bonnybank Road then along Ann Street towards the school, but as time went on she said she had to look for a job. There were hundreds of women now working in what were once looked upon as men's jobs. They went out every morning to the mills and factories, they even drove buses, and a lot of unmarried women had left the city to work in munitions factories.

According to reports in the newspaper, quite a lot of these women were happy to work outside the home. It gave them extra money, which they enjoyed having at the end of the week, but it also meant that the women filled the jobs that the men used to do before they were called up for the war. If it wasn't for the women, then industry and services would have collapsed years ago.

However, there was a great deal of unhappiness and grief in the city due to all the deaths over three long years of war. In fact, I had been embarrassed on my first day back at school in August when my teacher, Miss Price, had knelt down and, putting her arms around me, given me a hug. In the background, I could hear a few snatches of laughter, as some of my friends thought it was funny.

However, a few days later, four older boys in the school also lost family in the trenches in France – a father, two brothers and an uncle – and everyone felt sorry for all of us. I remember looking at the boys in assembly as we sang 'The Lord Is My Shepherd' and felt so sorry for them, especially when one of them began to cry.

This war had caused so much death, distress and hardship in our community, and it was a pattern repeated across the entire country. I read in the paper one day that over a few days of fighting, more than a million men had perished. I tried to visualise this amount but couldn't – until I realised my own father was one of those casualties. It wasn't the number of deaths but each personal one that mattered, each household either waiting for news or living with the news that a loved one had died.

Mum had worked in an office before her marriage but had often said she'd hated it, so she scanned the employment column in the paper to see what else was available.

I had overheard Granny telling one of her friends, 'Beth is so choosy, but she'll soon realise that she'll have to take whatever's available.'

I remember my cheeks burning with shame at Granny's words, but I never told Mum. I felt she had enough to worry about. In March of 1918 she managed to get a job in the millinery department of DM Brown's department store, a position I'm sure was wangled by one of Granny's cronies who worked in the dress and mantle department.

'Is the millinery department like a hat shop?' I asked.

Granny said, 'You'll love the position, Beth. DM Brown's is a great shop to work in and the customers are always so pleasant.' She looked at me. 'Please don't call it the hat shop, Lizzie.'

How Granny knew about the pleasant customers was a mystery because she hadn't worked outside the home since her marriage to my late grandfather, who had been a very successful solicitor in the town: a man who had worked at his desk right up till the day he died. That was a few months after Dad had left school. He had been planning on joining the Royal Navy, but Granny had persuaded him to join the family firm, as it had been founded by his great-grandfather, Peter John Flint.

I thought Granny resembled the late Queen Victoria. Like the late queen, she was tiny, plump and always dressed in black, and there was little in life that amused her. Her main interests were the church and her circle of friends. Every Sunday I would go with her to St Andrew's Church in King Street, where I would attend the Sunday school.

After the service we would head back to the house to have our dinner before four of Granny's friends visited her for afternoon tea and the knitting circle. Mum didn't go to church, in spite of Granny's remarks about heathen qualities. Mum always pleaded tiredness after six days on her feet in the hat shop – sorry, the millinery department – saying she liked a long lie in bed. I was always pleased to see Granny's reaction to this. Her eyebrows would almost disappear into her hairline and she puckered up her mouth in such a way that the tiny wrinkles around her cheeks made her look like a disgruntled elf.

Personally, I loved Sunday afternoons, because Mum and I spent them together. As soon as the women arrived at the door, we would be standing with our coats on, ready to leave. Mum was always pleasant to Granny's friends, saying, 'You have so much to talk about and you don't want a child running about the house.'

This annoyed me because I never ran around the rooms. I always made sure I walked normally, and because I read a lot of books, I was nearly always quiet. But as we walked down the stairs, Mum would take my hand and give me a big wink, which always made me laugh.

During the summer months we would go to the park and I would play on the swings while Mum sat on a bench and read the newspaper or her book. Sometimes we would walk along the Esplanade or go for a trip across the River Tay on the Fifie, which I loved. Also, now and again we would go to Magdalen Green, where lots of people gathered on a Sunday to either stroll on the grass or to socialise with friends.

During the cold winter and spring months, finding somewhere to go posed more of a challenge. Nearly all the shops were closed on the Sabbath, but there were a couple of small cafés attached to chip shops where we would crush into the tiny sitting area and eat chips with loads of salt and vinegar and drink hot cups of sugary tea.

Mum would always say on these occasions, 'Lizzie, Granny would have a heart attack if she knew we were eating chips, but do you know, I don't care.'

As far as I was concerned, however, the best trips were when we walked around the docks, making our way over tiny swing bridges and viewing the giant cargo ships that lay at anchor beside the wharves. I would write down in my small notebook all the exotic names, like *City of India*, *Benghazi* and *Peking Pearl*.

I tried to visualise these far-off ports and how glamorous they were, and sometimes dark-skinned sailors would make their way down wooden gangplanks and pass by, all chattering in wonderful strange languages.

I was still getting my postcards from Aunt Margaret and I knew Mum wrote to her every week, her face turning pink with pleasure when she received a reply.

'I suppose Aunt Margaret has seen all these foreign places?' I said one day.

Mum nodded. 'Well, maybe not all of them, but she has been in lots of different countries. Your dad wanted to travel like that and see lots of new places, but when your grandfather died suddenly he had to go and take over his business, much as he hated it.'

'He should have said he couldn't,' I said, thinking how easy that would have been.

'Well, life isn't always easy, Lizzie. Sometimes we have to make sacrifices and your dad made one when he said he would take his father's place in the office.' She frowned as she looked at her watch. 'It's time to go back.'

Once a month, Mum took me to the Eastern Cemetery on Arbroath Road. Her father, mother and Margaret's mother and father were all buried there and she liked to change the flowers on the two graves. She would tidy the place up and throw away the withered flowers from her previous visit and arrange the new foliage in the stone vases that lay in front of the headstones. I didn't understand why there were only two graves when four people had died.

'It's because my parents are buried in one plot, while Maggie, my stepmother, and her husband have their own plot. Your aunt Margaret arranged that.' She pointed out that another headstone that was inscribed 'Charles Bell and his beloved wife Margaret Bell Ferrier'.

She was scooping up small bits of litter that had blown in from the path as we made our way to the metal wire basket that held all the rotten debris from floral displays. There was always a strong smell from these baskets, and the stalks and dead flowers were all brown and soggy-looking. I always turned my head away if Mum asked me to put our rubbish in and I tried hard not to breathe in the decay.

'That is why I'm sure your dad isn't dead, Lizzie. I mean, if he was, why wasn't he sent back here to be buried? No, he's still alive and probably a prisoner of war and we'll see him again after this war is over.'

I hated visiting the cemetery, as the rows of weathered

headstones, these large, grey slabs of stone marking the last resting places of the dead, filled me with a terror I couldn't describe. Some had angels with outstretched wings guarding the plot and some had bushes planted as a remembrance.

When I mentioned these flowers, Mum said, 'They're hydrangeas, Lizzie. As you can see, some are pink and some are blue.'

'Why is that?'

Mum said she wasn't sure but it had something to do with the soil. I remember this answer vexing me all the way home because surely the soil was the same all over the cemetery. However, I was pleased that Mum was convinced Dad was still alive and I wanted to believe that so much.

Usually by the time we got back from our Sunday jaunts, Granny's four friends would be on the point of leaving. We would admire the pile of knitting they had done: navy-blue balaclavas, socks and gloves for the poor soldiers in the trenches. Sometimes they would also have a small pile of baby clothes for the poor families in the city. The church usually distributed these small garments to needy families, where I hoped they would be welcomed by the recipients.

This routine lasted for months until one cold day in September when Mum slipped on a step at work and twisted her ankle. It meant she was off work and that we were unable to go out on the Sunday.

'You can both stay and help with the knitting circle,' said Granny.

Mum didn't look too pleased, but she had no choice, so on the Sunday afternoon we sat by the fire waiting for Granny's friends.

The one person we knew was Mrs Mulholland from next door, but the other three were virtual strangers. Although we had met them every Sunday before going off on our excursions, we didn't really know them that well. Granny introduced them when they trooped in. 'This is Miss McMillan, Mrs Lawrence and Miss McKenzie.'

I heard Mum give a small groan under her breath, but she smiled at them as they sat down. Apart from Mrs Mulholland, who was in her fifties, the other three women looked as ancient as Granny.

The afternoon began with tea, sandwiches and small home-baked cakes; then the knitting needles and skeins of wool were produced from capacious cloth bags. It was my job to hold the skeins of wool while one of the women, Mrs Lawrence, wound it into large balls.

Mum concentrated on a knitting pattern for mitts while the five ladies nimbly slipped their stitches from needle to needle, chatting as they worked. Mrs Lawrence told Mum how her husband had died from influenza twenty years before.

'Have you any children?' Mum asked her.

'Yes, I have four, but they're all grown up now. Three are living in Canada and my daughter is married and lives in Glasgow.'

Granny said, 'Amy McMillan was a missionary in Africa.'

I gazed in awe at the shrivelled old woman sitting across from me, and even Mum looked interested.

Miss McMillan laughed. 'Oh, that was forty years ago, Mary. I came back to Dundee after I left the mission and I'm still here.'

I was fascinated by this revelation. 'Did you see any lions and giraffes when you lived in Africa?'

'I did see some when I went on a trip to Kenya, but it was monkeys I didn't like, Lizzie.'

'I always imagined monkeys were lovely creatures,' I said. 'I have pictures of them in one of my books and they are swinging from trees.'

'Yes, they do,' said Miss McMillan, 'but they can be very quarrelsome and sometimes quite vicious. We were always very wary of them if there were a group of them around the huts.' She stopped knitting and said, 'What to you want to be when you grow up, Lizzie?'

There was no hesitation on my part. 'I want to be a pirate.'

Granny looked at me with her forbidding, steely-eyed gaze. I could see she was not amused. 'Now don't be silly, Lizzie, you can't possibly want to be a pirate.'

'But I do. I want to travel all over the world on a pirate ship and jump from the rigging with my sword . . .'

I stopped because she was now glaring at me. I looked at Mum. She had turned her face away and it looked as though she was ready to burst out laughing. Miss McMillan began to cough and said, 'Excuse me, I think I need a glass of water.'

Granny got up and went to fetch it and when she came back, she said, 'I think you should train to be a teacher or work in a nice office like your grandfather did.'

I was amazed by the look of horror my mum gave her, but she turned her attention to Mrs Mulholland, who was sitting next to her.

'How is your sore back? I hope you are feeling better.'

Mum and I both knew that Mrs Mulholland was also a widow but was childless. Granny had said once that she hadn't been married for long when her husband died. I found it all very sad and I could see from Mum's expression that she felt the same.

Mrs Mulholland said she was much better now. 'I was making the bed when I felt the twinge, but thankfully the pain has gone.'

Granny said that was good news, but she still gave me her gimlet-eyed look. She then turned her attention to Miss McKenzie, who was a thin, white-haired woman with a sweet-looking face who had stayed silent all through the tea but had managed to knit a large pile of items.

'Are you keeping well, Amelia?'

Amelia smiled and said she was fine, thank you.

'And how is your sister? Is she feeling better now?'

'Yes she is, the doctor said she could maybe get up next week.'

Granny enlightened us. 'Amelia's sister has broken her ankle, but thank goodness she has Amelia to look after her.'

Later on when they had all left, Mum said, 'I didn't realise they are all in the same boat as we are.'

I noticed that she was crying as we got ready for bed.

I had overheard Granny mentioning my behaviour. 'Pirate indeed, what a lot of nonsense.'

I was surprised when Mum answered back. 'She's just a child, Mary, let her have a bit of nonsense in her life. After all, the reality of life is so much worse.'

I almost told Mum that it wasn't nonsense, but I knew she was upset so I stayed silent.

6

ARMISTICE

The town was abuzz with the news that the war would soon be over. Mum was overjoyed that Dad would soon be home and she set off for work with a new spring in her step.

Granny stayed quiet when Mum went on about how everything was now going to get back to normal and, although I wanted to believe Mum, I found Granny's behaviour out of character and I was suddenly afraid.

When word finally arrived that the Armistice would be signed at 11 a.m. on the eleventh day of the eleventh month, there was rejoicing all over the country. Mum read out the news from the newspapers, but the weather outside was dreich and depressing. Grey skies matched the cold grey pavements and buildings. Perhaps if the sun had been shining it would have been different, but cities, villages and hamlets had all lost their young men in the awful battles and Dundee was no exception. Nearly every family had been touched by the carnage of Loos, Neuve Chapelle, Ypres, the Somme and other battlefronts, and there wasn't any cause for joyous celebration in the homes to which loved ones would never return.

Oh, there were flags and bunting decorating some of the shops, and people thronged into the High Street on that wet November day in 1918. Men in flat caps and women jostled for space in front of the Town House, or the Pillars as it was better known, to hear the momentous news, but bereaved families went about their daily chores like grey shadows, glad that it was all over but, if the truth be told, it had been all over for them when their loved ones perished in the mud and gore of the trenches.

Mum mentioned this scene to us because some of the shop staff looked out of the windows in the department store that overlooked the street. As she was telling us the story, she sounded happy.

'I was telling Milly, my friend in the shop, that I hope it won't be long before Peter comes home. I wish now that I hadn't said it because I thought she was going to cry. Her brother and her fiancé were both killed at Loos. They were both in the Black Watch. And I feel very sorry for her. I'm lucky that Peter will be home soon and we'll be a family again.'

She made it sound like paradise, but once again Granny said very little and the fear in my heart grew stronger.

On the Sunday afternoon, the four ladies appeared again, bustling around as they took off coats, hats and gloves. I had the job of putting everything away into our bedroom, and by the time I got back, Mum was telling them that her husband would soon be coming home.

Miss McKenzie looked confused. 'But Mary said . . .' She stopped and went bright red when Mum looked at her. 'Oh, I'm sorry, I don't know what I'm talking about.'

Mum said, 'You probably heard that Peter is dead, but the telegram said he was missing in action so that can only mean he's still alive.'

Miss McKenzie said that she had got the story all wrong. 'I always get mixed up with stories, Beth, you must excuse me.'

Mum said she understood. 'I just like to put things right. After all, there's no sense in having wild rumours, is there?'

The women all nodded at the same time. It was like a synchronised nodding competition and it would have been so funny if it wasn't so worrying.

Granny said, 'Well, we won't have to knit for the war effort now that it's over, but we will still have our babies and families in need to cater for, so that means we can still keep busy with our knitting needles.'

Afterwards, when the ladies were busy getting into their coats, ready to face the rainy evening, I heard Miss McKenzie apologising to Granny.

'I'm so sorry, Mary, for coming out with the wrong thing to Beth. I hope I haven't upset her.'

Granny said it was all right, but as they passed me to go to the front door, Miss McKenzie was dabbing her eyes with a small white lace-edged handkerchief.

Almost right up till Christmastime, Mum kept writing to the War Office for news of Dad. She got one letter back that said there were hundreds of casualties in military hospitals but so far no Private Peter Flint was on the lists. However, they promised to keep checking and to keep in touch with us.

Mum had to work on Christmas Day, but Granny had decorated the house with paper chains. Her little decorative fairies and elves and a bunch of holly in a vase on the mantelpiece made it festive. I got three books: *Treasure Island*, *Little Women* and the *Big Book of Heroines*, which told the true stories of famous and courageous women. I also got a jigsaw in the form of a map of the world, which I loved. Now I could look at all the countries and see the places Aunt Margaret and her husband Gerald had visited with the British Diplomatic Service.

Mum had stayed positive ever since Armistice Day and I was so pleased to see her looking reasonably happy.

Aunt Margaret sent us a lovely Christmas card and a long letter. Mum opened it, eager to hear all the news from abroad. She read out snatches of it to me. 'They hope to be leaving Rio and coming to a posting in Europe. If that happens, then Margaret will be coming to visit us.' Mum looked so pleased.

'When are they coming?' I asked, thrilled to bits that Aunt Margaret was coming to see us.

Mum read the letter to the end before answering. 'She doesn't say, but it'll be wonderful to see her again. Maybe she'll be here when Peter gets home.'

Granny, who had been reading a book, gave Mum an odd look that alarmed me, but Mum was oblivious to it. She was too busy reading the letter again and dreaming of the reunion with Dad and her stepsister.

As I lay in my bed that night, I couldn't forget that strange look, and I felt cold and frightened but didn't understand what was wrong. Mum was adamant that Dad was coming home soon and I believed her, and I couldn't understand why Granny didn't share the same thought . . .

7

ANDY BAXTER

October 29th was Granny's birthday and it was a stormy day. The rain was bouncing off the playground as we all emerged from school, and by the time I got home I was soaking wet. Granny dried my hair with a rough towel and made me change into my flannelette nightdress.

She placed my school clothes on the airer, which hung from the ceiling in the scullery. 'I hope everything gets dry before tomorrow,' she said, fussing around and placing newspaper inside my wet shoes. 'You can set the table for the tea, Lizzie.'

Turning to look out of the window at the darkening sky and heavy rain, she said, 'I hope your mum has the sense to catch a tramcar instead of walking home in this weather.'

I felt it was a bit of an adventure being dressed in my nightgown at four thirty in the afternoon and I went over to the window to look out as well. People were hurrying along the pavement, which was awash with deep puddles, and the tramcars sent sprays of water over the unfortunate pedestrians passing at that moment.

At six o'clock, Mum arrived, and even although she had caught the tramcar, she'd still managed to get soaked before reaching the close. However, she refused to take off her clothes as Granny suggested, though she did remove her shoes and stockings.

'The shop was really quiet today,' she told us as we sat down to our tea. 'I suppose people didn't fancy coming out in the rain to buy a hat and I don't blame them.' She looked worried. 'We've been quiet for some days now and I hope we pick up soon.'

Granny said. 'I wouldn't worry too much, Beth. I always think women need to buy a new hat.'

Mum wasn't reassured. 'I don't know, Mary. Money and jobs are difficult to find these days and a lot of people are having a hard time making ends meet.'

I was too busy eyeing up the sugary buns from the baker's shop across the road that Granny had bought to celebrate her birthday. As a result I wasn't paying too much attention to all this talk about the state of the country, but I knew Mum was worried about money. She had her wage from DM Brown's, but I knew she didn't like relying on Granny to subsidise us.

After we had our tea, Granny opened her birthday present from us. It was a box of three rose-scented soaps, which we knew she liked. She thanked us profusely. 'It's just what I wanted, thank you.' She gave me a kiss on my cheek and I felt her thin, dry lips against my skin.

'I chose them, Granny,' I said proudly. 'We got them from the chemist's shop down the road.' Actually, I had wanted to get her the blue lacy wool cardigan I had seen in DM Brown's window, but Mum said it was too expensive and didn't I know that Granny liked to knit her own cardigans along with the children's clothes she knitted for the church.

At seven o'clock we were sitting by the fire when the doorbell rang. Mum looked surprised. 'Are you expecting anyone, Mary?'

Granny shook her head, but before either of them could get up, I was in the lobby and opening the door. I got such a shock when I saw the man standing on the landing. Dressed in a long army coat, he had a black eyepatch over his left eye. My first thought was that he was a pirate.

By now Mum had arrived beside me and she gave me a telling-off for running to the door. She then saw the man and almost slammed the door in his face.

'Mrs Flint, I'm Andy Baxter.'

Mum gasped and peered at him, her face turning a bright red. 'Oh Andy, I didn't recognise you. Come in.'

He hesitated. 'I don't want to bother you if you're busy.'

Mum had recovered from the surprise and said, 'No, come in. We're not busy.'

I was mesmerised by this man with his eyepatch and followed him into the living room, wondering who he was. Granny looked up as we entered and she was also surprised.

Mum said, 'This is Andy, he was a member of the swimming club that Peter used to go to.'

As he sat down, Granny said, 'I remember you, Andy. Weren't you the youngest member of the club?'

He looked uncomfortable sitting in the chair, but he nodded. 'Yes, I joined when I was fourteen and I loved the swimming and the competitions we used to go to.'

'Let me take your coat, Andy.' Mum stood beside him and took his coat into the lobby.

That was when I saw he had no left hand. He saw me looking and pulled the sleeve of his jumper down over the red-looking stub.

Mum offered him a cup of tea, but he said he didn't want anything.

'I just wanted to come and see you, Missus Flint. I wasn't sure of your new address, but Mrs Whyte told me where you lived.

Granny also saw the missing hand. 'Were you in the army, Andy?'

He nodded again. 'Aye, I was called up when I was eighteen and I've been in France.' He turned and looked at Mum. 'That's why I'm here. In 1917 I was in the same trench as your husband, Peter, and he saved my life.'

Mum put a hand over her mouth. 'You were with Peter.'

'Aye, I was. I was hit by shrapnel and I was lying in the mud when Peter ran out into no-man's-land and picked me up. I was taken to a hospital in France before being transferred back to Blighty. I lost my eye and my hand, but I'm one of the lucky ones.'

Andy stopped talking and wiped his face with his right hand.

'Was Peter injured as well?' Mum's eyes were bright with tears. 'It's just that he hasn't been sent home yet and we've had no word from the War Office.'

'When Peter carried me back to the trench, he heard another poor injured soldier crying out and he went back to save him.' Andy wiped his face again with a white handkerchief and it was a moment before he resumed his story. 'There was a bomb blast, Missus Flint, and when someone went out to look there was just a huge crater. No one could have survived that.'

Mum cried out. 'No, no, no, it isn't true. I know he survived and he'll be back home again soon.'

Granny tried to change the subject. 'Do you still live in Alexander Street, Andy?'

'Yes, I do. My father died when I was in France and Mum has gone back to work in Halley's jute mill.' He sounded bitter when he mentioned his father. 'I wish I could have said goodbye to him.'

Granny nodded. 'You've been through such a traumatic time, Andy, but your mother will be happy to have you home.'

Andy said that was true. 'I just wish I could find a job, but what job could I do? Anything manual is out of the question and I have to take one day at a time.'

Mum cried out again, 'I know Peter is alive, he is a survivor and he survived that bomb blast.' Her face was red as she realised she was repeating herself, while I stood in shocked silence.

Andy was distressed and looked at Granny. 'Well, maybe he did. Miracles do happen.' He stood up. 'I'll get off now, but I did want to see you and tell you that your husband was a hero.'

Granny got his coat and stood at the door speaking to him before we heard the door close and the key being turned in the lock.

When she came back into the room, Mum and I were crying. Granny looked shocked but, gathering up her courage, she said perhaps we should all go to bed.

'He's not dead, Mary. I don't believe it,' said Mum. She looked pale and her eyes were rimmed red with her tears.

Granny said maybe things would look better in the morning.

I thought Mum was going to protest, but she let Granny gently lead her to our bedroom. She waited until she was in bed. I lay awake to the sound of the rain on the window and Mum's crying.

After what seemed like hours, Mum eventually fell asleep while I was still awake. I could hear Granny moving about, so I quietly got up and went into the living room.

Granny was looking at a photo album, and she looked up in surprise when she saw me.

'I couldn't sleep, Granny,' I said. 'Do you think Daddy is dead?'

She didn't answer my question but said, 'I'm just looking at all the photos of your dad. Come and sit beside me and we'll look at them together.'

I curled up on the sofa beside her and gazed at the photos all neatly arranged in the album. There was one of the swimming club, and I felt tears in my eyes when I saw how young Dad looked as he held up a silver trophy from a swimming contest. He stood looking so proud and I was able to see the droplets of water from his hair. Standing behind him were the other members. They were all smiling with pleasure and I was shocked to see a very youthful-looking Andy Baxter. He had the world at his feet and couldn't have known what lay ahead of him. Nor could the rest of the team, Dad included. Now Andy was a broken young man with his terrible injuries and I felt so angry about this awful war.

'I think it's time for bed,' said Granny, standing up and putting the album back in the sideboard drawer. She still hadn't answered my question, but I went back to bed and lay awake for ages until tiredness took over.

I thought Granny was very courageous in her attitude to Andy's story. However, I noticed a change in her behaviour when she got ready for church on the Sunday morning. She always wore a black hat, but every week she would pin either a small bunch of artificial cherries or a small posy of silk flowers close to the brim, but on that Sunday and every Sunday afterwards she wore the black hat unadorned.

I knew it was her sign of mourning for a son, a husband and a father.

8

A LETTER FROM MARGARET

As the weeks went on, Mum went off to work looking like a ghost. She had always been slim, but now she had lost so much weight that her dress and coat hung from her slender shoulders. I knew Granny was worried about her, but after the fateful night of Andy Baxter's visit, Mum seemed resigned to the fact that Dad wasn't coming back from what the papers were calling 'the war to end all wars'.

Then suddenly, a week before Christmas 1921, she perked up and announced she was going out on the Thursday night to meet up with Milly, her colleague. She spent some time getting ready and at seven thirty she went out. I saw her standing at the tram stop across the road from our close. She waved before climbing aboard and I went back to my book. I was rereading *Treasure Island* and was immersed in the adventures of the characters, wishing I could live a life like them.

Granny was sitting by the fire, engrossed in her knitting pattern. I could see from the cover that it was a jersey for a child and I suspected it was a Christmas present for me. The pattern looked quite complicated, with a rope-like cable climbing up the front of the jersey. I wasn't enamoured with it, but I knew I would be expected to wear it.

Suddenly she stopped looking at it and said, 'Lizzie, did your mum say where she was meeting Milly?'

I dragged my eyes away from an exciting part of my book. 'I think she's going to Milly's house.'

Granny nodded. 'Oh, I see.'

I was in bed when Mum returned and I heard her speaking to Granny before she came through to the bedroom. Her cheeks were pink with being out in the cold wind and she didn't seem her usual self.

'Are you awake, Lizzie?'

I sat up in bed. 'Did you enjoy your visit to Milly?'

She didn't look at me as she climbed into bed. 'Yes, I did. We had a good blether.'

The next day brought some good news for her in the shape of a letter from Aunt Margaret. Gerald's posting in Rio was over and they would be travelling to his new post at Easter. They were heading to Lisbon, in Portugal, and Margaret said she was coming to see us before joining her husband.

Mum was thrilled at the thought of seeing her and so was I.

9

EASTER

It was Easter 1922 and Aunt Margaret was in the country. She was planning to visit us soon. Mum was so excited at the thought of seeing her after such a long time, and I was pleased to see that she seemed to be back to her usual self. Granny noticed this as well and she also looked pleased by the forthcoming visit.

I thought the time dragged by and I began to get impatient, but Mum warned me to behave. 'You have to learn to be patient, Lizzie. You know what people say: Rome wasn't built in a day.'

I was puzzled by her remark and wondered what Rome had to do with my aunt's visit, but I wisely stayed silent and just nodded.

The weather was lovely and sunny but with a cool breeze and Mum couldn't help saying, 'I hope it gets warmer when she comes, as she will notice such a difference from South America.'

I would soon be moving to primary seven at school and I planned to tell my aunt all my news. Mum, however, warned me not to hog all the conversation when she arrived because she was going to spend an entire week with us. I felt it was like Christmas instead of the start of the Easter school holiday and I was ready to burst with suppressed excitement.

Mum was still visiting Milly on a regular basis, and one night Granny asked her as she put on her coat to leave, 'Is Milly keeping well, Beth?'

Mum was just about to leave, but she stopped to look at Granny. 'She's fine, Mary, but obviously still heartbroken over the deaths in her family. Her mother has never recovered from the shock of hearing the terrible news and neither has Milly. They have a little shrine in their front room with the photos of both men and they mention it every time I visit.'

'Don't you find this upsetting, Beth?' Granny seemed to be concerned about these visits.

'Yes, I do, but I do my best to cheer them up.' Mum glanced around the house to make sure she had her bag, scarf and gloves before giving me a quick kiss on my cheek as she went towards the door.

'Can I come with you, Mum?' I asked.

She shook her head. 'It's too late for you to be out, Lizzie.'

Granny looked thoughtful, but when she saw me staring at her, she smiled and said it was time for my cocoa, then bed. I wanted to ask her why she didn't go with Mum; then I realised she had to stay at home to look after me.

Although I pretended to be asleep, I was always awake when Mum arrived home and I had noticed before her bright-eyed look, as if she had won some kind of victory, but I couldn't figure out what victory Mum could have won.

The week before Aunt Margaret's visit, however, she seemed distracted and pale when she arrived back, and I heard her suppressed sobs as she lay down in her bed.

I was alarmed. 'What's the matter, Mum?'

The crying stopped and she sat up. 'Oh, I thought you were asleep, Lizzie.' She searched for her hankie in the bedside-table drawer and wiped her face. 'I'm just crying with pleasure at the thought of seeing Margaret again.'

After counting the days till our visitor arrived, a taxi drew up outside the close and Aunt Margaret stepped out onto the pavement and glanced up at the window where I had spent the past hour gazing out. She waved, and Mum and I went downstairs to meet her.

I was expecting her to have loads of luggage, but all she carried was a small suitcase. Mum ran to greet her, while I stayed in the background.

'Margaret, it's so good to see you.' Mum was in tears as she spoke.

Margaret, in her usual practical fashion, said, 'Let's go upstairs, Beth.' She turned to me and took my hand. 'I hardly recognised you, Lizzie, you've grown so tall.'

I carried the suitcase upstairs and Granny was waiting at the door. Margaret laughed. 'What a great welcoming party I've got. I feel like the prodigal daughter returning to the fatted calf.' She gave Granny a big hug. 'How are you keeping, Mary? It's so good to see you all again.'

Granny and Mum had made a special meal for Aunt Margaret's homecoming: mince and mashed potatoes followed by rhubarb crumble and custard. Margaret gave a small whoop of joy when she was told what was on the menu. 'It's been years since I had mince and tatties and rhubarb crumble and custard.'

Margaret put her suitcase in our bedroom and hung her coat on the hook on the back of the door. She was quite tall, with short grey hair and a weather-beaten complexion. She saw me looking at her and she laughed. 'I've spent too many years living in a sunny climate, Lizzie.'

She wasn't as pretty and petite as Mum, but she was better dressed, with a grey woollen skirt and a white, high-necked crêpe de Chine blouse. Her black boots had a row of tiny buttons up the side – I wondered how long it took her to fasten them up every morning.

Then Mum came in and looked at the suitcase. 'Is the rest of your luggage arriving later, Margaret?'

'No, Beth, this is all I've got with me, as I've booked into the Royal Hotel for a few days.'

Mum looked disappointed. 'Oh, I thought you would be staying with us.'

Margaret put her arm around Mum's shoulder. 'I didn't want to put Mary to a lot of trouble with my visit, but we'll spend loads of time together.'

Then Granny called out that the dinner was ready and we all went through to the table by the window. Margaret enjoyed her meal, and afterwards when we were having a cup of tea she said, 'I'd forgotten how good Scottish cooking is. I really enjoyed that.'

I was impatient to hear all the stories about some of the countries she had lived in, but I remembered Mum's warning about me not bombarding her with my questions and childish chatter so I bided my time.

Later, when we were sitting around the fire, she produced three parcels from her case. 'It's just a small present for you all,' she said as she handed them out. Both Mum's and my parcels were small, while Granny's was larger.

When we opened them, Mum and I were delighted with a golden bangle each, while Granny had a very soft purple stole, which she put around her shoulders with a cry of pleasure.

'I've never felt anything so soft, Margaret,' said Granny, while Mum and I put our bangles on our wrists, where they almost glowed with magnificence.

'Your stole is made with alpaca wool, Mary; it's made from the fleece of a llama. And the bangles are made from South American gold, Beth. I hope you like them.'

We assured her that we were delighted with our gifts. I was on the verge of asking my questions, but she said, 'This visit is for two reasons, Beth: firstly I wanted to see you all, but I'm on a house-hunting quest as well.'

Mum said, 'What about Gerald's new posting?'

Margaret explained the situation. 'Gerald and I hope to come back here to live after he retires. He doesn't fancy going back to Edinburgh but wants a house by the sea. I'm hoping to find something suitable in Monifieth or Carnoustie.'

Mum was delighted by this news. 'When will this be, Margaret?'

Margaret laughed. 'Oh, not for a few years, but you know what he's like, he wants to be prepared when the occasion happens.' She picked up her bag and took out a brochure. 'I've booked into this hotel in Carnoustie for next week and I wondered if you would all like to join me while I look at houses.'

I jumped up. 'Can I come as well?'

She laughed. 'Of course you can.' She turned to Granny. 'I would love it if you could come, Mary.'

Granny shook her head. 'Thank you, Margaret, but it will be better if it's just the three of you, as you don't want a decrepit old body tagging along.'

I happened to glance at Mum and was dismayed to see a look of relief on her face. Thankfully, Granny didn't see it.

Mum said she would try to get a holiday from her work and it was all settled that we would head off to Carnoustie at the end of the week. The hotel looked quite grand and I was almost squirming with excitement at the thought of being away on holiday.

At nine o'clock, Margaret said she would have to get back to her hotel in Union Street, and Mum said she would go with her to see her settled in. I wanted to go as well, but Granny said it was my bedtime, so I had no choice but to go to the bottom of the close with them and stand and watch as they both boarded a tramcar.

The night had turned colder and I was freezing by the time I got back upstairs. Granny was cross with me for my foolhardiness in standing on the pavement.

'You'll catch your death of cold and then you won't be able to go to Carnoustie,' she warned me.

Appalled by this warning, I made up my mind not to get a cold, but once I was in bed and tucked up in my flannelette sheets and cosy quilt I soon warmed up.

It was almost eleven o'clock when Mum arrived back. Granny was asleep and I could hear Mum humming a tune as she got ready for bed. I was so pleased to hear Mum singing. I couldn't recall a time in the last five years when she had been this happy.

10

CARNOUSTIE

The plan was to leave for our holiday on Saturday evening after Mum had finished her work. Mum had been talking about nothing else since Margaret's arrival. She was a changed woman, and as she sat down for her tea on the Friday night she chatted happily about the plans for the coming week.

'Margaret said it would make the holiday seem longer if we left on the Saturday evening. That way we can have the whole day on Sunday instead of travelling and arriving in the afternoon.'

The excitement was contagious, and I was almost bursting with anticipation about the holiday. There had been one little incident earlier in the week when Margaret had tried to persuade Granny to come with us. I was looking at Mum when she said this and I was sure she was holding her breath.

Granny thanked Margaret and said, 'I would have loved to come, but I have an important meeting at the church on Sunday.'

I was worried when Mum visibly looked relieved again; in fact, she gave a huge sigh before covering her relief with a small cough.

Granny glanced over at her with a shrewd look. 'I hope you're not getting a cold, Beth, as it would be awful if you missed out on this holiday.'

Mum assured her it was just a slight tickle in her throat and nothing that a drink of water wouldn't cure.

Margaret looked nonplussed by this small exchange, but she

replied brightly, 'Well, Mary, you know you're welcome to come later in the week if you want to.'

Later, as we lay in bed, Mum said, 'I would love your granny to come and spend some time with us, Lizzie, but I do want it to be the three of us too. I hope I didn't give the impression I didn't want her to be with us.'

Mum had our suitcases packed by the Friday night. They sat in the hall and by the way Mum glanced at them with a smile every time she passed them, anyone would have thought they were icons of pleasure.

Thankfully the weather turned sunny and warm by the time we were ready to leave. Granny was standing on the landing as we hurried down the stairs on Saturday and on impulse I turned around and gave her a big hug.

'I wish you were coming with us,' I whispered.

She held me close and smiled. 'I'll maybe come with you another time. Now, away you go and have a great time on the beach.' She smoothed down my summer frock as if it was creased. 'Now you've got your shilling in your purse, so treat yourself to some ice cream.'

I held up my little purse that hung from a cord around my neck. 'Yes, I've got it here, Granny, and I'll see you next week.'

For some reason, I felt sad at leaving her behind, but as soon as we reached the East Station, where the train was due to depart for our destination, the feeling passed and once again anticipation took over. The platform was quiet, as most of the daily passengers or day trippers had long departed for home and we had a carriage all to ourselves. Mum let me sit by the window and I was engrossed by all the passing scenery. The sun was setting and long shadows began to appear as we swept past houses and fields until I finally got my first glimpse of the river.

White Sands Hotel was just as the brochure had described: a white-painted two-storey building set in a large garden that overlooked the sea. As we entered the reception area, a large grandfather clock chimed eight o'clock and a young woman smiled at us from behind a miniscule desk. Aunt Margaret signed the register, and then a young lad took our suitcases up to the two rooms that had been booked. Mum and I were to share one while Margaret had the small single room next to us. I had never been in a hotel before and I gazed out of the window with pleasure at the view of the sea.

Aunt Margaret had booked a meal for us, and after a quick wash in the bathroom along the corridor, we set off down the carpeted stairs to the dining room, which also had a sea view. The room was quiet, as most of the guests had already dined, and I felt so important as a large cardboard menu was placed in my hands by the waitress, who wore a simple black dress with a white frilly apron.

We all settled for fish in a white sauce, which was called sole mornay, with tomato soup to start and ice cream with peaches as a pudding. Mum and Margaret had coffee in the lounge while I had an orange squash. A three-piece band was playing a selection of popular tunes as the lady pianist sang in a lovely soprano voice. I felt so grown up and smart in this new setting. I was pleased to see Mum looking so relaxed, her foot tapping out the rhythm. At one point she even began to sing quietly along with the soprano and Aunt Margaret smiled.

At ten thirty we made our way upstairs, and I was soon tucked up in bed with the sound of the sea coming through the open window. Mum moved around the room, getting ready for bed, and I was pleased that she was still humming one of the songs that had been played earlier.

The next morning, after a breakfast served by the same waitress, we set off for the beach. I was wearing my swimsuit under my new dress and although the sun was warm, the water was very cold when I ventured in for a swim. I let the cold waves wash over me and after a few minutes I began to enjoy myself. There was a rock out at sea, maybe a hundred yards or so from the beach, and I considered swimming out to it, but Mum suddenly called out, 'Don't go too far out, Lizzie. Stay near the shore.'

I waved and lay on my back, looking up at the sky, which was like a blue arc above my head.

I knew Mum hated the water and she could never understand why my father had enjoyed his swimming so much. Obviously I had inherited his love of being suspended between the earth and the air with just water keeping me afloat.

Half an hour later I was ready to come ashore and I quickly made my way to where Mum and Margaret had placed their deckchairs in a sheltered spot.

Margaret was telling Mum about her search for a house. 'Gerald has given me an idea of the kind of place he wants and I have an appointment with a local solicitor this afternoon to see what's on offer.'

Mum was curious. 'Why is Gerald so keen to have a house by the sea, Margaret?'

'His grandmother had a house in Berwick and he spent a lot of his childhood there, but he's always fancied living in this area.'

Mum looked a bit dubious. 'Will you both be happy when he retires? You have to admit you've had an adventurous life living in exotic places and you might find it dull living in a small town.'

Margaret laughed. 'Oh, it's not all that glamorous, Beth. Yes, we've seen a bit of the world, but do you remember what your father always said? "East, west, hame's best."'

Mum nodded and she looked sad. 'Yes, I remember him saying it. He was always full of those pithy sayings.' She handed me a large towel. 'Hurry up and get that wet swimsuit off, Lizzie, because your arms and legs are turning blue.'

This was an exaggeration, but I wasn't happy having to strip off my wet suit in front of Margaret and another two people who were walking along the beach. I picked up the towel and my clothes.

'I'll change in the hotel if that's all right,' I said, looking at my aunt.

'That's a good idea, Lizzie,' she replied.

As I hurried up the beach, I heard Mum say that I was becoming more modest as I got older. Then she called out, 'Put your wet swimsuit in the wash hand basin.'

Margaret said this was a natural feeling. 'It took me months before I could get undressed in front of Gerald after we were married. He used to laugh at me.'

It was Mum's turn to laugh. 'Margaret, I don't believe a word of it.'

'You may well scoff, Beth, but it's true.'

I tried to visualise Margaret struggling to get undressed for bed, but couldn't.

Our room in the hotel was cosy from the sun shining through the window, and I was grateful for its warmth. I dressed quickly, combed my wet hair and hurried back to the beach, as I didn't want to miss a moment of this holiday.

The couple who had been walking on the sand had disappeared as I made my way back to the deckchairs. As I approached, I heard Mum's voice. It wasn't her usual tone but more like a loud whisper.

'Can I tell you a secret, Margaret?'

I saw my aunt turn slightly in her seat and look at Mum. 'Of course you can, Beth. Do you remember when you were young how you always told me about things that worried you?'

'Yes, I do remember, and that's why I have to ask you about something.' Mum hesitated, but she didn't look round to see if anyone was about.

There were clumps of rough grass growing on the sand, and I sat quietly down behind one clump, feeling so guilty at eavesdropping but unable to move away. It was the strangest feeling, like I was powerless to do anything but sit. It seemed ages until Mum spoke again: I thought she had decided to abandon any more conversation and that they had both fallen asleep in the warm sun. I was almost on my feet when she said, 'Do you know anything about spiritualism, Margaret?'

Margaret seemed to be confused. 'Do you mean seances or fortune telling, Beth?'

'No, it's nothing like that. It's a spiritualist medium who comes to a hall and gives messages from the dead.'

Margaret said she knew about things like that. 'In South America there are lots of people who believe in messages from beyond the grave, but I've never had any experience of it myself.'

'Milly, my friend at work, and her mother go to this hall in Lochee where they have these spiritualist meetings and I've been going with them. Milly's fiancé and her brother were both in the Black Watch and were killed at Loos. They hope to get a message from them, as they are grief-stricken over the deaths, especially Milly's mother, who has never recovered from the shock of her son's death. They asked me to go with them in case Peter wanted to contact me. I've told them he isn't dead but being held as a prisoner or he's been badly injured and he's in some hospital, but they say that can't be true as he would have been home by now.'

As I sat in the shelter of the dunes, I was saddened by Mum's revelations. I had overheard Granny tell Mrs Mulholland one day that Mum was tearing herself apart with all this false hope, but I also wanted to believe that Dad was still alive yet unable to come home.

Margaret had remained quiet throughout Mum's story, but she leaned towards her and said, 'I know there are lots of different cultures in the world that do believe that they can communicate with lost loved ones, but it's never been proved, Beth. One thing, however, is that the rituals of remembering the dead often bring peace and understanding.'

To my horror, Mum began to cry. 'I find these meetings very traumatic, Margaret. The hall is full of grieving women, for it's mostly women who go there and some get messages from beyond the grave. I've told Milly that because I've never had a message then that proves Peter isn't dead, because I know he would want to get in touch with me for a final goodbye. In fact, the last meeting I was at I felt so glad that there was nothing from him that I came home in a good mood.'

I remembered that night when Mum had a look of triumph on her face, and I was suddenly saddened by all this grief and longing and the thought that we would never see Dad again.

Margaret picked up her handbag, which was lying on the sand, and took out her handkerchief. 'Can I give you some advice, Beth?' Mum must have nodded because she went on. 'I think you should stop going to these meetings because they are upsetting you. I'm not saying the organisers are frauds, but I do think they are playing with people's emotions. These poor women who are clutching at straws to find some sort of answer to this dreadful and futile war; mothers, fathers, family and sweethearts who waved their menfolk away with banners and flags only to find that that was the last time they would see them. It must be an emotional nightmare, as it is with you and Lizzie. Have you discussed this with Mary?'

Mum sounded horrified. 'No, Margaret, I haven't, and promise me you won't say anything to her, as she will be mortified by my behaviour.'

Margaret said she would say nothing. She turned. 'I wonder where Lizzie is.'

On hearing my name I felt I had to stand up and not listen any longer. I scampered back along the sand and finally stood up and called out, 'I'm back'

There was silence from the women, but as I approached Mum smiled brightly while Margaret looked at her watch and said, 'I have to go and see the solicitor soon. Do you both want to come with me?'

'Oh yes, I do,' I said, but Mum didn't look too sure. I was hopping about, eager to go, so she finally agreed.

'We won't be in the way, will we, Margaret?'

My aunt smiled. 'You're never in my way, both of you. Of course I want you with me.'

We went back to the hotel, where we had our midday meal, then it was off to the solicitor, who had his office on the main street. We had to climb a flight of stairs, but the office was quite large and airy and overlooked the street. Mr Anderson was sitting behind a large desk, but he stood up when we entered. I think he was a bit surprised when he saw the three of us, but Margaret introduced us and we were shown to some comfy-looking chairs.

Mr Anderson had a thin file in front of him and he passed it over to my aunt. 'I have three houses that are suitable for renting or buying and you can go and view them anytime.'

Margaret said she could go right away and look at them. Mr Anderson left the room and quickly came back with three sets of keys. 'The file has all the relevant information, along with the addresses, and I can arrange for a car to take you to view them.'

'Are they all within walking distance, Mr Anderson?'

'Yes, they are, but please take your time and just let me have the keys back when you've seen them all.'

We emerged onto the street and Margaret turned to Mum. 'Do you feel like going to look at these houses, Beth?'

Mum said she didn't mind, so we set off to view the first one on the list. It was called Dene House, but when we eventually found its location, Margaret didn't like the look of it. It was tucked away down a narrow lane and surrounded by trees. The garden had a mossy, damp look, as if the sun didn't linger long. My aunt didn't even venture inside; she scored it off the list and we trudged on.

The next cottage, Willowbank, looked more promising, but it didn't have a sea view, although Mum and Margaret did say it had character. I loved it. It had low beamed ceilings and small windows that overlooked a well-kept garden, but, like Dene House, Willowbank was also scratched off the list.

The final house was a well-built stone house with a flight of stairs leading up to the front door. We all stood and looked out the window at the so-called sea view, but it was mostly hidden behind the roofs of the houses at the back. Oh, it had a tiny view of the sea, but Margaret wasn't pleased.

'I specifically asked for a detached house with an uninterrupted view, so I won't be considering this lot.'

Back in the solicitor's office, she mentioned this to Mr Anderson. 'My husband and I don't need the house right away, so if you can keep an eye out for the one I've described then you can get in touch with us.'

Mr Anderson said he would, but he explained, 'We don't get many houses like you've described coming up for sale or rent, but I will do my best to keep looking and I'll inform you if one does become vacant.'

Margaret said that would be fine and we made our way out of the office and back to the hotel. After our evening meal and an hour spent in the lounge with coffee and sherries for Mum and Margaret and a glass of lemonade for me, we decided it had been a tiring day and we went upstairs to bed.

I was reading my latest book, while Mum sat at the dressing table brushing her hair. Without meaning to, I suddenly said, 'Mum, do you think Dad is dead?'

She gave me a suspicious look. 'Were you listening to us on the beach, Lizzie?'

I thought about telling a lie, but I felt my face turn red. 'I didn't mean to, Mum, but I did hear what you said to Aunt Margaret.'

To my deep embarrassment I began to cry, and Mum came to sit on my bed, giving me a hug. 'I'm sorry, Lizzie, but I just don't know what to think any more. I do want to believe your dad is still alive, but I get so confused now and my thoughts are all over the place.' She gave me a serious look. 'I don't want to hurt and worry your granny with all of this, so you'll be a good girl and not say a word to her. Will you promise me?'

Although I didn't like the idea of not telling Granny, I nodded.

'You were just a wee girl when your dad went away to the war, but I hope you have lovely memories of him like I do. And another thing, I'm not going back to the meetings with Milly and her mother. They are too distressing.'

I nodded again, and later, when Mum had fallen asleep, I took the photo of Dad holding the trophy at the swimming baths, the one that showed the water dripping off his dark hair that was so like my own. I had quietly taken it out of the photo album that Granny had shown me – I fervently hoped she wouldn't miss it, at least for a little while. I kissed the image and placed it back in my book. I had memories of him, just small, fleeting things, like the way he used to laugh and tease me. I could almost smell the shaving soap he used to use, a tangy, smoky smell that I loved. I lay in bed and wished he was still a part of our lives.

Then there was the thought: maybe Mum was right. Maybe he wasn't dead but would someday walk back into our lives.

Years afterwards I was to recall that week with my mother and aunt. I remembered the sun glinting off the sea, the lovely sunsets and the comfortable hotel, but most of all it was the last time I saw Mum looking happy and carefree.

Within a few days of arriving back home, Margaret had to leave to join her husband. Mum and I went to the railway station with her to say goodbye. As usual, Margaret was practical and down to earth as we stood on the platform.

'I'll be in touch soon, Beth, so I want you to promise to look after yourself.'

I thought Mum would burst into tears, but she managed to smile as the train drew into the station.

Margaret gave us both a tight hug and smiled. 'I'll write soon and give you all my news, and when Gerald retires we will be home again.'

'Please send me postcards for my collection, Aunt Margaret,' I said.

She smiled. 'I'll send you loads and loads, Lizzie, and Uncle Gerald has bought himself a new camera so I'll send photographs as well.'

With a flurry of activity in putting her luggage on board before climbing into the carriage, we said our goodbyes as the train pulled away from the platform. We were left with the remnants of sooty steam and a small group of people who, like us, were seeing loved ones going on a journey.

Mum was crying but trying to hide the fact from me, and although I was dry-eyed, I was crying inwardly.

11

UNREST AND BAD NEWS

After Margaret's departure, Mum seemed to perk up. Granny noticed the change and remarked on it to Mrs Mulholland. 'The holiday has done the world of good for Beth, thank goodness.'

Mrs Mulholland said that this was a blessing and hoped it would continue. 'The poor lass has been through so much, with her husband missing.'

Granny didn't know I was listening, so I crept back to my bedroom and prayed with all my heart that Mum was finally getting better.

She still went out once or twice a week to visit Milly, but she said she didn't go back to the spiritualist meetings, although Milly's mother continued to go to try to get a message from her dead son.

After a few weeks, Mum became quiet and dispirited. Granny asked her if she was ill, but she just said everything was all right except she was worried about her job in the hat shop.

'Every day when I go into the town there are meetings of unemployed people gathering in the city centre, and it's getting worse. Cox's mill has laid off hundreds of workers and people are becoming angry that there is no work. I worry that DM Brown's will also lay off staff, and Milly says it's a possibility.'

Granny knew all about this unrest, as the newspapers were printing stories of the crowds of angry and hungry people.

'This government should be getting people back into jobs instead of sitting on their fat backsides,' she said one night as we sat down to our tea.

'There's been riots on some streets and shop windows broken and goods stolen,' said Mum. 'We could hear the noise from the store's windows and customers are keeping well away from the city centre. I honestly don't know where it's all going to end.' This was worrying news for me because Mum looked so pale and ill and all this uncertainty wasn't helping her. 'There are crowds of ex-soldiers joining in the protest, I heard. They're saying they fought a war to make a better world, but they've come back to starvation and no chance of any work. No wonder they are all so angry and bitter.'

We finished our meal in silence, then Granny said we were lucky to have food to eat, but Mum didn't answer. She got up and carried the empty plates into the sink, where she tackled the washing-up with a fierce expression in her eyes.

Margaret was reunited with Gerald, and she wrote long letters to Mum and sent postcards to me. I loved looking at the views of Lisbon and rushed through to my bedroom to put them in my box under the bed.

One day, Mum read out a letter from her and told me Margaret wanted to pay for my school fees at the Harris Academy, should I pass my qualifying exam. 'Would you like to go to the Harris Academy, Lizzie?'

Quite honestly I didn't care one way or another. My plan when I left school was to travel the world, and I didn't need good school marks to do that. However, I said I wouldn't mind.

My time at Rosebank School would soon be over and I felt sad about leaving it to go on to pastures new. Emily had been put back a year, which meant she wouldn't be leaving with me, and that was something else for me to miss, as we had been pals since our primary one days.

She said she would miss me as well, but she seemed happy enough to be staying on. One evening Mum said to meet her at dinnertime in the town and we would go to buy my new outfit. I waited outside the DM Brown's front door until Mum came hurrying out.

'We'll have to hurry, Lizzie, as I've only got an hour before I have to go back to work.' We headed for Reform Street and Caird's outfitter's store, where Margaret had deposited a cheque to cover the cost of my new uniform.

'We're very lucky to have your aunt pay for this,' said Mum, as we hurried along the pavement.

Inside the store we were served by an elderly, white-haired woman who quickly showed us the school blazer, the navy gym tunic with the gold and brown Harris school braid around the neckline, and a pair of black shoes.

'You must write to Margaret to thank her for her generosity, as it's not every girl who gets the opportunity to go to a prestigious school,' said Mum, who seemed quite out of breath with all the hurrying.

When I arrived home with my packages, Granny wanted to see what I had bought. She inspected the material of the blazer and gym tunic before nodding her appreciation. 'It's good quality, so mind you look after it,' she warned.

I couldn't believe how quickly my last term at school had gone, and I was ready to face this new chapter in my life. Because it would soon be my 12th birthday, I felt really grown up. In a few more years the world would be my oyster and I would be free to travel to exotic shores and realise my dreams.

I was busy doing my homework the day before my birthday, with my head full of far-off places instead of sums and spelling, when Granny announced she had to go to a meeting at the church with Mrs Mulholland.

'You'll be all right on your own until your mum gets home, Lizzie. Tell her I won't be long.'

I barely looked up as she put on her coat and hat before hurrying out the door. Later, when my homework was finished, I settled down with my library book, which was the tale of a couple of adventurous schoolgirls at a boarding school who were always getting into dangerous situations. I was so engrossed in the story that I didn't hear the front door open, but when I heard Mum crying, I quickly stood up in alarm and was standing nervously when she came in. Her face was pale and she was shaking as the tears ran down her cheeks.

I ran forward, as I thought she was going to faint, but she managed to sit on the chair. 'Mum, what's wrong?' The words came out like a whisper, as if I was afraid of the answer.

'Milly's mother died today.'

I was shocked, as Mum wiped her eyes with a handkerchief that lay like a sodden lump in her hand.

'A neighbour came to the store this afternoon and Milly had to go home. She was in a dreadful state, so I'll have to go and see her.' Mum stopped and looked around the room. 'Where's Granny?'

I mentioned the church meeting.

'Well, you'll have to go up to Mrs Mulholland's house and ask if she can look after you till your granny gets home.'

'Mrs Mulholland has gone to the meeting as well,' I said.

Mum looked confused and seemed undecided what to do. Suddenly she stood up. 'Get your coat, Lizzie, you'll have to come with me.'

I looked longingly at my book before hurrying to get my coat from the lobby cupboard.

As we made our way down the stairs, Mum took her powder compact from her bag and looked critically in the tiny mirror. 'Goodness, I look a right mess,' she said as she dabbed powder over her cheeks.

We quickly made our way to Dudhope Crescent Road. Milly lived with her mother in a flat on the second floor in the close next to the church. It was then I noticed with dismay that her window overlooked the old graveyard that Emily and I often dared one another to go into to hide behind a headstone. As I recalled, neither of us had done this, as the place had an overgrown appearance, with many of the gravestones covered with moss.

It was a stranger who answered the door and we could hear the voices of many people in the small flat.

Mum said, 'I work with Milly. How is she?'

The tall, thin elderly woman, who turned out to a neighbour, whispered, 'She's in a terrible state, poor lass. Her mother seemed fine when Milly left for work this morning, but just after dinnertime she was climbing the stairs after going down to the shop when she suddenly collapsed and died. It was terrible, because none of us could do anything for her.' She leant forward towards Mum, as if she wanted to whisper in her ear. 'If you ask me, she died of a broken heart because she never got over the death of her son and, of course, Milly's lad as well. That bloody war has a lot to answer for.'

I saw Mum's face grow pale and I was afraid she would collapse as well, but she walked resolutely towards Milly, who was sitting by the fireside and refusing the offer of more hot, sweet tea.

When she spotted us, she quickly stood up, and Mum hugged her as she began to cry again.

'Oh Milly, I'm so very sorry,' said Mum. 'What a terrible shock for you.'

I went and stood beside the window that overlooked the graveyard, and even though I was young, with little experience of life, I did recognise how terrible it must have been for the two women to have this reminder of death every time they left the house or looked out the window. Perhaps if the two dead men had been buried there, Milly and her mother could have comforted themselves by visiting the graves with flowers, but a son and a fiancé were now lying in another country and far from home.

The room had become unbearably hot, which was made worse by the kettle boiling on the stove and another teapot being filled from it. One elderly plump woman came and opened the window before sitting down on an empty chair beside me. She began wiping her face with a large red handkerchief. She turned to her neighbour and sighed.

'Aye, it's a sad day for the close. I was just speaking to Bella this morning and it's hard to believe she's dead.'

Her companion just nodded wordlessly and went to refill her cup from the teapot before retaking her seat on the wooden kitchen chair. 'I don't know what Milly will do now that she's on her own without any family left,' she said.

I noticed Mum coming towards me and I felt relieved that we would soon be leaving. She spoke to the plump women.

'I've asked Milly to come and stay with us for a few days, but she says she wants to stay here.'

The woman said that the neighbours would all look after her and Mum said, 'Thank you.'

As we went out the door, I glanced back at the scene of mourning. It was difficult to see Milly because of the crowd.

When we got back to Victoria Road, we saw Granny looking out the window, and when we reached the house she rushed to open the door. 'I've been so worried about you. Where have you been?'

Mum explained the sad news and Granny was shocked. 'That's terrible. How is Milly?'

'She has all the neighbours in with her, so they will be a great help to her, but later, when the news sinks in, I don't know how she'll cope. I did ask her to come here for a wee while, but she wanted to stay. She could have slept in my bed and I could have shared with Lizzie.'

Now, when I think of that night, I'm ashamed to remember how relieved I was that Milly hadn't taken up Mum's offer. I consoled myself later with thinking it was the selfishness of youth and not some horrid part of my being.

'Well, your tea is in the oven, but I think it's a bit dried up by now,' said Granny, bringing out two plates of bacon and eggs.

The bacon was crispy and the egg had a brown frilly edge and a hard yolk, but we were both hungry so we ate it up without complaint.

The next day was my birthday and I couldn't help thinking how similar it was to my sixth, when the news had come in about

Dad being missing in action. Six whole years, but the war was still responsible for victims of its violence.

I got a lovely nightgown from Granny, and books from Mum and Aunt Margaret. Granny made a small birthday cake, but somehow the pleasure of the celebration was missing.

12

A NEW SCHOOL

I was a bit apprehensive at the thought of going to a new school, but Mum said to look on it as an adventure.

'You're so like your dad, Lizzie, full of confidence. I often think you have none of my nature in you. Your dad liked going out and meeting people at the swimming and tennis clubs and he was always so full of life.'

I knew this was true because Mum didn't have a lot of friends, preferring to go out to work then stay at home in the evenings. Her sole friend was Milly, and I knew she was upset at not being allowed off work to go to Bella's funeral and be a support for her friend. But Milly understood that having a job and keeping it was very important in the city because so many people were unemployed and times were very hard.

Granny had offered to go to the funeral, and although Mum would have liked to have been there, it was important that one member of our family went to pay their respects. So Granny had put on her best black coat and hat and gone along to Milly's house, where the small service was held, and although she hadn't gone to the cemetery, she had stayed for a cup of tea and sandwiches, which she told Mum had been delicious. Mum said Milly had been touched by this gesture, while Granny said it had all been so sad, especially as Milly was now all alone in the world.

'The one good thing,' said Granny, 'is that she has good neighbours and they will look after her. I've told her she must come here for her tea whenever she wants to.'

So my new life at the Harris Academy coincided with Milly coming to the house two or three times a week. On these occasions I would go into the bedroom and do my homework before going back into the living room and listening to the conversation.

I wasn't the cleverest of scholars, although I did try hard to take in all the different subjects. It was so different from the primary school that at times I felt out of my depth. My favourite subjects were English, geography and history, and while I could manage arithmetic I didn't really like it very much.

Every morning Mum and I would catch the tram, and although she got off at the High Street I stayed on until it reached Tay Street, when I would race up to the playground in time for the bell.

There was just one thing worrying me and that came in the shape of Agnes Burnett. She was in the year above me, but I remembered her well from Rosebank School. She was a relative of Emily, some cousin or something, and she was a bully. She was tall for her age but had a plain, dumpling-like face and she wore glasses which seemed to magnify her pale blue eyes.

I had just finished my first month at school when she recognised me in the playground. 'Oh, it's skinny, dizzy Lizzie,' she said to the three girls who appeared to be her best friends. 'I wonder how you managed to get to this school, as you weren't the brightest girl in class, were you?'

I ignored her and turned my back to walk away. Enraged, she ran after me and poked me with her finger. 'Don't you turn your back on me, Lizzie Flint.'

I didn't turn round but kept walking away, and I heard her friends laugh. I was shaking with annoyance as I sat in my class. I realised I had made an enemy before I had had time to make a friend.

This name-calling went on every day for the next month, and

although I wasn't intimidated by Agnes and her friends, I hated the malice that was behind the taunts.

Back at home, Granny and Mum would quiz me on my day at school and I always tried to put on a bright, confident smile and tell them everything was fine. I didn't want to worry them by saying I hated it. I also got letters and postcards from Aunt Margaret asking the same thing and hoping I was enjoying the new experience. I decided to tell my aunt about the bullying, as I reckoned she lived so far away that my torment would remain a secret. I asked her not to say anything to Mum and, to my relief, she didn't.

It was one cold wet morning in October when things came to a head. I had arrived in the playground a bit earlier than usual and I didn't see Agnes or her three cronies until they came up behind me.

'Oh, here's dizzy Lizzie looking like a drowned rat,' said Agnes, and she gave me a hefty shove that landed me in a puddle of water.

'Ha, ha, ha,' laughed Agnes, while the other three sniggered. 'Dizzy Lizzie's wet herself. You'd better get Mummy to put some nappies on you.'

I stood up, and without thinking I grabbed Agnes by her jacket. Her blue eyes almost stood out on stalks in surprise.

'If you do that to me again, Agnes Burnett, I'll punch you so hard you'll wonder what hit you.' I was so angry. 'I remember how you pulled the head and arms off Emily's favourite doll, you horrible girl, and Emily cried for hours and hours until her mother told you to get out and not come back.'

Her pals looked on in amazement at this revelation. But Agnes walked away and said she was going to report me to the teacher. This was what I was dreading, and if the news got back to Mum then she would be so disappointed in me.

I went quickly to the cloakroom to dry my gym tunic, as the hem was soaking wet. I didn't realise a girl was following me until she stood in front of me.

'Hullo,' she said. 'I'm Laura. Don't let that wee monster worry you. I've noticed she always picks on the girls who are pretty. Perhaps it's because she has a face like a boiled gooseberry.'

I laughed and had a quick peek in the mirror. I hadn't thought of myself as being pretty, but this girl had said I was.

'I'm Lizzie. I don't think I've seen you in school.'

'No, I just started this week, but I've been watching that bully and her pals and if it's any consolation she picks on other girls as well. The pretty ones.'

I was so pleased to find out Laura was to be in my class and that I had found a friend at last.

Then a couple of weeks later we found out that Agnes and her pals had been in front of the headmaster and given a stern warning about their behaviour.

From then on, apart from receiving furious glares from my previous tormentors, life became happier. It was years later that I found out my aunt knew the headmaster from her own teaching days and that she had written to him about the situation.

Laura Niven lived in the Hawkhill and I often went home with her after school. Her mother would be baking when we went in and there was always the smell of home-made scones or pancakes smothered in strawberry jam, which we ate with relish.

Her mum would scold her: 'Leave some of the scones for your dad, Laura.'

Laura's dad, Wullie, was a joiner who worked in a small furniture factory, and he was a fervent socialist. We would be doing our homework while he spouted on about the state of the country. 'I'm lucky to have a job, but what about the thousands who are on the dole? There's a lot of anger in the country and it will all come to a head soon. Just you wait and see.'

Laura would giggle when he went on, while Irene, her mum, would calmly wash the dishes or sit down with her knitting.

'Are you listening to me, Irene?'

Irene would look up and nod. 'Yes, I'm listening to you, Wullie, and you're right.'

Appeased, he would sit back in his comfy armchair and read the paper.

I loved going to Laura's house after school, but one night Mum said I wasn't to bother Mrs Niven.

'Bring your friend here sometimes, Lizzie. After all, Laura's mum will have enough to do without you getting under her feet every afternoon.'

Granny was upstairs in Mrs Mulholland's house, so I told Mum I didn't like to bother her with my friend.

'You know how Granny has her own routine, Mum. Anyway, Mrs Niven says she doesn't mind me going to her house after school.'

Actually the main reason for not inviting Laura back was the fact that Granny was old-fashioned in her conversation and outlook and she would constantly question Laura about her lessons and what she wanted to do after leaving school. No, I much preferred the easy-going atmosphere at the Hawkhill, especially when Laura's dad arrived home from work with tiny curls of wood chippings in his hair and smelling of varnish and glue.

One evening I was on my way home to Victoria Road when I met Andy Baxter. He saw me but didn't speak, so I said, 'Hullo, Andy, it's Lizzie Flint. Maybe you don't remember me.'

He smiled and came over. 'I didn't want to bother you, Lizzie. How is your mother and Granny?'

I said they were both well. He didn't have his black eyepatch and I noticed he had a glass eye. He saw me looking at it and said ruefully, 'I'm not sure if this is an improvement on the patch.' His jacket and trousers looked threadbare and he was wearing a pair of sandshoes that were scuffed. I didn't mean to stare, but he looked embarrassed and said he had to be on his way home.

'Have you got a job, Andy?' I asked, but was immediately sorry for being nosy.

'No, I haven't, but I'm still looking and hopefully something will turn up.'

On that note he hurried up the Hilltown and I made my way home, feeling so sad for him and the hundreds of others who were unemployed.

I told Mum and Granny that I had been talking to him and they said the same thing, that it was a terrible world when so many people were living on the breadline.

The next evening at Laura's house I mentioned this meeting to her dad and he became so angry.

'There's going to be a lot of unrest coming and this government will have to get people back into work. That young man fought and was disabled fighting for his country and what thanks does he get? Bloody nothing.'

Mrs Niven looked at her husband. 'Mind your language, Wullie.'

Wullie made a snorting noise and disappeared behind his newspaper.

13

THE GENERAL STRIKE

The country was in a state of unrest. The miners were told that their wages were to be cut. Wullie Niven was solidly behind them.

'The miners are telling the government that there's not to be "a penny off the pay, a minute on the day", and they are right to call for a general strike.'

Irene was worried. 'What will happen if you have to go on strike, Wullie? How will we manage to live?'

'Well, we have to stand up to this government that wants to keep the working man down,' he said, but without much conviction.

Laura said afterwards that her father was big on conviction but still afraid of her mum's wrath when it came to money matters.

I have to admit we weren't too worried over this news because my old adversary at school was on the verge of leaving. Agnes Burnett, or Argy Bargy, as Laura and I had nicknamed her, hadn't really bothered me very much since her telling-off, but I still had to put up with her bulbous eyes glaring at me most days and I was often the person who got a shove from her now and again. However, I tried hard not to retaliate and that made her even madder, which gave me a feeling of satisfaction.

'Just think,' said Laura, 'maybe Argy Bargy won't manage to get a job because of all this unemployment and she'll have to go begging on the street, and what will we do? Well, we'll pass her by with a sneer.' For a moment, this thought pleased us.

The papers were full of the chaos caused by the strike, but then it turned out that volunteers were maintaining most of the services and trains. Trams and food supplies were almost at a normal level.

Wullie was annoyed about these volunteers. 'It's all right for these students and folk with money to step in and do the work of the strikers, but this country is rife with unemployment and folk are rioting on the streets because they don't have enough money to feed their families.'

Then it was announced that the Trades Union Congress, the miners' union, had decided to end the strike.

Wullie was enraged. 'The paper's saying the TUC is calling off the strike, Irene! It's a bloody . . .' He became silent as Irene gave him a stern look. 'It's a blinking disgrace, I can tell you,' he muttered, shaking the paper in disgust.

Laura and I had to muffle our laughter. He gave us both a hard look, but I began to cough and he seemed to think I had come down with the cold.

Still, what he said was true. We had witnessed the chaos on the Nethergate one day after school when an enraged crowd had tried to overturn a lorry that was being driven by a volunteer. It had been a frightening experience, and Laura had said she was glad her father was still working and not one of the mob that surrounded the lorry.

For a while now, Mum had been telling me to bring Laura round and I mentioned this to her one day.

'I would love to come to see your granny and mother.'

I glanced at her, thinking she was pretending, but she looked sincere, so the next night, instead of heading for the Hawkhill, we made our way to my house. I almost mentioned how quiet it would be and how Granny could be old-fashioned, but as things turned out I'd got everything wrong.

Laura and Granny got on like a house on fire. When she realised that Granny loved knitting, she asked if she could be shown how to do this. I had never enjoyed knitting, but Laura loved it and soon the two of them would be knitting and chatting while I did my homework and then read my latest book. After a while, I joined in and was soon knitting squares to be made up into blankets for the church, and I was ashamed to think I had ever thought it boring.

One evening, Granny asked Laura what she was planning to do after leaving school. Laura's face lit up. 'I'm hoping to be a teacher.' She turned to me. 'We can both become teachers, Lizzie, wouldn't that be great, and maybe we could be in the same school.'

I said that would be a great idea, but it was just to please her, as I didn't want to hurt her feelings by revealing my own hopeful plans for the future.

Mum also liked Laura's company and she would chatter on about her job and how her friend Milly was coping with living on her own.

One night I said to my friend, 'I hope you don't find us boring, Laura.'

She looked at me in amazement. 'Oh, I love the peace and quiet of your house. Don't get me wrong, I love my own home as well, but sometimes Dad gets carried away with politics and Mum has to calm him down. It gets hectic at times.'

It was my turn to be amazed. 'That's the reason I love being at the Hawkhill. It's so lively.'

Laura laughed. 'Maybe we should exchange houses then, Lizzie.' She then studied her knitting pattern for the matinee jacket she was knitting for the church, while I tried hard to get my knitted square finished. I had to admit to myself that I wasn't one of life's greatest knitters, but then I couldn't recall reading about any pirates who spent their lives at sea with their knitting needles, or any explorers, for that matter, because I had made up my mind that was what I wanted to do, as pirates were out of fashion.

14

MILLY MAKES A MOMENTOUS DECISION

Although the general strike was over, there were still families struggling to live on the breadline and the streets were always full of angry crowds gathering to protest about their poverty-stricken lives.

Even Mum, who was working, was feeling the strain, and I knew she was worried about keeping her job in the department store. Some nights when she came home from work she looked pale and worn out, and when Granny asked her how her day had gone she replied that it had been quiet in the millinery department and that some of the shop assistants were becoming worried about their future.

'It's just not in Dundee,' said Mum. 'It's the same all over the country.'

One afternoon Laura and I left school and caught the tramcar to Victoria Road. It had been a cold day with heavy showers and we were glad to be sitting in front of the fire. Granny had made cocoa and she laughed when we almost finished the plate of pancakes spread with butter.

'You haven't left much for your mother, have you, Lizzie?' she said as we sat at the table with our homework.

Laura and I must have looked guilty, but she said there were some more in the scullery.

We were still busy scribbling in our school jotters when Mum arrived home. She quickly took off her wet coat and hung it up in the lobby and she stood in front of the fire trying to warm her hands.

'I got soaked waiting for the tramcar.' She sat down and took off her shoes and put on her slippers. 'Oh, it's such a relief to be home when the weather is bad like this.' Turning to Granny, she said, 'Oh, by the way, Mary, Milly is coming round later. She was very quiet at work today, so I hope she's feeling all right.'

Laura was getting ready to go home when the doorbell went and Milly hurried into the room. She said she wasn't staying for long.

'I didn't want to mention this at work today, Beth, but I want you to know that I'll be leaving my work and my house and going to live with a cousin who lives in Glasgow.'

Mum and Granny were astounded.

'What's brought this on, Milly?' Mum asked.

Milly looked a bit embarrassed. 'Well, I'm finding it difficult to live on my own and pay the bills. I'm finding it gets harder every week. Then there's all this unrest about jobs, and what will happen if we lose our jobs, Beth?'

Mum started to say that this wouldn't happen, but Milly said it could and Mum had to agree that it was possible.

Granny said, 'Who is this cousin in Glasgow? Do you know her well?'

Milly said she didn't. 'The thing is, Jeannie my cousin lost her husband a couple of years ago and she's lonely, just like me. She wrote and asked if I'd like to go to visit her in Glasgow on Sunday and see if I'll like it there.'

While we all sat transfixed by this unexpected news, Laura, who had been sitting with her coat on, said, 'I'll have to get away home, Lizzie.'

I went and put on my coat and we went downstairs. 'I don't know how Mum will take this news, Laura.' I said. 'Milly's the only friend my mother has and I know they've shared a lot because of the deaths of my dad and Milly's fiancé and brother, who were all killed in the war.'

Laura was sympathetic. 'Your mum doesn't talk much about your dad, Lizzie.'

'That's because she's still convinced that he's alive and lying injured in some hospital in Germany.'

Laura looked at me sadly. 'That's awful. I knew you said your dad was posted missing in France, but I just assumed he was dead after all these years, and because you didn't say anything more I didn't like to ask. Mum and Dad asked me about him, but I told them you didn't like to talk about it.'

'No, I didn't say too much because I have to keep up this pretence that he's still alive, although Granny and I both know it's not true. My mum lives in a world of denial.'

'I know how you feel. My father joined up in 1915, but he was badly injured when a lorry overturned before he was sent abroad, so he was lucky that he didn't face the same carnage that other men faced.'

'Was he very ill when the accident happened?' I asked, feeling quite shocked by this revelation.

Laura nodded. 'I don't know if you've noticed that he has a limp when he walks. His leg was very badly broken and it took ages to heal. I remember Mum being so worried about him, but like your family, they never mention anything about those days.'

To be honest I had noticed his limp, but I had been so fascinated by his fervour about the state of the country that I hadn't thought any more about it, and Laura was quite right about this reluctance to speak about the war. I had met Andy's mother one day and she said he never mentioned the traumatic years of his army service. However, she did say he suffered from nightmares and he was shy around other people because of his injuries.

Milly was on the point of leaving when I got back upstairs and Mum was urging her to take her time about this momentous move.

After she left, Mum said, 'I've told her to think twice about moving, because she has her own house and it isn't easy leaving it behind to move in with someone.'

Granny stopped knitting and gave her a sad look. 'Is that how you felt when you moved here, Beth?'

Mum, realising her faux pas, said, 'No, we were glad to come here, Mary. You know that.'

Sadly, both Granny and I knew she lacked the conviction of her words. It would have been all right if Mum had had the sense to keep quiet, but she tried hard to rescue the situation, which made it worse instead of better.

'I mean, we couldn't afford to stay on in Garland Place, and it was so kind of you to offer us a home here.' She stopped for breath. 'Yes, we are both grateful, Mary, that's the truth.'

Granny seemed mollified by this grand speech, but I knew she was hurt because she began to dig her knitting needles into the stitches, which wasn't like her at all.

As we got ready for bed, Mum sat at the dressing-table mirror, brushing her hair. She caught sight of me looking at her in the mirror's reflection and she sighed.

'What a day it's been.'

Milly went off to Glasgow on Sunday on the morning train to visit this cousin she hadn't seen in years. Mum said she wouldn't like living in a strange house with a virtual stranger, but her words didn't sound convincing.

The next night Milly appeared at the house.

'How did you get on, Milly?' Mum asked as she busied herself with the teapot and the cups. Milly was dressed in her best dress and coat and was wearing her new pair of gloves.

'She's a lot older than me, Beth, but I think we'll get along fine. She has a nice two-bedroomed flat in Garnethill and it's not far from the centre of the town, and she says it should be easy to get a job in a department store because of my good references.'

Up till that point Granny had been sitting quietly, but she asked her, 'Do you feel you'll be happy living in another city, Milly?'

Milly didn't answer right away and Mum was about to speak

when she said, 'I'm not sure, Mary, but I don't think I've any choice. As I've said, since my mother died I've been finding things difficult and I know I can't manage much longer with my wages. No matter how much I try to cut down.'

'Well, Milly, you must go and do what you think is best for you. That's what I've told Beth.'

Mum gathered up the cups and saucers but didn't say anything. Milly stood up to leave.

'I'll have to think about it, but if I do decide to go then I must put my notice in to the store.'

Afterwards, when we were getting ready for bed, Mum said she was sure her friend had made up her mind to go.

'I'll miss her very much, Lizzie, but she has to do what's right for herself.'

15

THE WAR MEMORIAL
ON THE LAW

A month after that initial visit to her cousin's house, Milly was all ready to go. She had sold off the furniture and contents of her house, which gave her a tidy sum of money to start her new life. As she said, 'It's not as if I'll be beholden to Jeannie, at least not to begin with.'

On the Sunday afternoon before she left, Milly asked Mum and I to go with her to the new war memorial on top of the Law. Mum wasn't keen, but she felt she couldn't turn down this request from her friend. They had both paid a visit to the memorial on the day it was unveiled, but Mum had been very unhappy when she got home. It was as if the granite monument had been a reminder of all the deaths and she was still living in the hope that Dad would someday come home.

It was a cold, blustery day with some sharp showers when we made our way up the steep slope to the top, where the memorial stood looking out over the city that had lost so many of its young men.

Earlier, there had been a large article in the *People's Journal* that printed the photos of all the Dundee and district casualties of the war, and Milly treasured the paper, which showed the photographs of her brother Michael and fiancé Billy. I remembered the argument at home when Mum refused to allow a photograph of my father to be used. As a result his name was printed with a black silhouette and Granny had been so angry at this.

'Peter is dead, Beth. It's been years and he isn't coming back,' Granny had said.

Mum was furious. 'That's not true.' She looked at Granny, her face red with anger. 'Don't you want him to be alive, Mary?'

Granny went out of the door and I followed her. She was crying, but when I tried to speak to her she said she was fine. 'Go back in, Lizzie, and look after your mother.'

Now here we were, standing in the wind and looking at the memorial. Milly said what a great monument it was to the remembrance of the dead. I waited with bated breath, fully expecting Mum to lose her rag, but she turned away and said that it was indeed a great honour for the city to bestow upon the loss of so many fine young lives. Thankfully Milly didn't hear her murmur, 'It's a great pity this country allowed the war in the first place.'

We stood in silence for some time, then Milly said it was time to leave. I saw the look of relief on Mum's face as we slowly walked back down the hill.

Milly wiped the tears from her eyes and said, 'It's so sad looking at the war memorial. Don't you think so, Beth?'

'Yes, it is. It's a sad reminder of all the needless carnage.'

When we reached Victoria Road, Milly said she would come up for a quick cup of tea before leaving for the railway station that evening. Granny was pleased to see her.

'So you're all set for your trip, Milly? We hope everything works out for you in Glasgow.'

Milly nodded. 'Thank you for all your best wishes, Mary, and I think I'll be very happy.'

Mum brought the tea tray through and placed it on the table. 'Lizzie and I will come to the station with you and see you off.'

Later that night we stood on the platform, waiting for the train to arrive. I had carried the two suitcases that contained all Milly's worldly goods, while Mum seemed to be on the verge of tears. Thankfully she managed to keep her composure as Milly checked her handbag to make sure her tickets were safely inside. Then the train arrived, and as she boarded the train, both women began to cry.

'I'm going to miss you, Beth. Mind and look after yourself and promise me you'll come and visit me when I'm settled in.'

Mum said she would. 'You've been a good friend to me, Milly, and I'll miss you as well.'

Then the train began to pull away from the platform and we both waved until it reached a bend in the line and disappeared from view.

We turned and headed for home in silence. The rain had come on, a cold, wet drizzle, and we were glad to get back to the warmth of the house. Granny and Maisie Mulholland were busy with their knitting in front of a cheerful fire.

Maisie stood up as we entered and went to make some hot cocoa. Granny looked at us over the top of her spectacles. 'Did Milly get away on time?'

I answered, 'Yes, she did. The train was on time and her cousin is going to meet her in Glasgow.'

Mum quickly drank her cocoa, then said, 'I think I'll get away to bed, as I'm really tired.'

After Maisie left, Granny and I sat looking at the photo album again until I began to feel sleepy.

In the bedroom I tried to be very quiet getting undressed, as I thought Mum would be sound asleep, but when I looked at her, she was wide awake, her face turned towards the window.

When I spoke, she quickly closed her eyes, and I slipped into bed with a dark feeling of something I couldn't put my finger on. Was it fear or apprehension? I wasn't sure.

16

MILLY MOVES ON

It was not long after Milly departed for Glasgow that Granny and I became worried about Mum. We would be fine until she came home from work, but as soon as we had our tea she would start complaining about things like the small stain on my school skirt or something equally trivial.

One night I accidentally spilled some tea on my blouse and she exploded with anger. 'You're getting very careless, Lizzie. Don't you have any idea how much your clothes cost? I don't want your aunt Margaret to keep forking out good money if you're not going to look after things.'

I didn't reply, but went to get a wet cloth to wipe away the stain. Rolling her eyes in annoyance, Mum moved away from the table, saying she was going to bed as she was tired. Granny was silent, but I could see she was upset by this outburst, and after Mum went to the bedroom, Granny took out her knitting bag and began to pull out a skein of wool.

'You can help me roll this into a ball, Lizzie,' she said.

I obediently held the skein between my two outstretched hands and we sat in silence while she quickly unwound the wool into a large ball.

When she began to cast on her stitches for some new garment, I sat by the fire with my latest library book. It was a true story about a lady missionary who had travelled to Africa to spread Christianity to the natives of a small community in the wilds of the Dark Continent. By the time I was ready for bed I was filled with wonder at this adventurous pioneer and I wished I could be in Africa with her.

I also asked Laura if I could go to her house after school. I loved the hustle and vitality of her parents, even though Laura complained about her father always spouting on about social injustice. 'He's like a parrot,' she said one day, but she laughed as she said it and I knew she didn't mean it.

The time was drawing near when we would be leaving school and going into the adult world. I envied Laura because she knew what she wanted to do, but I had this restless urge and didn't know how to deal with it.

'Are you still planning to go to the teachers' college?' I asked her one afternoon as we made our way up the Hawkhill.

She was eating an apple, but she nodded. 'Yes, I am. Have you made up your mind what you're going to do?'

I shook my head. 'Not really.'

I must have sounded miserable because she looked straight at me and asked, 'Are you still planning a life of adventure, Lizzie?'

'I think so, but it all depends on how things are at home. Granny and I are really worried about Mum, but we don't know how to help her. I've told you how she's lived her life in her own little denial bubble, but the trouble is she doesn't make friends very easily. My dad was the outgoing, sociable person who was good at sport and had loads of pals while Mum was quiet and liked staying in the background. At least that's what Granny said.'

Laura was sympathetic. 'Well, everyone is different, aren't they?'

'Do you know what she did a few years ago? She went with Milly to a few spiritualist meetings hoping to get a message from Dad. When she didn't, she was convinced he was still alive and languishing in some foreign hospital.'

'Oh, I wouldn't worry too much about that. Our neighbour along the lobby regularly holds little seances for women who've

85

lost sons, husbands and fathers in the war. She always has a full house. My father says it's all a load of supernatural tommyrot, but Mum tells him she's heard it brings comfort to some people.'

The fact that other people were also seeking some contact with their dead loved ones consoled me, and I was pleased that Mum and Milly hadn't been paranoid and strange. It now seemed as if there were lots of women, for they were mostly women, all pursuing some sort of closure. Personally I thought it was distasteful, but that was just my opinion.

Then things came to a head one night. It had been a horrible day, with rain and a blustery wind that swept down the narrow streets, sending people scurrying from the wet pavements towards their homes or in my case onto a tramcar from the West Port to Victoria Road. I had to change out of my school clothes and dry my hair, but Granny made a pot of tea and we ate pancakes with honey. Then at six o'clock Mum appeared and she was in a foul mood due to the fact she had also been drenched in the rain.

'I've had a horrendous day, with three very difficult customers,' she said while pulling off her wet shoes and raincoat. 'Then I got caught in this awful weather and it's supposed to be summertime. I mean, for goodness' sake, it's May month and we should be having warm, sunny weather.'

One thing I had noticed lately was that Granny, when faced by Mum's wrath over difficult customers or rotten weather, would sit quietly until the storm passed; however, on this particular night it didn't pass and Mum raged all through our meal and afterwards. Even when Maisie appeared, she was still moaning.

Finally Granny had had enough and she said pleasantly, 'Maybe you should go to the doctor, Beth, and get something for your nerves.'

Mum exploded. 'My nerves . . . What's wrong with my nerves, Mary?'

Granny remained placid. 'Well, you always seem to be overwrought these days. Perhaps the doctor can prescribe something to help you.'

'I don't need anything to help me. All I'm looking for is some decent weather so I can wear my new summer frock, which hasn't been off its hanger since I bought it, and some cheerful customers who want to buy a hat instead of trying on all the stock then walking away without buying a thing.'

'Well, we can't pick the weather or make cheerful customers go into the millinery department, Beth, so we just have to put up with it.'

I didn't look up from my book when Granny said this and she didn't raise her eyes from her knitting. Then poor Maisie put in her pennyworth, as she tried to be helpful. 'I remember when I suffered from nerves a few years ago. I got a lovely bottle of tonic from the chemist and it only cost me sixpence.'

'Right then,' said Mum. 'Tomorrow Lizzie can go and get me some of this magic tonic from the chemist and we'll see if it helps my nerves.'

Later, when I went to bed, Mum was still awake and gazing at the ceiling. 'Do you think I need a tonic, Lizzie?' she asked me.

Unsure how to answer, I decided that truthfulness was best. 'Yes I do, Mum. You always seem so unhappy and pale, and you never eat enough but leave most of your food on the plate.'

She sighed listlessly, all of her former aggression now spent. 'Yes, I know. I'm beginning to be a pain to live with.'

'No, you're not. It's just that we're worried about you and want you to be happy again.'

She gave a mirthless laugh. 'Happy? I haven't been happy in years. But tomorrow you can get me this bottle of tonic and I promise to take it all and be a changed woman.'

The next afternoon I picked up the tonic from the chemist and carried it home like it was the Holy Grail. It was a huge bottle filled with a noxious-looking black mixture and I wondered how Mum would view it. After her tea – and I noticed with satisfaction she cleared her plate and even ate a slice of bread and butter with the cheese omelette – she took a tablespoon of her medicine, screwing up her face at the taste.

'This tastes awful,' she said, rinsing the spoon under the water tap.

Granny was pleased. 'The worse it is, the better it does you. That's a known fact.'

Over the week, the contents of the bottle grew less, and Granny congratulated Mum on taking the tonic every day. However, I knew better because I caught her on day two pouring the large tablespoon of the mixture down the sink and rinsing it away. She didn't know that I had seen her and I never let on.

Our exams were over and Laura announced one day as we strolled towards the school gate, 'I hope I pass my exam and I can apply to the teacher-training college for a place in the autumn.' She turned to me, her face glowing in the warm morning sunshine and her hair held back from her face with a ribbon. 'Have you made up your mind what you want to do, Lizzie?'

I hesitated, as quite honestly I hadn't. 'I'll wait till I get the results of my exams, Laura. After all I might have failed them.'

Laura shook her head. 'Rubbish, you're cleverer than me and I'm sure I've passed.'

I played for time. 'Do you honestly think that I'm clever?'

She laughed and ran towards the gate. 'Stop fishing for compliments.'

One night just before the school broke up for the summer holidays, Mum announced she was going to Glasgow on the Saturday night after work to see Milly. 'I'll stay the night and come back on the Sunday.'

Granny and I were both surprised because she hadn't mentioned this trip, although we knew she was still in contact with her friend. Granny said what a good idea it was. 'It'll be good to get a change of scene, Beth, and you can catch up with all Milly's news.' Then she added as an afterthought, 'Why don't you take Lizzie with you, as she'll enjoy the trip?'

Mum looked dismayed by this suggestion and I was suddenly annoyed with her for not asking me along in the first place.

'I don't think Milly can put us both up for the night, Mary, as it's not her house. Lizzie can go to Laura's house if you've got a meeting at the church.'

Granny shook her head and she also looked annoyed. 'No, I've nothing planned. It was just a suggestion.'

Before leaving on the Saturday, Mum had packed her small suitcase and said she would leave straight after work and be back on the Sunday night. For one terrible moment I thought she was planning to abandon me and go off, never to return. My mouth was dry and I knew I wouldn't be able to say goodbye without making my fears known. For the first time in my life, I suddenly felt afraid.

Then I came to my senses and almost laughed out loud at the ludicrous thought of being left behind. For one thing, Mum's suitcase was too small to hold all her belongings and she hadn't packed Dad's trophies. I knew she would never leave without them. Then I was struck by another disturbing thought. What if she was on a scouting mission to look for a job and a house in Glasgow? That would leave Granny all on her own.

When it was time for her to leave for the store, she smiled at us both. 'I'll see you tomorrow night and I'll give you all Milly's news then.'

I felt so foolish, especially when Granny picked up her shopping basket and announced, 'Let's go and get something nice for our tea, then we'll go into town and have a cup of tea in a café.'

Mum had been excited when she left and I thought she would be the same on her return, but when she appeared on the Sunday evening she looked tired and annoyed.

Granny gave her an enquiring look. 'Did you enjoy your visit, Beth?'

Mum sat down and gave a huge sigh. 'I thought Milly would be feeling unhappy in her new home, but she loves it. Her cousin Jeannie has a nice flat and Milly gets on well with her. She has also found a job in a ladies' fashion shop in Argyll Street and has become friendly with the owner's son, Albert. Milly says they go to the pictures together and she hopes it will lead to romance.'

Granny said that was good news, but Mum disagreed. 'Surely she can't have forgotten her dead fiancé, Mary.'

'But he died years ago. Surely Milly deserves some happiness and life has to go on.'

'Well, all I know is I could never replace Peter. Not then and not ever.'

Granny looked as if she was about to cry. 'No, Beth, I know you couldn't.'

As we lay in bed that night I suddenly realised that Mum was disappointed in Milly. Perhaps she had wanted her friend to be still mourning and weeping; instead she had found a new life and a possible new love.

Mum said, 'I thought Milly wanted to come back and that's why she asked me to visit her. Instead she wanted to show off how well everything has gone for her.'

'But surely you must be pleased for her,' I said.

Mum turned her back to me as she pulled the covers over her and I had to strain to hear her reply. 'Yes, I suppose I am. As your granny says, life has to go on.'

Her voice sounded so flat and dejected that I was afraid. Mum hadn't moved on with her life. She was still stuck in 1917, and nobody would ever be able to talk her into making a new life for herself or trying to make new friends and having a life outside of work and coming home every night to Victoria Road.

17

NEW HORIZONS

Laura and I spent our last week at school in the knowledge that we had both passed our exams with excellent marks, in my case much to my surprise. We spent that week discussing our futures, and for Laura the way ahead was as clear as it had always been.

'I'm putting my name down for a place at Dundee College of Education, Lizzie. What about you? Have you made up your mind what you want to do?'

I had to admit I hadn't, not that I hadn't thought a great deal about it, but the restlessness I felt was keeping me from making up my mind.

'I'm not sure about going into teaching, Laura, but I honestly don't know what I'll do,' I said truthfully.

Both Mum and Granny had tried hard to make me realise I needed to make a decision and make it soon.

'The places at university and the training college will fill up quickly,' Mum said one night when she was exasperated at my lack of commitment. 'It won't be easy to get a job either, as loads of people are unemployed and jobs are scarce.'

I knew that and I was annoyed at myself for my lack of forward planning. I wished I had Laura's clear-minded dedication, but I didn't.

Mum said, 'Why don't you write to Aunt Margaret and ask her for advice about the training college.'

So I did, but while I was waiting for a reply, Mum and Granny were worried I would be too late to be admitted along with Laura.

The long summer holiday lay ahead, and Laura and I had planned what we were going to do with these last few weeks of freedom before setting out on our chosen paths.

Perhaps I was looking back with rose-coloured spectacles when I recalled every day was sunny and warm because I know that wasn't true, but years later I was to remember those few weeks as a haven of sunshine and fun, with the shackles of school firmly cast off and the future still misty and unknown.

Every day we would set out on some adventure, sometimes going by the train to Broughty Ferry and swimming in the sea before lying on our damp towels on the sand eating ice cream, or spending days in the Barrack Park with our books. Once we borrowed two bicycles from a small bike-repair shop in the Hawkhill and pedalled into the countryside along with a picnic of sandwiches and bottles of lemonade. Another favourite outing was to the swimming baths, where after our dip in the icy-cold water we emerged shivering with goose-pimpled skin but laughing as we made our way home. However the best bit was the enjoyment and the freedom.

Three weeks into the holiday, Margaret replied to my letter. She was delighted that I was considering becoming a teacher. 'I know you want adventure, Lizzie, but you can always get a teaching post abroad after you qualify. The point is there is no future in setting off around the world without some qualifications to fall back on.'

After reading her letter I felt annoyed because she had been a head teacher in Edinburgh before her marriage to Gerald, so she was bound to say this was my best option. I said as much to Laura, but she said I was talking a load of rubbish.

'Your aunt knows what she is talking about, Lizzie, but if you don't want to take her advice, why did you write to her in the first place?'

I could have told her it was my mother's idea, but I didn't

because she would have thought I was making excuses like some five-year-old who couldn't think for herself.

'All right then, I'll put my name down for the training college, but maybe I'm too late.'

To be honest, I wasn't sure if this lateness was a good or a bad thing, but I was now committed and there was no way of going back.

18

DUNDEE COLLEGE
OF EDUCATION

Laura received her letter of admission to the training college during the summer holiday. She was going to start her studies towards her teaching career in October. I remember the day well when she appeared at Victoria Road with her good news.

'I've got my letter,' she said, her voice full of excitement. 'Did you get yours as well, Lizzie?'

Granny and Mum looked at me, disappointment showing on their faces when I said I hadn't.

'Never mind, you'll probably get it later because my application was in before yours. I can't see any problem, because we both did well with our exams and we both got our leaving certificates.'

Laura was quite certain this was the case, but I had my doubts, and judging by Mum's face, so did she.

'The best thing about it is we won't have to go into the accommodation hostel because we live in Dundee,' she said.

Later that night, Mum asked me if I really wanted to go to the college and I said I did.

But as the days went past I realised I wasn't going to be admitted along with Laura and I began to seriously think about my future. Jobs were very difficult to find. Granny said there might be an opening in my late grandfather's solicitors' office, but when she enquired it seemed they were fully staffed. However, they said perhaps if things changed I would be considered.

Granny was annoyed. 'If your grandfather was alive, he would have got you a position in the office, fully staffed or not.'

Unfortunately times had changed, and according to the newspapers most employers were now getting by with the minimum of workers. I tried to hide my worry, because Mum looked tired all the time and she had enough to cope with without my added burden. So much for my childhood fancies: I had to ruefully admit to myself that no one seemed to need pirates and explorers.

Laura and I still spent all our time together, but she seemed to be embarrassed by her good fortune. I told her not to be silly. It had been my own fault for dithering about my future.

One bit of pleasure during this difficult time was Laura's mum's piano. She had gone to lessons as a child and she had always wanted to own a piano but because of money being tight she hadn't been able to realise her dream.

I was at the Hawkhill one day and had been persuaded to stay for my tea because it was Irene's birthday. Wullie arrived home with a huge smile on his face. Irene gave him a suspicious look as she bustled between the cooker and the table, but before she could speak, Wullie announced he had bought a second-hand piano from a workmate.

'It's being delivered tomorrow, Irene. Happy birthday!'

Irene was speechless, but she went towards her husband and planted a kiss on his smiling face.

'Oh, thank you, Wullie. That's the best birthday present I've ever had.'

Wullie tried to look modest, but he was obviously pleased that his unexpected present had been greeted with such joy.

After our tea, Irene planned where to put the piano. She shifted a small table and chair and announced that this was the perfect spot for her new acquisition.

I made sure I was at the house the next day to see the piano. Laura and I stood on the stair while three hefty men manoeuvred the piano into the house, and after a cup of tea and a sugar bun to compensate for all their hard work, we stood and admired it.

Irene lifted the lid gingerly but was pleased to see it was in perfect order.

'It looks brand new,' she said, running her fingers over the keys.

Some of the neighbours came in to look at the new piece of furniture and Irene began to play some Scots songs. I had to admit she was very good, and even Laura looked bemused. Once again I stayed for my tea, and afterwards we gathered around and sang 'Comin' Thro' the Rye' and 'Flow Gently, Sweet Afton'.

Irene said she would have to buy some sheet music for some of the popular songs and we said we looked forward to singing them.

I had enjoyed myself and I went home with the sounds of the singing in my head. For a short time I had stopped worrying over my future, but no doubt it would be back with me by the time I got home.

I told Granny all about the piano and how Laura and I had joined in the singing. She was smiling as she held out a letter. 'This came for you, Lizzie.'

I half expected it to have come from Aunt Margaret, but it was in a plain white envelope with a British stamp. I opened it and couldn't believe my eyes.

Granny said, 'Is it good news?'

'Oh yes, it is. I've been accepted at the training college and I start in October along with Laura.'

'Did they say why your letter was late?'

'Yes, they have. This year's intake was full, but someone dropped out and I've been given her place. Isn't that good news?' I stopped. It was good news for me, but perhaps it wasn't good for the person who had cancelled her place. I hoped she had changed her mind about the course and that it wasn't anything bad that had stopped her from taking up the place.

I said as much to Granny, who agreed with me but added, 'One person's misfortune is another's good fortune.'

I could hardly wait to pass on my good news. When Mum arrived home from work, she was delighted to hear that I had been successful. She asked me, 'How long will the course last?'

'Two years unless I'm a university student. If that was the case, then I could take another year to gain a degree, but I'm happy just to have a chance of a job at the end of it.'

'Your aunt Margaret was a university student at the college, where she did three years training, but she came out with a degree and a Teacher's Special Certificate, which enabled her to teach English, Science and Languages. At the time I was just a small child, but I remember it well, especially as my father and Margaret's mother were so pleased at her success.' As usual when Mum spoke about Margaret, her face came alive, and I wished that she could look like that all the time instead of her tired, worn-out expression.

The next day I met up with Laura and she was delighted that we would both be together.

'Just think what fun we'll have, and at the end of it we'll both be teachers.'

I laughed. 'We have to study hard, Laura, and then pass our exams at the end.' I crossed my fingers when I said this as I didn't want to tempt fate by assuming all would be well.

Laura laughed out loud. 'Of course we'll pass our exams, Lizzie. We did well at school and it'll be no different from that.'

I smiled at her. That was what I liked about her, the infectious confidence – I hoped it would rub off on me. I envied Laura because she knew what she wanted to do with her life, and not once did she ever falter with her ambition of becoming a teacher, while I always had this restless feeling of not knowing what I wanted to do.

However, I wrote to my aunt that night and I knew she would be delighted at my news. I was grateful to her because she had told Mum that she would help financially with my education till I got a job, and I knew I was a lucky girl.

19

PARK PLACE

Laura and I were due to attend our first session at the college at noon on 3 October. The weeks leading up to this momentous occasion had been busy. We both had to have medical examinations, which we passed with no problems. Mum had made an appointment for me to see Dr Bennett at his surgery in Constitution Terrace. After his examination he said I was as fit as a fiddle, his exact words, and I came home clutching a certificate to prove it.

Laura went to see her family doctor, who lived in a large house on Blackness Avenue. She was also fit as a fiddle, but then neither of us expected anything else. After all, we were young women with the whole world at our feet.

We put in for and received a grant from the Scottish Education Department that would help out with our finances and help us not be a burden on our families. We also had to sign a declaration that we intended to follow the profession of a teacher in schools inspected by the education department, which made me a bit uneasy as I wanted to teach abroad after training. I said as much to Laura, but she advised me not to rock the boat.

'Just sign it, Lizzie. After all, we don't know what lies ahead of us in the future,' she said.

That left the problem of smart working clothes, but the problem was soon solved when Granny paid for an outfit suitable to attend the college. On the Saturday before I was due to go, we both paid a visit to DM Brown's ladies' dress department, where I was fitted out with a navy skirt, two white blouses and a navy-blue coat. We went up to the millinery department, where Mum was busy with an autocratic-looking elderly woman who didn't seem to know what she wanted. I thought Mum looked tired but was trying hard not to show it. Because Mum was busy, we got another young assistant who was very helpful. I wasn't very happy about wearing a hat, but Granny was most insistent that a lady had to have one. In the end I settled for a plain-looking cream-coloured cloche hat that didn't look too fancy or pretentious.

Afterwards we went up to the restaurant, where we had a cup of tea and a cake. I was meeting Laura later, and when I saw her we were both amazed at how similar our clothes were, even down to the same-shaped hats. This gave us a laugh, and we said we looked more like sisters than friends.

I was feeling nervous when the day finally arrived to present myself at the college. I had no idea what to expect, and Laura had said the same thing. We were two innocents about to enter the grown-up world of training, where eventually we would be in charge of young children and be responsible for their schooling. I felt as if my own childhood was being left behind, but I was also pleased that I was now on the first step to my new future.

Mum had wished me luck before leaving for her work that morning, and both Granny and Maisie Mulholland said everything would be all right and that I would be an ideal student for the next two years.

It was a typical autumn day as I made my way to Park Place. Although it was dry, the sky was overcast with dark grey clouds that threatened heavy rain before the day was out. There was a cold wind that whipped up the hem of my coat against my legs, and I hurried along the street, eager to be inside, where I hoped it would be warmer.

I had left Granny sitting by a warm fire whose flames lit up the cosy room, and the small lamp had been lit, which glowed softly on the polished wooden furniture. Suddenly I felt like I was going to cry and a sob caught in my throat at the thought of what lay ahead. I stopped for a moment to give myself a mental shake-up.

'Honestly, is this how pirates and explorers would behave before setting out for their adventurous journeys?' I asked myself before quickening my stride to meet up with Laura.

She was standing waiting for me at the entrance to the college. She gave me a quick smile before linking her arm through mine. 'Are we all set then, Lizzie?'

I nodded with a confidence I didn't feel and we went in through the door. The reception room was already busy with women, young girls and a small handful of men. At three o'clock, Professor William McClelland, who was the principal of the college and director of studies, made his appearance along with his staff, which included: Edith Luke, the warden and 'mistress' of the methods and practice of teaching classes; Margaret S. Malloch, the principal hostel warden; the Rev. James Smith, who taught religious instruction; and Robert Ash, the medical officer.

My head was reeling after all these descriptions, but I knew it would be fine once I was settled in. I glanced at Laura and I knew by her face that she felt the same.

After the speech by the principal, the students who required accommodation were told to gather at the door and they would be escorted to the Mayfield hostel in Small's Wynd. The girl who had been standing beside us picked up her bag and suitcase. She noticed that we weren't going to move.

She looked worried. 'Are you not going to the hostel?' she asked.

Laura said we lived in Dundee.

'Oh, you're lucky. I'm not looking forward to living in the hostel, but I'm sure I'll get used to it.' She held out her hand. 'I'm Pat Hogan.'

We introduced ourselves and she went on. 'My parents work on a farm near Kirriemuir, so it's not possible to travel here every day.'

She was quite plump, with short blonde curly hair and rosy cheeks that showed two dimples when she smiled. I thought she resembled the country dairymaid in the adverts for the Maypole Dairy. She wore a blue hand-knitted jumper and a dark-blue woollen skirt, and I got the impression she would be an energetic person and well able to control a classroom full of children.

Once again I had misgivings about being in college, but I was stopped from thinking too hard about this as Pat said goodbye. 'I hope to see you soon,' she said as she joined the queue of people who were being organised for their trip to the hostel.

Laura said she felt quite drained by all the activity, and to be honest I felt the same way. 'Hopefully things will be fine tomorrow when we start our course,' she said.

Mum and Granny were eager to hear how I got on, and I put on a bright expression and told them everything was going to be great. I mentioned Pat Hogan and Mum said what a blessing it was that I was able to come home every night, a sentiment I totally agreed with.

Over the next few weeks, Laura and I became very friendly with Pat and we spent a lot of our spare time together. Laura's mother invited Pat to visit any time she felt lonely at the hostel and we had some good nights at the Hawkhill, with Irene playing popular songs on the piano, with the three of us singing along.

I invited Pat to come to Victoria Road, but I did warn her our house was much quieter than Laura's. Once again I shouldn't have worried about our lack of social skills because Laura brought her knitting with her and it turned out that Pat was a whiz at doing crochet. Granny thought they were two very nice girls.

I would sit in our living room as Granny, Laura and Pat were busy with their handicrafts while I felt like an alien who had accidentally landed in Smith and Horner's wool department, and I felt that restlessness surge up inside me and I wished that the two-year course would soon be over, then I could look for something overseas, just as Margaret had suggested.

We also liked going to the pictures and secretly smoking a cigarette while watching the films that were now billed as 'talkies'. Smoking was a habit that we never really took to, but at the time it made us feel grown up.

One night Laura said, 'Do you remember when we used to be in love with Rudolph Valentino, Lizzie?'

I laughed. 'He was very handsome when he played "The Sheik".' I turned to Pat. 'We used to fall out over which one of us he would fall in love with. Do you remember that, Laura?'

'Oh, I do. I used to dream of him and wished I could be in the desert with him.'

Pat, being a country girl from a farm, confessed she had never seen him, although she had read about how women adored him.

At the time I was so busy with my studies at the college and our outings that I didn't notice Mum becoming more of a recluse. It was Granny who said one night that she should make an effort to go out more.

'You're a young woman, Beth. Why don't you go out with Lizzie and her friends to the pictures?'

Mum looked horrified. 'They won't want me hanging around with them, Mary. No, I just like listening to the wireless and reading my library books.'

I felt so guilty about not noticing how much Mum had retreated into a self-imposed shell.

'Why don't you come to the pictures with me one night, Mum? It'll be just the two of us, unless Granny wants to come as well.' I looked over, but Granny shook her head. 'We can look at the paper and see what films are on.'

Mum said she thought that was a good idea, so we made plans to see what film Mum fancied. That week we both went to the Plaza cinema on the Hilltown to see a Laurel and Hardy picture and we both laughed so loudly that Mum had tears in her eyes. When we arrived home, Granny seemed so pleased that she had enjoyed her night out.

'You should make this a weekly thing, Beth, as it's good to get out of the house for a change.'

Mum said she would think about it, but nothing came of it, so Granny and I just said that there was nothing else we could do about her. As a result, Mum sank back into her quiet life, listening to music and plays on the wireless, and reading her books.

I often looked at her when she was engrossed in her stories and I thought what a waste of life, because she was still a very pretty woman, with her light-brown hair, hazel eyes and a pale but clear complexion. I was quite sad about her, because I'm sure she would never have been like this if Dad had still been alive. It was as if her life had come to an end the day she got the telegram in 1917.

I wrote a letter to Margaret every week, giving her all the news from the college, and I looked forward to her replies. She said her husband would soon be retiring from his career and that they both looked forward to moving back to Scotland with a house by the sea. I knew that Mum would be a different person if Margaret stayed nearby.

It was coming up to December and the college was closing for the Christmas and New Year holiday from 13 December until 7 January. We were all looking forward to this break, although we wouldn't see much of Pat, as she was going home to the farm in Kirriemuir.

She was quite wistful a few days before the break. 'I'm going to miss all the fun and activity when I go home. There's nothing but fields where I live, although we do manage to get to the town now and again.'

Laura said she was welcome to come and stay with her for a few days if she got bored, but Pat said her mother needed her to help in the big farmhouse, where she had a job as a cleaner.

'My dad's boss and his wife always have visitors over the festive season, so Mum has a lot of extra work to do. I've always helped out before, so it'll be the same this year, I expect.'

Laura said to me later that we were lucky we didn't have to fetch and carry for visitors and clean a big old farmhouse, and I agreed.

The weather had turned cold and wet, but there was no snow, so Pat managed to catch her train and we went to see her off.

'Have a lovely Christmas,' she said as she humped her suitcase into the half-empty carriage.

'The same to you, Pat,' we called in unison as the train puffed out of the station.

We wandered up into the High Street to look at the shop windows, then went into Woolworth's store to look for presents. I didn't know what I wanted so I said I would leave it until the following week and Laura agreed. We were full of plans for the holiday and I knew we would be spending time together in each other's houses. Granny loved Christmas and she always decorated the house with paper chains and the festive ornaments she brought out from below her bed, like the fairies with gossamer wings and the elves with their green trousers and red hats. Then when New Year was over she would carefully wrap them in tissue paper and shove the box back under the bed.

Christmas Day was a normal working day for Mum, but she was planning on having a good rest at the New Year holiday, when the store closed for two days. The week before Christmas, Mum got a card from Milly with a letter. She told us about it at teatime.

'Milly is getting married at the New Year to the son of the owner of the shop she works in. She wants me to be a witness at the quiet ceremony they've planned, but I don't think I can manage it.'

Granny said, 'That's wonderful news, Beth, but I do think you should reconsider being with Milly on her big day.'

Mum turned the letter over in her hand before slipping it into her pocket. 'It will be difficult to travel to Glasgow over the holiday, as I'm not sure about the trains.'

Granny picked up her knitting and she seemed immersed in the complicated pattern, but she said softly, 'Well, think about it, Beth.'

I was disappointed, as I felt it would have done Mum the world of good to be among people and enjoy their company. Granny felt the same thing, but we both knew not to push Mum into something she didn't want to do. It was a lesson we had learned over the years.

20

A WEDDING IN GLASGOW

Laura and I were very busy during the next couple of days, as we were both in a quandary about buying gifts for our families.

'I've got a book of Ivor Novello's music for Mum, as she likes his songs, but I've no idea what to get for my dad. I could get him a new spirit level or a chisel, I suppose.'

I looked at her and she laughed.

'I'm just joking.'

I said I was in the same boat. 'I've seen a lovely brooch in Marshall's jewellery shop, but it's too expensive, and I haven't a clue what to get for Mum.'

We were walking down the Wellgate at the time when I gave a sigh. 'Why do we always give presents at Christmas anyway?'

Laura looked shocked. 'It's because of the gifts brought to the baby Jesus from the Three Wise Men.'

I laughed. 'I know that. I'm not stupid when it comes to stories from the Bible, but that all happened thousands of years ago.'

Laura just gave me one of her famous looks that spoke more than a hundred words and we continued to gaze in the shop windows.

Later, when I got home, I saw Granny was excited about something.

'What do you think, Lizzie?' she said. 'Your mother has changed her mind about being Milly's witness and we will be going to Glasgow after Christmas. I've written to a guest house and booked two rooms for two nights.'

I said nothing but was perplexed about the 'we'.

'Oh, I forgot mention that I'm coming as well.'

'When did Mum change her mind?' I asked.

'Just before she left for work this morning, but I went to see Maisie before you got up, and when I got back you had left to go and see Laura. Isn't that good news?'

I said it was great news.

When Mum arrived home that night, I tackled her about her change of mind.

'Well, I've been friends with Milly for years and I thought I had to be with her on her wedding day. Your granny wanted to come as well, so we've planned to stay for two nights, then be home in time to bring in the new year here.'

I wasn't sure how to broach the subject of money. 'How much will it cost, Mum?'

'Granny is paying for the rooms at the guest house and I'll pay for the train tickets and the wedding present. I've bought a pair of Egyptian cotton sheets for the gift, as they were on offer at the store.'

I wasn't sure about mentioning the cost of Christmas presents in the face of this new financial plan, but time was running out and I had to get my shopping done in the next few days.

'I was going to buy Granny a lovely brooch I saw, but it's too dear.' I hesitated. 'Do you think we can buy it together as a joint gift?'

Mum said that was a good idea, but added, 'You're not to spend money on anything for me, as I know you need all your money for your course at the college.'

On Christmas Eve we decorated the house with the usual paper chains that Granny kept in the wooden box under her bed and I bought a bunch of holly from the florist in Victoria Road. Later, I went round to Laura's house to exchange our presents and we sang Christmas carols round the piano. Irene then produced a small bottle of port and we had some with lemonade, clinking our glasses together and wishing each other a merry Christmas.

It was a cold, misty night as I walked home. The streets were thronged with people, and small shops were still busy with customers. At that moment I experienced such a feeling of well-being and happiness that I almost stopped in my tracks. I couldn't ever recall feeling like this and I almost cried.

When I got home, Mum and Granny were sitting with cups of hot cocoa and the firelight glimmered off the paper chains and the bunch of holly that was placed in a vase on the mantelpiece. After they went to bed, I took Dad's photo out of my handbag and saw once again the droplets of water dripping from his dark hair. He looked so alive that it was hard to believe he was lying somewhere in France in an unmarked grave. 'Happy Christmas, Dad, wherever you are,' I said before going to bed.

The next morning Granny was overcome with her lovely brooch, and Mum and I laughed when she pinned it on her night-gown. Mum looked delighted at the two books I gave her. Granny gave me an angora jumper and Mum also chose books for me, while Laura's present was a fountain pen. This was something I had been going on about during the time at the college, but I didn't realise she had noticed. I hoped she liked the bracelet I had chosen for her and I smiled at the thought of the well-wrapped chisel her father might be opening at this very minute.

Later, Maisie Mulholland joined us for our evening meal, and she was pleased with her small present of three handkerchiefs with her initial on the corners.

On the Sunday morning Mum, Granny and I left for the train station to go to Glasgow. Mum had packed the wedding present and the suit she was going to wear, while Granny and I had our clothes in her suitcase. The train station was busy when we arrived, but the train was on time and we were pleased to get a carriage all to ourselves.

'Milly said she would meet us at Glasgow,' said Mum. 'She said it's to be a small wedding at the registry office and we'll be going for a meal afterwards.'

'Have you met Milly's future husband, Beth?'

Mum shook her head. 'No, I haven't. I only know he's the son of the owner of the shop where she works.'

I had a window seat and was quite content to sit and watch the wintry scene as the train swept through little villages and larger towns. There had been a fall of snow overnight, but it was just a slight sprinkling over the fields. Then before long we were going through the outskirts of Glasgow before finally coming to a stop at the large station that was bustling with people and trains.

Mum spotted Milly standing on the platform and she hurried along when she saw us. She gave Mum a big hug, saying how pleased she was that Mum had agreed to be with her on her big day.

'I've booked a taxi to take you to the guest house, and after you get settled in I want you to come to the house for your dinner and to meet Albert and his father. Albert and I are going to stay with him after the wedding.'

Mum gave Granny one of her looks, but nothing was said until we were in the guest house, which was near Sauchiehall Street.

Mum looked worried. 'Milly didn't say anything in her letters about living with her father-in-law.'

Granny said it was probably a temporary arrangement until they could maybe get their own house.

At one o'clock, the taxi came back and we all piled in. We thought we would be going to one of the tenement houses that surrounded the guest house, but the driver drove out towards Kelvingrove before turning into a drive that led up to a large stone-built house with a veranda and a beautiful garden. At least it would be lovely come the spring and summer.

Milly was at the door and she looked radiant in a blue dress with long, wide sleeves that seemed to be in the height of fashion. Standing beside her was a man who looked about forty years old, of medium height, and with hair that was beginning to thin. However, he had a pleasant, smiling face and was also well dressed.

We gazed out of the window with amazement, but Granny broke the silence. 'Milly's landed on her feet here.'

We were ushered into a hall that had a lovely tiled floor before entering the lounge, which had big windows overlooking the garden. There was a blazing fire burning in the grate and there were comfortable chairs and sofas placed around it. The only other occupants in the room were an elderly man with silver hair and a slight stoop to his shoulders and an older, plain-looking woman who was dressed in black.

Milly made the introductions. 'This is my cousin Jeannie and my future father-in-law Alfred Bernard.'

Alfred came over and shook our hands, while Jeannie nodded her head. The door opened and Milly's fiancé entered the room carrying a tray with glasses of sherry. She turned and gave him a loving look. 'And this is Albert.'

Albert said he was so pleased to finally meet his fiancée's friends and he thanked Mum for agreeing to be a witness at their wedding.

Mum sat in one of the chairs nearest the fire, clutching her glass of sherry. She looked slightly amazed at her surroundings, while Granny looked totally dumbstruck, which amused me because I had never seen her like that before.

After our sherry we all went through to the dining room, which also overlooked the garden. The table was large enough to seat about a dozen people. The meal started with soup, followed by steak pie, which was brought in from the kitchen by Milly. The wedding was the main topic of conversation, and Mum mentioned the weather and hoped it wasn't going to be snowy or wet. Afterwards we all went back to the lounge for coffee, tea or more sherry. Granny and Mum had another sherry, but I wasn't keen on the taste of it, so I settled for a cup of tea.

Later in the afternoon when the light began to fade, the lamps were lit and we said it was time to leave. Milly announced that she was coming back to the guest house with us in order to discuss further the wedding arrangements with Mum, so we emerged out into the cold winter's afternoon and back into the taxi.

Milly looked so happy as she discussed the plans for the following day.

'The ceremony is at one o'clock and then we'll go to the Royal Hotel for a meal. It's a hotel not far from the registry office and there will only be eight of us, as we didn't want a big wedding. Robert Davidson, Albert's friend from his schooldays, is the best man, but he couldn't be here today. He is the manager of the shop in Tollcross. You'll meet him tomorrow.'

Mum was keen to hear all the news.

'Does Albert work in the shop along with you?'

'No, he does the office work and is the general manager of the three shops, but after I'm married I will still work as well, as I enjoy being in the shop.'

'I didn't know he owned the three shops, Milly. Are they all in Glasgow?'

Milly said they were. 'Mr Bernard, my father-in-law, is the owner, but Albert does all the work, plus there are ten assistants in the three branches. We are very busy because they are good-quality shops.' She turned to Mum. 'They're not big stores like DM Brown's, Beth, but we sell ladies' clothes, hats and shoes.'

Granny said, 'You made the best decision to leave Dundee, Milly. Look how well it's turned out for you.'

'I know, I sometimes feel I'm dreaming. I never imagined it would end like this, but I'm very lucky to have met Albert.' She looked down at her hands, which were clasped tightly around her small handbag. 'I know I'll never forget Michael and Billy, but it's not often you get a second chance of happiness like I have. The one regret I do have is that my mother couldn't be here with me on my wedding day.'

We gazed at her silently until Mum said, 'I know how you feel, Milly, but you've got the rest of your life to live and you can't live on memories.'

She stood up. 'Well, I'll see you tomorrow. The taxi will pick you up at half past twelve and take you to the registry office.'

Mum went to see her off, then came back in. She was rubbing

her hands. 'It's got a lot colder, so let's hope it's a nice day tomorrow.'

When we woke up the next morning, the sun was shining brightly, but there was a white frost on the pavements and there was a cold wind. Mum spent ages getting ready. She had brought two outfits with her and she was in a quandary as to which one to wear. As the time was marching on, Granny settled her dilemma for her.

'I think you look good in the lavender skirt and jacket, Beth, and the cream hat goes well with it.'

Mum had a final look in the mirror, turning one way then the other before stating she would wear the lavender outfit. With that big decision made, there was just a short time left before the taxi came, so we sat in the small lounge while the owner brought us a pot of tea and some biscuits.

It was so cold when we went outside that our breath was misted up, but we hoped the sun would warm things up a bit.

I enjoyed looking at the buildings as the taxi made its way to our destination and, like Dundee, the streets were busy with people shopping or going to work. The registry office was situated in a lovely old building in the city centre, and we were shown to a room that had chairs in front of a large, heavily decorated table with a big vase of flowers placed at the side.

Jeannie, Albert and his father were sitting down with another young man who we assumed was the best man, and Granny and I joined them while Mum waited in the corridor for Milly's arrival.

We didn't have long to wait before the door opened and Milly and Mum entered. The bride was dressed in a soft blue dress and jacket and she looked so happy. Albert stood up, along with his best man, and the bridal party faced the desk, where the registrar, a middle-aged man in a dark suit, smiled and welcomed them.

The service didn't take long, but I found it very relaxing and simple and I made a mental note that should I ever get married then this was the service I would like to have. Then it was time to leave for the hotel, as another couple were waiting to be married, so it meant we couldn't hang around. As we stood on the pavement, three young girls came forward and handed a silver horseshoe to Milly before throwing confetti over the bride and groom – confetti that was soon whisked away by the cold wind.

Albert smiled and Milly gave the girls a hug. 'We'll see you all tomorrow night,' she said.

We all got into the waiting taxis and within a few minutes we were in front of the hotel, which looked like it had been a large house at one time. It faced the river and the water looked cold and grey on this winter's day, so we were glad to be inside, where a lovely log fire was burning brightly.

A small room had been set up for the wedding party and a two-tier wedding cake sat on a small table beside the round table with its flowers, glasses and silver cutlery on the white tablecloth. Two waitresses dressed in black outfits with small white frilly aprons handed out sherry for the women and whisky for the men; then we sat down for the wedding breakfast.

Mum was sitting next to the best man and he introduced himself, saying he was the manager of one of the shops, and he also explained that his friendship with the groom went back to their schooldays. Mum didn't mention that Milly had already explained everything, but she smiled and nodded her head as he spoke.

The meal was delicious and Granny whispered that she hadn't realised how hungry she was. Afterwards, the best man stood up and made a speech that was humorous and everyone laughed. He mentioned incidents from his and the groom's youth before turning to Milly and saying Albert was a very lucky man that she had come to work for him, and we all agreed as we drank the toast.

I overheard Mum asking Milly if they were going away for a honeymoon, but Milly said no, not at the moment, but they did intend to take a few days away after the January sales. 'The shops are always busy then, so we have to stay till they're over. Tomorrow night we're having a party here for the staff from the three shops. The three girls today who gave me my horseshoe were members of staff, but we couldn't invite them all to the wedding because we couldn't close the shops. But with the New Year holiday the day after tomorrow we intend to see everyone at the party.' She looked at Mum. 'I was hoping you could all stay another day and come as well.'

Mum said she was sorry, but we had to leave tomorrow morning as there might be no transport on New Year's Day, and she added, 'Lizzie has made plans to meet up with her friend Laura on Hogmanay, Milly, but it's been a wonderful time and I'm glad to have been at the celebration of your wedding.'

Milly took out a small lace-edged handkerchief and dabbed her eyes. 'Oh, Beth, I feel so happy I want to cry.'

'Well, that's what weddings are for, Milly, to have a good cry.'

At that statement both women began to laugh so heartily that Albert and Robert looked over with a smile, especially Albert, who was beaming with joy as he gazed at his new wife.

Then it was all over. Albert and Milly were booked into the hotel for the night, so we said our goodbyes at the door. Jeannie thanked us for coming.

'I'm so glad she's happy,' she said as she got into the taxi to take her back home. 'I was a bit worried when I asked her to come and live with me, but it's all turned out well.'

'It been lovely meeting you, Jeannie, and we've had a wonderful time,' Mum said as we waved her goodbye, then we set off for the guest house for our final evening in Glasgow.

We caught the morning train the next day and were back home for early afternoon. Mum carefully put her outfit away in the wardrobe and kicked off her shoes, while Granny bustled about making tea and hot toast.

Both women sank into the armchairs with a sigh.

'It's good to get away, Beth,' said Granny. 'But it's also good to get home.'

Later that evening I got ready to go out to meet Laura, as we planned to be in the city centre to bring in the New Year. When we arrived at eleven o'clock, the streets were already busy with revellers. I told Laura all about the wedding and she laughed when she said that someday it could be our own weddings we would be arranging.

At twelve o'clock the bells began to chime and there was a lot of hugging and kissing strangers. We had arranged to visit Victoria Road first and we found Mum and Granny half sleeping by the fire. Granny jumped up and gave us glasses of raspberry cordial, shortbread and sultana cake before saying they would soon be going to bed.

Later we stepped out into the street, which was still busy with first-footing revellers, and we hurried up to the Hawkhill. Laura's house was so different from mine. There was a host of neighbours in and Irene was handing out sandwiches, black bun and shortbread, while Wullie was laughing with his neighbours. He was wearing a brightly coloured tie and a new pullover, which I admired.

'Do you like my outfit, Lizzie? It's my Christmas present from my wee girl.'

I looked at Laura and she had the grace to blush. I whispered as I passed by, 'What happened to the gift-wrapped chisel?'

About three o'clock in the morning Irene produced a huge steak pie, and we all sat at the kitchen table as if we hadn't seen any food in weeks. I stayed there that night, squeezing in beside Laura, who complained I was hogging all the blankets. I think she was joking.

21

CYCLING AROUND PERTHSHIRE AND ANGUS

It was great to be back at the college and to catch up with all the news from our friends. Pat was also glad to be back, as she said she had been working in the big house for most of the Christmas holidays.

We were studying hard and time seemed to go so quickly. At the beginning of March I decided to go with Granny to the church every Sunday. I had gone to Sunday school when I was younger, although I wasn't a regular member, but in view of the emphasis on religious education at the college I thought I should make the effort.

Granny was delighted when I mentioned this, so every Sunday morning we made our way down the steps from Victoria Road to King Street and attended the morning service at St Andrew's Church. I found the experience so peaceful and I loved singing the hymns and psalms.

Mum never joined us, as she liked a long lie in bed after her work all week. Maisie Mulholland came with us, then afterwards we went back home, where she joined us for tea and rolls with bacon. The knitting group was still busy every Sunday afternoon, but I usually curled up in a chair with my college notes or a favourite book while Mum stretched out on her bed with her library book.

One day Laura said, 'We'll have to plan a holiday when the college breaks up. I thought we could have a cycling holiday, staying at the youth hostels.' She looked at me and Pat. 'What do you think about that?'

There was only one small flaw in the plan, as I explained to her. 'I don't own a bike, Laura.' I turned to Pat. 'Do you have a bike, Pat?'

Pat said there was an old bike in the cowshed at home, but she didn't think it was very roadworthy.

Laura rolled her eyes in exasperation. 'I don't own a bike either, but we can hire them for the week. Remember where we hired the two bikes in the summer, Lizzie?'

Pat wanted to know where this was.

'There's a shop on the Hawkhill that sells bikes, but the owner also hires them out. We can go and look at them on Saturday.'

So it was all settled, and on the following Saturday morning the three of us trooped up the hill to the small bike shop. I hadn't visited the shop in the summer, as Laura's father had brought the two bikes down to the house, but we saw the shop was full of wheels and chains and oily cloths. There were a few new bikes on display, but the owner took us out to the shed in the back court, which was stuffed full of bikes of every size, from kiddies' tricycles to large black sturdy machines that looked heavy enough to support a hippopotamus.

We chose three that looked reliable and they came with the added bonus of a basket in front and a leather bag at the rear. As he pushed one of the bikes around the yard, he said, 'These bikes will carry you around the country for miles.' He gave a loud cough and patted the bike affectionately. 'Aye, lassies, my bikes won't let you down.'

That guarantee was enough for Laura, who stepped forward. 'That's great, Mr Wilson. Can we hire three for a week during the holidays?'

Mr Wilson gave us an appraising stare before announcing that as long as we looked after them properly, he would hire them out for what seemed a small amount of money. Well, it seemed reasonable to me, but I had no idea what the going rate of hiring a bike was.

The weeks leading up to the summer break were filled with plans of where we would go, what food and clothes would be needed, and looking at a map of the relevant youth hostels.

One day I asked Laura, 'Have you been to any of these hostels?'

She shook her head. 'No, I haven't, but just think what fun we'll have on the open road and cooking for ourselves.'

The plan was to go the first week after the college closed, as Pat had to be home to help out on the farm for the rest of the holiday. Mum thought I was mad, going away with a big heavy bike and probably living like a tramp, but by now we were all filled with anticipation of the adventure.

It was raining on the day of departure and Laura almost did a U-turn and cancelled the plan, but we had prepared all our food for a couple of days and stowed it in the rear saddlebags, so complete with raincoats and sturdy shoes we set off on our way to our first stop, near Alyth. The rain swept into our faces as we made our way towards our destination, and we were soaked by the time we reached the grey stone building, which was a welcome sight to our eyes.

We half expected the hostel to be empty in this awful weather, but were surprised to find three young women cooking their tea in the communal kitchen. I'd never thought I would find the aroma of baked beans so appealing. We had stopped under the shelter of a tree a few hours earlier and had eaten our sandwiches, but now we were all starving.

The women turned out to be very friendly and we were surprised when they said they were office workers from Pullar's dye works in Perth out on a weekend jaunt. As we opened our bags to take out sausages and eggs, they asked us to sit with them at the long table in the common room. Pat brewed the tea and I was in charge of the frying pan, while Laura spread the bread with butter. Never before in my life or since have I enjoyed a meal so much.

The women told us they regularly cycled to the hostels at the weekend. As we chatted, Roberta, Ann and Cathy said they would be going back the next day, but the hostel was always busy, so there would be lots more people coming in.

I said we would be leaving as well, as we were planning on moving on. With our wet coats hanging over chairs to dry, we moved to the common room and were soon exchanging stories about training to be teachers. Laura said it was the only job she wanted to do and Pat agreed with her. Ann looked at me and asked if I also felt it was my vocation.

I said yes it was. After all, I wasn't going to explain my silly notions of swashbuckling adventures, but Laura laughed and said, 'Lizzie wanted to be a pirate or an explorer when she was young.'

I glared her, but everyone seemed to find it amusing. Roberta asked when our training would be finished, but before Laura could answer, I said, 'We're going into our second year in October.'

Pat came through with the teapot and filled up our cups. The tea was sweet and hot and it warmed us up. The rain had turned to mist and it had turned much colder. She sat down beside me.

'I love my training and it's hard to believe that I'm now going into my second year. It just seems like yesterday when I started.'

Roberta laughed. 'Just wait till you're teaching twenty unruly kids, then every day seems like a month. At least that's what my sister tells me, as she's a teacher.'

When we looked at her with dismay, she laughed again. 'Sorry, I'm just joking.'

Later it was time for bed and to be honest we were all ready for it. My legs felt as if they were on fire. The bedroom held several bunk beds but because the hostel wasn't full we had a choice. The room was cold, but once we were in bed I soon warmed up. Just before dropping off to sleep, Laura sighed loudly.

'It's freezing in here and I miss my warm, cosy bed at home. Whose idea was it to come on this holiday?'

I heard the bed creaking as Pat sat up. She was indignant.

'It was your idea, Laura, so stop moaning.'

'I'm not moaning, I'm merely asking a rhetorical question.'

I think I muttered, 'It's all your fault,' but I can't be sure because the next thing I remember was waking up with the sun shining through the window. Our three companions were already up and preparing breakfast, and after a quick wash we joined them.

Cathy was clearing the table. 'Well, where will you be heading today?'

Laura piped up, 'We're hoping to go to Glenisla.'

As they left, they called out, 'Good luck on your travels.'

Within the hour we were also on our way, glad the rain was off. It looked like it would be a promising day of sunshine. We seemed to pedal for ages, and after two hours I asked Laura if she knew where we were.

'Look at the map?' I suggested.

Laura stopped and hunted in her saddlebag, but the map had disappeared.

'I can't find it.' Then, as if she had had a brainwave, she groaned, 'Oh no, I was looking at it last night and I think I've left it in the hostel.'

I couldn't believe we were lost, and as there were no signposts around we weren't sure if we should turn back or go on. Suddenly a small van passed us and the driver stopped when we waved frantically at him. He looked bemused at us three girls with bikes who were not shipwrecked but lost on the country roads.

Laura gave him a big smile. 'We're looking for the hostel at Glenisla.'

'Aye, you're on the right road, so just keep going and you'll see the sign for the hostel.'

It was teatime when we found the hostel, and we gratefully parked our bikes and entered the building. There was a warden in charge and she said we should have booked, but because it was late on the Sunday, most of the hostellers had left. We had enough sausages, bacon and eggs for our tea, but there would be nothing left for breakfast. We decided we would tackle that problem in the morning.

Pat said we could easily cycle to her parents' house the next day, where her mother would make something for us, and we agreed that would be wonderful. There was also the knowledge that we would know where we were, instead of cycling around the countryside like wandering minstrels.

'I thought you would know your way around these roads, Pat,' said Laura. 'After all, you live in the area.'

'Well, I've never been on this road before. I know the roads to Alyth, Blairgowrie and Forfar, and we sometimes go on the bus to Dundee, but although I know about Glenisla, Glenshee and Glen Doll I've never been to any of these places.'

Laura sounded grumpy. 'Well, I wish I had known that before making our travel plans, otherwise we could have gone somewhere else.'

The next day on our journey we came across a house by the side of the road that was also a small shop. We bustled into the small room that held shelves filled with groceries. We quickly bought three Fry's Chocolate Cream bars, three Mars bars and three bottles of lemonade. We sat down by the side of a stream and scoffed the lot.

Much later we were relieved to see Pat's house. Her mother looked surprised as she opened the door. Her hands were covered in flour, and the most delicious smell wafted out of the kitchen.

Pat introduced us and said, 'We were going youth hostelling, Mum, but we decided to come to see you and Dad.' There was no mention of the missing map or the non-existent food in our bags.

Pat's mum was also called Pat, and she ushered us into a large kitchen, where a wooden table held wire racks of scones, pancakes and a large fruit cake.

'Sit here at the table while I put the kettle on. It's lucky it's my baking day so there's lots to eat. Your father is working on the hay, but he'll be home for his supper.'

There was a fire burning in the range, and a large tabby cat stretched out on the rug. It was so homely and welcoming and we gratefully sat around the table. To begin with, we politely ate one scone each before Mrs Hogan said to tuck in, as she was planning on baking some more. Well, we needed no second invitation and I felt the butter run down my fingers as I ate my fourth warm scone. In fact, we all ate so much that I seriously thought the wheels on my bike would collapse with all the extra weight.

After finishing our fourth cup of tea, Pat said to her mother, 'Can we stay here for the night, Mum?'

I felt embarrassed at foisting ourselves on the poor woman, but she smiled and said it would be no bother at all.

'You can sleep in your room, Pat, and Lizzie and Laura can have the spare room in the attic.' She then carried another tray of home baking from the range and set it on the table. 'Your dad will be home about seven, so we'll have our supper then.'

Pat said she would show us round the farm, so we set off into the farmyard, which had hens running around. We then walked up to the big house, which looked magnificent, with its grey stone walls and shining windows.

'Our farm is part of the estate and this is the owner's house. They're very nice people, who do a lot of entertaining, and there are lots of people who come to stay. Mum helps out with the cleaning and I work during the holidays.'

I was amazed as I thought about the kitchen filled with home baking and now this extra heavy job on top of it.

'What a lot of hard work for your mother, Pat.'

'Yes, it is, and she seems to enjoy it, but she's made sure I don't end up like her. That's why she encouraged me to go away to be a teacher. She said she didn't get the chance for education, but she made sure I did.'

It was seven o'clock when we heard the kitchen door opening and a man's gruff voice call out, 'I almost fell over three bikes, Pat. Who put them there?'

Mrs Hogan shouted back, 'We've got Pat and her two friends come to stay, Davie.'

Davie came into the room in his stocking soles. He was a tall, gaunt-faced man with strong-looking sinewy arms that spoke of hard work and heavy lifting. His face lit up when he saw his daughter, and he smiled at me and Laura.

'I'll just get washed before supper,' he said, as Pat brought out a large casserole dish of cottage pie and vegetables.

'Supper's on the table, Davie, so don't be long.'

In all the years that followed I have never forgotten those three glorious days we spent with the Hogans. Davie told us some hair-raising tales from the farm.

'Aye, I mind one old chap who stood on a pitchfork and it went right through his foot. It was a right mess, I can tell you.'

Pat's mum said there was to be no more talk of the farm as she carried over a huge apple pie and custard for our pudding.

Laura looked at it in amazement, and Pat, noticing the look, whispered to us, 'Now you know why I'm so plump.'

Davie went to bed at nine o'clock, as he said he had to be at work by five o'clock the next morning, but we stayed up until ten before making our way up to our attic bedroom. It was a lovely room, with a tiny window that overlooked the fields beyond, and the double bed with a plump pink quilt on the top looked so comfy.

Laura sighed with pleasure as she got into bed. 'What a great holiday, Lizzie.'

As I got in beside her and snuggled down, I agreed.

After another couple of days of overeating, it was time to leave. We thanked Pat for all her hospitality.

'It's no bother, my dears. Pat's told me how much you've helped her at the college and it's been a pleasure to have met you.'

We then set off on the road home. It was a pity Pat had to return the bike, as she had to be back at the farm afterwards, but she said she would enjoy the last day of the holiday before catching the bus back to Kirriemuir.

When I arrived back home, Mum and Granny were having their tea. Mum said I was sunburned and asked if I had enjoyed my trip before adding, 'There's some food in the oven for you.'

After all the food I had eaten, I said, 'No thanks, Mum, I've had my tea.'

Pat had left her bike at Laura's house and we went to see her off on her bus. 'We'll see you in October, Pat,' we said, as the bus set off.

We returned the bikes the following day and the holiday faded into a lovely memory.

22

A HOLIDAY BY THE SEA

At the end of July Granny announced that we should have a holiday. Mum had been suffering from a sore throat and a bad cold, so Granny suggested a few days by the seaside.

'We can maybe go to Broughty Ferry or Carnoustie,' she said. 'That way Beth won't have to travel far.'

To start with, Mum was against the idea, but Granny went ahead and booked the three of us into a small guest house in the Ferry that had been recommended by one of her friends from the church.

We set off on the Friday morning with our two suitcases, while I had the money belt I had bought to go on the cycling trip. Laura had laughed at the time, but I felt it was a great idea and saved me putting any cash in the saddlebag.

The guest house was on the Esplanade and had a wonderful sea view, and with the sun shining on the river the water shimmered in the noon heat. Mum was still coughing as we arrived, but she seemed impressed by the view.

Mrs Robb, the owner of Ferryview, opened the door and welcomed us with a smile. 'I've got the rooms ready for you, and after you've unpacked please come down to the dining room for your dinner.'

The food was plain but very tasty, and afterwards Mum said she would like a look at the town and Granny went with her. I had brought my college studies with me, but it was too nice a day to have my head stuck in a book, so I went for a walk towards the castle.

There were lots of benches facing the water, but most of them were filled with visitors. I walked towards the beach but it was also crowded with families enjoying the sunshine. I strolled further along until the beach gave way to grassy dunes, and there was a lone empty seat.

I sat and watched boats sailing towards the North Sea, my head full of plans for the future. After the end of the training course I knew I had to go to one of the Education Department's schools, but hopefully after teaching there I would be free to travel overseas.

Filled with my dreams of travel, I retraced my steps, stopping at a kiosk by the beach and buying an ice cream. I had to fiddle with the cash in my belt, but it was great not to have to carry a handbag.

When I arrived back at Ferryview, Mum had gone to bed with two aspirin and Granny was in the lounge knitting. She held up a ball of blue wool. 'I found the most wonderful wool shop in the town, so I bought this. Beth's throat is still sore, so she went for a lie down, but she said she would be down for her tea.' She stopped knitting and looked at me. 'I'm really worried about your Mum, Lizzie. She always looks so pale and I don't think she eats as well as she should.'

I said I was worried as well, but Mum was really stubborn when anyone mentioned going to the doctor. 'If this sore throat lasts much longer,' I said, 'then I'm going to make her get medical help.'

Granny's needles clicked as she knitted something that resembled a five inch length of blue stitches. 'It's a great pity she's never got over Peter's death, but I've read there are hundreds of families still mourning their lost sons, husband, fathers and sweethearts.'

Up till then I had been engrossed in my studies, but suddenly the spectre of the day we learned Dad was missing came back and I felt a shiver up my spine. I looked over at Granny, but she was now studying a pattern.

She saw me looking and held up the paper. 'It's a baby's matinee jacket.'

I mumbled something like, 'It's lovely,' but the afternoon had been spoiled by bad memories.

Later Mum appeared. Her face was flushed, as if she had a fever, but she managed to eat most of her tea, which was fish and chips with bread and butter and a huge pot of tea.

Mrs Robb said she normally served cocoa and biscuits before bedtime, but I was the only one who went downstairs, as I didn't want the woman to be left with her pot of cocoa.

The next day wasn't so hot. Granny said she needed more wool and asked if we wanted to go with her into town. I thought Mum was going to refuse, so I said I would come, but as we were leaving Mum appeared and we set off. A breeze was blowing from the river, and the smell was invigorating as we made our way up the street.

We spent ages in the wool shop with Granny, chatting to the assistant and buying more wool, before deciding to go into a café. It was quite busy, but we found a table and Granny ordered tea and scones while Mum gazed listlessly out of the window. I noticed Granny giving her a concerned look before the waitress brought our order.

Back at the guest house, Mum said she would go for a lie-down and Granny sat at the window of the lounge with her knitting.

'I'm going for a walk,' I said, and I made my way back to the dunes and the empty bench. Hordes of seagulls were flying overhead, and I imagined myself on a boat with seabirds swooping and wheeling as the ship ploughed through the ocean waves to some magical faraway land.

I was brought back to earth as I looked at my wristwatch and saw it was time for our midday meal. Mum didn't come down for that, but she did appear for tea, and Granny and I thought she looked much better.

'Yes, my sore throat has gone and I feel a bit better,' she said.

We left after breakfast the next morning, but I was pleased to see Mum had some colour in her cheeks, and she said she was looking forward to going back to work.

When we arrived back at Victoria Road, I was already missing the smell of the salty air, and the noise from the street was so different from the Ferry. Tramcars clanged up and down while carts filled with bales of jute and pulled by huge Clydesdale horses clattered up towards the jute mills on Dens Road.

Before we had left to go away to the Ferry, I had arranged to go to the pictures with Laura and we were to meet at the Plaza. I saw her hurrying up the hill and she arrived all flustered with a red face.

'I've managed to get a wee job in the grocer's shop downstairs from the house,' she said as we went in to buy our tickets. 'It's just for a few weeks till the start of the new term at college, but it'll help me out with money.'

I was slightly envious. 'Oh, that's great, Laura. I wish I could get a job as well, but there's so many folk unemployed that I don't think that will happen.'

She nodded as we headed for our seats. 'I know I'm lucky, but it's just for three hours in the afternoon and it'll only last for the next few weeks.'

Later as we headed home down the hill, her face went red as she said, 'There's this super-looking young lad working in the shop and he's asked me out to the pictures one night.'

I stopped and looked at her. 'I think you're blushing, Laura. Are you going to go out with him?'

She tried to look nonchalant but failed. 'I might.'

When I got home, I suddenly felt bereft. I wondered if our friendship could possibly survive this romantic involvement. I mentioned this to Granny and she gave me a stern look.

'You'll probably meet a young man as well, Lizzie. That's what happens to friends, but hopefully you'll still have time for each other.'

I decided to spend most of my time before the start of my second year in my studies. I so desperately wanted to do well in order to get a job overseas. I had read somewhere that teachers were needed to teach English to foreign students and I was hoping that would happen.

It was now September and my days of freedom would soon be over. I noticed that Granny appeared to be tired most days. She often had to sit down, and although I did most of the work around the house she would still make an excuse to go to bed early.

Of course, Mum didn't notice anything out of the ordinary, but then she was only home in the evenings and didn't see Granny having to put down her knitting and take deep breaths. One day I told Granny I was worried about her, but she just said she was fine and it was the colder weather that was making her more tired than normal. 'I'm always like this in the autumn, when the nights begin to draw in.'

I almost said I hadn't noticed this during all the autumns we had lived with her, but I could see from her expression that the matter was closed.

I hadn't seen much of Laura during these last few weeks, but on the night before we were due to start our second year's course, she arrived at the door.

Granny was visiting Maisie and Mum was in her room. 'Well, it's back to the training college tomorrow,' she said. 'It'll be great to see Pat again.'

I said it would. Laura then leant forward and whispered, 'I've been seeing Mike, he's the lad working in the shop for the summer, and we've been to the pictures a few times and we sometimes go for a walk on Sunday. He's gone back to Glasgow University, where he's training to be an engineer, but we said we would write to each other.'

'That's wonderful news, Laura. I'm so pleased for you.' Although I was sincere, I somehow knew life was changing and we couldn't stay as we were.

Pat was wearing a new hand-knitted pink jumper when we saw her the next morning. Her cheeks were rosy and she looked full of life, and Laura couldn't wait to tell her about her new romance.

Pat's eyes were like saucers as she listened, and then she said, 'I'm glad to be back. It's been hard work on the farm and in the big house, but maybe Lizzie and I will meet two nice lads this term. What do you think, Lizzie?'

'I suppose anything's possible, Pat.' On that flippant note we joined the rest of the class.

One morning at the end of October, the weather turned very cold and the wind promised the threat of snow. Granny was still in bed when I left, which surprised me, but as she was sleeping I didn't like to wake her.

It was mid-afternoon when one of the tutors entered the room and asked to see me in her office. I was so taken aback, wondering what misdemeanour I had committed, that I followed her like an automaton. I do remember Laura and Pat staring at me as I went past, but I shook my head at them as if to say I had no idea what was happening.

Mr Robert Ash, the medical officer, was in the office and he asked me to sit down. 'Miss Flint, I'm sorry to have to tell you that your grandmother has had a heart attack and she's been taken to the Royal Infirmary.'

I stared at him for what seemed ages. 'I saw her this morning and she was fine,' I stuttered.

'Well, I suggest you make your way to the infirmary right away, and we are all very sorry to have to give you this bad news.'

I rushed to get my coat and bag and was lucky that a tramcar was turning the corner of Tay Street, although it seemed to take ages to travel to the foot of the Hilltown. As I hurried up the road to the infirmary, I hoped that Mum had also been told, but when I arrived she was nowhere to be seen. However, Maisie was sitting in the waiting room and she had been crying.

'I went to see your granny this morning and I found her lying on the floor. I called the doctor and she's now in with a consultant. I went out to the telephone box and called the college, as I wasn't sure what to do.'

I told her she had done the right thing, but I was annoyed at myself for not contacting Mum. 'I should have stopped at

DM Brown's to tell Mum, but I'll wait till I speak to the doctor before going.'

The waiting room began to fill up, as it was the afternoon visiting hours, but the doctor appeared at the door and asked me to come with him to his office. My heart was hammering against my ribcage, but I managed to smile weakly at Maisie, who had turned her anxious face towards the man.

The office was small, but he ushered me towards a chair and I sat with my hands in my lap, desperately trying not to twist and turn them in my anxiety. The doctor was medium height and middle-aged with a round, cheery-looking expression, which changed when he looked at me. Alarm bells began to ring in my brain, but I fought hard to keep composed.

'I'm afraid I have to tell you that your grandmother is very ill. She suffered a heart attack, but I hope she'll recover with rest and medication.'

A feeling of relief washed over me. 'Can I see her?'

'No, not at the moment, but she was asking about your mother and yourself, so I've told her it might be possible for you both to visit tonight.'

I was feeling better by now, and back in the waiting room I told Maisie what the doctor had said. She dabbed her eyes with her handkerchief and said simply, 'Thank goodness.'

As it was coming up for five o'clock, I decided to wait till Mum came home before telling her the news, but I couldn't sit at peace and kept going to the window to look out for her arrival. At five thirty I couldn't stay in the house any longer, so I wrapped up warmly in my winter coat and went downstairs to wait for Mum. I spotted Maisie also looking out of the window and I gave her a wave.

It was nearly six o'clock when I spotted Mum hurrying up the road, and she looked at me in surprise when I ran to meet her. 'Granny's been taken to hospital, Mum, and we've to go and see her.'

Mum was confused, as anyone who had been suddenly accosted on the pavement would be. 'What's wrong with her, Lizzie? Has she had an accident? She was perfectly all right this morning when I left for work.'

I told her about Maisie finding her lying on the floor.

Mum seemed exasperated. 'I've noticed she has got a bit shaky on her feet recently. I bet she tripped over something.' She gave me an accusing glance. 'Have you left something lying on the floor? You always have these binders with notes and you put them on the floor.'

I said I hadn't left anything, but I was afraid to mention the heart attack in case Mum panicked, as she often did. By this time we were on our way to the infirmary. The wind was bitingly cold and it whipped against our faces as we made our way along Garland Place. Mum gave a long glance at our old house, but she didn't say anything.

When we reached the front door of the infirmary, the porter, who had a small office right beside it, asked us what we wanted.

'We've come to see Mrs Mary Flint, who was admitted this morning,' I said.

The porter said there were no evening visiting hours today as there had been afternoon visiting earlier.

'The doctor told us to come back tonight to see Mrs Flint,' I said, getting slightly annoyed by this obstacle of a man at the entrance.

'What doctor was that?'

I suddenly realised I hadn't registered the doctor's name. 'I'm sorry, but I don't know it. But my granny was admitted with a heart attack.'

Mum heard the word 'heart' and she began to cry. 'You never said anything about Mary's heart. I thought she had tripped.'

The porter, now that I had given him some information, said, 'That'll be Dr McNab. I'll give him a buzz and get him to come down.'

I said to Mum that we should have a seat in the waiting room, but she was still annoyed at me for withholding information. Thankfully, the doctor arrived within a few minutes and we went back to his office. Mum was trying to dry her tears as we walked along the corridor.

When we were seated, the doctor took off his glasses and I knew at once the news wasn't good. 'I'm afraid to have to tell you that Mrs Flint died at five thirty this evening. I'm so sorry.'

I grasped Mum's hand, hoping she wouldn't become hysterical, but she looked shell-shocked at this sad news.

'But you said you thought she would get better with rest and medication, doctor,' I said, my voice coming out all squeaky with shock.

'Yes, that was my diagnosis this afternoon, but your grand-mother took another heart attack at five thirty this evening that proved fatal.' He gave us a kindly look. 'I'm so very sorry. We were going to get in touch with you as soon as we could.'

He began to tell us about getting a death certificate, but I didn't take it all in. His words seemed to come from a distance, as if I was somewhere else listening to an echo.

Afterwards, I'll never forget trying to get Mum home. The rain had come on and I had to support her, as I felt she was about to collapse on me, but somehow we made it back to Victoria Road.

Maisie must have noticed our approach from her window because she was waiting at our door. She opened her mouth to speak, but when she saw my expression she remained silent and she quietly followed us into the sitting room, where she had lit the fire.

Mum still hadn't said a word, but I quickly removed her wet stockings and shoes while Maisie made tea. Suddenly there was a roar of pain and Mum began to cry. It wasn't a gentle cry but harsh sobs that seemed to come from deep in her soul. Maisie tried to comfort her, but she would have none of it.

'Granny died at five thirty this evening, Maisie.' I didn't add that at that time I had experienced the awful feeling of anxiety and agitation. 'We never got the chance to say goodbye to her.'

Maisie said, 'I think we should get Beth to her bed.'

I agreed and we tried to get her to go to sleep, but the awful crying wouldn't stop. I painfully remembered a similar time when Mum cried like this, when I was six and Dad was posted as missing. Maisie said we would have to call the doctor out tomorrow if Mum was still distressed, and I agreed.

'I'll sit up tonight with her, Maisie, and hopefully she'll fall asleep with exhaustion.'

Maisie left, but she put her hand on my shoulder. 'We'll all miss your granny, Lizzie. She's been my neighbour and friend for years but I didn't get a chance to say goodbye to her either.'

I felt my chest constrict with emotion, but I didn't want to cry in front of her. She wasn't the only one who hadn't said goodbye, as Mum or I hadn't either, and I was furious with myself for not waking Granny up this morning. Perhaps if I had I would have noticed she was ill, and if I had then maybe she would still be alive.

Mum finally fell asleep around midnight, but as I lay down on my bed I couldn't sleep. Then at three o'clock in the morning Mum awoke and told me to send a telegram to Margaret before another bout of tears made her body shake as if she was in the throes of a fever. She got back to sleep before dawn, and mercifully I fell asleep as well.

We didn't get up till after nine the next morning, and Mum sat in the chair looking as white as a sheet and rocking gently to and fro. I tried to get her to eat some toast, but she ignored me. Maisie appeared, and I said I was going to get the doctor and also send a telegram to my aunt.

Thankfully the post office was empty of customers as I handed over the telegram. The man behind the counter gave me a sympathetic look, but I knew I couldn't have handled any questions if I ran into Granny's neighbours and friends.

I phoned the doctor's house from the telephone box down the street, and he said he would come round as soon as possible. When I got home, Mum had burst into another flood of tears and Maisie was trying to comfort her.

I sat beside Mum and said, 'I've sent the telegram to Margaret and the doctor will be coming in soon to help you.'

She clutched my arm. 'Did you tell Margaret to come quickly?'

I nodded, although I hadn't actually said as much.

The doctor arrived mid-morning, and when he saw the state of Mum's grief he prescribed a sedative. 'This will help to sedate Mrs Flint and it will also make her sleep better.'

Laura and Pat turned up that evening, but they didn't stay long. 'We just want to say how sorry we are, Lizzie.'

The next morning, Mum was still asleep when Margaret's reply to my telegram arrived. It said simply that she was on her way and would soon be with us.

I sat at the window and gazed down on a wet and windy street. A few people with umbrellas were out and about. As I sipped my tea with the telegram on my lap, and with a numb feeling of helplessness and grief, I silently said a prayer of thanks.

23

THE FUNERAL

Two days later, Margaret arrived at seven o'clock in the morning. She had travelled from Lisbon to London, where she caught the overnight sleeper, but when she appeared at the door on that dark autumn morning she looked as if she had only travelled a short distance instead of the many hundreds of miles from Portugal.

I was so grateful to see her. As she took off her coat and placed her suitcase in the lobby, she asked how Mum was coping with the shock of Granny's death. As it was I had been up most of the night with her, but she had finally fallen asleep at five o'clock.

Margaret said not to wake her up, and she sat at the fire while I cooked bacon and eggs, as I expected she would be hungry after her long journey. After breakfast, which she enjoyed, she asked about the arrangements for Granny's burial.

'I've been in touch with the funeral director's business on the Hilltown, but I haven't manage to do much more, Margaret.'

She said she would get in touch with the authorities, and I was relieved to have that burden lifted from my shoulders.

Mum must have heard our voices because she suddenly called out, 'Margaret, is that you?'

Margaret went through to the bedroom and Mum began to cry again, but Margaret's soothing words seemed to help, and within minutes they both appeared. Mum's hair was dishevelled and she was wearing her dressing gown, and her red-rimmed eyes were a sharp contrast to her ashen complexion.

'Would you like some bacon and eggs, Mum?' I asked.

She gazed at me with a glazed expression and shivered. It was as if I had offered her some boiled octopus, so I just made her a cup of hot sweet tea, which she didn't drink.

Margaret took charge immediately. 'Now, Lizzie, I think you should go back to the college today, and they will give you the day off for the funeral.'

I opened my mouth to protest, but she said, 'I remember when I was at the college and they didn't like any absences. Don't worry, I'll be here to look after Beth.'

So that was arranged, and to be honest I was grateful to get out of the house and leave everything in Margaret's capable hands.

As I walked along the wet pavement to the college, I was feeling depressed. All my plans to go and see the world were now in tatters, as I realised I could never leave Mum because I feared she wouldn't be able to cope on her own. I would get a job in a school in Dundee and that would be my life. Then I felt guilty at having these thoughts. After all, she was my mother and it was my duty to look after her.

When I appeared at Park Place, the first person I met was Pat. She looked surprised to see me.

'Should you be here, Lizzie? What about your mum?'

'My aunt has arrived from Portugal and she said she would take over everything and look after Mum.'

'Well, I'm glad to see you and I felt really sorry for you both that night Laura and I came to see you after your granny's death. Your poor mother was so distressed and we felt so helpless.'

'Yes, I know. I feel like that as well, so that's why I'm so grateful Margaret is here, as she copes so well with anything.'

Laura then appeared and the three of us went into our classes. Before I left that afternoon, I went to see my tutor to arrange time off for the funeral, and with everything settled I set off for home.

Mum was sitting in the chair wearing a clean dress, and her hair was newly washed and combed. She looked so much better now that Margaret was here. I couldn't help but marvel at the change in her, and I wished that my aunt could stay with us forever and not have to go back to Portugal.

Margaret explained that they had been busy that day. 'We went to see the funeral director and the funeral will be the day after tomorrow. We also went to see the solicitor, and Mary's will states that she wants to be buried beside her late husband at Balgay Cemetery. The minister from the church came here this afternoon and everything is settled.'

I looked across at Mum and she seemed to be so relaxed. It was such a contrast to her earlier state of mind. It was when Margaret and I were taking the cottage pie out of the oven that she whispered, 'I called the doctor in again and he's given Beth some sleeping pills to help her until after the funeral.'

As she scooped the pie onto the plates I noticed the fine lines on her face and that she looked tired. 'Margaret, please don't do too much, because you look tired.'

She laughed. 'It's just the journey catching up with me. I'll be fine by tomorrow.'

After tea, Margaret and Mum discussed some things about the funeral service. Mum and I had arranged for Margaret to live with us instead of booking into a hotel, and she seemed pleased about that arrangement. As I didn't want to sleep in Granny's room, I said I would sleep on the sofa. Margaret said that Maisie had offered me a spare bed in her house, but I said I was happy with the sofa. For the first night since Granny's death, Mum slept right through the night, but I was too restless to sleep, although I did doze off in the early morning.

The funeral was to take place at eleven o'clock, and it turned out to be a misty day. The church was packed with Granny's friends and fellow parishioners, and it was with a feeling of unreality that I followed Mum, Margaret and Maisie to the front pew.

Thankfully Mum was calm, but she looked so fragile in her black coat and hat that I had to hold back my tears.

The minister gave a wonderful eulogy about Granny, saying

what stalwart members she and her late husband had been and how she had knitted hundreds of items for the soldiers in the trenches and latterly for needy families. He mentioned the tragedy in her life, with the loss of her husband and son. Especially her son Peter, he said, who had died like thousands of other soldiers in the war. His condolences went out to his young widow and daughter and all the family. I noticed Margaret was holding Mum's hand, while Maisie cried quietly into her handkerchief. The hymns were the 23rd Psalm and 'Abide With Me', and it was at this point I almost burst into tears. I was trying to hold my grief in, as I knew I would upset Mum and I didn't want her to break down.

I vaguely remember people coming up and speaking to us afterwards, but everything still felt unreal. It was to be a private burial at Balgay, so the car took the three of us, plus the minister, to the cemetery. Margaret had arranged refreshments back at the house for anyone who wanted to come, and Maisie had volunteered to be there until we returned.

The mist shrouded the gravestones, giving them a ghostly appearance, but the service at the cemetery was brief, with the minister saying a final prayer. I watched as Granny's coffin was lowered into its narrow slot. I had never been so sad as this in my life, but as we turned to leave the many wreathes were placed on the spot, and because they were mainly arrangements of chrysanthemums in shades of gold, russet and yellow, the grave seemed to glow with colour and light. I knew the sharp tang of their perfume would remain with me for the rest of my life.

Back at the house, Maisie was busy handing round sandwiches and tea to Milly and Albert and Andy Baxter. I then noticed Wullie and Irene sitting on the sofa with Davie and Pat Hogan.

Andy, Wullie and Davie were dressed in their dark-coloured suits and white shirts with starched collars. There was a faint smell of mothballs, and I knew the men had put on their best clothes for the funeral, which filled me with emotion. These were men who were more at home working with wood and farming, but they now sat in awkward silence as their wives quietly spoke to each other. It made me feel humble that they had come to say farewell to Granny, a woman they had never met.

I went to sit beside them while Mum went to sit with Milly, Albert and Andy. It was easy to see that Albert worked in the clothing trade because his suit of dark-coloured worsted looked fashionable.

'Thank you so much for coming,' I said. 'We really appreciate it.'

Wullie said, 'We wanted to come, Lizzie. Laura and Pat didn't want to ask for time off from the college, but they'll be round tonight.'

Pat expressed the same sentiments, as she looked at Davie. 'You've been so good to our Pat, and she always said she loved coming here to see you all, especially your granny.'

Davie's calloused, weather-beaten hand was holding one of Granny's china cups and saucers, but he placed it onto the little table beside the sofa as Margaret came over and I introduced her.

'This is my aunt Margaret, she's travelled from Lisbon to be with us.'

I left them to go and speak with Milly. She had been crying, but apart from that she looked well. I gave her a hug and she started crying again. 'I hope Beth will be fine, Lizzie. You know how sensitive she is, and I do worry about her.'

'Yes, I know, Milly, but Margaret and I will keep an eye on her.'

She grasped my hand. 'I know you will, and she's a lucky woman to have such a caring daughter.' She hesitated and glanced over her shoulder. 'Can I tell you a secret, Lizzie?'

My mind was still numb, but I nodded.

She was smiling. 'I'm expecting a baby next year, but I don't want to mention it to Beth just yet, but can you tell her from me?'

'That's great, Milly. What does Albert think about your news?'

'He's thrilled, and so is my father-in-law. They both hope it will be a boy and I would like a girl, but it honestly doesn't matter as we'll have our own first child.'

Andy was sitting with Mum and she was trying to make

conversation, but I saw from her face that the sedative was wearing off, so I went over. Before I reached them, Margaret came and said that Pat's and Laura's parents were leaving, so I turned around to say goodbye and thank them once more for their support.

Davie said, 'Your aunt very kindly offered to get us a taxi to take us to the station, but it will only take us a wee while to catch the tramcar.'

Pat and Irene took my hand as they went through the door. 'Now remember, Lizzie, we're here for you and your mum any time you need us.'

'Thank you.'

I watched from the window as they emerged onto the street, but the mist had thickened and they were just a blur as they got on the tramcar.

Andy was also standing up to go and I went to have a word with him. I thought he looked well; he had a black leather glove over his missing hand.

'How are you keeping, Andy?' I asked.

'Things are looking up for me, Lizzie. I've got a job at Lord Robert's workshop in Meadowside. He set it up to give work to people disabled in the war, and I've been lucky to get a place there.'

I was so pleased for him and I said so.

'It means that my mother has some extra income coming into the house now, and I've also got a girlfriend. At the moment we're just friends who go to the pictures together, but I'm hoping it will become a more serious relationship between us.'

'Congratulations, Andy. You deserve some happiness after all you've been through.'

'I wouldn't have had all this if it hadn't been for your father, Lizzie. I owe him my life, but it's a terrible tragedy that you're both now living without him.'

I was so choked with emotion that I couldn't speak, so I just took hold of his good hand and clasped it tightly.

Thankfully Milly said they had also to go and catch the train back to Glasgow. I thought Mum wouldn't let her go as they hugged one another, but finally they all left, including Maisie, who had been a tower of strength all afternoon. She said she appreciated our heartfelt thanks. 'I would have done anything for Mary, as we've been neighbours for years.'

Margaret sat down with a loud sigh. 'Would you both like something to eat?' she asked, but Mum said if we didn't mind she would go to bed.

Margaret made cheese omelettes and toast. We sat at the window, but this time the curtains were closed against the cold, foggy night air.

Pat and Laura arrived about seven o'clock, but Mum was still in bed. Margaret entertained them with stories of her teaching days and her life in foreign countries, and we all reminisced about Granny and her prolific knitting. It was nine o'clock when they left, and that just left Margaret and me with our memories.

24

MUM MAKES A CONFESSION

I found life very hard after Granny's death, but Margaret made things bearable. I shudder to think what it would have been like if she hadn't been there. Every Sunday we both made our way to the cemetery, where we cleared the withered wreaths and laid fresh flowers on the grave. Afterwards, if the weather was dry we would sit on one of the benches and discuss how Mum would cope after she went back to Lisbon.

'I have to be back by the end of November, Lizzie.'

'Yes, I know, Margaret, but hopefully Mum will be able to get on with her life.'

As it was, Mum seemed to get a new lease of life and she looked much better for it. She had been to the solicitor's office with Margaret, and Granny had left her life savings to Mum with a small bequest to me. It wasn't a huge amount of money, but it would cushion Mum's life quite a bit. The house was rented, but the local factor transferred the lease to us, so that was one worry less.

Margaret had found a hairdressing salon in the Nethergate that stayed open one evening a week, so both she and Mum regularly had their hair washed and cut. Margaret's grey hair was styled in a fashionable Eton crop, while Mum had a softer, curlier look. Mum bought some Pond's cream from the beauty counter at DM Brown's for her face, and she began to look like how I remembered her as a child.

Laura and Pat came round regularly, even though I saw them at the college every day, but we enjoyed listening to Margaret's stories of her foreign travels and her teaching career, especially me.

One evening, Laura asked her how she managed to cope in the classroom. We were learning the rudimentary lessons at college, but we had yet to experience the real thing.

'Well, I did three years' training, Laura, because I was a university pupil. My first job was at Butterburn School, which I loved. Later I applied for a teaching post in a private school in Edinburgh, and I stayed there for a few years before finally becoming the headmistress. In the beginning I had this class of eight-year-olds, and there was one girl in particular, Abigail Lee, whose parents were American. She was so smart she was in danger of turning round and cutting herself. One day I misspelt the word "believe" and she called out loudly that it was wrong. I couldn't let this minute whippersnapper get the better of me, so I said, "Well done, Abigail Lee, I wondered who would be the first one to notice it. You are a clever girl."' Margaret laughed at the memory. 'She was so pleased she sat up straight with a priggish smile and looked at her classmates. Then a month later her parents went back to America. I often wondered what became of her. I personally think she's the head of some big firm and struts around all day lording it over the poor workers.'

We all laughed, and even Mum was amused, which gladdened my heart. One day Pat asked me if Margaret was Mum's sister, but I said no, she was a stepsister. Yet in my mind she was more than that: she was more like a mother to her, and Mum just blossomed when she was around.

One night Mum confessed to us that all the time she had lived at Victoria Road she had felt like the lodger. I was shocked, and Margaret said that couldn't be true because Mary doted on us; in fact, she had said as much to Margaret.

'But that's how I felt, Margaret,' Mum said. 'I had to leave my own home behind and move here because I had no choice, but it was never my own house.'

After Mum went to bed, I said, 'I never thought she felt like that. Granny was always so kind to us, and I'm sure there were times when she wished she had the house to herself.'

Margaret said not to worry. 'Beth has always been a sensitive person, so I'm sure she didn't mean it.'

Actually I thought she had, but we left it at that.

I was dreading the weeks going by, and before long it was time for Margaret to leave. Mum put on a brave face and said she would be fine.

'I've got Lizzie, so don't worry about us, Margaret.'

On the last Friday in November, Margaret and I went to the railway station, where she had booked a place on the London sleeper train. I helped her with her suitcases and we stood on the cold platform as the train got up its head of steam. I tried to be brave, but it was hard to keep from crying.

'You'll soon be finished at the college, Lizzie, and you'll do well as a teacher. Gerald and I are still hoping to buy a house by the sea, and in a couple of years we'll be back for good.'

'Oh Margaret, I'm going to miss you, and I know Mum is feeling the same way.'

The guard began to shut the doors and my aunt stepped onto the train.

'I'll write every week, and if you need me then let me know and I'll come back, because Lisbon isn't as far away as Rio de Janeiro.'

Then the train chugged forwards, and I stood and waved until it was out of sight.

I walked home along the wet streets, but when I got home Mum was in bed, so I sat at the window with my cocoa and photograph of Dad and wondered what life would have been like if he hadn't died in that needless and cruel war.

We didn't really celebrate Christmas that year, and I didn't decorate the house with Granny's paper chains or bunches of holly or her little fairy figures. Margaret sent her usual lavish hamper from Keiller's shop and the treats inside lasted until the New Year. On Hogmanay we didn't even wait up for the bells, but were in bed by eleven.

Laura had asked me to go to her house, but I said I couldn't leave Mum on her own and she said she understood.

On New Year's Day I went to the cemetery and laid a big bunch of holly on the grave.

As I stood looking at the inscribed headstone, I said softly, 'Happy New Year, Granny . . .'

25

MILLY'S GOOD NEWS

After Margaret's departure I was frightened Mum would revert back to her former depressed state, but I was pleasantly surprised that she still seemed to be enjoying life. She still went to the hair salon every few weeks, as she said the attention of the hairdresser made her feel relaxed.

Because she seemed to be coping so well, I was able to go with Laura and Pat once a week to the pictures. Our favourite film star was Douglas Fairbanks; we all thought he was so handsome. Pat said that he was married to Mary Pickford, another film star, but that didn't stop us swooning over him.

We were coming out of the Plaza cinema one night when Laura remarked, 'I can't get over how quickly the last two years have gone. Just think, we'll soon be finished our course, and it only seems like yesterday when we started.'

'I wonder where we'll be teaching this time next year?' I said.

Laura was philosophical. 'It doesn't really matter. The main thing is we'll have a job. Not like all the poor folk who are unemployed. My dad was saying that he was lucky to be in a job, but quite a few of our neighbours have husbands and sons searching for work.'

Pat said that it was different in the countryside, as most of her parents' friends and neighbours all worked on the farm or in the owner's big house.

After a while I began to relax, and I must say I enjoyed my last few months at the college. I had resigned myself to working in Dundee and my dream of travelling was only a fantasy. I still read my library books on travel and I marvelled at all the wonderful and exotic places in the world, but my childhood plans were only a distant memory.

One night Mum said that she was going to get rid of Granny's old furniture and replace it with new things from the furniture store in the Wellgate. I was appalled.

'We can't get rid of Granny's lovely things, Mum,' I said, looking around at the well-polished sideboard and the table and chairs.

Mum said that was nonsense. 'I've been looking in the shop and they have all this modern furniture and the room will look really fresh and new.' She glanced around the room disdainfully. 'This is all so old-fashioned and . . . and Victorian.'

She made it sound as if the furniture was ugly, which it wasn't, but she was adamant that it all had to go. When she mentioned this to Maisie, her reaction was the same as mine.

'But Mary cherished all these things, Beth, and she polished everything once a week.'

'I know that, Maisie, but I want new things.'

Maisie looked at me, but I just shook my head. When Mum got an idea into her mind, then nothing would change it. It was just the way she was.

'When I buy my new things, Maisie, you can have what you want for your house.'

Although I was annoyed at her, to be honest I was too busy at the college to pay much attention to Mum's plans. She would sit at the table with a writing pad and pencil and mark down the prices she had been given by the salesman and shake her head as she counted everything up.

Thankfully after a few weeks she seemed to drop the idea, and I was relieved. Granny's inheritance was there to be used for essentials and living expenses, but it was Mum's money, so if she wanted to use it to change the look of the house then that was her decision. In the end, I think it was the fact that she might run short of money if she went on with her spending spree that settled the matter. So life went on much the same as before and Mum never mentioned the old-fashioned and 'Victorian' furniture again.

It was coming up to the end of our training, and we were excited about our futures but also sad that we would soon be saying goodbye to the college and all our tutors. Pat had the added problem of looking for accommodation when she took up a post at a school, but Laura said she could stay with her until she found somewhere to live.

In June we were given our teacher's training certificates, and to celebrate the three of us went to the tearoom at DM Brown's for high tea. We looked in at the millinery department, but Mum was busy with a customer. She glanced over and we smiled and waved. She didn't smile back, and I saw the tiredness on her face and was suddenly worried. The euphoria of Margaret's visit was gone and she was back to her usual listless self.

At the beginning of July, Milly wrote with the news that she had given birth to a son.

'His name is Albert, but we're calling him Bertie,' she said. 'I would love you to be his godmother, Beth, when he gets christened.'

I thought Mum would be pleased with the news, especially the fact that Milly wanted her to be the baby's godmother, but Mum said she was going to write back and say she couldn't manage it.

I know she had come down with a bad summer cold, and I'd hoped she would feel better, but she didn't. Instead she began to take days off work, and at the end of the month, she said, 'I'm going to ask the store if I can do three days a week, Lizzie.'

Alarm bells began to ring in my head, but she said she couldn't get rid of the cold and the cough that she seemed to have had for ages, but with fewer hours to work she would soon be feeling better.

Milly wrote back and said she was disappointed, but if Mum wasn't feeling well then she understood. She was going to ask her cousin Jeannie, the one she had left Dundee to go and live with, and when Bertie was a bit bigger she would come through and visit us.

Laura, Pat and I were waiting for confirmation of placements in schools, and as it turned out, even though I had been a reluctant student to start with, I had a letter saying that I had to begin my teaching career after the summer holidays at Ann Street School. I would spend a term under the guidance of one of the teachers who was due to retire.

I was sorry for the looks of disappointment on my friends' faces. 'I thought we would all be placed at the same time,' said Laura, who seemed a bit disgruntled with my news.

Pat remained silent, but I hoped that they would also hear from the education department soon.

I didn't go far that summer, as Mum's request had been granted and she worked at the store on Thursday, Friday and Saturday, so I felt I had to be with her the rest of the week. I wrote to Margaret with our news, thinking she would be worried about Mum, but she said perhaps it was better for her, as she had never been a strong woman. Of course, she was delighted with my placement and said I would go far in my career.

Then much to my relief, Laura and Pat also got placements. Laura was going to Tay Street School and Pat to Hill Street. We met up and shared our worries and plans.

Laura was worried about taking over a class of small children. 'What if they don't behave themselves and don't listen to a word I say?'

Pat said not to worry, as we had been trained to do this job and we would all manage. 'There will be other teachers in the school and they will help us with any problems,' she said.

I bought a new skirt and blouse for my first day and I pinned my hair up to make me look more mature, but I didn't sleep very well the night before the new term, which started on a Monday. Mum wasn't working, but as I left that morning she was still asleep. I could have done with some support, and once again I wished Margaret was here, but she wasn't, as she had her husband and her own life to lead.

Walking into the playground at Ann Street was a strange feeling. The children were all running around and calling out to their friends. A few of the mothers had gathered at the school gate and they stood around gossiping with each other.

The first person I met was Miss Annie Hendry, the teacher who was due to retire, and she took me to the small staff room, where I met the other teachers and Mr Drummond, the headmaster. He was a tall, thin man with a severe expression and hair slicked back with Brylcreem. He welcomed me and said he hoped I would be happy in his school.

My knees were shaking, but I wanted to portray a look of confidence. However, my smile went unnoticed as the school bell began to ring. Miss Annie Hendry was a woman of around sixty, with glasses that hung around her neck on a chain. She had a round, cheery-looking face and her hair was swept back in a large, heavy-looking bun.

She took my arm. 'You'll be fine, Miss Flint. We will be teaching primary three and you'll find the children well behaved.'

We walked into a classroom that held twenty desks with seats attached and a huge blackboard that stood beside the teacher's desk. Twenty pairs of eyes swivelled in my direction as she introduced me.

'This is Miss Flint, who will be teaching along with me for a little while. What do we say to our new teacher?'

Twenty little voices chanted, 'Good morning, Miss Flint.'

I answered them and the day's work began. Looking back, although I didn't realise it at the time, this was one of the happiest times of my life. I loved the children. Most of the little girls sat so primly in their seats, their hair tied up with bows, while the boys were a bit noisier but still well behaved.

One little lad put his hand up. Miss Hendry sighed.

'What is it, Charlie?'

'I think it's braw having twa teachers instead of just you, Miss Hendry, and she's much prettier than you.'

I was mortified, but she told him to sit down and get on with his sums. She whispered, 'That's Charlie: he always says what's on his mind and he's a rascal.'

As the days went by I found I loved working with this experienced teacher. As we sat having a cup of tea in the staff room, she told me she had been teaching for forty years.

'I'm going to miss it, but it's time for me to go and have a well-earned rest.'

The children were a mixed bunch with their reading and sums. I found the girls were better able to do their lessons than the boys, and Charlie in particular seemed to have problems with his reading. No matter how hard I tried to get him to read his book, he still stumbled over the words.

Just before Christmas I brought in my own book, *Treasure Island*, and when the rest of the class were busy with their work I would sit beside Charlie and get him to read along with me. He was fascinated by the story of Jim Hawkins and the black spot, and when we reached the part with Long John Silver his eyes lit up.

One afternoon he asked me if he could take the book home with him. I said he could, but warned him that he had to look after it, as it was a special present from my aunt. Every time we had a reading lesson he would tell me how far on he was with the story.

'I'm at the part when the baddies on the boat are planning on da'en awa' wi' the crew and Long John Silver and his parrot Captain Flint are egging them on.' He gazed at me with shining eyes. 'Are you named efter the parrot, Miss Flint?'

I assured him I wasn't, but I said I was pleased that my name was in such a great story.

'I would love tae be a pirate, Miss Flint.'

'Oh, Charlie,' I thought, 'we're kindred spirits,' but I said that he would be better learning all his lessons first, especially his reading, which was coming on well.

On Saturday afternoon I usually met up with Laura and Pat, and we would exchange gossip about our classes and pupils.

Laura sighed. 'I never thought it would be so tiring teaching children.' When she saw the look on my face, she replied, 'Oh, don't get me wrong, I love it, but I've got a few unruly boys in my class and they're hard going.'

Pat said she was coping all right, but she did say the training hadn't catered for the actual job of teaching kids, some of whom didn't want to learn. 'What about you, Lizzie, how are you getting on?'

I said I was lucky to have Miss Hendry for a few weeks to begin with and on the whole the children were well behaved.

As we sat in the small café with our tea and scones, the talk then turned to other topics. Laura had been a bit downhearted a couple of months previous when Mike, the boy from the grocer's shop in the Hawkhill, had left to go back to university in Glasgow.

I hesitated to ask her if she had heard from him, but as I was dithering, she said, 'I haven't had a letter from him for three weeks, although he did say he was busy with his studies.' She gave a deep sigh and placed her hand under her chin like one of the Hollywood film stars from the pictures.

Pat smiled at me and I nodded. We both knew Laura liked to pose like Mary Pickford or some other heroine of the silver screen.

The Christmas holiday was soon coming up, and I was dreading it. Mum was still tired and listless, and personally I thought it had been a bad idea to just work for three days. At least when she was at work she had to put her job before herself, but now she just sat around all day in the house with only Maisie for company. I had found out by accident that Maisie was also going to the shops for her, and this annoyed me. Maisie was much older than Mum and she had developed arthritis in her legs, which made it painful for her to climb the stairs. Still, the one consolation was that I would be around during the school holidays and I intended to make sure Mum got out and about.

Margaret's hamper arrived on Christmas Eve and once again it was filled with luxuries we couldn't afford. I was pleased that Mum had given some items to Maisie and we invited her down for her dinner the next day.

I still hadn't the heart to decorate the house, but I put the best cloth on the table and used Granny's china cups and saucers. I had bought a ready-made steak pie from the butcher and an apple tart from the baker, and Maisie said she hadn't had such a feast for ages. I was alarmed at how little Mum ate, but she said she would have the rest of the pie for supper. I knew she wouldn't eat it so late at night, and I was right. She went off to bed with her hot-water bottle and her book, and the pie had to be put into the larder, where we would have it for dinner the following day.

Laura had invited me up during the holiday, but I didn't like to leave Mum on her own. The one bit of good news was that Pat had found lodgings with an elderly woman who lived in Strathmartine Road, which meant she only had a five-minute walk to school.

On Hogmanay, Mum and I opened the box of chocolates and bottle of sherry from the hamper and we saw in the new year. Before going to bed, Mum did her usual ritual of winding up the various clocks in the house.

'I love the sound of ticking clocks,' she said as she placed the clock keys back in the sideboard drawer. 'I always think they are the heartbeat of a house.'

On that note, we greeted 1932 with the grandfather clock chiming one o'clock while her little carriage clock followed a minute or two later with its delightful musical notes. Then in the morning I heard the loud ringing from the alarm clock.

26

ANN STREET SCHOOL

I was glad when the new school term started. Up till then I hadn't realised how much I missed the children, and as I gazed at my pupils I could see quite a few new hand-knitted jerseys, scarves and gloves.

I knew most of their parents didn't have a lot of money, apart from a few who had a father who was lucky enough to have a job. I saw some of the mothers as I went through the school gates and their coats were well worn, but they still wanted their children to get something new for Christmas.

'Good morning, boys and girls,' I said.

They all chanted at once, 'Good morning, Miss Flint.'

'Now, before we do our multiplication tables, perhaps you would like to write down what you did over the holiday.'

As I sat at my desk I saw little heads bent over their jotters, and I had to smile at Charlie, who sat chewing the end of his pencil with a furrowed expression, as if trying to remember any highlights.

After half an hour, I asked if anyone wanted to tell me what he or she had done.

I wasn't surprised when Betty's hand shot up. Out of the whole class, she was by far the brightest pupil. 'I helped my mother make paper chains for our kitchen. We cut them out of old newspapers.'

'That was lovely, Betty, and did you put them away till next year?'

She shrugged her thin shoulders. 'No, Miss Flint. My wee brother tore them when we took them down, but Mum said we could always make more next year from other newspapers.'

For the next hour I listened to stories of new ribbons being bought or jumpers knitted, and most of the children had received a small stocking with a thruppeny bit and some sweets. I looked at Charlie when he raised his hand.

'I got a book from the libry. It was all aboot pirates, but I had to take it back because I only got a loan of it.'

'That's great, Charlie, but the word is "library".'

He was indignant. 'That's whit I said, Miss Flint, the libry.'

I let it pass, and we went on to recite the five times table. When they all chanted the figures, I looked out of the window at the weak sunshine and hoped it would stay dry, as Mum had said she would go to the shops to get some groceries, but I had left her asleep and as usual she didn't look well.

I was brought out of my reverie by Polly Watson, who taught the class next door. She was looking for the ink bottle to fill up her inkwell. For some reason, some of the supplies were housed in one of my cupboards.

The children were still reciting the tables, but as it was coming up for their playtime I told them to put their jotters in the desks and make their way to the cloakroom for their coats. I was busy putting some books away when I saw Charlie standing by my desk. He had my copy of *Treasure Island* in his hand. 'I've brought back yer book, Miss Flint, and I really liked reading it.'

'Thank you, Charlie, I'm glad you liked it, and I'm pleased that you've gone to the library, where you'll be able to reads lots of books.' I was also pleased that his reading skills had improved.

'Aye, my dad likes the libry because he reads loads of murder stories, but he said he would look oot for pirate books for me.'

He then ran out to join his pals in the playground, and I put my book in my bag before going to join my colleagues in the staff room for a cup of tea.

Later, when I got home, there was no sign of Mum. I thought she must have left the shopping till later, but half an hour later she appeared. She wasn't wearing a coat and she looked red-faced and flustered.

I was annoyed at her. 'I hope you didn't go out in the cold without your coat, Mum?'

Her hand shot to her mouth. 'Oh Lizzie, I forgot about getting the groceries. I went to see Maisie and I didn't realise it was so late.' She went into the lobby to get her coat, but I made her sit down by the fire, which had died away to glowing embers.

'Put some coal on the fire and I'll go to the shop.'

We normally went to the Home & Colonial shop in the Wellgate, but I went across the road to the small grocer's shop run by Queenie McGregor. I liked this tiny shop with all the goods stacked on shelves, with the butter and cheese on a marble counter and the tea and biscuits in tins by the side of the counter. She weighed every thing on a small scale with brass weights and it took that much longer to get everything we needed, as she kept adding things like sugar to the bag then shoving the scoop into it to remove some, watching until the scales went down with a satisfying thump.

Once back in the house, Mum stoked up the fire while I set about getting our tea ready. As I was setting the table, I happened to glance back and I saw Mum had been crying.

'What's wrong, Mum?' I asked. I realised my voice was harsh, but I was worried.

She dismissed my query with her hand. 'It's nothing. I got something in my eye, I think it was a small spark from the fire. That's why I was with Maisie; she looked at it and bathed my eye with tepid water.'

After tea I inspected her eye, but everything looked fine. Maisie had obviously done a good job with her tepid water.

I was surprised how quickly the days went by, and I soon got into a routine of work and looking after the house. At the end of January we got a letter from Margaret. The solicitor had sent her details of a house in Carnoustie and she asked if we could possibly go and see it.

'I can't get away at the moment,' she wrote, 'but I like the sound of this house and would appreciate it if you could go and look it over. The solicitor will go with you.'

Mum panicked at this suggestion. 'How will we know if the house is all right, Lizzie? What if the roof falls in after she's bought it? Then we'll get the blame from Gerald.'

I said Margaret had thought of that and that if the solicitor was to be there with us then we could ask him questions.

'Questions? What kind of questions?'

'I don't know. We can ask if the roof is likely to fall down, and if he says it isn't and it does then it's his fault.'

She gave a look that said 'don't be frivolous'. 'When are we supposed to go to see the house? I'll be working on Saturday and that's the only day you will be off and we can't go in the evening as it's dark by four o'clock.'

'Right then, I'll go to Carnoustie on Saturday,' I said. 'I'll phone the solicitor tomorrow and arrange it.'

This seemed to placate Mum. 'Yes, that's the best idea. You can take notes and send them to Margaret and Gerald, and it will be up to them to decide.'

Mum never mentioned it again that week, so on the Saturday morning I set off for the East Station to catch the train. The solicitor said he normally worked in the morning on Saturday, but he was happy to show me round.

It was a strange kind of day as I made my way into the town. Even although it was almost the end of January, the weather had turned mild and the sun shone from a blue sky. The newspaper had said there was a storm coming after a short period of high pressure, but that was hard to imagine on a lovely day like this.

I always enjoyed travelling by train, and as I reached the solicitor's office he was ready and waiting for me. He picked up a bunch of keys from his desk. 'The house is half a mile from the town, but we can go in my car.'

His car was small but incredibly clean, with shining bodywork, and we soon reached the outskirts of the town and travelled along the coast road.

The house stood on its own, and although it was set back from the road by a small garden enclosed within a stone wall, it still had panoramic views of the beach and the sea. On a day like this the sea was calm, but I wondered what it would be like in stormy weather. There was quite a large expanse of beach, so I didn't think the waves would reach the house, but I assumed it would be a terrifying sight when huge waves smashed against the sand.

It was a lovely stone-built building with two windows downstairs and three above, but what I liked was the wooden veranda that stretched the length of the frontage. Inside, the rooms were small but cosy-looking, with a small kitchen to the back that overlooked a large garden. The three bedrooms upstairs were next to a small bathroom with an ancient-looking water geyser.

'Should Mrs Cook buy the house, I would advise the removal of this geyser and having a new one installed. Otherwise everything is in excellent condition.'

I had brought a notebook with me and I took down all the details, even drawing sketches of both the outside and inside of the house. Every room was empty of furniture and floor coverings, but the floorboards were solid. No doubt Margaret would want to redecorate it, as the wallpaper was faded and old-fashioned, but that was just my opinion.

'Will you be sending details to my aunt?' I asked. 'I'll send her my opinion and the notes I've taken.'

'Yes, I'll get in touch with her on Monday with all the relevant information.'

We then got back in the car and he drove me to the station, where I sat on a bench until the train arrived. I dropped in at DM Brown's on my way home, but when I saw Mum was busy I went home and wrote to Margaret, including my notes and sketches, before walking down to the post office.

When Mum arrived home that evening, she looked really exhausted, but I had the tea ready. The first thing she did was put on her slippers.

'My feet are killing me and I'm sorry I bought those new shoes,' she said, sitting down in the chair with her feet on the footstool.

As usual she didn't eat much, even though I had bought a steak pie from the butcher. Again, I was worried by her lack of appetite. I knew she had never been a big eater, but she was getting worse, and I planned on having a talk with the doctor about it.

Two days later the forecasted storm arrived, and the rain and wind were ferocious. Mum said she was glad she didn't have to go to work, but I got soaked going to the school. Polly arrived at the same time as I did and Mr Drummond was already in his office. Then Jane Andrews, who was the infant teacher, came in like a drowned rat.

'What a day,' she said as she dried her hair with the cloakroom towel. 'Thank goodness I've got my mackintosh, which my parents gave me for my Christmas.'

Polly said it was a lovely waterproof coat, and I agreed.

It was in the middle of the following week before we heard from Margaret. Her letter thanked us for going to look at the house, and on the recommendation of the solicitor and surveyor she had gone ahead and bought it. She added that she was due back for good in May, with Gerald following later in the year.

Mum greeted this news with delight. 'It'll be so good to have Margaret back in this country and also to meet up with Gerald again. I haven't seen him since they were married in 1913.'

I was surprised by this. 'Hasn't he come back to this country since then?'

'No, he's travelled to loads of places with his work. That's why I'm surprised he wants to come back to the seaside to retire. I would have thought he would want to stay somewhere abroad.'

I also thought it strange, but as I had never met him I had no idea what he was like, apart from a photograph that Margaret had shown me years ago. He was tall and slim, with a small moustache and dark hair.

Margaret had also mentioned in her letter that she was going to get in touch with Justice's furniture shop in Whitehall Street to supply furniture for the new house and that the solicitor would arrange for a plumber to come and replace the ancient water heater. She asked if I could maybe arrange to be in the house to oversee to the deliveries.

I wrote back saying it would have to be on a Saturday, and Justice's said they would be in touch when they were sending out their van.

Two weeks later I was back at the house and was amazed when the carpets were laid in the rooms and linoleum laid in the kitchen and bathroom There wasn't a lot of furniture, but Margaret had obviously chosen it from a catalogue and each room had the basics. I let the delivery men place everything in each room and I knew Margaret could always place things to her own taste. The plumber had been and lovely new water heaters were installed in the bathroom and kitchen.

When I got back home, Mum wanted to hear how it had all gone, and I spent a couple of hours telling her how the house now looked.

The snow came early in February, and it was a relief to arrive inside the school every morning. The children would come in with snow-encrusted gloves, scarves and coats, and the cloakroom floor was covered in small puddles.

I was really enjoying my job and becoming more confident. To start with, I was nervous when Annie Hendry retired, but as the days passed I felt I had chosen my true vocation. I got on well with the other teachers, and the headmaster and I looked forward to me being here for a long time.

Looking back, I knew I shouldn't have become complacent. After all, I had experienced a feeling of well-being at Christmas before, but since Granny had died festive times were tinged with sadness. I should have known not to be smug.

It was at the end of February when the bombshell hit. I had

arrived home, feeling shivery with a bad cold, when Maisie asked me to come to her house. It was one of Mum's non-working days and she was dozing in the chair.

I had a cold feeling in my stomach and I just knew something was up. When we were inside Maisie's house, she began to cry.

'What's the matter, Maisie?' I asked, wondering what had happened to our neighbour to upset her.

She wiped her eyes. 'I'm sorry, Lizzie, but I have to tell you something, although your mother has sworn me to secrecy.'

I suddenly felt sick with fear but tried to keep my voice steady. 'What is it, Maisie?'

Maisie kept twisting her hands. 'I promised not to say anything, Lizzie.'

I told her to sit down. 'Don't worry about keeping anything a secret. I want to know what's wrong.'

She looked directly at me. 'A few months ago your mother came to see me, as she was worried about something.' She stopped, as if considering whether to go on, then the words came out in a rush. 'Your mother has a lump on her breast, but she won't go to the doctor. I begged her to tell you and also to get medical help, but she was adamant it would go away, but it hasn't and it's getting bigger. You must have noticed how tired she is and how she's now working three days a week. Well, today she told me she's giving up her work as she can't carry on.'

I was in a state of shock. I felt as if the ground was shifting below my feet. Everything now made sense, and I had been too stupid to see it.

'Why didn't she tell me?'

Maisie looked unhappy. 'She didn't want to worry you. She said it was something that would disappear and she would be well again.'

I left Maisie and went to see Mum. She was awake when I went in.

'Heavens, Lizzie, is it that time already?'

I went and sat beside her. 'Mum, why didn't you tell me about the lump in your breast?'

She was indignant. 'I told Maisie to keep it a secret and she should never have said anything. Anyway, the lump is getting smaller and I'm feeling so much better.'

I made her open her blouse and I was shocked when I saw the lump and how misshapen her breast had become. If this was a lump that was getting smaller, then it must have been huge before.

'I'm going round to see the doctor, Mum, and I hope he can come to see you tonight.'

She began to cry. 'I don't want to see the doctor, Lizzie.'

I took her hand. 'You must get treatment. It won't disappear by itself.'

Dr Bennett's wife answered the door when I called at his house, and when I explained everything to her she said he would come round as soon as possible.

We didn't make any tea that night in case he arrived, and at five thirty he appeared with his large black bag. Mum began to say there was nothing wrong with her, but he said he would have a look and make a diagnosis for himself.

Mum went through to the bedroom and I sat on the edge of my chair. Poor Maisie stayed in her own flat, and I reckoned she was too frightened to come in. It had cost her a lot to break her promise, but I was grateful she had.

The doctor came into the living room, but Mum stayed behind. His face was grave, and I knew it was bad news.

'Mrs Flint should have come to see me when she first noticed the lump. I'm afraid it has either developed into something very serious or, on the other hand, it could be a benign lump. I have mentioned a visit to the infirmary to examine her to see which it is, but she's adamant she doesn't want that.' He stopped and opened his bag. 'I'll leave this sleeping draught so she can get a good night's sleep tonight. I'll be back tomorrow to make another examination.'

After he left, I went into the bedroom. Mum was lying wide awake. 'I told you, didn't I, Lizzie, that there was nothing to worry about. I just have to get a good sleep, that's all.'

Maisie arrived later, when Mum was sound asleep. I told her

what the doctor had said. 'He never said what treatment he'll give her, but can you ask him tomorrow when he comes back? Mum says she's fine, but she's always lived in this world of denial and she won't change now.'

I spent a sleepless night, but thankfully Mum slept soundly, as all I could hear in the darkened bedroom were soft snoring noises.

The next morning I tried hard to persuade Mum to go to the infirmary.

'Please, Mum, it's for your own good to get proper treatment, so do what the doctor suggests.'

She gave me a sleepy look and said she would.

Maisie was going to be with the doctor and I said I would see him after school, but I set off with my mind in turmoil.

I tried my best all day to concentrate on my work, but the vision of something seriously wrong with Mum wouldn't go away, and I was glad when it was time to go home.

Maisie had made some tea and Mum was trying to eat a shortbread biscuit, but the crumbs kept sticking in her throat, so she gave up and sat quietly sipping her tea. I looked at Maisie and she gave a slight nod.

I tried to be light and unconcerned. 'Well, Mum, what did the doctor say?'

'He wants me to go for an examination at the infirmary at the end of the week. I tried to tell him I was fine, but he said, wasn't it better to know what is wrong with me to stop us all worrying about something that might be trivial?'

I said that was the best thing to do and I knew I would have to go with her. 'I'll ask Mr Drummond if I can stay off so I can go with you.'

I spent another sleepless night, but the next morning the headmaster was very understanding. 'Of course you must go with your mother,' he said.

On the Thursday morning we set off for the infirmary. Dr Bennett had said Mum would be admitted for a few days, so I had packed a small suitcase with her soap bag, slippers and nightgown.

As we walked along the street, she said, 'What a lot of fuss over nothing, Lizzie. I'm only doing this to please you and Maisie, as you've both been lecturing me for days.'

'We're only thinking about your health, Mum.'

I heard her muttering, 'I should never have told Maisie.'

'What did you say?'

She pulled the hood of her raincoat over her head and said, 'Nothing. I didn't say a word.'

At the infirmary, a nurse took her into the ward and the doctor met me in the corridor. He was quite a tall man and very distinguished-looking, and I knew this would impress Mum. It was one thing to be poked about by Dr Bennett but quite another thing to be a patient of this aristocratic-looking man.

'We'll do some tests, Miss Flint, and we'll let your doctor know the results.'

I said that would be fine. 'How will I know when she's coming home, doctor?'

'We'll let your doctor know and he'll be in touch with you. If she's still in over the weekend, then you can come and see her at the visiting times.'

She was still in on the Saturday and Sunday, so Maisie and I went to see her. I took a *Good Housekeeping* magazine and some chocolates, while Maisie had three oranges in a brown paper bag.

Mum was sitting up in bed when we arrived and I thought she looked really annoyed.

'I'll be glad when I get out of here.'

I asked her what the doctor had said, but she said she hadn't been told. 'But I'm getting home on Monday, so didn't I tell you there was nothing wrong with me?'

I felt so relieved at this. Obviously the lump in her breast was maybe a blocked gland or something equally innocuous. 'Oh, I'm so glad, Mum, and isn't it better to know that everything is fine?'

She nodded. 'I suppose so, even though I was right.'

Maisie went to the infirmary on the Monday and took her home. I felt so guilty I couldn't do it, but I didn't want to ask for another day off from the school.

When I arrived home that afternoon, Maisie met me on the stair.

'I saw you coming down the road, Lizzie, and the ward sister told me at the infirmary that you have to go and see Dr Bennett tonight. I didn't want to tell you in front of Beth.'

'Thank you, Maisie. I think I'll go right now. He'll have the hospital report and hopefully I'll have some good news for Mum when I get back.'

I hurried along the street to the doctor's house and waited in his small surgery in the garden. He came in with a folder and I didn't like his expression. Cold fingers of fear settled in my stomach, but I didn't try to avoid his gaze. Whatever the truth was, I knew I had to face it.

He fiddled about with his glasses and finally opened the folder. 'I'm afraid I have very bad news about Mrs Flint.' He didn't look at me but kept turning the few pages in front of him. He then settled a worried gaze on me. 'The test has come back and your mother has a malignant tumour which I regret to say is too far advanced for surgery. I'm so very sorry.'

I sat in a daze, like I was in some kind of nightmare. I was almost too afraid to ask him anything. 'What . . . what happens now?'

'It's just rest and care now, and it's difficult to say how long she will live. She hasn't any pain at the moment, but when she does I can deal with that. I'll come round every few days to check on her. Do you want me to tell her or will you?'

'No, no,' I whispered. 'I'll do it, but not at the moment. I don't want her to know how ill she is.'

The doctor nodded. 'Yes, that's often the best thing to do. However, it depends on the patient. Some people want the truth, but others don't.'

'I don't think my mum could cope with the truth, at least not yet.'

It was raining when I walked home and I was glad, because it covered up my tears. I had to stand for a few moments at the front door of our house to compose myself, and when I entered,

Mum was asleep. Maisie looked at me and I shook my head. As she left to go back to her own flat, she patted me on the shoulder.

'I'll see you tomorrow, Lizzie.'

That night I wrote a letter to Margaret and gave her all the ghastly news but said Mum didn't know anything so not to mention it when she wrote back.

The Easter holidays weren't far off, and I knew I would have to leave the school to care for Mum. I honestly didn't know what the future held, but when Mum woke up she seemed so bright and cheerful that I found it so hard not to burst into tears.

'Did the doctor get the report from the infirmary, Lizzie?'

I said he had.

'And didn't I tell you everything was fine?'

'Yes, Mum, you did, and you were right.'

For a moment, there was a look of triumph on her face.

After she went to bed I sat down and made a list of things that needing seeing to. First of all I would have to finish at the school come the Easter holiday, but until then Maisie said she would come in and sit with Mum. Then I had to go to DM Brown's and tell them that Mum would no longer be working her three days. I would have to see Laura and Pat to warn them not to let my secret out and just to carry on as usual should they come to the house.

At that point I missed Granny and Margaret so much, but as we had no other relatives I could call on it was all down to me, at least for the moment.

I can't remember much about that time, as I seemed to be in a daze, but I do remember being sad at having to tell Mr Drummond that I could no longer work in the school. I wasn't sure how I stood with not having worked for even a year, but I had no choice.

Everyone was so helpful and sympathetic. Polly, Jane and everyone in the school were a huge help as I struggled during the last few weeks to hold onto my teaching job and to face up to the reality that Mum wasn't going to live for much longer.

But like everything in life, be it anticipated joy or dread, the time arrived when the school was breaking up and it was my last day. The children had only been told that I was leaving to look after my mother, and I was in tears when they gave me a bunch of daffodils. Polly, Jane and Mr Drummond gave me a lovely brooch and they all wished me well. No one said they hoped to see me back at work soon because that would mean Mum was no longer with me, but I was grateful for all their support.

It was snowing as I walked down Cotton Road on my way home, and although I was crying I knew I could always blame the cold wind and not the heartbreak I felt at this tragic turn of events in our lives.

27

THE LAST SUMMER

It was May 1932 when Margaret arrived, and I had never been so pleased to see anyone as I was to see her reassuring figure appearing at the front door a few weeks after the Easter holiday. I had warned her that Mum didn't know how ill she was, and she came in with her usual brisk manner and beaming smile.

Mum sat up in her chair with a delighted smile. 'Margaret, come and sit beside me.' As Margaret pulled her chair up close to her, Mum said, 'You better not sit too close to me because I've got this terrible influenza, and I don't want you to catch it.'

Margaret gave me a long stare before turning her attention to her stepsister. 'It's so good to see you, Beth, and I'm home for good. Gerald won't be coming back till the end of the year, when we hope to have a long retirement by the sea.'

I said, 'I'll put the dinner on, Margaret, because you'll be hungry after your long trip.'

Margaret said she was hungry and I was pleased I had made a pot of broth with cold brisket and potatoes to follow. Mum ate very little, although Margaret tried her best to get her to clear her plate.

'I'll eat it later,' she said. It was the usual excuse, as I told Margaret later. It normally went into the bin, I said.

Margaret said her luggage was still at the station's left-luggage office and she planned to get a taxi in the morning to take it to her new house in Carnoustie. I saw her looking at the single bed in the living room.

'I brought it through so that Mum could look out of the window and also because this room is cosier than the bedroom,' I said as we sat around the fire with our cups of tea.

'I've been thinking, Beth', she said. 'Why don't you both come and live with me in Carnoustie?'

I was taken aback. 'What about Gerald? He won't want us cluttering up his house when he comes home.'

'Well, he's not coming till the end of the year. In fact, I often wonder if he wants to retire, because he loves his job so much. When he does come home, then you can go back to Victoria Road. If you want to, just look on it as a holiday by the sea.'

Later, when Mum was asleep, Margaret said, 'Beth can't go outside because of the stairs, Lizzie, and if we all go to Carnoustie then she'll get lots of fresh air and she'll love the sea views.'

So it was settled. Next morning when Margaret suggested the move, Mum said she didn't mind where she lived as long as Margaret was there. Over the next few days my aunt went to see the house and also made sure everything was in place for us.

'I've turned the dining room into a bedroom for Beth; it has great views over the garden and the sea.'

I was worried about Dr Bennett. 'He comes in to see Mum three times a week and I don't think he'll manage to make the trip to Carnoustie.'

'Go and speak to him, Lizzie. Ask if he wants to come or if he would prefer another doctor to take over Beth's medical care.'

So I went that morning and he said a local doctor would be preferable. 'Your mother's health will deteriorate, so a local man will be better to have near at hand.'

By the end of that week we were ready for the move. Margaret had seen the local doctor and he said he would take Mum on as his patient. Maisie was upset when we said we were moving, but she understood the need for it. Mum had asked for Dad's trophies to come with us, so I wrapped them in newspaper and put them in a cardboard box, and then we said goodbye to the flat.

For a brief moment, I was overtaken with a feeling of sadness as I recalled our first day here away back in 1917 and how Granny had made us so welcome.

Margaret put her arm around my shoulder. 'You're not giving it up, Lizzie. It will still be here any time you want to come back.'

I also said a tearful goodbye to Maisie, who promised to keep her eye on the house, and we slowly half-carried Mum down to the waiting taxi. Margaret told Maisie to come for a few days' holiday any time she felt like it and also said to tell her if anything needed done in the house when it was empty.

I gazed out of the window at the busy street and I had a premonition that I wouldn't be back for a long time, if ever. The sun was shining, but Mum fell asleep by the time we reached the outskirts of Dundee and it was then I realised how time was running out for her.

The taxi driver carried our luggage and boxes into the house, and by that time Mum was gazing at the sea. The garden, which had had a neglected look when I came to see it, was now full of colourful flowers and the lawn was neatly trimmed. The wooden veranda now had a new coat of paint and there were three reclining chairs with fluffy padded cushions.

Inside was also freshly decorated, and sunlight filled the living room and what was to be Mum's bedroom next door. I couldn't believe how much work had been done, but to be truthful I wasn't surprised. Margaret had the knack of tackling anything – maybe not with her own hands, but with her methodical nature and skill at acquiring workmen and furniture suppliers.

We decided on a picnic on the veranda for our midday meal, and Mum looked so comfy lying on her padded chair. Although it was a lovely day, the sea was a bit choppy and gulls wheeled over the beach, which was deserted, mainly because it was too far from the town. We were still sitting on the veranda when the doctor arrived. He was a plump man with a round, cheery face and he wore his spectacles on the bridge of his nose. He was dressed in a pair of navy trousers and a light-grey jacket, and he wore a linen hat on his head.

'Good afternoon, ladies,' he said, removing his hat to reveal a shiny bald head with a fringe of white hair. 'I'm Dr Smith and I've had a letter from Dr Bennett.'

Margaret asked him if he wanted some tea, and he sat down at the small table. 'Thank you, I would love a cup of tea.' He smiled at us and deep creases formed at the corners of his eyes. He looked around him. 'I must say, you've done wonders with the house, and I'm so glad, as it's been empty for some time.'

He chatted on about the joys of living in Carnoustie – 'It's great for the sea air and the golf, if you like the game' – but I noticed he kept looking at Mum, especially when she drifted off halfway through his chatter.

After he left, we made our way into the house. Margaret had arranged two single beds downstairs, and I was pleased because I wanted to be near Mum through the night. Another bonus to the room was a shelved alcove, on which I placed Dad's trophies, where she could see them from her bed.

As the days lengthened and became warmer, Mum's face took on a rosy glow and she appeared to be in better health, so much so that I began to harbour hopes that she was getting better. Margaret had found an advertisement in the paper for a wheelchair, and when she went to collect it we all laughed. It had a wicker-like seat with wheels, so with Mum tucked up in it and me pushing we all had some marvellous trips into the town.

Margaret had arranged for the grocery order every week, which was delivered in a small van with a cheery young man bringing the boxes to the door. He always spent some time chatting to us and this cheered Mum up. Then the fish van called once a week as well and the milkman every morning, so we weren't cut off from people.

And during trips into town with the wheelchair, we were able to look into all the small shop windows and to buy fresh bread and cakes from the baker, as well as going into their small café and having a morning coffee. This meant we got to know quite a few people, and their conversations with us made us feel part of this small community.

Dr Smith would also pop in every week and stay for a cup of tea and a blether with Mum and Margaret while I would go and do some work in the garden, which I found to be therapeutic. I especially loved the roses and I would cut a few and bring them into the house, where their scent filled the air. I always placed a small vase by the side of Mum's bed, which she loved.

Sometimes Laura and Pat would pay a visit on a Sunday, and Margaret would tell them tales from her teaching days, which often left us all howling with laughter. But later when they left and I walked with them to the station, they would express their sympathy for Mum. As we hugged one another before the train came in, Laura would say, 'I think your Mum looks a lot better, Lizzie,' while Pat would agree and add, 'Maybe she's getting well again, with all this lovely sea air. Mind and tell her my parents are asking after her.'

Laura said that Wullie and Irene were also thinking of us, and for a brief moment as the train pulled up to the platform I wished everything was back as it was before, with Irene at the piano and Wullie arriving home with sawdust and woodchips in his hair. But of course it wasn't, and I smiled as I waved them away.

At the end of June, Milly arrived with wee Bertie and I saw the shock on her face when she saw Mum, a look that quickly passed before she smiled brightly.

'Beth, it's great to see you, and I've brought Bertie to say hello.'

Bertie was just under a year old, but he was on his feet, walking slowly over the floor on his two plump, pink legs with a helping hand from his mother.

We all made a fuss of him, but after a wee while he became bored and began to cry. Milly was telling Mum and Margaret about her life in Glasgow and how happy she was, but she picked her son up and tried to stop his wailing. Margaret had brought through the tea tray so I said I would take him down to the beach.

He didn't want to leave his mother and was clinging to her skirt, but when I picked him up and said we were going to look at the water, his little face beamed and he twisted his head towards the door.

Milly was concerned. 'You'll be careful with the water, Lizzie?'

I said I would just let him play on the beach. A few days earlier I had found a small tin bucket and spade in the shed, so we crossed the road and sat on the sand. Bertie was delighted with the spade and after I showed him how to fill up his small bucket, he began to do the same, with the sand going everywhere.

After a while at this ploy, I picked him up and walked down to the sea. He was fascinated by the water and tried to prise himself loose from my arms. 'No, Bertie,' I said. 'The water is too cold.'

Just then, a ship passed on its way to the North Sea and he pointed a chubby finger at it.

'Do you see the boat, Bertie? It's sailing away to a far-off land.'

He turned to look at me, then gazed once more at the ship. He wasn't the only one watching it, as I gazed at it as well, wondering where it was heading for.

I recalled watching the ships in the harbour at Dundee when I was a child, wishing I could stow away on one towards a life of adventure and new countries. Granny always said to be careful what you wished for, in case it ever came true.

'Right then, young man, let's get you back to your mother in case she's worried about you.'

He carried the bucket and spade and I felt them dig into my ribs, but we didn't have far to walk.

As I approached the house I decided to let him play in the garden for a while, which meant I came back into the house through the back door. I stopped when I heard Mum's voice.

'I've been so stupid, Milly. I should have done what you've done and let go of my memories of Peter and made a life for Lizzie and me. It's just that I always thought that one day he would walk through the door, even though I was told that he had died.'

Milly sounded sad. 'No, Beth, there's nothing wrong in always having hope. You had a wonderful marriage and it must have been hard for you to think Peter wouldn't come back.'

'That's the worst thing about war,' said Mum. 'It doesn't only affect the soldiers on the battlefields but all their loved ones waiting at home. If I had my way, there wouldn't be any more wars, but that will never happen.'

'I know,' said Milly. 'It killed my mother. She never got over the death of my brother or my fiancé, and there are hundreds of mothers and sweethearts all over the country who feel their lives are over.'

I hated eavesdropping, so I coughed before going through the door, while Bertie banged his bucket and spade together. When she saw her son, Milly stood up.

'I'm sorry,' I said, 'but he's got sand in his hair, Milly.'

'That's all right, we'll soon comb that out.'

Bertie stretched out his arms and his mother carried him back to her seat.

Then it was time for them to leave. 'I'll be back soon to see you, Beth,' Milly promised. 'So just concentrate on getting well.'

Mum said she would, and once again I walked with them to the train.

'What is wrong with your mother, Lizzie? I didn't like to ask her.'

I decided to tell her the truth. 'She has only a few months left, Milly. In fact, the doctor is amazed she has lived as long as she has, but it's all down to Margaret and all the care she gets here.' I was quite dry-eyed when I said this, but I had to choke back a sob.

Milly was sympathetic. 'Poor Beth. She is my best friend, yet there's nothing I can do to help her.' She began to cry, making Bertie whimper, and she held him closer. 'It's all right, Bertie. Mummy has got some sand in her eyes.'

'I didn't tell her what the doctor said, Milly, and I feel so guilty about that, but I just wanted her last few months to be happy, and thankfully I think Margaret and I have managed that.'

They gave me a wave from the carriage window, with Bertie smiling and raising his chubby little arm. Once again the tears weren't far away as I walked back home.

Years later I was to remember that summer as a magical time.

We sat on the veranda with the sun warm on our faces, smelling the salty tang of the sea, and our lives seemed to be in slow motion. The days were lazy and we didn't have any timetable for things. We ate when we were hungry, and the only ritual was just before our evening meal, when Margaret liked to sit and look at the view with her glass of gin and tonic with lime juice.

'No matter where we lived,' she said, 'Gerald and I would have our drink before our evening meal.' She turned to Mum, who was propped up on her reclining chair. 'Would like to try one, Beth?'

To start with Mum said no, but as that summer wore on she began to have a weak gin and tonic and said she felt better after it.

'It's called "mother's ruin", Beth, but as I've never been a mother I can't say if it's true. What do you think?'

Mum smiled and said a little of what you fancy couldn't possibly ruin anyone, and we all laughed.

It was late August when Maisie visited us for the last time. She would sometimes arrive out of the blue and stay for a couple of hours, but on this final visit (although we didn't know it would be then) she stayed for a meal. As she was leaving, she suddenly turned back and embraced Mum. 'Goodbye, Beth,' she said simply as she walked away from the house.

After Maisie's departure, we stayed on the veranda. The day had been sunny and warm, but now dark clouds had gathered over the sea. Now and then a shaft of sunlight would break through the clouds, and I said, 'Do you remember telling me that these shafts of sunlight were the angels peeping through the sky with their torches?'

Mum laughed. 'Imagine you remembering that. You were just a tiny child when I said that, but yes, I still think it's angels with torches.'

Margaret came and sat beside us. 'Yes, I always thought the same thing.'

That night Mum awoke in pain and cried out. Margaret called the doctor early that morning and he gave Mum an injection.

'This will take away the pain,' he said to me. 'I'll call in every day to see Mrs Flint.'

I overheard him talking to Margaret as he walked down the path. 'I'm afraid this is almost the end, Mrs Cook, but she won't be in pain, as I've given her some morphine.'

I was devastated. I knew there wasn't going to be a happy ending, but now that Mum's life was ebbing away I didn't know how I would cope without her. I stayed up every night with her, dozing on the chair by the side of her bed. Her small carriage clock would chime the hours throughout the night, and in the morning the sun would shine on her bed and her face, but she slept soundly.

Margaret would tiptoe into the room with a breakfast tray, and we both sat with cups of tea until she woke up. She was always groggy and didn't want anything to eat. I tried giving her sips of water, but most of it would dribble down her chin. Then one morning she awoke and we were amazed when she sat up and gave us a clear-eyed look, although her voice was feeble.

Margaret took her hand. 'How are you feeling today, Beth?'

Ignoring the question, Mum grasped Margaret's hand.

'Margaret, I want a private funeral with just Lizzie and you there.'

I almost fell off my chair. Margaret said to her not to talk nonsense, but she lifted her head slightly. 'It's not nonsense, Margaret. I've known for ages that I'll never get better. Now promise me about the funeral.'

We both said we would abide by her wishes, and she slumped down on her pillow and fell asleep. The doctor arrived later and gave her another injection.

I didn't want her to hear me crying, so I ran out into the garden and sat on the bench beside the roses. Margaret came out and we both sat quietly, then I said, 'I never thought she knew how ill she was, but she's known for ages.'

Margaret nodded. 'Beth was always a smart woman. She was trying to protect you, Lizzie, and you were doing the same for her.'

That night I sat beside Mum and was alarmed when her breathing became ragged and she started to cough. I went to give her a sip of water, when she suddenly sat up with a wondrous look on her face.

'Peter, I knew you would come back.'

Taken aback, I turned my head quickly to the door, but there was no one there. Moonlight filtered in through the window, casting shadows over the floor, but there was no one else in the room except us.

I went to get Margaret, and she hurried in and sat by the bed. 'Beth, it's Margaret and Lizzie here.'

Mum opened her eyes and she looked so happy.

'I've met Peter again.'

There was a strange noise from her throat. Margaret leaned over the bed and placed her fingers on Mum's neck. I suddenly thought she looked old and tired as she said, 'I'm afraid Beth's dead, Lizzie.'

I didn't believe it. 'She spoke just a minute ago and she seemed so happy; she can't be dead.'

I remember Margaret helping me out and making me go to bed, and for the next few days everything passed in a tearful blur. I knew this day had to come, but I'd still harboured hope that somehow Mum would get better. But she hadn't.

As usual, Margaret was her efficient self and she made all the arrangements. Although we had promised Mum a private funeral, Margaret thought Maisie and Milly should come if they could.

Quite honestly I was incapable of thinking, so I said yes, they should come.

It was decided that a small service would be held in the EJ Watson's funeral parlour in Ann Street and the funeral director arranged for a minister to conduct it. Maisie and Milly were already seated when we entered, and although we were a small party the service was short but very moving. We then went off to the Eastern Cemetery in Arbroath Road, where Mum was to be buried beside her mother and father. Before we left the house I had gathered a huge bunch of roses from the garden, which we placed on the grave. They were white and yellow roses, and I laid them beside the granite headstone that was inscribed 'To Eliza, dear wife of William Ferrier, died 1891, and later to the said William Ferrier who died 1912.'

We stood gazing at Mum's last resting place. For ages afterwards, the scent of roses reminded me of that sad day.

We thanked the minister, who declined our invitation to come back for refreshments, as he had another funeral to conduct, so the four of us went back to Victoria Road for a cup of tea, which Maisie had arranged. I was so grateful to her for her thoughtfulness.

Later, Laura and Pat arrived, and the three of us burst into tears. Mum would have been forty-two on her birthday, and later it struck me that I was now an orphan at the tender age of twenty-one.

Margaret said she would arrange for the stonemason to inscribe Mum's name on the headstone at a later date, and as the sun was setting we set off for Carnoustie with sad hearts.

28

FAMILY SECRETS

I was dreading going into the house after the funeral, but Margaret said although Mum was no longer there, all our memories of her were, and of course as usual she was right. Mum loved lily of the valley perfume, and before going to bed that night I sprayed some over my bedclothes and it was as if she was with me in the room Also her little carriage clock chimed the hours and I heard every hour until five o'clock, when I finally fell asleep.

Margaret took over the cooking the next day, and I felt guilty for being so lethargic, but she said it was a recognised part of coping with grief, so that made me feel slightly better. Later that night after our evening meal, Margaret went into one of her travel cases and brought out a thick photo album. It was not unlike the one Granny had had, which I now kept in my dressing-table drawer, but it was much bigger.

We both sat on the sofa while Margaret turned the pages. The first ten pages were filled with people I didn't know: people in Edwardian clothes, the ladies with enormous hats that made me think of Mum's job in DM Brown's 'Hat Shop'.

There was one photo of a lovely young woman with an innocent-looking face that had an ethereal quality about it. Underneath it simply said 'Eliza'. Margaret said this was my grandmother, who had died when Mum was one year old, leaving my grandfather, who was in his late forties, with a baby to look after.

'Your grandfather was a teacher at the high school, but he managed to employ a woman to look after Beth. After a year, your mum was two, she had to leave. My father was also a teacher at the high school, but he died of pneumonia when I was thirteen. Your grandfather offered my mother the job as a housekeeper and she accepted. I was fourteen when we went to live with Beth and her father. Later on they got married and I was so pleased to be part of the family.'

Margaret stopped and placed a finger on the photo of a tiny child smiling at the camera. 'This is Beth, and I loved her immediately. I would take her out in her pram to the park, and I adored her even although I was twelve years older than her. She loved me as well and would cling to my skirts all the time.'

Then I saw what looked like the wedding photo of Mum and Dad, with Margaret as the bridesmaid. I didn't recognise the best man. I said I had never seen it before, which I thought was strange, and Margaret nodded.

'Beth never liked this photo, that's why you've never seen it.'

I couldn't understand this. 'Why didn't she like it? I know she looks a bit plump in it, but surely she wasn't that vain.'

'No, it wasn't vanity, Lizzie. Beth met your dad when she was eighteen. He was in his early twenties and had recently started work in his late father's office, which, incidentally, he hated because he wanted to join the navy. When Beth told her father she was getting married, he objected to it, but they got married when she was twenty. Your grandfather, William Ferrier, was convinced she was expecting a baby, so when she got married he told Peter's mother, Mary. They were both very angry, but Beth told them it was all nonsense. Then you were born eight months after the wedding and the anger erupted again. Mary said she couldn't mention the birth to her church friends and your grandfather said the same about his school colleagues.'

I was angry when I heard this. 'What a lot of fuss over nothing, Margaret.'

Margaret said no, it wasn't over nothing. 'You've got to imagine what life was like then. It was a huge stigma, but Beth said she and Peter were in love and that's all that mattered. Of course I was on their side, but I was already teaching at a school in Edinburgh, so I wasn't around very much.

'Then a year later your grandfather died and my mother joined me in Edinburgh. Sadly, she died before my marriage to Gerald. Mary started to come round to the house when you were a bit older, but I don't think Beth ever really forgave her or her father. With your grandfather dead, Peter and Beth stayed in the family house in Garland Place, and they were so happy until the war started.'

'The house in Garland Place where we stayed was my grandfather's house? I didn't know that.'

'There was a lot of things your Mum hid away, one of them being this wedding photo.'

'Well, it's not going to be hidden away any longer: I'm going to buy a picture frame for it and put it beside my bed. After all, Dad was taken away from us when I was six, so I want to have this to remind me of you all.'

Margaret stood up and went over to the sideboard. 'I never usually have more then one gin and tonic, but I'll make an exception tonight. It's looking back on all these memories that's so sad.'

I looked at the photo again. It was obviously taken in a studio because they all looked so formal, standing beside a potted palm with a misty background of hills. 'Who is the best man?'

Margaret put on her spectacles again. 'I can't remember his name, but he was one of Peter's tennis-club friends. What I do recall, however, is the slight feeling of envy I felt when Beth married such a lovely, handsome man. But I was pleased for them, as they were so much in love.'

'Were you married to Gerald when the photo was taken?'

'No, I met Gerald a year later at a dinner party in Edinburgh. At the time I was headmistress of a private school for girls. We liked one another right away. He had just returned from Belgrade, where he was with the British Diplomatic Service, and he told me his next posting was to Rio de Janeiro. A few weeks later I mentioned to him how much I had wanted to visit Rio, and soon after he proposed to me. I accepted and we both sailed off for South America.' She turned the page of the album. 'This is Gerald.'

He was standing in front of a building, looking so upright and distinguished, with dark, swept-back hair and with a serious expression on his face, which no doubt was the usual expression of a diplomat.

Margaret showed me more pictures taken in Rio and he looked the same in every one. I didn't want to comment on this, but she laughed. 'Gerald's face never changes, no matter what the circumstances are. I used to tell him that even if he was in a custard-pie fight with Charlie Chaplin he would just look like he was sucking a lemon.'

She had such a fond look on her face when she said this that I said, 'You'll be glad when he comes here to stay.'

'Yes, I will, but I sometimes think he'll never want to settle down with his slippers and pipe. He was born in India, where his father worked for the British government. He was sent back to Scotland for his schooling and he spent his holidays with his maternal granny in North Berwick. However, he loves living abroad and I can't see him being happy settling down here, although he said that's what he wanted.' She closed the album. 'That's enough memories for tonight, I think.'

She looked so sad that I suddenly felt sorry for her.

The next day I went into the town and bought two picture frames from the small gift shop on the high street. I put the wedding photo in the larger one and the photo of Dad with his swimming trophy in the other. As I placed them next to my bed, I felt so happy looking at them, and I had a warm feeling that maybe I was in the wedding photo as well – that is if the rumour was true about Mum's pregnancy

It was in September when the stonemason added Mum's name to the gravestone. It said 'Beth Flint, daughter of the above Eliza and William, born 1890 died 1932'.

As we walked away after leaving more roses on the grave, I said to Margaret, 'I hope she is with my dad now.' I had mentioned Mum's cry at the end of her life, and Margaret had said that a lot of people believed in an afterlife and that she had witnessed scenes like this in Rio and Lisbon.

I hoped there was an afterlife and that Mum and Dad were now reunited, but even if there wasn't one, at least she was at peace.

Margaret gave a backward glance at the stone. 'What we should have had inscribed is "A Victim of the Great War" because it's not just the men on the battlefield who die but also their loved ones. I know I've said it before, but there is never a truer word. It's a different kind of death from being blown up with a mortar shell, but dying of a broken heart is every bit as fatal . . .'

29

ELSIE LOMAX

October started with an autumnal storm. The rain battered against the windows and the sea was rough, with huge waves pounding on the beach. I was so restless in the weeks following Mum's death, but I knew I had to go back to work or I would go mad.

Margaret had made quite a lot of friends in the town and she was often out visiting them or having a coffee with them in the small café on the high street. She did ask me to come with her, but to be honest I didn't feel like company or indulging in the local gossip. As we were having breakfast one morning, I said, 'I'll have to go back to Dundee and try to get another teaching job, Margaret.'

She poured out another cup of tea and nodded. 'Yes, I think it's time for you to get back into the routine again, Lizzie.'

'I'll stay at Victoria Road and hopefully there will be a job in some school. Laura is still at Tay Street and Pat at Hill Street. It would be great if there was an opening at either of them for me.'

Margaret looked thoughtful as she took a letter from her pocket. 'I got this letter the other day from two of my ex-colleagues from Edinburgh. Marie Macbeth and Sandy McFarlane now run a school in Hong Kong and they have a teacher called Jean who's planning on coming back to Scotland at the Christmas term.' She looked at me over the top of her spectacles. 'Would you be interested in going there? It's mostly British pupils in the school, but there are also some Chinese students.'

I almost choked on my toast, and after I had stopped coughing, I said, 'Hong Kong?'

Margaret nodded. 'Well, you always said you wanted to be a pirate or an explorer, and although at Marie's school you'd be neither, at least you'll be in a different country. Just like your travel books from the library.'

Hong Kong! After getting over the shock, I was beginning to like the idea.

'I haven't been teaching for very long, though, and maybe they want someone with more experience.'

Margaret was pragmatic. 'No, I don't think they do. You'll probably get experience as you go along, and Marie will help you, as will Sandy.'

'I'll think about it, Margaret.'

Margaret went back to reading her newspaper and said, 'That's fine, Lizzie.'

That night in bed my mind was in a turmoil over my future, and the more I thought about Hong Kong the more I liked the idea. Next morning I said I was interested in going abroad, and Margaret said she would write a letter and get it posted that morning.

We were well and truly into autumn now, and the garden, which had been such a joy during the summer, was looking windblown, with just a few hardy flowers still blooming. I was full of nervous tension, wondering if the job was still vacant. What if Marie Macbeth advertised locally for a new teacher? Margaret had told me Britain had leased the island from China and it had a cosmopolitan population, so no doubt there must be teachers living there.

I had almost given up hope about hearing when the postman delivered the letters one dark and rainy November morning and I saw the airmail letter with the foreign stamp. I took them through to Margaret and she held up the letter.

'*Voilà*,' she said. 'Greetings from Hong Kong.'

I held my breath as she slit the top of the envelope with her silver-handled letter opener.

'I'll not keep you in suspense, Lizzie. Marie says you'll make an excellent teacher and you can travel out when it suits you.'

Now that I knew I had the job, I was suddenly filled with nervousness. Margaret noticed this. 'You'll be fine, Lizzie, so stop worrying.'

'I'm not worried,' I said. Then, looking down at my hands, I noticed I had twisted the corner of the tablecloth so tightly that it now lay curled up in an untidy ball.

Margaret laughed. 'Oh yes, I can see you're not worried, but the poor tablecloth has other ideas.'

It was then arranged that I should travel to Hong Kong as quickly as possible, but first I had to get a passport and have inoculations against foul-sounding diseases. I seemed to spend the following weeks in a blur of activity, but then everything was arranged. I had my passport and passage on a ship from the P&O shipping line, plus all my medical checks.

A few days before leaving I met up with Laura and Pat, and we went out for our tea to Franchi's tearoom in the Overgate.

Laura sounded unsure about my new job. 'I hope you're not going into the white slave trade, Lizzie.'

I laughed. 'Don't be daft, Laura. The teachers at the school are Margaret's ex-colleagues, and anyway, I think I can look after myself.'

Pat remained silent, but as we were leaving, she said, 'Laura's right to be worried, Lizzie. After all, you're heading for the Orient, and none of us know anything about the Far East except what we've read in the geography books.'

I said I would be fine and that if anything was not as it should be then I would come straight home.

We said goodbye at the train station, promising to write often to each other, but as the train drew away from the platform I suddenly felt a pang of wanting to cling on to the tried and trusted. Margaret was waiting up for me with hot cocoa, and as I went off to bed the nervousness returned. I didn't want to leave Margaret or Scotland behind, but I was committed and there was no way back.

I broached the subject of not leaving the next morning. 'Margaret, I really don't want to leave you here by yourself. I can easily cancel all the arrangements.'

She was adamant that I should leave. 'Gerald will be coming back soon, so I won't be on my own. Just go, and if you don't like it then you can always come back here.'

When I made up my mind to go abroad, I had suggested to Margaret that I should give up the house in Victoria Road. 'Do you think that's a good idea?' I asked.

She gave this some thought. 'Yes, I think you should. After all, when Gerald and I aren't here any longer this house will be yours.'

'Oh Margaret, don't speak like that, not when I'm going a thousand miles away from you.'

'Well, these things happen, Lizzie. I just want you to know you will be well provided for.'

I almost burst into tears when she said that.

It didn't take too long to give the house up. It was rented so I didn't need to put it up for sale, and Margaret took most of the furniture to Carnoustie, which pleased me, as I didn't like the idea of Granny's things going to strangers. I asked Maisie to come and take what she wanted. She said she'd always loved Granny's Lloyd Loom wicker chair and ottoman, and along with household items we carried them into her flat.

Maisie cried when I said goodbye. 'I remember you coming to stay here all those years ago when you were a wee lassie. I felt so sorry for your poor mother, God rest her soul.'

'I'll write to you, Maisie, and give you all my news, and maybe I'll not be away too long.'

After she left I gazed around the empty room, remembering how sad Mum and I had been on coming to stay here. I knew Granny had been good to us, and even if Mum had never really forgiven her, I do know she had done her best for us, and in her own way had spent her life making up for the cruel things said about my birth.

The noise from the street filtered up into the room, and for a moment I was filled with such sadness at the memories. I then turned and walked out, locking the door and leaving my childhood behind.

My last two visits were to the Balgay and Eastern cemeteries. I carried two bunches of chrysanthemums to lay on both graves, and I stood in the cold November chill and said my goodbyes to the two most important people in my life.

Margaret was waiting at home when I arrived back, but she didn't need to ask me where I had been. She saw it in my face. She had given me one of her large travelling cases and all my clothes were already packed. I had placed my passport and essential documents in my money belt, the one I had bought to go on the cycling holiday, which seemed so long ago now.

When Mum died, I had wanted her to be buried with the gold bangle that Margaret had given her, but my aunt had persuaded me to keep it. 'If you ever go abroad, gold is the same as having money, Lizzie. Keep it safe, along with your own bangle, and I'll feel happier knowing you have something to fall back on should you need it.'

So both bangles were also now in my money belt. I couldn't believe how quickly the time had gone, and it was now my day of departure. Margaret had booked me on the sleeper train to London and I would take a taxi to the dock, where I would board the ship.

It was a typically drizzly November evening when I left the house. Margaret came with me as far as Dundee. She had originally wanted to come to London with me, but she had developed a bad cold a few days earlier, so I told her it wouldn't be wise to travel and she reluctantly agreed.

We had to get from the East Station to the Tay Bridge Station to catch the sleeper, but Margaret had organised a taxi to be waiting for us, so it only took a few minutes to travel the length of

Dock Street. For a brief moment as we stood on the platform, I suddenly got cold feet and decided I wanted to stay.

Margaret said not to be foolish. 'You must go and live your own life, Lizzie. If you're unhappy in Hong Kong, then do come home, but if you stay here you will regret it all your life.'

I held onto her as the train drew in and didn't want to let go. She pulled my arms away from her and she gently pushed me onto the train. 'Now mind and write to me often, as I want to hear how you are. Will you promise me?'

The guard blew his whistle as I called out, 'I'll write every week, Margaret. Thank you for everything.'

The steward took my case to my sleeping quarters, where I sat down and cried. 'What have I let myself in for?' I said quietly through my tears. Once in bed, however, the rocking of the train soon sent me to sleep, and the next thing I remembered was the steward bringing me my morning cup of tea.

'We're just coming into London, Miss.'

For a minute I couldn't think where I was; then the full realisation struck me as I stumbled out of the berth and had a quick wash just as we pulled into the station. A porter took my case to the waiting taxi, and I looked out onto the foggy London streets as we sped across the city towards the docks.

When we reached my destination, the ship was waiting for the passengers to embark. It was called SS *China Rose* and the long-ago memories of walking around the harbour at Dundee with Mum came flooding back. I had chirpily exclaimed then how I wished I could be a pirate and I remembered Granny telling me to be careful what you wished for because it might come true. Now here I was being confronted with my childhood wish and I suddenly felt terrified.

The dock was busy with people and luggage, and there was a cacophony of noise as sailors, men, women and a few children walked up the gangplank, busy turning to look at friends or relatives who stood on the dock, some of whom were smiling and waving, but a few were crying as they said goodbye to their loved ones.

Ahead of me was a large woman dressed in a thick woollen coat with a huge fur collar and carrying an enormous leather handbag. She was urging a young blonde-haired woman to get a move on. 'Hurry up, Elsie. I'm freezing, standing here while you dither about.'

Elsie turned an apologetic face to the woman. 'I'm sorry, Mother, but I feel a bit queasy.'

The older woman snorted. 'Don't be stupid. We haven't sailed yet.'

With this comment, Elsie sprinted up the gangplank and stood by the ship's rail, gazing down at the sea of faces that surged forwards in order to get a better last look. She had a very pale face under a grey cloche hat and she looked very unhappy, as did her mother when she joined her.

'I hope that steward doesn't bang my case on his way to our cabin,' she said as she followed the case's departure through narrowed eyes, her lips clamped together with displeasure.

By now I was beginning to get excited at the thought of this long sea voyage, and when I saw my cabin I was enthralled. It wasn't a big space, but it was all I needed, with a neat bunk bed, a desk that doubled as a dressing table, a wardrobe and a small bathroom. Margaret had said she had paid extra for my passage, for which I was grateful.

The first thing I unpacked was Mum's small carriage clock. I had asked Margaret if she wanted to keep it, but she had said no.

'I remember that clock, Lizzie, and Beth always loved it, even as a child, but now it belongs to you.'

I was pleased that Margaret had made room for Granny's furniture, especially the grandfather clock, but I had packed Granny's photo album along with my two framed photos, and I soon had the cabin looking more like my bedroom at home.

I went up to the deck and stood looking as the ship slowly slipped its anchor. To begin with, we passed wharves where there was a strong smell of fish, oil and wet wood. Hordes of men stood on the docks while high cranes lifted crates from the ships' holds. Once on dry land they would be loaded on trucks and wagons to be taken to the many warehouses that lined the river. The air was filled with the voices of the dockers as they negotiated the cargoes.

Shortly, we left all that behind as we headed into the open sea and began the journey into the unknown. I could smell the salty tang of the sea, and the river changed from brackish, oily water to white-tipped waves as the ship headed into the wind.

I had the feeling I was beginning a new stage of my life. I was still grieving for the mother and granny I loved, but Margaret had been right, as she usually was: life had to go on, and it wasn't what you did with your life but what you didn't. That was where true regret lay.

I looked around as I stood at the rails, but apart from a few hardy men who were taking a brisk walk along the deck it appeared as if most of the passengers had elected to stay in their cabins or in the lounges, where I had noticed comfy-looking chairs and tables. Perhaps the wind was too cold for them, but I relished the thought of the journey ahead and I also wanted a last look at the receding land I was leaving behind.

30

THE ADVENTURE BEGINS

Margaret had given me some tips about etiquette aboard a ship, so on the first evening I wore a silver-grey satin dress with matching sandals as I made my way to the dining room. It was almost three-quarters full when I entered, and the waiter showed me to my table, where two women and an elderly man were already seated.

I thought I would have had a single table, but most tables held four or six passengers, so it looked as if everyone was sharing. I noticed Elsie and her mother were sitting next to an elderly couple and Elsie's mother was talking loudly to them. Either they were deaf or this was her natural tone of voice.

My companions turned out to be a retired major by the name of James Watters, who was travelling to India, and two middle-aged ladies, Ada and Hannah Jones, who were disembarking at Port Said.

'We're going to join our brother David in Egypt,' Ada said.

Hannah added, 'Yes, he's working on an archaeological dig there and we're going to visit him for the winter.' She turned to her sister. 'It gets so cold in Wales, doesn't it? So we thought it would make a nice change to get away to the sun.'

Major Watters said he didn't mind a bit of cold weather. 'I believe it gets too hot in Delhi, where I'm going, but I won't be gone long, as I'm taking my brother back with me to Edinburgh because he hasn't been well. He's retired from his job as an army doctor and we hope to return back home to the family house.'

Three pairs of eyes looked at me, asking me to tell them my story, but my life seemed very mediocre compared to theirs, so I simply told them my mother had died and I was now going to teach in a school in Hong Kong.

Hannah looked at her sister. 'Doesn't that sound wonderful, Ada? Going to the Far East.'

Ada said it was and they then tried to put names to the rest of the passengers as we ate our meal, which was delicious. I went back to the lounge with them, where we had coffee while the colonel had a brandy. I looked at my watch and wondered if Margaret was having her gin and tonic, and I suddenly felt homesick. I noticed Elsie and her mother were sitting together with their coffee and the older woman was doing all the speaking, although I couldn't hear what she was saying. Elsie looked miserable and I felt sorry for her.

Later, before going to bed, I walked around the deck. The moonlight was shining on the water, looking like a long silver road, and I stayed outside until I felt cold before going into my cabin.

I was beginning to enjoy my time at sea until a couple of days later I awoke and I felt the cabin floor swaying. When I went outside, the sea was very rough, with large waves. 'This must be the Bay of Biscay,' I thought. Margaret had warned me it was always a very rough passage here.

I made my way to the dining room and was surprised to see it almost empty. I had the table to myself, and as I ordered breakfast the waiter said, 'I see you're a true sailor, Miss.'

'I'm sorry, but I don't understand,' I replied.

He waved a hand over the empty tables. 'Most of the passengers are in their cabins. Seasick they are, poor souls.'

It was the same all that day, and the next, and it wasn't until we were almost at Gibraltar that people started to appear. I was lounging on a deckchair when Elsie walked past. She looked even paler than when she had first boarded the ship.

She glanced at me as she passed, then turned back.

'Hullo, do you mind if I sit beside you?'

I said I didn't mind, so she stretched out beside me. The sun was much warmer now and she sighed.

'I'm so glad it's getting warmer and that I'm finally getting over that awful seasickness. Did you have it as well?'

'No, I was lucky, and I had the entire dining room to myself.'

She looked at me in amazement. 'You were able to *eat*?'

I said I had, and I introduced myself. 'I'm Lizzie Flint.'

She held out a slender white hand. 'Pleased to meet you, Lizzie. I'm Elsie Lomax.'

I almost said I knew her name. I noticed the wedding and engagement rings on her left hand, and she saw me looking at them. 'I'm Mrs Elsie Lomax.' She sighed. 'My mother is still under the weather, and although I feel fine now I don't think I can stomach anything to eat.'

'Where are you travelling to, Elsie?' I said, thinking they were just going on a short trip to the sun.

'I'm going to Shanghai.'

I almost fell off my deckchair. 'What? Shanghai in China?'

'Yes, I'm going to join my husband, Ronnie, who works there.' She opened her small handbag and took out a photo. It showed a tall, young, good-looking man in a striped blazer and flannels gazing insolently into the lens. 'This is Ronnie. His father owns cotton mills in Lancashire and China. He sent Ronnie out there to manage those mills. He isn't happy there and wants to come home, but I have to go and join him because his father has told him he has to stay there for some time. We met at Edinburgh University and got married six months ago. Poor Ronnie wanted to be an artist, but his father said that was a namby-pamby thing to do and that he would be better off running the mills in China.' She looked so unhappy as she put the photo away.

'I'm really sorry to hear that, Elsie. Could he not have told his father he didn't want to go?'

'Actually he did, but his father said he would stop his allowance if he didn't go, so he had no choice.'

I didn't agree with that, but I stayed silent. Elsie's husband could have defied his father and looked for a job in order to support himself and his young wife, but hadn't.

'Is your mother going to stay with you both when you get to China?'

She shuddered, as if caught in a chill wind. 'Oh lord, no. She's coming with me in order to see where I'm going to be staying and make sure the place is safe. She wrote to Ronnie's father and demanded a return fare for herself in order to scrutinise the arrangements in China, so Mr Lomax came up with the ticket.'

I tried not to smile. The thought crossed my mind: 'I bet he did.' When it came down to Mr Lomax versus Elsie's mother, it would have been no contest.

'Where are you heading for, Lizzie?'

'I'm going to teach in a school in Hong Kong and I'm really looking forward to it.'

'I wish I felt the same as you, but I'm dreading going to Shanghai. I'll be glad to see Ronnie again, but China's on the other side of the world and I'm trying hard not to think about it.' Then she suddenly said, 'Here comes my mother. She'll be wondering why I've left her alone in the cabin.'

Elsie's mother was an imposing figure as she strode towards us. 'Elsie, I was wondering where you had got to.'

For a brief moment, I had an amusing thought. Where on earth did the woman think her daughter had gone? After all, we were in the middle of the sea on a ship.

'Mother, this is Lizzie Flint. We were just sitting in the sun and having a chat. Lizzie, this is my mother, Mrs Burton.'

Mrs Burton was the kind of woman who gave one a good look-over before speaking. I must have passed muster because she inclined her head. 'Pleased to meet you, Miss Flint.' She turned to Elsie. 'I thought we might have a stroll along the deck, then I might manage a cup of coffee.'

Elsie stood up, but before she followed her mother's back, which was still clad in the thick woollen coat, she said, 'Maybe we can meet up later in the lounge and have a coffee.'

I smiled at her. 'I'll look forward to that, Elsie.'

As the two women walked off I was able to return to my book.

The next few days passed in this lazy fashion, and Elsie and I spent a lot of time together, either lazing on the deckchairs or sitting in the lounge. I was also enjoying the company of my dinner companions. Major Watters mentioned he had fought in the war.

'I try not to think about it too much,' he said one evening. 'They're calling it the Great War, but there's nothing great or glorious about it. I've enjoyed my army career, but I'm also glad I'm out of it, because I think there will be another war in the near future.'

The two ladies looked horrified, and Ada said, 'Oh, don't say that, Major. The last one was bad enough and we don't want any more young men slaughtered.'

I felt tears spring to my eyes.

Ada looked alarmed. 'Are you all right, Lizzie?'

I said I was. 'It's just that my father was killed in 1917 and his body was never found.' I almost added that it killed my mother too, but I didn't.

The major put his hand over mine and his voice was rough. 'So sorry to hear that, Lizzie, but there were hundreds of men who died like that, with no known burial site.'

Hannah and Ada looked at me with concern and I tried to lighten the situation. 'Tell me about your brother, David.'

Ada said, 'He loves pottering around the temples and ruins in Egypt and they've found some really ancient relics.'

'He met Howard Carter,' said Hannah. 'It was just after he discovered Tutankhamun's tomb. David wrote and told us about the wonderful things found with the mummy. Then there was the tragic story of Lord Carnarvon being bitten by a mosquito and dying. David said a lot of people thought it was a curse from the tomb.'

I remembered how Granny, Mum and I had been reading about this wonderful discovery and I mentioned this to them.

'We were the same, weren't we, Ada?' said Hannah.

Ada said they were, and we all agreed what a great find it was as we ate our meal.

31

SHIPMATES

We were approaching Port Said, and Elsie and I were standing on the deck with Ada and Hannah. We were all excited at the thought of being on land again. The two sisters said their brother was coming to meet them to take them to Cairo, where he had booked them into a hotel.

'It'll be so good to see him again, as it's been over ten years since we met up with him,' said Hannah. Ada was busy checking their luggage and I noticed a few people were going to disembark there as well.

Elsie leaned on the rail and surveyed the scene. We had both decided to go ashore for a few hours, but Mrs Burton had objected. 'I don't want you to get lost in a foreign land, Elsie.'

'I'll be going with Lizzie,' she said. Mrs Burton gave me a look, as if to say that wasn't a good recommendation, but Elsie stood her ground. 'You can always come with us.'

Mrs Burton gazed at her daughter with a horrified expression. 'What? Go ashore to be amongst a crowd of sailors and pedlars and goodness only knows who else?'

Then Major Watters said he would accompany us, and Mrs Burton relented. The hot sun was beating down when we stepped ashore, but we were wearing large straw hats that shielded our faces from the heat. The major helped the two ladies with their luggage, and when the brother arrived in a battered-looking car, they introduced him to us. He was in his fifties, with a thin, sunburnt face and a lovely smile. He was dressed in shorts and a short-sleeved shirt, and I noticed his arms were thin and sinewy, as if they were used to excavating his digs.

I gave Ada and Hannah a hug. 'I'm going to miss you both, as I've enjoyed hearing the stories about the excavations.'

Hannah took out her handkerchief and wiped her eyes. 'We'll also miss you, Lizzie. Now mind and take care of yourself in Hong Kong and maybe we'll meet again.'

The major and Elsie said goodbye and the car drove off in a cloud of dust. The three of us explored the streets behind the port, but we were surrounded by children begging us to buy their wares. Elsie opened her handbag, but the major said it was best to ignore them, otherwise we would be mobbed by more pedlars.

The sun beat down on our heads, and after a couple of hours we all decided to go back to the ship. Mrs Burton gave us a look of triumph as if to say, 'I did warn you, didn't I?'

It was just me and the major at the table that night, and although I liked him, he didn't have the same sociable manner of Ada and Hannah. However, I was so excited to be sailing through the Suez Canal, and after the meal Elsie and I stood and watched as the ship negotiated the locks.

The next night we were surprised to have Elsie and her mother sitting beside us. 'I couldn't stand having another conversation with that elderly couple we were sharing a table with because they are both deaf, so I asked if we could be moved here,' said Mrs Burton to the major.

Elsie gave me a shy glance while the major looked mortified. I was pleased to have Elsie as a companion, but her mother was a bit overbearing. She immediately launched into a tirade about her son-in-law and his father.

'What father sends his only son to China just a few months after he marries my daughter? I wrote and told him what I thought, that his son is a bit immature, but he says Ronnie has to learn the business of cotton weaving and that he has sent one of his trusted managers to the Shanghai mills who will look after him and Elsie.' She looked at the major as if hoping he would agree with her, but he just nodded.

Afterwards in the lounge he normally only drank one brandy, but that night he had two. He drained his glass under the gimlet eye of Mrs Burton.

As the ship sailed eastwards, I missed the company of Ada and Hannah, and I wondered if they were enjoying their sightseeing trip to the archaeological dig with their brother. I know the major wasn't pleased having Mrs Burton as a table companion, although he liked to chat with Elsie.

Mrs Burton took umbrage at this attention, and one morning I overheard her telling Elsie to watch out for the old goat, as she didn't like him trying to seduce her.

Elsie was mortified. 'He's old enough to be my father, and he's just being polite.'

Mrs Burton wasn't going to be told otherwise. 'I know Lizzie eggs him on, so maybe he thinks he can charm any young woman.'

When I heard this, I was furious at this stupid woman and, like the major, I wished they hadn't foisted themselves on us at Port Said. I turned to go and find a quiet deckchair but almost knocked Elsie over as she hurried around the corner away from her mother.

She saw me and she sat down beside me. 'I wish my mother hadn't come with me, Lizzie. She gets quite obnoxious at times and she's just had a go at Major Watters. Thankfully he wasn't there to hear her.'

I didn't mention I had overheard her. 'Never mind, Elsie. When you're reunited with your husband, you'll be much happier, especially when your mother travels back to Edinburgh.'

Elsie sat in silence for a few moments, twisting her wedding ring. 'Lizzie, can I tell you something in confidence?'

'Of course you can.'

'I'm not sure how things will work out with me and Ronnie. I haven't seen him for months. What if he's changed?'

I wasn't sure how to answer this question, as I didn't know the man, but they had obviously been in love with one another when they got married and surely nothing had changed apart from moving to another country.

I took her hand in mine. 'I'm sure everything will work out for you and Ronnie. It's just a matter of getting used to living together again and getting to know your new surroundings.'

She nodded, but she still looked worried.

That evening at dinner, the major complimented me and Elsie on our dresses. 'You both look lovely.'

Mrs Burton glared at him and in a loud voice announced that he should keep his compliments for someone his own age. 'You're a bit of a gigolo, Major, trying to seduce two innocent young girls.'

The Major looked at her in shock, especially as the people on the surrounding tables stopped eating and glanced at him. Then, to my dismay, he stood up and walked out of the room.

Mrs Burton gave Elsie a gloating glance. 'That's sorted him out,' she said as she cut up her fish, putting a large forkful in her mouth while her daughter looked embarrassed.

I later found him in the lounge with his brandy.

'I apologise for that awful woman, Major Watters. Please don't let her annoy you.'

He smiled. 'No, I won't let her do that, Lizzie.'

The next morning he was sitting at another table, with the deaf couple, and he remained there for the rest of his journey. I felt like joining him, and I would have done so if it hadn't been for Elsie. That was one of the drawbacks of a ship. There wasn't anywhere you could go to avoid someone, and I knew I would be glad when we reached Bombay, where the major was disembarking. Then it was on to Hong Kong.

Later, looking back on that long sea voyage, it still rankled that it was spoiled by Elsie's mother. What should have been a wonderful, relaxing trip was suddenly full of annoyance at having to bite my tongue and not let my feelings show when Mrs Burton launched into some tirade.

Thankfully, and I'm sure the major felt the same, we soon reached Bombay, and quite a few of the passengers were disembarking. The major was standing on the deck with his luggage when I went up to say goodbye to him.

'It's been lovely knowing you, Major Watters, and I hope you and your brother have a more pleasant journey back.' I gave him a kiss on his cheek

'It's been such a pleasure to meet you, Lizzie, and I hope you find your heart's desire in Hong Kong.'

I stood at the rail as he went down the gangplank, but at the bottom he turned and waved. I hadn't noticed that Elsie had come to stand beside me. She waved back and called out, 'Goodbye, Major Watters.'

We both turned to find that Mrs Burton was standing behind us. She looked livid, but Elsie walked past her with a small smile on her face. It was afterwards that she told me she had had enough of her mother's bossiness.

'I told her I was a married woman and I could speak to anyone I wanted without her commenting on it. I also told her to keep her opinions to herself in future.' She laughed. 'She hasn't spoken to me since, but that is a bonus. She's going around with an injured expression, as if she's looking for sympathy from anyone who'll tell her what a horrible daughter she has. Funnily enough, no one has.'

I had to laugh as well, and from then on the voyage became more congenial, as I was now sitting with a family who had embarked at Bombay and were bound for Singapore.

32

HONG KONG

Hong Kong. I couldn't believe that I was here at last after my long sea journey. The dockside was abuzz with what seemed to be hundreds of people who were pushing barrows, lifting crates and generally making a lot of noise.

I used to think the Wellgate in Dundee on a Saturday was busy with pedestrians, but I thought it was possible to multiply the scene below by a hundred or more. Elsie had come to see me off, and as I scanned the horde of humanity bustling around on the jetty I had a moment of doubt. How would I ever find the address of the school amongst this crowd? It was Elsie who spotted the man and woman standing and scanning the passengers who were leaving the ship.

'I think they look like your new employers, Lizzie.'

I glanced over and the man caught my eye. He waved and said something to the woman, who also lifted her arm in a welcoming gesture. My luggage was being uplifted by one of the seamen and I was now on the brink of stepping ashore in this strange foreign land.

Elsie began to cry. 'I'm going to miss you, and I wish you were also going to Shanghai. I don't think I'm going to cope on my own, especially if Ronnie is at work all the time.'

'You'll be fine, Elsie,' I said, giving her a hug. 'Everything will look much better when you see your husband again.'

'I probably won't see you again, Lizzie, but I hope everything goes well for you.'

I gave her hand a squeeze. 'Say goodbye to your mother.'

She laughed. 'Yes, I will.'

As I stepped onto the dock I turned and waved at her, but her face was just a white blur. Although it wasn't raining, it was very humid and so unlike the weather back home. I could feel sweat on the back of my neck and I just knew my hair would be a mass of frizzy curls.

The man and woman approached.

'Miss Flint? I'm Sandy McFarlane and this is Marie Macbeth.'

Marie was dressed in a beige-coloured raincoat. She had a very plain, weather-beaten face and her short grey hair was cut in an unfashionable style, while Sandy was slimmer and taller. He was wearing a rumpled-looking cream-coloured suit, a white shirt and a cream hat with a red band.

'We've got a taxi waiting,' he said, taking charge of my trunk. We managed to weave our way through the crowds and into the waiting car, which looked a bit bashed, but the Chinese driver flashed a wide smile at me and helped me into the back seat.

I was fascinated by all the activity on the streets. Small shops with apartments above were thronged by people, and the taxi had to weave its way through carts, bicycles and rickshaws, and pedestrians who wandered in front of the car. Some were loaded down with baskets and boxes, one of the boxes being full of squawking chickens.

Sandy saw that I was looking at the rickshaws and said, 'I wanted to pick you up in one of those, but Marie was dead set against it, weren't you, Marie?'

Marie didn't answer but merely scowled at him before turning her attention to me. 'I hope you've had a pleasant journey, Miss Flint, and I also hope you'll be happy working in the school.'

'Oh, I'm sure I shall, Miss Macbeth.'

Sandy took his hat off and used it to fan his face. 'It's damn hot today, but rain is forecast for later, so that should cool it down. Aren't you too hot in that raincoat, Marie?' he asked.

She replied that there was going to be heavy rain later and it was best to be prepared for it.

Sandy turned his attention back to me. 'Now tell me, how is your dear Aunt Margaret? It's been a few years since we last saw her.'

'She's doing well and is busy getting her new house ready for Gerald coming home from Lisbon. She sends her love to you both.'

Marie looked out of the window. 'Ah, here we are at the school.'

I followed her gaze. The school was a large building set on a busy street. The school wasn't what I expected – I thought it would have been a stand-alone building with an open space for a playground, but instead it was a large building that looked like any other on the busy street. Sandy saw my surprise.

'It's not what you were expecting?'

I smiled. 'No, it isn't. It's just so different from the school I was teaching in, in Dundee.'

Sandy said, 'It's miles away from the school Marie and I were teaching in, in Edinburgh. We had a large imposing building there, with acres of green playing fields, but space is at a premium here in Hong Kong, as you'll find out.'

Marie paid the taxi driver, who gave me another wide smile, and Sandy carried my trunk through the wooden door. Once inside I was pleasantly surprised by the interior, as it was larger than it looked from outside. We moved through the three roomy classrooms, with their desks, chairs and big blackboards, into a kitchen and bathroom before climbing a wooden stair to the rooms above.

Marie opened the door to one of them. 'This is your room, Miss Flint, and there is another bathroom along the corridor that is beside our bedrooms. The children are all day pupils and you will be teaching the two youngest classes. We have sixty pupils at the moment and most of them are British, although we do have quite a few Chinese children who speak very good English.'

I didn't say anything but was secretly relieved that the children spoke English, as I didn't understand Chinese.

She took her coat off and I was surprised to see she was dressed in a woollen jumper, thick tweed skirt, beige-coloured lisle stockings and brown lace-up shoes, which was in sharp contrast to Sandy, who had bare feet thrust into leather sandals.

'This isn't a boarding school, but we have pupils from a lot of the families who live near us.' Marie explained. 'Tomorrow is Sunday, which means there is no school, so you'll have a day to get to know your way around. I go to the church in the morning and if you would like to come with me then let me know.'

Sandy jumped in. 'I'll show Miss Flint around the place, Marie. I'm sure she would like to see the local scenes.' He gave me a huge smile and I'm sure he winked at me, but maybe it was something in his eye.

Marie gave him a baleful glance. 'Now don't be going into any shady-looking places, Sandy, and don't let Miss Flint eat any of the food prepared on the street. You never know where it's been cooked or even what it is you're eating.'

Sandy grinned. 'Scout's honour, Marie.'

'I have a policy here, Miss Flint, of trying to keep our Scottish habits alive and well. We eat sensible food. We have a good cook called Mrs Kydd who comes in every day who's the wife of a Scottish grocer who manages to get some of our provisions shipped in from Scotland.'

Later, I was able to confirm this diet, as we had in the evening a meal of mince and dumplings with tinned peas. Breakfast in the morning was porridge with powdered milk, Keiller's marmalade on toast, and tea with sugar and more powdered milk.

After Marie, dressed in her jumper, skirt, raincoat and rain hat, left for the church, Sandy said it was time for some sightseeing. 'It might be better to take a coat in case it rains, as we get heavy showers some days,' he said.

I noticed with amusement that he was still dressed in his crumpled suit and hat but had changed into a clean blue shirt.

The first thing he did was hire a rickshaw. To start with, I was a bit appalled that a little old Chinese man was pulling us along, but Sandy said he had been doing this for years and it was a good source of income to him and his family. Mollified, I sat back and enjoyed the trip. When we reached the harbour, I was amazed to see that it was packed tightly with sampans. It was difficult to see any water between these boats, and the entire area was a hive of activity. Men, women and children were busy doing their chores on board the boats.

Sandy said, 'It's quite a sight, isn't it?'

I nodded. I had never seen anything like it before.

'These families are born and live and die on board these sampans,' he said. 'A complete circle of life on the water.'

I couldn't imagine living like that, but for the people themselves it was their way of life.

Sandy rubbed his hands. 'Right then, let's go and get something to eat. I'll take you to my favourite vendor, Mr Song, who has a cart on the street.'

'But Marie said . . .'

He snorted. 'Never mind what Marie said. She likes to have her little paradise around her, a slice of Skye as recalled by her. She won't wear anything but woollens and tweeds and sensible shoes. It's as if she is still tramping the hills of the Western Isles, and as for the food . . . I only manage to exist here because of my love of Chinese cuisine.' He winked again and this time there was no doubt about it. 'So let's go and sample the delights of Hong Kong, but don't tell her. Don't get me wrong, I am fond of her and respect her as a good teacher, it's just her taste in food I dislike.'

We soon found Mr Song's cart and Sandy ordered prawns on slender bamboo sticks, which came with a thick glutinous sauce. It was delicious.

Sandy smiled. 'Didn't I tell you it beats that awful porridge and powdered milk into a cocked hat?'

I had to agree.

Sandy was a great guide, and as we toured the streets and small shops I was enjoying myself so much. Before going back to the school, he took me into a dark cave of a restaurant, where we ate dim sum and more prawns served with bowls of fragrant rice.

Back at the school, we found Marie had returned from the church. 'Did you have a good time, Miss Flint?'

'Please call me Lizzie. Yes, we had a wonderful time, thank you.'

She looked me straight in the eye. 'I hope you didn't eat anything, as you won't be able to eat your dinner.'

I hated lying to her, but Sandy was making signs behind her back, so I prevaricated.

'What are we having for our dinner?'

'Mrs Kydd has made a lovely steak pie with carrots, and for pudding there's semolina and jam.'

Sandy looked appalled, and I had to laugh. Marie gave me a suspicious look, but I said, 'That's my favourite meal.' It was a pity, as I had to eat everything on my plate and I felt quite nauseous afterwards.

The next day was my first day teaching, and I faced the rows of small children, who were all wearing white shirts and short trousers, with the girls in white blouses and grey skirts. There were ten Chinese children and I was pleased that they were also in the same uniform. Obviously Marie was a stickler for conformity, and I agreed with her.

'Good morning, boys and girls. My name is Miss Flint and I'm your new teacher.'

'Good morning, Miss Flint,' they said in unison.

'Now, I will get to know all your names as the day goes on, but if you open your reading books we will begin with that.'

For a brief moment, I had a sudden longing for Dundee and Ann Street School, and I wondered how Charlie was getting on and if he was still keeping up with his reading.

As I got to know them better, I soon found the children were so well behaved. I was glad I had made the decision to come here, as my time at the school was turning out to be a happy experience.

I wrote to Margaret every week and I sent her photos that I had taken with my new camera, which I had bought in a small photographic shop run by a Chinese family that appeared to have ten children, who all worked in the business.

Margaret replied that she was well and that Gerald was on the point of reuniting with her. I was pleased when I read this, as I still harboured a worry that I had abandoned her. I mentioned this to Sandy one evening and he laughed.

'Nobody can abandon Margaret, Lizzie. She's a self-made woman and quite capable of living by and looking after herself.'

I agreed but added, 'Still, I'll be glad when Gerald finally retires and they can settle down in their house by the sea.'

He nodded. 'Well, I hope Gerald does retire. What do you think?'

I had to confess I had never met him. 'Have you met him?'

'Oh yes, we know him. Margaret was the headmistress of the school we taught in and we all got on well. One night she went to a dinner party given by a mutual friend and she met Gerald. Then, to our amazement, she married him. As I said to Marie, "Marry in haste, repent at leisure," but she seems to be happy with him.'

'Don't you like him, Sandy?'

'Yes, I like him, but he's such a dry old stick. He's a good few years older than Margaret and he's a proper diplomat. I bet he asked her permission to kiss her on their wedding night and that Margaret just told him to get on with it.'

I felt myself go red and he laughed again.

'You're just joking, Sandy,' I said.

He gave me one of his looks that said 'would I lie to you' and held up his hand. 'I tell the truth, the whole truth and nothing but the truth,' he said solemnly.

I had to laugh at him, because he was such a witty man and very good company.

It was a month later that I was to recall that flippant conversation when I received a letter from my aunt.

I've just returned from Lisbon, where Gerald has been buried after suffering a heart attack. It was all so sudden that I really can't take it all in yet. He left instructions in his will that he was to be buried in the country he was currently living in. The graveyard in Lisbon is a very peaceful and beautiful place and the service was as dignified as he would have wished it. It is just so sad for this to happen on the eve of his retirement, but when I think about it perhaps this is what he wanted, as I always knew in my mind that he would never settle down to a normal retirement. Travelling the world was in his blood.

I was shocked when I read this and I rushed through to the kitchen, where Marie and Sandy were having their mid-morning cup of tea. Sandy saw my tears and he jumped up.

'What's the matter, Lizzie?'

'I've just got this letter from Margaret. Gerald has died of a heart attack and has been buried in Lisbon.' I handed the letter to him.

He sat down, and after he had read it he handed it to Marie, who looked shocked.

Sandy said, 'What an awful thing to happen, to make plans to leave a country and end up being buried there.'

I was still crying as I sat down to answer Margaret's letter. 'I'm going to go back, Marie, back to Scotland to be with her.'

Marie said she understood, but Sandy disagreed.

'Look, Lizzie, Marie and I know Margaret very well, and I don't think she'll want you running back there.'

I looked at Marie, and she agreed, but she said, 'Write to her and ask her if she wants you to return to be with her, Lizzie. Margaret is a very self-sufficient woman and well enough able to cope with whatever life throws at her. Tell her you'll return when you hear from her.'

I was torn in half. One part of me wanted to get on the next ship back to Carnoustie, but another part wanted to experience life here in Hong Kong. So I wrote and waited for Margaret's reply.

The days that went past were filled with a mixture of grief at Gerald's death and pleasure at teaching the children in my class, but before long Margaret replied and told me to stay where I was and to make the most of my life.

Gerald and I had a wonderful life together and he always enjoyed his work. Travelling the world was like an addiction to him, and I want you to fulfil your dream of living abroad and making the most of that dream. Please thank Marie and Sandy for their condolences and give them my best regards. Your loving aunt, Margaret.

When I told them what she had said, Sandy nodded.

'I knew she would say that, Lizzie. If I know Margaret, then I guess she has made loads of friends where she lives, so you're not to worry about her.' As he went out the door, he turned. 'I still feel guilty about laughing at Gerald that day. I didn't mean any harm and I regret my words very much.'

I said I felt the same. I knew he was just being funny about the man I had never met and never would meet now.

Life settled down again to the usual daily routine, with Sandy and I still going out in the evening to sample Hong Kong cuisine.

One of my favourite shops was Mr Wang's Wonderful World of Books. Sandy had introduced me to it and I spent most of my spare time there. The shop was situated down one of the narrow streets that was always a hive of activity even until late at night. Mr Wang's shop was deceptive. From the street, it looked like just another one of the businesses that traded there, but when you went inside it was like entering a cavern filled with book-lined shelves that stretched from the floor to the ceiling. Little benches were placed beside these shelves, and it was possible to come in and read a book without having to pay for it.

During my childhood I had often seen pictures of Chinese people and Mr Wang fitted my image of a Chinaman. He had a long, stringy, grey beard and he wore a fabulous embroidered coat and hat. He sat behind a desk that was situated just inside the door. By his side was his abacus, which he deftly used to count the purchases of his customers, and he would nod and smile when one entered and did the same when they left, regardless of whether they bought a book or not. I adored him, and he always made me feel welcome.

'Miss Lizzieeeee,' he said, making it sound as if I had ten e's attached to the end of my name.

'Mr Wang, how are you tonight?' I always asked him, and he would nod and smile. I always bought a few books from him, as I didn't like the idea of forever sitting in his cavern reading his stock.

In the beginning, Sandy would come in with me, but after a few visits he disappeared into the shop next door, which sold bottles of beer.

'I only have the two bottles of beer,' he said. 'If I go over that, Marie will know what I've been doing.'

I said I didn't believe him, but he laughed.

'Believe me, it's true. Marie is able to smell alcohol from a distance of a hundred yards, unless it's downwind – then it's half a mile.'

I gave him one of my disbelieving looks, but he said, 'Trust me, I'm an ex-Scout.'

I didn't mind, because I was in my element sitting amongst all these books, with Mr Wang's kindly eye on me unless he had another customer, and then his abacus would go *click, click, click*.

33

THE YEAR OF THE DOG

It was the Chinese New Year: 14 February 1934, the Year of the Dog. The school was closed for the celebration, as were a lot of the small shops. Sandy, Marie and I were standing outside watching the dragon parade as it slowly made its way down the narrow streets followed by what looked like the entire population of Hong Kong. Fireworks were cascading into the night sky over the harbour, colourful rockets shooting upwards in a multitude of sparks. The smell of gunpowder lay thick in the air. I had never witnessed anything like it.

I recalled how Laura and I had spent New Year's Eve in Dundee and how we both thought at the time how busy and noisy it was, but compared to this spectacle it was a very minor event. Families with young children and babies were out on the streets, laughing and chattering about the new year ahead of them.

Sandy explained how the Chinese calendar was made up of twelve animals and how the Year of the Rooster was now over and the Dog was in the ascendant. 'The Chinese people put huge faith in the elements of each animal year,' he said. 'Every year has different elements.'

Personally, I was fascinated by everything, but when Sandy suggested we should go along with the dragon parade, Marie said she was going back inside.

'I think Lizzie would like to see the rest of the parade, Marie, so we'll just go out for a wee while.' He took my elbow and said to stay close to him, as he didn't want me to get lost in the crowds. 'Marie will kill me if I lose you.'

As we neared the harbour, I could see crowds of people standing on the banks, and the little sampans were all lit up, with the families gathered on the decks watching the fireworks.

Sandy said that Mr Wang's Wonderful World of Books was to be open, as two authors were due to visit it and sign their book. He asked me if I wanted to go and I said yes, I would love to. The shop was busier than usual and there was a large poster in the window advertising *Dragon Land*, a book by author Jonas O'Neill with photographs by Alex Garcia.

Mr Wang sat at the desk and gazed at the waiting queue with his usual inscrutable air, but he nodded his head when he saw me. I sat on my usual bench and had a good view of the two authors, who sat at a large table surrounded by copies of their book.

I had no idea which one was which, but I assumed the Italian-looking man with the black, slicked-back hair was Alex Garcia, which meant his companion must be Jonas O'Neill. He was tall and very slim with light-brown hair and blue eyes, and I liked the way he spoke to the customers with his soft Irish voice. It was difficult to say how old he was, but I reckoned he was in his early thirties.

Mr Wang's abacus was clicking away due to all the sales of the book, and after the crowd had thinned out a bit, I joined the end of the queue. I had noticed that most of the customers were Chinese, but there was a smattering of British people buying the book.

When it came to my turn, Jonas O'Neill gave me a direct look and he smiled.

I held out my copy. 'Can you sign it to Lizzie Flint, please?'

His eyes screwed up with laughter. 'Certainly, Lizzie Flint, and it's a grand name you have.' After he signed it, he held the book open for Alex Garcia to sign, and I was taken aback by the dark-haired man's American accent. I thanked them and went back to my seat.

I must have sat for a good hour reading the book, as it was a fascinating account of life as lived in China, with wonderful photographs by Mr Garcia. Every few minutes I would look across at Jonas O'Neill, but when he caught my eye I blushed like some immature schoolgirl. I didn't know why I felt drawn to this stranger, as he wasn't especially handsome, but I was. I tried to look at him less in case he thought I was some forward hussy.

I went over to Mr Wang to pay him and he said, 'Miss Lizzeeeee, you seem to like Mr Jonas?'

'Oh no, Mr Wang, I don't even know him.'

'Ah, but Mr Wang knows you do, and he likes you, I can tell.'

There was still no sign of Sandy, so I resumed my seat and held the book up to make it look as if I was reading it. I felt someone's eyes on me. It was Jonas, who was studying me with a quizzical look. I tried to look nonchalant and kept glancing at my watch. Thankfully Sandy appeared, and he said he had been standing at the door waiting for me.

'You seen to be taken with that author chappie, Lizzie,' he said with a smile.

I felt my face go red again, but my voice was steady. 'What author chappie are you talking about, Sandy?'

'You know damn well who I mean, so stop trying to deny it.'

I gave him a steady look. 'How many beers have you had tonight?'

'As a matter of fact I've had three, but that's because it's the new year and tomorrow I might need the hair of the dog, which is funny because it's the Year of the Dog.'

I gathered up my book, and without a backward glance at the author chappie I walked out of the shop, with Sandy following behind. Mr Wang called out, 'Happy New Year, Miss Lizzieeeee.'

I turned around. 'Happy New Year, Mr Wang.'

Then I saw Jonas O'Neill and Alex Garcia gathering up the leftover books, and as I caught his eye, he waved. 'Goodnight, Lizzie Flint.'

Sandy gave me one of his looks. 'I told you, didn't I, that you've made an impression on him.'

'Nonsense, Sandy,' I said, but I felt my heart hammering in my chest and couldn't for the life of me think what had happened to me that night.

When I got home, Sandy made straight for his room, no doubt dodging Marie, who would smell the beer on his breath, but I sat up with her and we had a small sherry each to celebrate another year.

Later, in bed, I sat up with my book. I couldn't put it down. It was full of the history of China, from the opium wars to the Boxer Rebellion. It told of the slow demise of the emperors in their Forbidden City with all its concubines, and of the warlords and civil wars. It told the story of the famines, and of the incredible cruelty but also the beauty of this fabulous land, all told in words and great pictures. I turned to the back cover and found the photographs of the two authors: Jonas O'Neill, born in County Cork and a graduate of Dublin University, and Alex Garcia, born New York and a photographer of merit. Both men were now residing in Shanghai, where they were freelance reporters for a Shanghai newspaper.

It was 3 a.m. when I closed the book, but when I woke up next morning I was mortified to recall the dream I had had of Jonas O'Neill.

34

MR WANG'S WONDERFUL
WORLD OF BOOKS

After the New Year celebrations were over, life at the school seemed rather flat: a feeling that wasn't helped by the weather, which was wet and humid. By the end of the day all I wanted was a bath and clean clothes, and I noticed Sandy wasn't his usual cheery self.

For some time now, ever since Gerald's death, I had been toying with the idea of going back home to see Margaret. All her letters were full of how well she was keeping and her social life in Carnoustie, but I was still worried about her.

I was also still thinking about Jonas O'Neill, and I had no idea why I felt like this. It had never happened to me before. I mentioned it when I wrote to Laura and was shocked when she replied that I was in love with the man. 'What nonsense,' I thought, 'and so typical of Laura's romantic nature.' How, I asked myself, could I possibly be in love with someone I hardly knew and had only spoken a dozen words to?

I was worried about leaving Marie and Sandy in the lurch, as the new school term had started, so I said nothing about leaving. At the beginning of March, Sandy announced one morning that the two authors of *Dragon Land* were coming back due to the popularity of their book. He had given me a bland look as he ate his porridge with its powdered milk, then said, 'Oh by the way,

Lizzie, I was talking to Mr Wang and he's having another book signing with those two author chappies.'

I nearly choked on my toast, and Sandy looked triumphant. 'I knew you would be pleased.'

'I'm not pleased, Sandy,' I said indignantly. 'It's just that I never expected them back here in Hong Kong when there's the entire country of China to go round with their book. And another thing: why didn't Mr Wang tell me?'

'Well, I expect they have been doing that, but they obviously have enough customers here to warrant another trip. Or maybe they've got another motive. As for Mr Wang, he said to tell you, and I'm telling you now.' He scooped the last spoonful of porridge into his mouth with a grimace. 'Good Lord, Marie, this powdered milk tastes atrocious.'

She looked at him over the top of her spectacles. 'Well, I must say it's taken you a long time to come to that conclusion, Sandy. You've been eating it for years.'

'I know, and my stomach has finally gone on strike, so I won't be eating any more of it.'

'Are you sure your stomach isn't rebelling against that awful junk you eat every night?' she said tartly.

I had to smile. Sandy had eaten two helpings of fried rice and prawns along with two bottles of beer last night, and Marie's words echoed my thoughts.

Although I hadn't said anything to Sandy, a few weeks earlier I had written a letter to the publishers of *Dragon Land*, hoping they could pass it on to the two men. It was a short letter stating that I wanted to thank them for such a super book and how much I had enjoyed it. I hadn't had a reply, but then again I wasn't expecting one.

I could barely wait to get to Mr Wang's shop, and I found him putting up a poster about the book. The event was on the Saturday, which was three days away.

On Saturday I was in two minds whether to go or to stay in the school. I tried on three different outfits, but all the time my mind was on the letter I had sent. Would Jonas O'Neill and Alex Garcia think I was some starry-eyed youngster? Why had I written it, I wondered? The answer was that I'd never expected to see either of them again. I finally made up my mind I wasn't going to go, but when Sandy popped his head round the door I found myself walking out with him into the crowded streets.

'I'll not bother coming into the shop with you, Lizzie. I'll just pop into the wee restaurant down the road, as it's a special menu on tonight.'

I started to panic. 'Can you not come in for a minute or two, Sandy?'

He laughed. 'No, if it's a toss-up between Mr Chan's sticky ribs and rice and Jonas O'Neill's book, then the rice wins hands down.'

I hesitated by the door and was almost on the verge of leaving when Mr Wang called out, 'Miss Lizzieeeee.'

I saw Jonas turn round and he smiled. 'Hello, Lizzie Flint, nice to meet you again.'

I picked up a copy of the book and walked towards him. 'Can you sign this, please? Put "To Margaret from Lizzie".'

I watched as the now familiar flourish of a signature was scrawled across the page, and Jonas handed it to Alex, who also signed it.

'We want to thank you for your letter, Miss Flint,' Alex said. 'It's always good to hear how well our readers like the book.'

Jonas didn't say anything and my heart sank, but when I looked at him he smiled. 'I was hoping your father would give you our special invitation.'

'My father . . . ?'

'Yes, the man who was with you the last time we were here.'

'Oh, he's not my father. We're both teachers at the same school, but yes, he did say you were both coming back.'

As I went to pick up the signed book, Jonas touched my hand.

'Can you wait till we're finished here? I would like to take you out for a meal.'

I thought, 'Will I wait? Why, Jonas, I've been waiting a lifetime to meet you.'

Instead, I smiled back. 'Yes, I'll wait.' I pointed to the bench. 'I'll be sitting over there.'

The shop began to fill up. There was a huge queue in front of the table and I could hear Jonas's voice as he chatted to the customers. When Sandy appeared, I said, 'Hello, Father.'

He laughed out loud. 'I didn't want to let on to that author chappie that I'm not your father. I hope you don't mind.'

I said I didn't mind at all and explained about having a meal with Jonas.

Sandy looked worried. 'I'm supposed to be looking after you, Lizzie, and I'm not sure about this chappie's intentions.'

'I'll be fine. I'm a big girl now, and I promise I'll not stay out too long.'

'Well, mind and remember that. I won't mention to Marie anything about this. I'll just tell her you're still at Mr Wang's shop.'

Earlier on I had noticed a lovely Chinese girl sitting quietly on one of the other benches, but as the signing came to an end she got up and went to the table.

Jonas came over.

'I'm leaving my book with Mr Wang,' I said, 'and I'll collect it later.'

Jonas took my arm. 'There's someone I would like you to meet,' he said as we went over to where Alex was sitting with the girl. 'This is Sue Lin Crawford, Alex's fiancée.'

She said, 'Hello, Lizzie, nice to meet you,' and she laughed when she saw my surprise that she had a Scottish accent. 'I lived in Scotland for twelve years and went to Glasgow University.'

I told her I was from Dundee and had been a teacher there before coming out to Hong Kong.

As we left the shop, Mr Wang beamed a huge smile at me. 'Goodnight, Miss Lizzieeeee.'

'Goodnight, Mr Wang.' I could sense his gaze following me as the four of us stepped out into the street.

As we walked along, Jonas explained that Sue Lin and Alex were going back to the hotel, and if I didn't mind, there was a small seafood restaurant on the same street that we could go to.

I didn't tell him that I would follow him to the moon and back, but just nodded.

The restaurant was tiny, but we got a table by the far wall, and a tiny Chinese lady came and took our order. It was all so surreal. One day I was working away at the school and now I was sitting here with a virtual stranger, and the strange thing was, I was loving every moment of it.

After we had eaten, we sat with tiny bowls of fragrant tea and talked.

Jonas said, 'I originally come from Cork, in Ireland, where my father has a small farm and also breeds and stables horses. I'm afraid I'm a disappointment to him, as I didn't want to stay on the farm or in Ireland. My uncle has a farm in the Scottish Borders, and I didn't want to go there either. I came to Shanghai ten years ago and I love the life there as a freelance journalist and now an author. I sometimes worry about my father, as my mother died five years ago and I haven't seen him since I went back for her funeral. What about you, Lizzie, what brought you to Hong Kong?'

'My father was killed in the war when I was six and my mother never recovered from it. My granny and mother are both dead, but I've got my aunt Margaret to thank for coming out here. Her friends run the school I teach in. I've always longed for adventure. When I was a child, I used to shock my granny by saying I wanted to be a pirate.'

He burst out laughing. 'A pirate?'

'Or an explorer, I didn't mind which.'

He became serious. 'You must all have missed your father very much.'

I said we had. 'My mother always said the war had a lot to answer for, with all the families left behind to mourn their loved ones, and she was right. In the end it killed both my father and my mother.'

He sighed. 'The worst thing is there's no end to conflict. There's a war brewing in China, with the Japanese armies taking over the northern part of the country. Then there's Chiang Kai-shek with his army and the Communists under Mao Zedong fighting one another, and the Japanese have their sights on the rest of the country.'

I was shocked. 'But people said the conflict of 1914 to 1918 was the war to end all wars.'

'Well, they're wrong. It will happen all over again. Not just here, but in Europe as well.'

This statement depressed me. Surely there had been enough killing and, judging by Jonas's book, there had been enough in China as well.

'Let's speak about something cheerier,' said Jonas.

'What a lovely girl Sue Lin is. When are she and Alex getting married?'

'Well, tomorrow if Alex had his way, but Sue Lin loves her job as a journalist on the newspaper, and with Alex and I always travelling and looking for news, as well as starting another book, they just never seem to set a date.'

I said I was surprised by her Scottish accent.

'Her father is a doctor from Glasgow who came out to China to do missionary work. He met Sue Lin's mother in Shanghai and they were married. She takes her looks from her mother. They moved back to Glasgow when Sue Lin was a girl. When she got the job on the newspaper, she came back to Shanghai and her birthplace.'

I looked at my watch and was alarmed to see it was almost twelve o'clock. I stood up. 'I must get back to the school or Marie, she's the other teacher, will be worried about me.'

'All right, Cinderella. I'll walk back with you and make sure you get home safely.'

The streets were still crowded with people, and I wondered if the population ever slept more than a few hours. The rain had cleared, and it was a pleasant night as we headed back. When we reached the door, he said, 'Alex, Sue Lin and I are here for a week, and I would like to see you again. What about tomorrow night?'

'Yes, I would like to see you again as well, Jonas.'

I turned to go, but he put his arms around me and gave me a gentle kiss. 'Goodnight, Captain Flint,' he said softly.

I laughed. 'Just make sure I don't scratch you with my talons.'

He was still laughing as he walked away down the street.

When I went inside, I almost fell over Sandy. He was wearing his dressing gown and he whispered furiously, 'Where have you been, Lizzie? I've been worried about you.'

'I'm fine, Sandy. Please don't worry about me. I'm seeing Jonas tomorrow night, but I'll tell Marie about it.'

As he walked away, I overheard him say, 'Well, I hope you know what you're doing.'

Jonas came to the school the next night, and I introduced him to Marie before we left to go out. We were going to the hotel to meet up with Sue Lin and Alex, and we found them waiting for us in the hotel bar.

Sue Lin wanted to hear about Scotland. 'It's been ages since I was home, but I keep in touch with my parents. Maybe one day we'll go and live there. Won't we, Alex?'

For the short time I had known Alex, he hadn't said much, but he smiled at her and said it would either be there or Shanghai or New York, he didn't mind. I loved his American accent. He said he had been born in Brooklyn to Italian parents who had left Italy for a better life. Sadly they were both dead now and he didn't feel like Brooklyn was his home any more.

'I think we might stay in Shanghai, Sue Lin. I've got my photography business and you have your career.'

'What about you, Lizzie? Will you stay here?' he asked.

'I don't know. I've been thinking of going back to Dundee to see my aunt, but I haven't made up my mind.'

Sue Lin said she led an exciting life following up stories for the paper. 'I travel quite a bit, but it's nothing like these two do. They're always travelling to far-off places for their scoops, and also for their book.'

I said it all sounded dangerous and asked if Shanghai was a dangerous city to live in.

'We live in the International Settlement, which is run by the British, and there's a large population of different nationalities,' said Jonas. 'It's just like living in London or any large city.'

Later, as we walked home, he asked me, 'Are you really thinking of leaving Hong Kong?'

I hesitated for a moment. 'Well, I've been thinking about it since the New Year. Marie has a new girl starting this month. Her parents have just arrived here. Her father is in the army and she's looking for a teaching post, so I won't be leaving them without a teacher.'

'Why don't you come to Shanghai with me?'

I was speechless for a moment.

'I don't think Marie and Sandy would like that, Jonas. They told my aunt they would look after me. Not that I need looking after, you understand,' I added. 'I wouldn't like to worry my aunt that I was going off with someone I hardly know to a strange country. For all I know, you could be a married man with children.'

'Well, I'm not, and I'm not asking you to come and live there forever if you don't want to. Just come for a holiday.'

'I'll think about it, I promise.'

I was desperate to join him, but my feelings for him were too intense and I thought I might not want to leave after my holiday.

He kissed me again, but this time I returned the kiss and held onto him like I never wanted to let him go. My emotions were all over the place, so I quickly opened the door.

'Goodnight, Lizzie. I'll see you tomorrow.'

'Goodnight, Jonas,' I said as I quickly went inside.

The next morning I casually mentioned going on holiday to Shanghai. Marie looked shocked, as did Sandy.

'Are you going with Jonas?' he asked.

I was amused by this. It was now Jonas instead of 'that chappie'.

'Yes, but only for a holiday. I thought when June comes to work here then I could maybe have a few weeks off.'

Marie gave me a stern look. 'I don't like the idea of you going to Shanghai. Oh, I expect it's a wonderful city, but I've heard stories about the place and I don't think Margaret will be happy about it.'

I had the same thoughts, so I said it was merely an idea.

That evening when Jonas met me I told him I couldn't go with him, but that I would still like to keep in touch.

He said he'd thought I would turn him down. 'I'm leaving in two days' time with Alex and Sue Lin, but yes, we will keep in touch, Lizzie.'

That night in bed I was almost crying. I reread *Dragon Land* and wished with all my heart I could be with Jonas. Not just for a holiday, but forever.

Two days later I said goodbye to Alex, Sue Lin and Jonas at the docks and watched as they boarded their ship for Shanghai. Jonas said he would write and keep in touch, but I didn't believe him. Once he was back in his own environment he would soon forget me. But would I forget him?

I think Marie and Sandy were pleased that he had gone. Sandy organised an evening out again, but my heart wasn't in it. Although I didn't mention it to Marie, as I wanted to wait till June was settled in the job, somehow Hong Kong had lost its fascination for me and I made up my mind to return home.

35

JONAS O'NEILL AND
DRAGON LAND

June was an efficient young woman, and as my assistant in the classroom she was proving to be a good teacher. I was pleased about that, as it meant I could go ahead with my plan to go back home. I had posted Jonas's book *Dragon Land* to Margaret, but had said nothing about leaving Hong Kong, as I was sure she would tell me to stay and enjoy the experience of living in another country.

Jonas was as good as his word and he wrote a lovely long letter when he arrived back in Shanghai. I was missing him terribly, but he sounded more friendly than besotted with love in his letter, so I didn't answer it for a few days. When I did, I said I was thinking of leaving and going back to Dundee. I never mentioned how much I missed him, but tried to write my letter as more of a friendly note from one friend to another.

A week went by, then another, and he didn't reply, so I thought he wasn't interested in keeping up the friendship. Sandy noticed both how I hurried to the letter box every time the mail was delivered and my downcast face when there was nothing for me.

'No letter from Shanghai yet, Lizzie?' he asked.

I shook my head but said nothing. I thought he was being flippant about Jonas, but one morning he said, 'I'm really sorry it hasn't worked out with you both. Maybe you should have gone with him when he asked you.' He stopped as if giving this some thought. 'Well, maybe not, Lizzie. Anything could have happened to you in China, and Marie would never have got over that. Nor would I.'

I gave him a hug. 'Thanks, Sandy, you've both been very good to me, but I've made up my mind to go home. I wouldn't have left if you'd had no one to replace me, but June will be able to take over my class.'

'Actually, Marie and I are planning on retiring next year, so we'll be giving up the school. Marie wants to go back to Skye, and I might just stay here. I haven't made up my mind yet.'

This news came as a shock.

'I thought you both loved the school and I always thought you would both be here for a long time.'

'Well, if we were both young then we would be, but we're getting old, so retirement is on the cards, I'm sorry to say. Just one thing, Lizzie: don't say anything to Marie, as she thinks I don't know about her plans to return to her misty island.'

I was depressed about receiving no letter from Jonas. It was as if I had met my soulmate only to have him disappear from my life. And now Sandy was talking about retirement. It was all too much.

'You can always take June out in the evening when I've gone,' I told Sandy, but he shook his head.

'I don't think so, Lizzie. She's a nice girl but very dull in her outlook. Anyway, she goes home to her parents very night and I think she does embroidery with her mother as a hobby.'

I laughed. He was incorrigible. 'Why do you think that?

'She showed me a handkerchief she had embroidered and she said that was how she and her mother spent their leisure time. Quite honestly I had to pretend to go into raptures over it. No, Lizzie, she's nothing like you.'

I was overcome with emotion when he said that. 'Well, I've enjoyed every minute of our outings, Sandy, and I'll always remember them, even when I'm old and grey-haired.'

'By then I'll probably be ancient.' However, he said it with a smile.

My one consolation was Mr Wang's bookshop. With Sandy disappearing on our nightly visits for his beer, I spent ages in the shop. Mr Wang looked so ancient and wise, and he would tell me about his previous life in Canton.

'I came here years and years ago, but I want to go back to Canton one day,' he said.

'That makes two of us, Mr Wang. I'm planning on going home as well.'

He shook his head. 'No, Lizzieeee, you'll live in China with Mr O'Neill.'

I was taken aback by this statement. 'What makes you say that?'

He gave me a smile. 'I just know it.'

'Well, if Mr Wang knows it, why doesn't Jonas?' I thought.

It was two weeks later, a day I will never forget, when Sandy came into my classroom. He whispered that someone was waiting to see me. When I looked puzzled, he said to June, 'We won't be long.'

I followed him out and he gave me a conspiratorial grin. 'He's in the kitchen with Mrs Kydd.'

'Who is?' I asked. But I was talking to myself, as Sandy hurried off to his own classroom.

I could hear Mrs Kydd clattering her pots as she took them down from the high shelf, making preparations for the evening meal. I could also hear her talking to someone, and I had the insane notion that it was Margaret. I knew she loved travelling and I wondered if she had come to see Marie, Sandy and me.

That was why my mouth fell open when I saw Jonas standing by the kitchen table. He had a huge bunch of flowers in his hand, and when he turned and smiled at me I felt my knees begin to shake.

He came over with the flowers and said, 'These are for you.'

'Surely you didn't come all this way to give me flowers, Jonas,' I said.

He laid the flowers down by the sink, and Mrs Kydd said she would find a vase for them. He gave her a charming smile and I was amused to see her blush. It was obvious he had this effect on women.

'Let's go outside, Lizzie,' he said, tucking my arm through his.

'I've got a class of children, Jonas. I can't just leave them.'

'Sandy said you have a new teacher, so of course you can leave them for a short time.'

We went to the small café across the road, and once seated I asked him, 'Are you back signing books, Jonas? Is that why you're here?'

He shook his head. 'No. I've come here especially to see you and to tell you not to leave and go back to Scotland.'

I must have looked idiotic as he said that. 'You've come all the way from Shanghai to tell me that?'

'No, I've come all this way to ask you to marry me and come back with me as my wife.'

I stared at him. 'Marry you?'

He grinned. 'Yes, you know, get the minister to join us in holy wedlock.'

'I don't understand, Jonas. Why do you want to marry me? You hardly know me.'

'Ah, well, when I was a young lad in County Cork, I went to the fairground one day and old Mrs Donaghue, our local oracle and fortune teller, told me I would get married one day to a pirate. She was well known in Cork as being in league with the leprechauns and the little folk, so she was always correct with her predictions.'

I laughed. 'I don't believe it.'

He looked sheepish. 'Well, maybe I'm wrong about the leprechauns and the little folk, but she did say I would marry a woman with strong connections to the sea, and a pirate has that, hasn't she?' He took my hand and became serious. 'What do you say, my beautiful little pirate?'

I wanted to scream out loud, 'Yes, yes, yes,' but I composed myself and said, 'I suppose we can't have Mrs Donaghue have a faulty prediction, can we?'

'So that's a yes then?'

'Yes, it is.'

All at once I was laughing and crying. As we made our way back to the school, Sandy and Marie heard the commotion, but when they heard the good news they both congratulated us. I thought Marie's good wishes were a bit subdued, but Sandy made up for it by shaking Jonas's hand and slapping him on his back.

The next few weeks were a whirlwind of activity and planning. Jonas left most of the plans to me, and I said I wanted to be married in the small church that Marie attended every Sunday, so we went to see the minister and he readily agreed to marry us. I did ask Jonas if he had any preference for the service, but he said he didn't.

'I was brought up a Catholic, but I haven't been to a church in years, so I don't mind where it is,' he said.

'What about having the wedding meal in the seafood café on the docks?' said Sandy, who was fond of the food there and was a regular customer.

I said no, we were planning a meal in the Oriental Hotel with just a few guests.

The wedding day was fast approaching when we hit a snag. Sue Lin and Alex were to be our witnesses, but they were both away on business for the newspaper that took longer than expected, which meant they wouldn't make it to Hong Kong in time.

I said to Jonas, 'I'm sorry your two friends can't be here, but what about having Sandy and Marie as witnesses?'

Jonas said he didn't mind. All he wanted was for us to get married and he wasn't concerned about the details. 'I would have liked Alex and Sue Lin to be here, but they've promised us another reception when we reach Shanghai.'

To start with, I was unsure how Marie would take to the idea, but when I mentioned it she seemed pleased, while Sandy was delighted. I also asked Mrs Kydd to come to the church, but she said she couldn't manage as she had another engagement that day.

'I'll buy myself a new suit,' Sandy said before looking at Marie. 'You'll have to buy something nice as well. Lizzie doesn't want you turning up in your woolly jumper and thick tweed skirt with those clumpy shoes you wear.'

'I beg your pardon, Sandy, but I'm well aware what to wear, thank you very much.'

Jonas smiled at this spat, but I was a little bit worried. Marie was a lovely person, but her wardrobe was very limited and more suitable for the Highlands of Scotland than humid Hong Kong.

However, I needn't have worried. I chose a white dress with a matching hat. On my wedding morning Marie appeared in my bedroom wearing a very smart cream suit, court shoes and a little hat with a flower.

Sandy couldn't believe his eyes. 'Good God, Marie, you look wonderful, and I didn't realise you were so good-looking.'

'Well, that's just because you never looked hard enough,' she said.

I had written to Margaret to tell her my good news and had received a letter saying how pleased she was for us both and asking me to send some photos of the day.

The wedding was due at midday, and before we set off for the church, Marie gave me a small box with a silver St Christopher medallion on a thin chain.

'This belonged to my mother, Lizzie, but I want you to have it. I hope it will keep you safe in Shanghai, as St Christopher is the patron saint of travellers.'

I was overcome with emotion. 'Thank you, Marie,' I said as I placed it around my neck. 'I'll treasure it forever.'

The wedding ceremony was brief, but as we emerged from the church Jonas and I were man and wife. It all felt so unreal, as if I was living in a dream. We went to the hotel, where I was hoping Mr Wang would be waiting. I had invited him to the ceremony, and while he said he couldn't manage it he said he would be at the hotel. He was sitting in the lobby, but he stood up when we approached.

'I can't leave the shop for long, Lizzieeeee, but all the blessings on your marriage.' He shook hands with Jonas and then handed me an intricate-looking box. 'It has a hidden message inside, but you have to figure out how to open it first.'

'Oh, thank you, Mr Wang. You have been one of my best friends since coming here and I will always treasure this gift.'

He inclined his head, wished us all good day and walked out of the hotel.

'I wish he could have stayed,' I said to Jonas. 'He's been a dear, dear friend to me.'

Sandy had arranged for a bottle of champagne to be served with our meal, and as the food was all Chinese cuisine I supposed he had ordered what he liked. Marie ate very little, but she said she enjoyed everything except the champagne, saying she normally just had a small sherry now and again, so Jonas ordered some for her.

It was six o'clock before we finished; then with a flurry of goodbyes, Marie and Sandy left to go back to the school.

'We'll come down to see you both off tomorrow,' said Sandy. 'When does your ship sail?'

Jonas said it was eleven o'clock in the morning.

Marie looked at Sandy and said tartly, 'That should give you time to get over all the food and drink you've eaten.' She turned to me and gave me a hug. 'Goodbye, Lizzie. I hope you'll be very happy in your new country.' She shook Jonas's hand. 'Goodbye, Jonas.'

We were then left on our own. Jonas said, 'Let's go for a walk.'

I put my jacket over my dress and we set off towards the harbour. There was a full moon and the water shimmered in its glow. Lights from the moored sampans also lit up the sky, while the shops had small lanterns outside their doors. It was magical, and I felt so alive walking beside my husband. He took my hand, and at the end of the street was Mr Wang's shop, so we went inside.

Mr Wang wasn't there, which surprised me. A young girl was behind the counter, and when I asked her about him she said, 'I am Mr Wang's niece. He has retired to his bed early.'

This statement worried me. 'Is Mr Wang all right?'

She smiled and nodded. 'He has a headache, but he will be down in the shop later. He has had too much rice wine.'

As we walked towards the hotel, we were laughing. 'I didn't know Mr Wang liked his rice wine,' I said.

Jonas laughed. 'His niece said he had a bottle behind his cash desk and he's ill because he doesn't usually drink. She said he's going to miss you very much and he was drinking to celebrate your wedding.'

I felt touched by this and knew I would miss Mr Wang very much too.

Jonas had booked a room at the hotel for the night, and as we went in through the front door I suddenly felt apprehensive. A few months ago I had been a single teacher who had never had a boyfriend, and here I was now, a married woman.

I had bought a lovely new nightgown for my honeymoon, which we were spending on the ship going to Shanghai, and as I slipped it on after my bath, Jonas was standing by the window.

He turned as I entered and came across and held me tightly, giving me such a passionate kiss I almost fainted. But I managed to kiss him back, and I knew I had been waiting all my life for this wonderful moment as we slipped into bed together.

I awoke later in the night and the moon was shining through the window. Suddenly I recalled a film I had seen with Laura and Pat about such a scene and at the time we almost swooned. Later, Pat said it was all Hollywood fantasy and quite slushy. I made a mental note if I should ever see her again to tell her it wasn't a fantasy and it certainly wasn't slushy; it was romantic and full of love, celebrating the commitment we had both made.

The next morning we headed for the docks, where the ship was waiting to take us on our journey to China. Sandy and Marie were already standing on the wharf as our luggage was loaded on board.

Sandy said I looked radiant, and I blushed, much to his amusement, but Marie was her usual efficient self.

'Now remember and write to us, Lizzie, and let us know all about your new home.'

I said I would. 'Thank you so much for all you've done for me, both of you, and I promise I will keep in touch.' I put my hand over my St Christopher necklace. 'Thank you for my lovely present as well, Marie.'

Then with a final hug from her and handshakes from Sandy, Jonas guided me up the gangplank. He turned as we reached the top.

'Don't worry, I'll look after her, and thanks for everything.'

Marie began to cry. She wiped her eyes, as if feeling guilty at her emotion, but I saw Sandy put his arm around her shoulders.

As the ship slowly moved away from the dock, we stood at the rail and waved a farewell, not only to Marie and Sandy but also to Hong Kong. For a brief moment, I wondered if I would ever see it again, but my life now lay in Shanghai with my new husband and I couldn't have been happier.

36

SHANGHAI

The last time I had been on a sea voyage I was alone, but I was now travelling as a married woman with my husband and there were still times when I felt I was existing in a dream. Everything had happened so fast that the reality hadn't hit me yet. One thing, however, was clear in my mind. I loved Jonas, and I realised I had done so since the very first moment I saw him in Mr Wang's bookshop. Up till then I hadn't believed in love at first sight, thinking it was just a figment of the imagination in books and in the films, but I now knew it was real.

As we sailed on the South China Sea, Jonas told me about his life in Shanghai.

'I'll be away a lot, Lizzie, as a freelance writer. Alex and I travel around looking for the news stories for the paper and also for our next book.' He gave me an anxious glance. 'I did mention that, didn't I?'

I laughed. 'Of course you did. You pointed out all the pitfalls I would face, but you also mentioned all the joys, so don't worry, I want to be with you, no matter where you live.'

He sighed. 'Well, that makes me feel a lot happier. Marie kept giving me some worried frowns, almost as if I was abducting you to live a life of debauchery.'

'I wouldn't worry about that, Jonas. It's part of her upbringing to be cautious about everything foreign. Sandy, on the other hand, embraces everything oriental. No matter where he lives in the world, he will love the local culture and especially the food.' I stopped. Thinking about Sandy suddenly filled me with nostalgia. He had been such a delightful companion on our many evenings out and I was grateful for those memories.

Jonas was describing our house. 'It's not a large place, but it's situated on Bubbling Well Road, that's the road to Nanking, and our neighbours are a lovely couple: Zheng Yan and his wife Ping Li. You'll like them. We'll be living in the International Settlement, and although we are in China we'll be under the jurisdiction of the British government. There's a large population of Britons, especially in the police force, so there will no problem with coping with a foreign language.'

I said it all sounded wonderful, but I secretly hoped it would be more like the China I had read about all those years ago in the library in Dundee.

We were nearing Shanghai and were now sailing up the Huangpu River. Jonas was keen to point out the various landmarks, but when the ship docked at one of the wharves, all I could see was the Bund.

'This is the financial centre of the Settlement,' he said. 'This is where all the money is made.'

Jonas had described it to me, but seeing it with my own eyes was another matter. He pointed out various buildings, but to be honest I was a bit disappointed. Though it was huge and teeming with life, the buildings were just like those in any other western city. I had expected to see temples and fragrant gardens.

I was hoping for a rickshaw ride, but Jonas got a taxi to take us to the house. He must have seen my face, because he smiled.

'Never mind, Lizzie, you'll see the Chinese way of life as well. Tomorrow I'll take you on a rickshaw ride around the city.'

As the taxi wound its way into the city, I was pleased to see hundreds of Chinese people going about their daily lives. The taxi driver had to dodge the rickshaws and the carts piled high with goods. I also saw some little men carrying two heavy loads on bamboo poles that they had placed across their shoulders. I felt so sorry for them, as they looked ready to collapse as they made their way forward with bowed backs. Apart from that I was fascinated by the scenes that flashed by the car window, and before long we arrived at the house on Bubbling Well Road.

Jonas carried our luggage up the small drive to the door. It was a single-storey house with a wooden veranda that ran the length of the front, and I was immediately struck by how similar it looked to the house in Carnoustie.

The garden was a fragrant mixture of flowers and bushes, and I noticed that the windows and their shutters were clean and shining. I wondered briefly if Jonas was the cleaner, but he had been in Hong Kong for a few weeks before our marriage and everything looked spick and span.

The front door opened and we were met by a tiny Chinese woman dressed in what looked like cotton pyjamas. Her hair was jet black and tied back in a loose bun. It was difficult to guess her age, as she could have been anything between thirty and sixty.

Jonas called out, 'Hello, Madame Zheng, I want you to meet my wife, Lizzie.'

The woman came down the steps with her arms outstretched and a big smile on her face.

'Lizzie, I'm Ping Li, and I welcome you to Shanghai,' she said, bowing her head.

I wasn't a tall woman, but faced with this tiny person I felt awkward as I towered over her.

'I'm so pleased to meet you, Ping Li. My husband has spoken of you and your husband so much that I feel I already know you.'

Her face broke out in another smile that caused tiny wrinkles to form around her eyes.

'Please come in. My husband is at work, but you will meet him tonight. I have prepared tea and rice cakes for you.'

I was pleasantly surprised when I stepped over the threshold, as everything was clean and tidy. Either Jonas was a domestic god or this tiny woman had spruced the place up for our arrival. There were vases of fragrant flowers on a few of the well-polished surfaces, and she disappeared into the small kitchen before reappearing with a tray of tea.

Jonas said it was great to see her again.

'Thank you for cleaning up all my untidy mess, Ping Li.'

'So he isn't a domestic god after all,' I thought. We drank the tea from small china bowls, and the small rice cakes were delicious. I wondered if the Zhengs shared the house with us, but Jonas said, 'Zheng Yan and Ping Li live in the house next door and they're wonderful neighbours.'

Ping Li smiled. 'Thank you, Jonas, and I hope to be a wonderful neighbour to Lizzie. Now I must go back and prepare the evening meal for my husband.'

'Where does he work?' I asked.

She looked very proud as she answered. 'Zheng Yan is the head shipping clerk at the British Shipping Company. You would have passed by his office when you arrived at the dock.'

Jonas said he hadn't seen him, but that the office looked very busy.

'Yes, he told me a lot of ships were due in today, so he will have been busy with all the extra work.' She looked at me. 'A great deal of China's trade comes into the docks of the Huangpu River, so my husband has a very responsible job.' She stood up. 'I hope we will become good friends, Lizzie.'

'Yes, I'm sure we will, Ping Li, and I look forward to meeting your husband.'

After she had gone, Jonas showed me round the rest of the house. There were two bedrooms, a small kitchen and bathroom, and it was simply furnished, but I was enchanted with it.

Jonas looked worried. 'I hope you like it, Lizzie. You can throw out the furniture and buy new things if you want.'

I said I was happy with everything and I wouldn't dream of throwing anything out. All I wanted in my life was Jonas, and the house was secondary to him.

Before I could ask him what he would like for his evening meal, he said, 'I hope you don't mind, but Sue Lin and Alex want us to join them at the Palace Hotel tonight.'

I said I didn't mind.

Before getting ready for our meeting with Alex and Sue Lin, Zheng Yan arrived home from work and came into the house with his wife. He was a small man, around five foot three inches, only a couple of inches taller than his wife, and he was dressed in a dark-coloured suit with a white shirt and blue tie. He looked very smart, and his wife gazed at him with a proud look on her face.

Jonas went and put his arm around his shoulders. 'Zheng Yan, come and meet my wife, Lizzie.'

He was very formal as he shook my hand and bowed. 'I'm pleased to meet you, Lizzie.'

Ping Li hovered in the background, but I asked them to sit down and have some tea.

Jonas asked Zheng Yan, 'Have you had a busy day?'

'Very, very busy, Jonas. Lots of ships coming in with their cargoes, and of course I have all the paperwork to fill in. Then there are the passenger ships, but they are someone else's job.'

Jonas said he had noticed that. 'I looked out for you when we arrived, but you must have been busy.'

'Yes, yes, I was very busy.'

I put the tea tray on the table and we all sipped the bowls of fragrant tea.

I asked them, 'Have you always lived here in Shanghai?'

'No,' said Zheng Yan. 'I come from Hong Kong, where I worked with the British Shipping Company, but I came to supervise the offices here.' He looked at his wife. 'Then I met my wife, who comes from Shanghai, and we got married ten years ago.'

Ping Li nodded. 'It was a fortunate move for my husband to come here and meet me. Now we are both very happy.'

I was amused by her statement, but I kept a straight face. I liked the way she spoke for both of them and the way he beamed at her when she said something.

'I make dresses for the Star department store. It is a high-class shop and my dresses sell very well.'

'That's wonderful, Ping Li. I must go and see this shop, as my mother also worked in a department store in Dundee. She was in the millinery department – we always called it the hat shop!'

Ping Li clapped her tiny hands together. 'Then we have so much in common, Lizzie, and we will be great friends.'

'Oh, I do hope so,' I said with feeling. I suddenly felt a rapport with my neighbours and I was glad that I had them living in the next house.

After they departed, it was time to get ready to go to the hotel. 'Is it a very grand hotel?' I asked Jonas.

He shook his head. 'I really don't know much about it, as I don't normally go out to hotels, but it certainly has an impressive frontage, so maybe we had better dress for the occasion.'

I went to look out my silver-grey satin dress that I had last worn on board the ship to Hong Kong, as I wasn't sure if I should wear my white wedding frock or not. Jonas came through wearing a light-coloured suit that made him look so handsome, but he was muttering about it being a bit tight.

'I don't normally wear suits like this, as I like being casually dressed.'

I told him he looked great in it, and he looked in the mirror and said, 'Do I really?' He still sounded unsure.

By now I had decided on the silver-grey dress, and I pinned my hair up and caught it in a lovely clasp I had bought in Hong Kong. It was shaped like a dragon, and I had loved it when I spotted it in a small shop in the bazaar, but this was the first time I had worn it.

Jonas stood behind me and caught my eye in the mirror. 'I'm so glad I met you that night in Mr Wang's shop, Lizzie. I fell in love with you that night, but I didn't want to tell you in case it frightened you away. Then when you wrote to tell me you were leaving to go back home, I realised I couldn't let you go.'

I turned and held his hand. 'I fell in love with you that night as well, Jonas, but I was also frightened you maybe had a wife and children and I would embarrass you with my protestations of love.'

'Well, it's all turned out for the best,' he said. 'We'll have years and years of happiness to look forward to.'

I felt a sliver of ice in my stomach. I didn't like predictions like this, especially after my mother's experience, but I smiled at him. 'Of course we will,' I said with my fingers crossed.

We got a taxi to the hotel, as rain had begun to fall quite heavily, but when we arrived I was surprised at the grandness of the building. The reception area was quite spectacular and the dining room was busy with people sitting eating at tables covered with white tablecloths and shiny silver cutlery. It was a far cry from the street carts and small restaurants Sandy and I had frequented, and I suddenly felt a bit overwhelmed.

Thankfully Sue Lin and Alex appeared, and we were seated at a table by the far wall, which gave us some privacy. Alex looked handsome in his black suit, white shirt and grey striped tie, and his hair was slicked back like it had been the first time I saw him. Sue Lin looked lovely in an exquisite dress of deep-blue satin with silver flowers embroidered on it, and she also had a silver clasp holding her dark hair back from her face. I couldn't reconcile her Chinese looks with her Scottish accent when she said, 'Congratulations, Lizzie and Jonas, on your marriage. Alex and I hope you'll both be very happy.'

Alex smiled. 'Hopefully it'll be our turn next, Sue Lin,' but she just squeezed his hand and picked up the menu.

I noticed Jonas giving Alex a look, but Alex just shrugged his shoulders as if to say, 'Well, I tried.'

I felt so sorry for him, as he was certainly besotted with her, but maybe Sue Lin wasn't ready for marriage.

The food was delicious and we drank some champagne to celebrate our marriage, and the evening was turning out to be a good time with friends. I don't know what made me look over my shoulder, but I noticed the couple who were sitting at a table in the centre of the room were looking in our direction.

Jonas saw me and said, 'That's the aristocracy of Shanghai. He's Conrad Hamilton and that's his wife, Lorna-May. They're

241

American, and he's the head of the American Bank here in Shanghai.'

Before I could answer, they stood up and came over to our table.

'Good evening, Jonas, Alex and Sue Lin,' said Conrad. 'And this lovely lady is your wife, I believe?'

Jonas said I was. 'This is Lizzie. We arrived back today.'

Conrad shook my hand. 'Pleased to meet you, Lizzie. This is my wife, Lorna-May.'

She was wearing a beautiful gown of pale silver and she had a sparkling necklace around her neck that looked like it was made of diamonds, but surely, I thought, they were fake.

She gave me a cool, appraising look. 'Pleased to meet you, Lizzie.' She turned to Jonas. 'You've been a dark horse, Jonas. We all thought you would never get married.'

Jonas gave her a crooked smile. 'Well, I never met the right woman, but I have now.'

Conrad laughed. 'Just like the old Jonas. Full of Irish charm.'

Before turning away with her husband, Lorna-May said in her seductive drawl, 'Perhaps we'll see you again, Lizzie.'

I almost said 'I hope not', but I smiled and said I would look forward to that.

We then resumed our conversation. The two men had been speaking about the Japanese takeover of the northern part of China.

'They're calling it Manchuria,' said Alex, 'and they're also causing diplomatic rows that give them the excuse to take over more land. They're a nation that needs watching.'

Jonas agreed, and Sue Lin said she was doing an article on the refugee problem.

'There are hundreds of refugees fleeing from the north and they're ending up in Peking and Shanghai.'

When there was a lull in the conversation, I asked Jonas, 'Do you know a woman called Elsie Lomax, Jonas?'

The three faces looked at me, and Sue Lin said, 'Is she Ronnie Lomax's wife?'

'Yes, she is. I met her on the ship coming from London to Hong Kong and she said her husband was in charge of his father's cotton mills on the banks of the Huangpu River. Her mother was with her, but I expect she has gone back home by now.'

Jonas laughed. 'Yes, she has. She caused an incident with her son-in-law at the mill and told him she was taking her daughter back with her and not leaving her in the fleshpots of Shanghai.'

I said that sounded very much like Mrs Burton.

'Has Elsie gone back with her?'

Jonas said she was still here and lived on Bubbling Well Road. 'Her house is much larger than ours, but it's between us and the palatial place of the Conrad Hamiltons.'

'I do hope she's happy, as she was very nervous about coming out here,' I said, but no one said a word.

Then Jonas said, 'We don't really know her that well, Lizzie, but why don't you pay her a visit? I'm sure she'll be glad to see a friendly face.'

When I said I would, the three of them glanced at one another, and although I was slightly puzzled by this, Sue Lin gave my hand a squeeze and she smiled. 'Elsie Lomax will be so pleased to see you again, Lizzie.'

37

ZHENG YAN AND PING LI

Jonas and I spent the next few weeks settling into our house. Although I had said I didn't want to change anything, I moved some of the furniture around and bought new curtains for the windows, as I thought the old ones were too dark and a bit threadbare.

Jonas was working with Alex on another book, and they spent hours together discussing it and sifting through the photographs Alex had taken.

I put my mother's carriage clock on the sideboard, along with Mr Wang's box. Neither Jonas nor I had been able to unlock the mystery of opening it, but I knew we would manage it sometime. I often looked at the photograph album and sometimes got a little bit nostalgic about my previous life in Dundee, but I was so happy here with my husband that this soon passed.

I wrote letters to Margaret and Laura and Pat and looked forward to all their news. I was amused when Laura replied to my letter telling her I was married. She wrote back saying she always thought she would be the first of the three of us to get married, and I thought she sounded slightly miffed that I had beaten her to the matrimonial gatepost. She was still teaching but was now at Rosebank School, the primary school I had attended as a child along with Emily. But thinking back to those days reminded me of the sadness of my father's death.

I still had a letter I'd found in Mum's box after her death. It was dated November 1918 and it verified that Dad had died that July day in 1917. But even with this evidence in front of her she still didn't believe it. She had written 'not true' on the letter and continued to live a life of denial, which was so sad but so typical of her. I had shown this letter to Margaret and she said Mum had let her see it.

Margaret had said, 'Your mum knew your dad was probably dead, but because there was no body or burial, a part of her hoped he was alive. She told me that if she saw someone who looked like your dad she had renewed hope that he could still be alive, and that small spark of hope never left her. That's the tragedy of this war, Lizzie, that not all the dead had a Christian burial.'

I put the letter back in the box.

Pat had sent her congratulations and also her parents' good wishes. She was now a teacher in Kirriemuir, which meant she was living on the farm instead of in lodgings. I also had a letter from Irene and Wullie, and I recalled the happy times I spent in their house in the Hawkhill and all the singsongs we'd had. Maisie also wrote with her congratulations.

Ping Li was a great friend, and I spent a lot of my time in her house, where she sat at her sewing machine making her dresses. I got a bit homesick when I saw her machine was a Singer made in their factory in Glasgow, but that soon passed as well. Some days we made our way to the Star store with her deliveries and spent time browsing in the different departments.

Most evenings after our meal, Jonas would go into his study with his typewriter and I would hear him typing away, and on other nights Ping Li and I would sit on the veranda while Zheng Yan and Jonas played mah-jong, the gentle click of tiles blending with the sound of birdsong from our garden.

After our meal at the Palace Hotel the night we arrived, I made a point of contacting Elsie. I was upset when I first met her, as she looked really depressed. Her hair wasn't brushed and her dress looked like she had worn it for days. She had been surprised to see me and had jumped up.

'Lizzie, I can't believe you're here in Shanghai. When did you leave Hong Kong?'

'I got married there, but my husband lives here,' I told her. 'His name is Jonas O'Neill.'

She looked surprised. 'Not the Jonas O'Neill who wrote *Dragon Land*?'

'Yes. It's the same man,' I said. 'I met him at a book signing in Hong Kong.'

I always like to think she cheered up from that first meeting, as she confessed she hadn't made any friends.

'What about your husband, Elsie? He must know lots of people. Does he take you out to meet anyone?'

Her face fell. 'No, he doesn't, Lizzie. The kind of people he meets aren't suited to me, he tells me. Anyway, I hardly see him for days on end. He goes out drinking in the American Café every night, and although he comes home in the early hours of the morning, he's gone out by the time I get up.'

One afternoon Ping Li and I were sitting on the veranda when a car drew up. Lorna-May Hamilton stepped out.

'I was passing and I thought I would hand this invitation to you instead of posting it.'

She was dressed in a cream linen dress with cream sandals and cream cotton gloves. She looked as if she had stepped out of the front cover of a magazine.

'Hello, Mrs Hamilton,' I said. 'May I introduce my neighbour, Madame Zheng.'

She cast a cool gaze at Ping Li, but made no welcoming gesture to her.

Ping Li stood up. 'I must get back, Lizzie. I'll see you later.'

Lorna-May waited until Ping Li had disappeared through the garden before sitting down. 'I'm having a birthday party next Saturday at the racecourse and I would like you and Jonas to come.'

'A birthday party?' I was surprised she had come here to ask us, as I was sure we weren't in her social circle.

'Yes, it's my twenty-eighth birthday and Conrad wants to celebrate it with our friends, so please tell me you'll both come.'

246

I wasn't sure what Jonas's plans were for that day, so I said I would ask him and let her know.

'Just drop me a letter if you can come, and please call me Lorna-May.' She leaned forward in her seat. 'Can I give you a bit of advice, Lizzie?'

I nodded.

'I couldn't help but see you've become friendly with the native servants.'

I was confused. 'The native servants?'

'Yes, that Chinese woman who was sitting here. I personally never get friendly with my servants and I don't even know their names. I have girl one and girl two, plus the cook, who is just called the cook.'

'Madame Zheng isn't my servant; she's my good friend and neighbour.'

'Well, we must keep ourselves to ourselves here in the International Settlement and not consort with the Chinese population.'

I was furious at this attitude. 'Lorna-May, has it never occurred to you that it's us who are living in their country and not the other way round?'

Her eyes narrowed and she clamped her scarlet lips together. 'I hope you're not a Communist, Lizzie.'

I was speechless.

'It's just that here in China there is the National Army under Chiang Kai-shek and the rebel army led by the Communist Mao Zedong. Conrad and I have met Chiang Kai-shek and his wife Meiling. She is part of the powerful Soong family.' After that statement she stood up. 'Well, I must get away as I have an appointment with my hairdresser, but let me know if you can come to the party.'

That night I mentioned the visit to Jonas.

'I've never gone to any of her parties,' he said, 'but maybe we should go to this one, as you'll meet lots of people. And another thing: as far as I know Lorna-May has been twenty-eight for the last five years, so it should be a laugh.'

'She called me a Communist, Jonas, because I'm friendly with Ping Li.'

Jonas laughed. 'Well, you'd better watch out she doesn't set Chiang Kai-shek onto you, as she keeps peppering her talk with his name. It's almost as if they are old friends.' He became serious. 'I want you to meet as many people as possible because when I have to go away I want you to have friends you can call on if you need any help.'

So it was arranged that we would go to the birthday bash at the racecourse. Jonas said it was the place where the rich and powerful members of Shanghai society gathered. 'They go there to the races, or to play cricket or join the swimming club. It's the social hub of Shanghai.'

Personally I didn't want to be part of the social set, but if it meant meeting as many people as possible, I thought, then perhaps I should make the effort. The only thing was I didn't own a suitable wardrobe of fashionable clothes. Ping Li came to my aid, however, and made me a lovely evening dress of purple shantung silk.

'I bought the material at the department store and you will look wonderful at the party,' she said. When I went to pay for it, she shook her head and held her hands together as if in prayer. 'No, no, it is a gift from me to you because you are my neighbour and my friend.'

I mentioned to Jonas the dilemma over payment, but he said I should accept the gift. 'You can always repay her some other time with a favour or something of the kind.'

With that in mind, I gladly accepted the dress. It fitted me perfectly. Ping Li had to make a slight adjustment to the waistband, but everything else was fine. I bought a pair of purple suede ankle-strap sandals from the store and I looked forward to Lorna-May's party.

On the Friday, I asked Elsie what she was going to wear on the night, but she shook her head. 'We've not been invited, Lizzie.'

I was puzzled. 'But Lorna-May said it was her friends and neighbours who were going, and surely you and Ronnie are neighbours.'

'I really don't mind not being asked. We went to one party when I first arrived, but Ronnie became so drunk that I was embarrassed and we've never been asked to another one.'

'Maybe Ronnie will take you out for the evening instead, Elsie.'

She looked evasive and said, 'Maybe he will.'

On the Saturday night, Alex picked us up in his car. He looked despondent. 'Sue Lin can't make it, as she is away following up a story for the paper.'

Jonas was in a joking mood when he said not to worry, we would sit together with me in the middle, but Alex didn't laugh or even smile.

I thought it would be an informal party with guests mixing with each other, but when we arrived at the club we found a huge dining table set out. There were place names on the table, and after we were handed a drink by the white-coated waiters we sat down at our allotted places.

To my surprise, I found out I wouldn't be sitting between Jonas and Alex but was placed next to Conrad Hamilton. I looked at Jonas when I sat down, and he shrugged his shoulders, as if to say he had nothing to do with it.

Lorna-May made her entrance like a film star. She was wearing a figure-hugging silver dress and high-heeled sandals. Her face was perfectly made up, with red lips and thin pencilled eyebrows. I don't know about the rest of the women at the table, but she made me feel like a country bumpkin, with my hair curling around my ears and wearing no make-up.

Jonas was sitting next to Lorna-May and Alex was placed beside a plump woman in a puce-coloured dress. I had only met Conrad once that night at the hotel and I had no idea what to say to him. However, by the time the first course was served I found he was a modest, charming man and very easy to talk to.

'Lorna-May tells me you've come here from Scotland?'

'Well, I left Dundee to work in Hong Kong, but after I married Jonas we came here.'

Conrad looked at me with surprise. 'I don't believe it. My great-grandfather came from Dundee originally. He was called

Robert Conrad Hamilton and he worked in a bank there before emigrating to America as a young man. He was the one who made the family banking dynasty as it is now. Well, would you believe it, what a surprise.'

I had to tell him all about my life there and my family history, and before I knew it the meal was over and the company moved into the large room where a small band was playing for dancing.

As Jonas swept me across the floor, he said, 'You were having a great conversation with Conrad. I think Lorna-May was jealous, not only because of Conrad's attention but you were easily the most beautiful woman in the room.'

I said he was biased, but added, 'You won't believe this, Jonas, but his great-grandfather was a Dundee man who emigrated to America and founded the family fortune.'

'I always said if one stood on the street in Shanghai you would meet people from every corner of the world, and that goes to show how true it is.'

I noticed Alex sitting alone and we went to join him. When he mentioned he was going home, we also thanked our hosts and made our way back to the house. Alex dropped us off, but said he was tired and just wanted to get home. I knew he had a small apartment above his photography workshop and that Sue Lin often spent the night there, but she wouldn't tonight, obviously, and Alex must have felt depressed by her absence. I wished they could get together as a married couple, but Sue Lin seemingly put her career first, or maybe she had an aversion to marriage.

The next morning while Jonas shut himself away with his typewriter, I sat on the veranda with Ping Li and Elsie and told them everything about the previous night.

'Your dress was admired, Ping Li, and I wouldn't be surprised if you get loads of orders for dresses'.

'I wouldn't make them, Lizzie. I just make things for my good friends and the customers at the department store.'

38

THE MISSION

A fortnight later, at the beginning of July, Jonas and Alex set off to cover a story about Japanese activity in Manchuria, now called Manchukuo, but before he left he said he would be back in time to celebrate our first wedding anniversary in August.

I watched as the car set off, with Alex's camera and tripod in the back, and I suddenly felt so alone. Jonas had warned me that he would be going away from time to time, as it was his job as a freelance journalist to write the stories while Alex captured the scenes on his camera.

Ping Li had gone to the store with a box of her dresses, so I decided to go into town and look around the shops. It was late afternoon when I dropped into one of the cafés for a cup of tea and was surprised to see Lorna-May sitting at one of the tables. She waved me over.

'I've had such a hard day with shopping,' she said, pointing to the pile of packages at her feet, 'so I just dropped into the nearest place for a cool drink.'

I was also feeling the heat, as it was an unusually warm autumn day, but Lorna-May looked cool and unruffled and not in the least hot and bothered.

'I should have brought the car with me, but I find the streets so crowded with people and carts and rickshaws that it's too much of a bother. I'm waiting for Conrad to come and pick me up.'

I ordered tea when the waitress came for my order, but was surprised when Lorna-May ordered a gin and tonic with lime juice.

She saw my face and she said, 'I'm just worn out, so I need a reviving drink.' She lit up one of her cigarettes and sipped her drink while I finished my tea.

'Will Conrad be coming soon for you?'

She shrugged her slim shoulders and blew smoke out from her cigarette. Just then I spotted Elsie as she stood hesitantly at the door. I waved, and she walked past the tables to where we were sitting, but came to a stop when she noticed I wasn't alone.

Lorna-May looked annoyed and whispered, 'Oh, don't let that wishy-washy woman come over here. She never looks after herself and it looks like she has been wearing that dress in her bed, and as for her hair . . .' She made a little moue.

Determined to ignore her, I called Elsie over. 'Come and have a cup of tea, Elsie.'

Elsie sat down on the edge of her seat.

I gave her a smile. 'I was going to come to see you later today, as Jonas is away for a week or two.'

Lorna-May had nodded to Elsie when she sat down, but she now ignored her as she took out her powder compact and touched up her lipstick, which, in my opinion, needed touched up judging by the bright-red lipstick ring on her glass.

Thankfully a car drew up and Lorna-May stood, gathering her packages, and went out of the door.

I let out a sigh of relief, and Elsie laughed. 'She's the kind of woman you're always ready to see the back of.'

I asked her if she was all right. 'Were you looking for someone, Elsie?'

Her face went bright red. 'I was hoping to catch Ronnie after his work and before he goes into the bar of the American Café, but he didn't show up, so I'll just go home on my own.'

'Why don't you come back with me and have a meal, then maybe we can go to the cinema. What do you think?'

'Normally I would love to do that, but I usually go to the

Mission church school this evening. I help out with the refugee children once a week.'

'Why don't I come with you?' I said, and she nodded eagerly.

I had heard of the Mission church and school, but had never been there. Elsie explained as we walked along the busy street, dodging hand carts and the pyjama-clad Chinamen with their loads on the bamboo poles.

'The two women who run it come from Edinburgh and the minister is their brother. I got to know them when I first arrived here, as my mother said she knew them. Their names are Betsy and Jeannie Miller, and the brother is David.'

When we reached the Mission, it was crowded with children and families who were lined up waiting for some food. Elsie put on her apron and handed one to me, and we dished out portions of rice into the waiting bowls.

Betsy introduced herself and said, 'There are a lot of people coming from the north where the Japanese have set up their new territory.'

I asked her where all these people would end up.

'They'll have relatives here in Shanghai or else they'll move further south to some of the other cities, but it's a tragedy that they've had to leave their homes behind.'

Afterwards as we walked home, I said, 'I knew there was a problem with refugees, Elsie, but I never imagined it was this bad until I saw it at the Mission. It's a terrible world.'

'A lot of them will disappear into the back streets here, and hopefully they'll get work and food and somewhere to stay. If not, they have the Mission to help them.'

When we reached my house, Elsie said she wouldn't come in. 'Maybe Ronnie is at home,' she said, but I noticed there was no enthusiasm in her voice.

I spent a sleepless night without Jonas lying beside me, and in the early morning I was sitting on the veranda with my tea when Elsie came to the gate.

'I thought we could maybe spend some time going round the Yu Garden,' she said. I got dressed, and by the time we were ready to leave Ping Li appeared and we asked her to come with us. Looking back years later I was to remember that happy time as we explored the garden and the temples, and then the little side streets where Ping Li knew the best places to shop.

'I grew up around these streets,' she said, 'but sadly my parents are dead and as I was an only child I have no relatives living here.'

Elsie and I looked at her with sympathy.

'I know how it feels, Ping Li, to have no parents, as mine are also dead, but I do have a wonderful aunt,' I said.

Elsie screwed up her face. 'I still have my mother, but she can be a right menace at times.'

Ping Li sounded shocked. 'No, Elsie, you must be grateful you still have her to cherish and look after you.'

Elsie muttered that she was grateful, but as it was lunchtime we stopped being morbid and made our way to a tiny restaurant that I would have passed if Ping Li hadn't mentioned going inside. The interior was dim and cave-like, but the tables all looked clean. The owner came to greet us and she welcomed Ping Li as an old friend. We had bowls of soup with tiny dumplings and it was delicious.

Elsie said Ping Li was teaching her to cook like this and I said I would like lessons as well. Ping Li looked gratified, as if we had paid her a huge compliment, and she said she would show us some basic Chinese meals.

One thing that surprised me that day was the fact Elsie was able to buy some jewellery in the bazaar. It was only a short time ago she had said her husband didn't give her any spending money.

As if she knew what I was thinking, she explained. 'I got frustrated with no money to call my own, but Ronnie was adamant he held on to the purse strings, so I wrote to his father a few weeks ago and told him about my situation. I said I wanted money put into my own bank account every six months and I got my first instalment last week.' She looked so happy when she told us this. 'I've not to let Ronnie know about it and I don't intend to tell him.'

I wondered what kind of marriage she had, with secrets and subterfuge. I couldn't imagine keeping anything from Jonas, but I had to admit that Ronnie Lomax was a bully and an absent, controlling husband.

The day soon passed and we had loads of laughs, and these trips continued until Jonas was due to come home. In the evening Elsie and I would go to the cinema and watch American films. We especially liked Tarzan films and we both giggled at Tarzan's athletic body. Elsie said if he appeared at her front door she wouldn't turn him away, and we both laughed so loudly that some of the cinema patrons turned round to look at us, which set us off again, only this time we tried to muffle our laughs.

Then, two days before our first wedding anniversary, Jonas arrived back with Alex. He looked tired and pale, but after a few hours in the house he was back to normal. I asked him if he was ill, but he said it had been a harrowing journey because of some of the sights they had witnessed. When I quizzed him, he just said that the Japanese army in the north was quite ruthless and he hoped they wouldn't be coming out of their territory, Manchukuo.

I had made a special meal for our anniversary and had lit two candles to give the room a romantic look. I had a special reason to make everything perfect. Jonas grinned when he saw the candles, and after the meal he produced a bottle of brandy.

'Let's drink a toast to the wonderful first year of marriage,' he said, going to look for the glasses in the cabinet.

'I won't have a drink Jonas, but you have one.'

We settled on the sofa and I said, 'I've been to see the doctor in the hospital and we're going to have a baby. It's due next April or early May.' I felt a bit apprehensive as I didn't know how Jonas would take this news, but he gathered me in his arms and said that it was the best news he had heard in weeks.

He lifted his glass. 'A toast to our baby, Lizzie, and to a wonderful family life for the three of us.' He drank his brandy and I had a glass of water.

The next night we had Zheng Yan and Ping Li in for a meal

and Jonas announced he was to be a father. Zheng Yan shook his hand.

'That's good news, Jonas and Lizzie.'

I looked at Ping Li, but she merely nodded. 'I guessed as much ages ago,' she said.

'But you couldn't have,' I said. 'I've only just found out myself.'

'Do you remember the dress I made for you, the purple one?' When I nodded she said, 'I made the dress to the measurements exactly as I took them a few weeks ago, but then on the night I had to enlarge the waistband a bit. So I guessed that was the reason: a baby.'

Zheng Yan smiled at her. 'There's not much gets past my wife, Lizzie.'

I had to smile. I remembered her taking my measurements before Lorna-May's invitation, but that had been for a dress I had planned to buy at the Star store.

The next day I told Elsie, and although she looked pleased she also seemed a bit wistful, as if this was what she wanted with her husband. I also wrote letters to Margaret, Maisie, Laura, Pat, Marie and Sandy, so the news was out. Jonas and I were thrilled that we were to become a family.

39

LORNA-MAY'S
NEW YEAR PARTY

Lorna-May came to the house after Christmas to invite us to her New Year party at the Palace Hotel. 'We like to keep our western culture alive here and celebrate our New Year on the 31st of December. Conrad and I hope you can both come.'

By now I was five months pregnant, and although I didn't have a big bump I wasn't in the mood for going out socially. 'I don't think we can manage to come, Lorna-May, as we just planned a quiet time with Elsie and Zheng Yan and Ping Li.'

Lorna-May looked at me as if I was daft. 'You and Jonas must celebrate the end of 1935. It's one of the biggest social events of the year and it's usually myself who organises it.'

I said I would ask Jonas and let her know, and she left in a huff. 'Well, I have to know the numbers so the hotel can cater for it,' she said as she got into her car.

I watched as she drove away, then went to see Jonas, who was in the study. I mentioned the invitation. Jonas said it was up to me, but maybe it would do me the world of good to have a night out. I said I would think about it.

Elsie arrived the next morning, clutching a thick piece of cardboard. 'We've been asked to Lorna-May's party and I'm not sure if I want to go. Ronnie said he is going, so no doubt I'll have to make the effort, but I'll not enjoy it. Are you going, Lizzie?'

She looked so uncertain that I knew she was hoping we would be there to keep her company.

'Well, maybe we'll go for a few hours, but we won't be staying long.' Lorna-May's parties tended to last well into the early morning and there was usually a lot of drinking at them. 'I'll have to explain to Ping Li that we'll not be able to see them, but I do know she's planning a meal for the Chinese New Year and we'll definitely go to that.'

'I wonder why the Chinese have a different new year from us,' said Elsie. 'You would think it would be the same everywhere at the end of the year.'

'When I was in Hong Kong, an old friend, Sandy, explained it all to me. According to Chinese culture it's to do with the twelve animals. This is the Year of the Dog and next year it will be the turn of the Boar. My baby will be born under that sign and Ping Li is making a horoscope for him or her. I don't really believe in it myself, but she does, and I don't want to hurt her feelings.'

Elsie sighed. 'I sometimes wish I was having a baby, but when Ronnie comes home drunk then I'm glad I don't.'

I was wondering what to wear at the party, but when I tried on my silver-grey dress I was delighted to find that it still fitted me.

I could hardly believe another year was almost over and that this time next year we would be a family. Before going to the hotel we spent a couple of hours with Zheng Yan and Ping Li.

'I'm sorry we can't spend the evening with you,' I said, but Ping Li said it wasn't important.

'Our New Year is the main time and we will be together that night.'

Alex and Sue Lin came to collect us with their car and we set off for the hotel. By the time we got there at nine o'clock, the hotel ballroom was full of revellers. Sue Lin looked beautiful in a shimmering turquoise, tightly fitted dress and I felt so plump standing beside her.

Lorna-May and Conrad came over and welcomed us, and I

looked around the room to see if Elsie had arrived. The band was playing a foxtrot and quite a few couples were on the dance floor, but the four of us found a comfortable seat and sat down to watch them.

At ten o'clock there was still no sign of Elsie, and I assumed she had changed her mind. Then a commotion arose at the far end of the room and I saw it was Ronnie. He had obviously been celebrating earlier in the evening and he was arguing with the waiter. Elsie was standing by his side, and even from that distance I could see her face was flushed with embarrassment.

Conrad went up to Ronnie and led him to a seat in the far corner, while I waved to Elsie. She hurried up and came to sit with us.

'I didn't want to come, Lizzie,' she said. 'Ronnie has been drinking all day, but he made such a scene when I said I wasn't going. He said we would never be accepted by Shanghai society if I didn't mix with them.'

Alex and Jonas looked at each other but said nothing, while I was annoyed at Ronnie for making out it was Elsie's fault when it was obviously his. I looked over at him as he sat slumped on his chair. He was dressed in a smart suit, and he was certainly very handsome, with his dark hair flopping over his brow and his boyish face. I could well imagine Elsie falling in love with him during their university days.

At twelve o'clock, balloons cascaded down from the ceiling and champagne corks popped loudly as we all wished each other a Happy New Year. Elsie looked as if this new year would be unhappy, like the previous ones, but Alex kissed Sue Lin and Jonas put his arm around me.

'Happy New Year, Lizzie,' he said softly. 'This year we will have our son or daughter.'

'Do you mind if it is a girl, Jonas?'

He laughed 'I don't mind at all.'

We left soon after, but we had to take Elsie with us, as Ronnie had disappeared. 'He's probably sleeping it off in bed at home,' she said. However, when we dropped her at her house it was all in darkness, so Jonas went in with her. When he came back to the car, he said there was no sign of Ronnie, but Elsie had said she would go straight to bed.

The next day we had a meal with Zheng Yan and his wife. Ping Li wanted to know how I was keeping. She asked me this at least once a week, much to Jonas's amusement.

'I think she'll be a nervous wreck by the time the baby is born,' he said.

During the meal I was worried about Elsie, but it wasn't until the early evening I managed to go and see her. She wasn't in, and I was on my way back home when she came up the road. She looked pale and tired, so I went back home with her.

'Is everyone talking about Ronnie's behaviour last night?' She sounded so weary that I felt sympathy for her.

'I don't know, Elsie. I haven't spoken to anyone who was at the party. We've spent most of the day with Zheng Yan and Ping Li. What did you do today?'

'I've been at the Mission all day, helping Betsy and Jeannie. You know something, Lizzie, this is an awful place. We're living in relative luxury while the Chinese refugees don't have a roof over their heads or know where their next meal is coming from. It makes me want to cry, it really does.'

I linked my arm in hers. 'Come on, I'll make you a cup of tea and you can relax after your busy day.'

The house was still empty when we reached the door. She stood inside the living room. 'If you don't mind, I think I'll go straight to bed.'

I left her and returned home. Jonas was sitting reading a book. 'How is Elsie?'

I was so angry. 'If I could get hold of that husband of hers, I think I would knock some sense into him.'

'It wouldn't work, Lizzie. I remember when her mother was here and she tried to do that, but she didn't succeed, so what chance does anyone else have? Elsie will have to work her problems out for herself, I'm afraid.'

I went into the kitchen for a glass of water and the baby gave a mighty kick. I put my hand over my stomach and counted my blessings.

It was just before the Chinese New Year when Lorna-May called at the house. Jonas and Alex were away on a story, but they said they would be back before the festivities. Jonas loved this Chinese festival, with its dragons and fireworks and general merriment.

Lorna-May said, 'I'm driving over to the French Concession for a bit of shopping. Would you like to come?'

If Jonas had been at home, I would have said no, but as I was on my own I went to get my jacket. Lorna-May was a good driver and she was able to dodge all the obstacles on the road.

'I learned to drive in New York when I was eighteen,' she said. Her voice became wistful. 'I wish I was eighteen again, Lizzie, don't you?'

I said I was quite happy at the age I was now.

'That's because you have a loving husband and you're about to become a mother. Oh, don't get me wrong, Conrad's a good husband, but his work comes first, and as for becoming pregnant, well, I wouldn't want to ruin my figure. It's a well-known fact that women go fat after they've had children.'

I was shocked. 'Surely that doesn't matter as long as you've got a healthy baby.'

'Well, maybe you don't think so, but I do know it matters.'

I was glad she changed the subject as we drove into the French Concession. The streets were wide and tree-lined and it looked like a very pleasant place to stay. I said as much to Lorna-May.

'Oh yes, it is. The streets are set out like French boulevards and I would love to live here. I did ask Conrad to buy a house here, but he likes being near his work.'

She parked the car and we set off down one of the streets that were lined with shops. Lorna-May spent ages looking in the windows before deciding on going into a classy-looking ladies' dress shop, where she bought a lovely day dress. When I heard the price, I almost fainted. It was as much as my monthly household accounts, but she said as we came out of the shop, 'Conrad likes to see me looking well dressed.'

We got back into the car and drove back through the leafy boulevards to the International Settlement.

After she left, Ping Li came in with bowls of tea and I told her about my trip.

'Although I was born here,' she said, 'I've never been to Frenchland.'

'Frenchland?'

She nodded. 'That's what it's called.'

40

THE YEAR OF THE BOAR

I was grateful I was feeling well during my pregnancy, and apart from a few bouts of nausea in the early months I didn't feel any different from normal. I did feel a bit tired in the evening and I was glad to put my feet up on the sofa, but I remembered my mother telling me one day that she had suffered from early morning sickness when she was expecting me and for some reason I had thought I would be the same. Thankfully I wasn't. Elsie and I would go to see the doctor at the hospital every month, where he was pleased with my progress. I was relieved about that, because I had no idea what lay ahead. I knew the basics of childbirth, but I felt what all expectant mothers feel: how will I cope with a tiny baby?

During those final months I felt I was on a kind of hiatus, as if the rest of the world was passing me by. Jonas was still busy with his book. Alex was a regular visitor to the house, but if I went out it was usually with Ping Li or Elsie.

Then on 4 February, just as the Chinese community in Shanghai was getting ready to celebrate the New Year, I was laid low with a bad bout of influenza. Every bone in my body ached and I was glad to stay in bed, which was so unlike me.

Jonas brought me hot drinks and Ping Li carried in bowls of herbal tea, which she swore by. 'This is the remedy for influenza,' she said as I sipped the bitter liquid. Whether or not it was because of her faith in the cure, I did begin to feel better, but I was very weak and had a high temperature.

Jonas called the doctor in, and he said it would just run its course and that the baby was fine. That was our main worry, and I spent sleepless nights fretting about the future as the rest of the city celebrated the Year of the Boar.

I hadn't felt the baby move very much over the last couple of days, but as I lay awake with Jonas sleeping soundly beside me and the sound of fireworks exploding in the night sky, I suddenly felt a vigorous kick in my abdomen and I relaxed. All was well, I thought. As if to make up for the days of inactivity, the baby turned and moved as if he or she had been wakened up by all the noise.

Thankfully, after almost ten days in the house, I felt well enough to go outside, and although the air was humid and sticky it was better than being cooped up. Jonas said he was taking me to the Yu Garden to recuperate. We left in the early morning, when we knew the gardens would be quiet, and it was so peaceful sitting on a stone bench looking at the temples.

Jonas held my hand. 'Are you happy living here, Lizzie?'

I looked at him in surprise. 'Yes, I am. I would be happy anywhere as long as you were with me.'

'It's just that I see the worst side of China with my work. All the fighting between the Communists and Chiang Kai-shek's Nationalist army, and now Japan seems intent on making inroads in the north and I have a fear they won't be happy with that.'

'But this is the International Settlement, so surely they couldn't come here with their armies.'

He smiled. 'Let's hope not. I sometimes worry about having a young baby growing up with all this conflict, and it's not only happening here but in Europe too, with the rise of the Nazi Party.'

I suddenly felt cold. 'Surely Germany won't start another war, not after the carnage of the last one. My father died in the trenches and my mother never got over his death. I can never understand why people can't live in peace with one another.'

'Let's go and have some tea in one of the teahouses,' Jonas suggested. 'It'll stop me being pessimistic.'

We moved through the garden, which was beginning to get busy, and went into the teahouse. Although the tea was hot I still felt cold, and I was glad when we got back home and I was in familiar surroundings again.

Later that week, Elsie and I went for my first visit to the hospital after my bout of influenza. Once again I was relieved when the doctor said all was well. 'You're a strong young healthy woman, Mrs O'Neill, and you'll have a healthy baby.'

It was when we were walking back that Elsie suddenly stopped and looked across the road. I followed her gaze, but the street was bustling with people and traffic and it looked very much like it always did.

'What's wrong, Elsie?' I asked.

She shook her head. 'I thought I saw Ronnie.'

'Do you want to go and see if it's him?' I suggested, but she said no.

'Maybe I made a mistake, but it looked like him. The strange thing is he was with a dark-haired woman and she was holding on to his arm.'

'But surely he will be at work in the mill, won't he?'

'Yes – at least that's what he said when he left this morning.'

'Well, maybe, if it was him, the woman could be a colleague from the mill. You did say there was an English manager in charge. Maybe it's his daughter or wife.'

Elsie gave a deep sigh. 'Yes, that's probably it, and I'm not sure now if it was him.'

So we continued along the road until we reached the house. I asked her to come in and we were soon sitting on the veranda with our tea.

'Can I tell you something, Lizzie? I wouldn't want it to get out.'

'Oh, I wouldn't repeat a confidence, Elsie.'

She sat without talking for a while, just staring at her cup. Then she took a deep breath and said, 'Ronnie and I don't have a normal marriage, Lizzie. For the past six months or so he's been sleeping in the spare bedroom. He doesn't get in until the early hours of the morning and then I only see him for a half-hour before he goes to work. I've tried talking to him, but he says everything is all right and that once we leave Shanghai our marriage will get back on track. He says it's just because he's unhappy living here and working in the mill.'

I didn't know what to say, but I knew I had to comment on her distress. 'Can he not write to his father and tell him about this unhappiness? After all, his son's marriage is more important than running cotton mills.'

'I suggested that, Lizzie, but he just shouted at me and said if I went behind his back with my stories he would leave me right away and I would have to fend for myself.'

'Charming man,' I thought to myself. 'Well, you mustn't give in to him, Elsie. You must get him to agree on a solution to this horrible situation.'

As she left she said she would have another talk with him, but we both knew it wouldn't make any difference. The house felt quiet after she had gone, but I couldn't stop worrying about her. Ronnie seemed to be one of those young wealthy oafs who thought of nothing but themselves.

As I stood up, I felt the baby give another kick.

41

THE NEW ARRIVAL

I was ten days over my due date for my baby's birth, and although I wasn't worried I knew Jonas was. He was due to go off with Alex to Nanking, where rumours of people dying from hunger were coming through.

'I've told Alex I can't go,' he said. 'I don't want to leave you on your own when the baby arrives.'

I would have liked him to have been with me as well, but I had married him knowing what his work was, so I said I would be fine. 'I'll have Ping Li and Elsie to help me, so you're not to worry about me.'

He hesitated, and I repeated that I would be fine, so he reluctantly phoned Alex to say they could leave the following morning.

After he went I was suddenly not so confident, but I knew I was a strong woman who could stand up against anything – before it struck me that the baby could be born in the night, when I would be alone.

I mentioned this to Elsie, and she said she would move in with me until after the birth and I was so grateful to her. I was worried what Ronnie might say, but she dismissed this by saying he probably wouldn't notice, which I thought was very sad. Later that afternoon she arrived with a small suitcase and I told her she could have the small bedroom.

By seven o'clock that evening I had started to have some pain, but it didn't seem to be caused by the contractions I was told I would have, so I went to bed as usual at eleven o'clock. At four o'clock in the morning I knew I had to get to the hospital, but by then Elsie had woken up and had ordered a taxi.

She fussed around, getting me dressed and making sure I had everything I needed in my suitcase. When she was putting my shoes on, I felt a wave of pain that made me gasp out loud and Elsie rushed to the window to see if the taxi was there.

'I told them a baby was due so to make sure they hurried up,' she said, looking anxiously towards the door. I had another pain and had to sit down, but thankfully we heard the sound of a car drawing up and she rushed to the door.

I found it hard walking down the path, but the young British driver helped me, while Elsie followed behind with the case. It wasn't a long drive to the hospital, but at the time I remember thinking it took ages, as one contraction followed another just minutes apart.

As I was taken to the delivery room I silently thought how stupid I had been letting Jonas go away. So much for being a strong-minded woman who knew all the answers. I would have laughed, but I didn't feel like it at the time. The pain seemed to take over my body, and I was glad when I was lying in the bed and the doctor, who was Scottish and originally from Inverness, was by my side, along with the Chinese midwife.

'The baby's isn't coming yet,' he said, which surprised me so much I must have groaned out loud.

I managed to lift my head to look at him. 'I thought the baby was going to be born either in the taxi or the house, doctor.'

He smiled at me. 'First-time babies usually don't come that quickly, but you're in the best place and it won't be too long now.'

Another wave of pain. When he said it wouldn't be long, I wondered how long he meant. The midwife was soothing, as she kept me informed about what was happening. I had read a lot of books on childbirth, but of course they'd never mentioned this level of pain.

I wondered if Elsie had taken the taxi back home and hoped that she had, especially as I was convinced the baby was going to be born before I reached the hospital. I remembered telling her over and over again that I wasn't going to make it in time. Now the doctor seemed amused by my prediction.

It was a hot, humid night and my gown was sticking to my body, but the midwife cooled me down with a wet cloth. I was grateful to her, so much so that if I had been dying at that point I would have left her my gold bangles in gratitude.

The delivery room was small, with white tiled walls and a bright light overhead. I asked if I could have a drink of water, and the woman went to a small sink and filled a small glass. I gulped it down like I was lost in the desert and then immediately felt terrible that I was losing control of my manners. Then another, stronger pain engulfed me and the midwife hurried from the room only to return with the doctor.

'Ah, yes,' he said. 'Baby's about to enter the world, Mrs O'Neill!'

I almost said amen to that, but his statement was followed by another two waves of pain before I heard the cries of my baby.

'You've got a lusty wee lad, Mrs O'Neill. He's got a great pair of lungs on him.'

The midwife placed my son beside me and I gazed in wonder at this scrap of new life I had brought forth into the world. I couldn't explain my feelings, but I was bursting with pride.

Within the hour I was in a small side room and Elsie came in to see me. I was so pleased to see her I almost burst into tears, but instead I smiled weakly. 'Jonas and I have a son, Elsie.'

She smiled at me. 'Yes, I know, the doctor told me. He was born at seven o'clock on the tenth of May.'

Seven o'clock. I had lost all sense of time. I had been in labour for over three hours. 'I thought he was going to be born when I woke up with that awful pain, Elsie. If I had known, I wouldn't have rushed you like that. And that poor taxi driver, what a fuss I made.'

'It's better to be in hospital in time, Lizzie. After all, how do we know how long it takes for a baby to be born?'

I laughed. 'You're right. I'll know next time what to expect.'

After she left I fell asleep but was woken up by the nurse, who was carrying my baby in a woollen blanket. 'It's time for your baby's feed,' she said cheerfully. I could hardly keep my eyes open.

Later that day I had Elsie and Ping Li visit me. Ping Li had made a beautiful set of baby clothes, which were very much admired by the nurses when they came into the room.

'Do you have a name for the baby, Lizzie?' asked Elsie.

I shook my head. 'I'll wait till Jonas comes home and we'll choose one together.'

After they left I had a visit from Betsy and Jeannie Miller, who said they had seen the baby in the small nursery and he was lovely. 'He was crying when we saw him, Lizzie. He's got a great pair of lungs on him.'

I smiled at them. 'That's what the doctor said.'

The following day I was beginning to feel less tired, when Lorna-May swept in bearing a large bunch of sweet-smelling flowers. 'How are the new mother and baby doing?' she said, gazing at my nightgown, which was stained with a small patch of dried-on milk.

'It's the most amazing feeling, Lorna-May. I can't really describe it to you, but to have a new scrap of life brought into the world is earth-shattering.'

'I see, so you're feeling well.'

'I've never felt better.'

She stood up. 'Well, I'll give these flowers to the nurse to put in a vase, and I'm glad you're looking so well. Oh, by the way, Conrad sends his regards.'

'Dear Lorna-May,' I thought, 'did you think you would find me looking like I'm at death's door?' Then I remembered how I'd felt like I was at death's door during the birth, so I couldn't blame Lorna-May for thinking that I would look as if I was.

A couple of days later Jonas rushed in, looking contrite and worried. 'I knew I should never have left you, Lizzie.'

'Have you seen our son?' I asked.

'Yes, I have, and he's crying. The nurse says he has a good pair of lungs on him.'

I burst out laughing. 'The doctor said that to me and the nurses said the same thing to Elsie and Ping Li. He seems to be famous in here for his good pair of lungs.'

Jonas had also brought a bunch of flowers, and I asked the nurse to put them where I could see them.

'The doctor said you can go home tomorrow, so I will come and pick you up.' Just as he reached the door, he said, 'Were you all right with the birth, Lizzie?'

'Do you know, Jonas, I don't remember much about it.' The truth was I didn't remember the pain or the waiting; all I recalled was the moment the baby was placed beside me.

'I love you, Lizzie,' he said, 'and I love my son. I'll be back in to see you tonight and then tomorrow we'll all go home.'

'That will be wonderful, Jonas. I love you too, and our son, and we'll be a family when we get home.'

42

PETER FLINT O'NEILL

I had ordered a cot and pram from the department store, and Elsie said she would be in the house to catch the delivery man when he came. When she came to see me on my last day in hospital, she said everything had been delivered.

'You should have seen the delivery man, Lizzie. He was a five-foot-tall Chinese man of about seventy years old, and it was so funny seeing him wheeling the pram up the path. When the cot came, he had another old man with him to help carry it. I gave them a good tip, and they kept thanking me and saying they hoped I had a lovely son.' She had been laughing when telling me this, but her face fell at the last sentence.

'You'll have a family as well, Elsie, it just takes time,' I said, wishing I could wave a magic wand and give her a loving husband like Jonas and a child of her own, but even I knew it wasn't likely to happen.

Jonas came with Alex's car to take us home, and we found Ping Li had filled the house with flowers. The baby was sleeping as Jonas carried him into the bedroom and placed him in his cot. Ping Li had made a beautiful quilted cover, and as we both stood looking down on our baby, I suddenly filled up with emotion and held tightly to Jonas.

'I sometimes think I shouldn't be so happy, Jonas, not when other people are unhappy.'

He took my hand and led me into the lounge and made me

sit with my feet up on the sofa. 'I'll make us a cup of tea, so just you rest.'

When we were sitting with our tea, Jonas said, 'I know how you feel, Lizzie. Alex and I see so much tragedy and suffering amongst the Chinese people. In the countryside around Nanking there's been a famine and people are starving, but what do the warlords do? Raise the rents for the farmers, that's what they do.'

'We really are blessed, Jonas. We live in their beautiful country, but we are cocooned from all the hardships they suffer. It isn't fair.'

Jonas's mouth twisted in disgust. 'I know, but when is life ever fair, Lizzie? I've seen babies die of hunger, and although I've always had so much pity for the people, now I have you and my son I don't think I can bear anything happening to either of you.'

I took his hand. 'Nothing will happen to us, not when we have you to look after us.'

I suddenly wanted to lighten his mood. 'We must choose a name, because we can't keep referring to him as a baby, especially when he's going to college: his peers will laugh at him.'

Jonas smiled. 'That's what I like about you, Lizzie. You make everything so much fun.'

I decided to tease him. 'Is that all you like about me?'

He blushed deep red. 'No, it isn't, as you well know.'

Gratified, I said, 'Well, what about our son's name? Do you want to call him after yourself?'

Jonas said he did not. 'I was nicknamed Jonah the whale at school, and although I always laughed about it, I didn't like it. What about your side of the family?'

'My father was called Peter, and I would like my maiden name as well.'

'Well, that settles it. Peter Flint O'Neill it is.'

'Won't his grandfather in Cork like to be included in his grandson's name?'

'No, I don't think so, because he is also called Jonas, as was his father before him. Anyway, as I said, I haven't had much contact with him since my mother died. He blamed me for her death, because he said that I broke her heart after I left to go to university.'

I hadn't heard that story before and it saddened me. 'Surely he didn't believe that?'

'Maybe not now, but he did at the time and he said some nasty things to me, so I left Ireland after university and came here. I do have an uncle and aunt who have a farm in the Borders near Dumfries and I got on well with them. The thing is, although I'm a writer I can't be bothered writing letters, which I know is awful.'

'Well, I will write to both your father and uncle and tell them about Peter and they'll be delighted.'

During that week we registered our son's name with the clerk in the registrar's office.

Ping Li came in every morning and she fussed over Peter like a mother hen. The slightest whimper from him had her rushing over and checking him to see what was wrong. She often came over in the evening, as she liked to help bathe him in his baby bath, then when it was time to put him down she would sit on the small nursing chair I had bought and sing him a lullaby. I had to keep a straight face, as she had a high-pitched sing-song way of singing, and Peter would open his eyes and gaze at her as if mesmerised.

'Ah, Peter likes Ping Li to sing to him, don't you, Peter?'

Zheng Yan would come with her to play mah-jong with Jonas and he kept telling his wife not to monopolise Peter.

'I do not monopolise Peter,' she said huffily. 'He likes me singing my lullabies.'

Those times were the stuff of lasting memories – I knew I would never forget those days.

Elsie was also a frequent visitor and she also liked to hold Peter, but she didn't sing to him; she merely rocked him to sleep with a contented smile on her face. She rarely mentioned Ronnie on these visits and I didn't want to bring back unhappy memories for her, so I didn't mention him either.

Most days I put Peter in his pram and Ping Li, Elsie and I would take him for a stroll along the Bund. It was a lovely place to walk, with the buildings on one side and the river on the other. It was always busy with pedestrians and traffic. The cotton mills lined the banks of the river, and the wharves and docks were a hive of activity, with people loading and unloading cargoes from the ships.

One day I was surprised when Elsie said she would go into the mill and see her husband. 'I'll give him a surprise and maybe he'll take me out for a meal, as he says he goes out to a café every day to eat.'

Ping Li wasn't with us that day, and as Elsie left, I turned and began to walk home. I had hardly gone a hundred yards when I heard the sound of running feet behind me. I turned and saw Elsie trying to catch up with me. She was crying.

I was alarmed. 'Is everything all right, Elsie?'

She shook her head and wiped the tears from her eyes. 'I spoke to the manager and he told me that Ronnie hadn't been into work for over a week.' She caught hold of my hand. 'It was so embarrassing, Lizzie. The man thought I knew he wasn't working, but when he saw how distressed I was he was so sympathetic. I feel such a fool. I should never have gone in.'

'You weren't to know. Have you any idea where Ronnie has been going instead of work?'

Her eyes grew hard. 'Oh, I have an idea, all right. He'll be at the American Café or the gambling tables somewhere. Another thing: when he came home last night, he left his shirt to be washed and it had lipstick on it and was smelling of perfume.'

I didn't have an answer to that. Instead I said, 'Let's go home, Elsie.'

'Home, is that what I call it?'

We walked in silence all the way back, but when we reached my house she said she wouldn't come in but would see me later.

I didn't realise how wonderful yet so demanding a new baby could be. The days seemed to pass in a daze. I spent that summer looking after Peter and Jonas, and writing letters and sending photographs to Margaret, Laura, Pat, and Marie and Sandy. I also got in contact with Jonas's father and uncle, and I was pleased when they wrote back with congratulations about Peter. I think Jonas was pleased to hear from his father, and I was grateful that we were in touch with his side of the family. As usual, Laura was miffed that I had beaten her in the motherhood stakes and she complained that her latest boyfriend didn't appear to be the marrying type.

I had asked her about Mike, but she said he had gone to a job in England after leaving university and although they still wrote to one another she felt they were drifting apart:

I've met this teacher who teaches at the Morgan Academy. His name is John and he is really very clever, but at the moment we are just friends. At least that's what he wants to be. Just friends.

I wrote back and said just to give him time, or that maybe Mike would come back to Dundee, as I knew he seemed really keen on her when they first met. I didn't tell her that her trouble was her impatience, as she wanted everything to happen right away.

Elsie never said anything more about Ronnie. I thought about how difficult relationships could be and was thankful I had met Jonas.

Alex was another one who was suffering from unrequited love, as Sue Lin, although she was always affectionate and friendly with him, was a true career woman who loved the life she was living. Some days she would dash in, give Peter a quick kiss and tell him what a lovely boy he was before drinking a cup of tea and rushing out again to follow up some story or other.

'I have to write up the latest incident with the Japanese. They were saying a delegation was insulted by Chinese civil servants and it's going to lead to a diplomatic row,' she said.

Ping Li had been sitting listening to her and she shook her head. 'That girl should learn to slow down and not rush about like that. One day it will be the death of her.'

'Jonas told me she's always been like that. I feel sorry for Alex, because he worships her.'

When I mentioned this to Alex, instead of laughing it off or shrugging his shoulders at her impetuousness, he became serious. 'This is what the Japanese government are doing: causing diplomatic incidents in order to take over more territory. I wouldn't trust them, as they are a dangerous lot.'

At that moment Peter started to cry, so I didn't answer him, but the remark hadn't gone unnoticed and I was worried about the serious expression on his face.

After his initial bouts of crying in the hospital, Peter became a placid baby and I couldn't help noticing how much he resembled my mother. Perhaps it was the colour of his eyes and hair, which were like hers, but sometimes I also caught an expression on his childish face that strengthened my belief.

I mentioned this to Ping Li, who said, 'I resembled my mother when I was a child, but now I'm not sure who I look like.'

Zheng Yan, who was sitting on the veranda with us, said fondly, 'You look like my wife, Ping Li.'

It never ceased to amaze me how simple the Chinese people were in their speech. To Zheng Yan, it didn't matter who Ping Li resembled. In fact, she could have looked like one of the dragons that fluttered on banners around the city; to him, she would just look like his wife.

Jonas and Alex had been busy on their new book and by the end of the year it was published. The title was *The Beating Heart of the Dragon* and it was a wonderful story about the ordinary people of China as they went about their daily lives, sometimes in the harshest of conditions and environments. Alex had taken stunning photographs to illustrate the people getting on with their work and leisure. Like their first book, it was a mixture of beautiful, placid scenes and horrendous places.

I was so proud of the both of them, and both the Chinese and foreign populations queued up to buy it.

One day Jonas said quite casually, 'Alex and I have to go to

Hong Kong to do some signings. Would you like to come with us?'

'Yes, I would, but can we take Peter with us?'

Jonas didn't look happy. 'Do you think Ping Li could maybe look after him, as we'll only be gone a week or two. It will mean a sea voyage and he might not like it.'

I said I wasn't sure, but I would think about it.

Ping Li was delighted when I mentioned this, but I didn't want to be separated from my son, although I didn't say so.

Jonas was pleased that I was going with him, but I wished I had an excuse not to go. It was strange how being a mother had made me so protective about our son. Before he was born I would have leapt at the chance to go with Jonas on a sea voyage, but the idea didn't seem so tempting this time.

I had our bags packed and we were planning on leaving the next day when Peter began crying through the night. When I picked him up, he had a fever.

'I must call the doctor out, Jonas,' I said, and he agreed.

The doctor came round and said Peter's temperature was over a hundred degrees. 'Just keep him cool by sponging him down with tepid water and I will call back in the morning.'

I stayed up all night and Peter slept in my arms.

Jonas tiptoed through. He looked worried. 'I think you should stay here with him, Lizzie.'

I nodded. Much as I loved my husband, there was no way I would have gone away, leaving Peter like that.

At dawn, Alex came round and Jonas said goodbye to us. He hesitated at the door. 'I think we'll postpone the trip, Lizzie, as I don't want to leave you both here on your own.'

'Honestly, Jonas, we'll be fine. The doctor will be here soon and I think Peter's temperature is down.'

By now Peter had fallen asleep, and although his face was still flushed he didn't seem to be so hot. I stood at the window and waved the two men away. Part of me wanted to go with them, but another part didn't. I knew I was responsible not only for myself but also for this small child who was now in his cot.

The doctor arrived at nine o'clock, but by then Peter seemed to be back to normal. I apologised to him. 'I'm sorry to have called you out through the night, but I was worried.'

The doctor said it was all right. 'Children do run these high temperatures. Sometimes it's serious and other times it's not. Peter seems to be fine now, but bring him to the surgery if he becomes unwell again.'

When Ping Li came in, Peter was playing with his toys and she looked disappointed at not having to look after him.

I said, 'Maybe you can look after him today, Ping Li?'

Her face broke into a smile as she picked him up and carried him to her house. She started to sing to him and he gave her his wide-eyed look, while I thankfully went back to bed.

43

THE CHRISTENING

Jonas had never mentioned getting Peter christened, but I broached the subject one morning. 'I'm thinking of asking the Reverend David Miller if he will christen Peter. What do you think, Jonas?'

He looked up from reading the morning paper, which was delivered by a small Chinese boy who was as thin as a stick and had spindly little legs that seemed to buckle under the weight of his paper bag. I always gave him a few coins as an extra, and he would place the paper on the veranda as if it was a precious relic, smoothing it with a thin hand and placing a rock on top to keep it from blowing away in the breeze.

I repeated myself. 'What do you think about the christening in the Mission church?'

'I don't mind, Lizzie, and I think it's a good idea.'

'We will have to have godparents. Have you anyone in mind?' I asked.

He put the paper down. 'Well, I would like Alex and Sue Lin.'

I wrote this down. 'I thought of asking Elsie and Ping Li. Do you want to come with me to the Mission church?'

He stood up. 'Let's go now, as Alex and I will be very busy with the book, so we'd better get the christening done as soon as possible.'

We met the Reverend Miller in his little house beside the

church and he welcomed us into his study. His desk was awash with papers. 'I'm writing this week's sermon,' he said, scooping them up and putting them on another table by the wall.

I explained why we were there. 'I know we should have had him christened before this, but we were unsure about the ceremony in a foreign country.'

He assured us it was all right. 'We have our own little bit of Britain here, as well as the other nationalities that go to make up this settlement, and I have done quite a few christenings over the years.' He took out his diary. 'I can manage it a week on Sunday, if that's fine with you?'

I looked at Jonas, who nodded.

Reverend Miller beamed at us. 'Well, I'll put it in my diary, and may I say how pleased I am that you've asked me to do it. Most of the expatriates go to the grander Episcopalian church.'

I said I wanted Peter to be christened in the Church of Scotland, and the minister beamed again. 'Right then, that's settled.'

I was aware that Peter was no longer a tiny baby – he was coming up to his second birthday – but I was glad it was happening. I hadn't broached the subject before because neither Jonas or myself were members of any church. I had grown very fond of Betsy and Jeannie but had rarely met their brother, so I was pleased he had been so helpful.

I had a lot to do in the run-up to the Sunday. Elsie and Ping Li were thrilled to be asked to be godparents, while Jonas said he would ask Alex and Sue Lin. Alex said yes immediately, but Sue Lin was away and couldn't be contacted, so I said to Jonas I was going to ask Zheng Yan.

I was amused by Jonas's attitude. He was a typical man when it came to planning family matters and he was content to leave everything to me. I wanted a quiet baptism, then to have a few of our friends back to the house. I sent a note to Lorna-May and her husband, and she appeared at the door the following morning.

She was dressed in a very chic-looking dress and looked like she was off to some function or other. 'Oh no, this is my everyday dress,' she said when I commented on it. 'I'm thinking your house will be too small afterwards. Let me book the Racecourse clubhouse, as it's grander, with lots of room.'

I didn't want to hurt her feelings by telling her I preferred my own house, so I made up a little white lie. 'I'm sorry, Lorna-May, but Jonas has planned it and I don't think he'll like his plans changed.'

She wasn't happy, but I knew she was the kind of woman who always deferred to her husband, and she wouldn't want to offend Jonas by telling him his house wasn't grand enough. I was waiting for her to criticise the church, but she said nothing. Maybe she thought Jonas had also planned this and that silence was the best policy.

On the Sunday we all made our way to the church. It was a warm, humid day, but the interior of the small church was cool. There was a large congregation, a mixture of expatriates and Chinese residents, and the service, although simple, was lovely. Alex looked so serious as the minister read out a godparent's duties, but Elsie, Zheng Yan and Ping Li nodded as he spoke.

I spotted Lorna-May and Conrad in the congregation, as their fashionable outfits made them stand out like exotic flowers amongst the plainer clothes of the parishioners.

I had hired a couple of young Chinese girls to serve the food and drink, which they did with their usual smiling faces, and the day was a success. During the service I missed Margaret and wished she could have been with us, and I also thought of my mother and Granny and wished they could have been there to see Jonas and Peter.

Betsy had played the organ for my favourite hymn, 'By Cool Siloam's Shady Rill' and she now stood with her sister and brother, getting their photograph taken with Peter. Alex had started his godparent's duties right away by offering to take all the photos, and I knew I would treasure this day forever.

Elsie gave Peter a silver rattle, while Alex handed over a silver teething ring. Lorna-May held Peter for her photo, and her gift was an inscribed silver cup in a satin-lined box. I thanked them all for their generosity and for coming to our family occasion. It was at the end of the afternoon when Zheng Yan and Ping Li were leaving that they handed me the most beautiful parchment scroll with Peter's date of birth and the attributes of a child born in the Year of the Boar. It was all written in Chinese calligraphy and I hung it up above his cot.

As we went to bed that night, Jonas and I stood looking down on our sleeping child, and I couldn't help but think what a very fortunate little boy he was.

When the photos were developed, I sent copies off to Margaret, Maisie, Laura, Pat, and Sandy and Marie.

Margaret wrote back saying she wished she could have been with us on our special occasion, a sentiment I endorsed, while Laura asked who the two tiny Chinese people were. 'They look so cute, as if they should be on top of a wedding cake,' she said.

I wrote back and told her they were my dearest friends, and although they might look 'cute', as she said, I would gladly put my life in their hands if the need ever arose.

44

REFUGEES AT THE MISSION

Elsie, Peter and I continued going once a week to the Mission to help Betsy and Jeannie with the influx of refugees. As Betsy said, there didn't seem to be an end to the stream of displaced people from the northern regions. Some of the families had walked hundreds of miles, but they waited with patience and good manners until they could all be fed with a bowl of rice.

Elsie never mentioned Ronnie again after her disastrous meeting with the mill manager, but I was worried about her. She had seemed so alive at the christening, but now she was pale and tired-looking. Some days her dress was wrinkled, as if she had slept in it or hadn't ironed it, which I knew couldn't be the case, because we both sent out our laundry to the local Chinese laundry. Every week a wizened old woman would call at the house and go away with our bundle and return later that day with it all beautifully washed and ironed. As with the paper boy, I always gave her some extra money and she would bow to me as she handed over the washing.

The Chinese people seemed to work for a pittance and on the busy streets it was common to see old men almost bent double with bamboo poles slung across their shoulders and huge bundles of goods hanging from them. It was the same in the shops, which stayed open from morning until late at night, with entire families working in them; in workshops, tiny children with dark hair and large, luminous eyes bent over sewing machines or served food from the street carts and small restaurants.

I knew Dundee had its jute workers who stayed in slum housing and worked long hours in the many jute mills, and they were similar to the maze of narrow streets that led off from the Bund and the river. There were dark, poky houses that seemed to overflow with people and street markets with live chickens, thin mangy-looking dogs and food all mixed up beside the stalls.

Ping Li and I would walk through these streets as she bought swathes of material for her dresses, and we would hire a rickshaw to take us back to Bubbling Well Road. I sensed a tension in these streets, but thought I was imagining it until Ping Li said the same.

'People are afraid of the Japanese armies. Stories are arriving here with the refugees and they hope the armies don't come to Shanghai.'

'But surely this is the International Settlement under the British, American and French governments, Ping Li.'

'The Japanese don't recognise any treaties. They work to their own agendas. That is what Zheng Yan says.'

On Peter's birthday on the tenth of May we took him to the zoo. I could hardly believe he was two years old. He held out his chubby arms when we passed the cages and waved his hands at the monkeys as they capered in the trees in their compound. I had a slight pain in my side and thought I had pulled a muscle, but it went away. Still, I was glad when we headed for home to the birthday tea and a cake with the two candles.

Peter gazed in delight at his cake, but he kept blowing bubbles instead of blowing the candles out, so Jonas did it for him. His little face crumpled when the lights went out, so I relit them and he managed to blow them out by himself.

'Who's a clever little boy?' He looked at me and I said, 'Peter's the cleverest little boy in the whole wide world.'

He put his fist into the cake and it came out all sticky with sponge and jam, and Jonas and I laughed.

45

THE JAPANESE TREATY

Although life went on as usual by July 1937 there was a different atmosphere, felt by not only the Chinese population but also the expatriates. The tension was like the threat of thunder before the storm breaks.

This tension wasn't helped by the arrival of Japanese naval ships anchored in the river or the fact that Chiang Kai-shek refused to join forces with Mao Zedong's army in a joint display of strength against the Japanese threat. Zheng Yan was incensed by this.

'You think he would put the safety of the people before his hatred of the Communists,' he said bitterly.

Then word came through that the Japanese army was fighting a battle with Chiang Kai-shek's Nationalist army on the outskirts of Peking.

Jonas gave me a searching look. 'I won't go if you don't want me to, because you and Peter are my main concerns and not my job. Alex can quite easily go alone and take his photographs.'

I so much wanted Jonas to stay with me and Peter, just our little threesome in our own house, but I knew when I married him what his job was, so I said I would be fine. 'I don't suppose the Japanese will attack the Settlement.' Although I sounded confident, I certainly wasn't.

As he packed his bag and stowed it into Alex's car, he made me promise not to stay if there was any danger. 'Now you must listen,

Lizzie, and take Peter away from here if anything does happen. If they advise the women and children to evacuate, then you must go, either to Hong Kong or back to Scotland.'

I couldn't believe what I was hearing. 'I don't want to leave you here, Jonas, and return home. This is my life now, with you and Peter.'

He held me close. 'Promise me you'll go if you have to. No matter where you are, I will come to be with you. Now, do you promise me?'

I tried hard not to be upset, but I whispered, 'I promise.'

'You'll have Elsie and the Miller sisters to help you if you need it. Zheng Yan and Ping Li will help as well.'

So I stood on my veranda and watched as the car slowly drove away, with Jonas's face gazing at me till it disappeared from view. When I went to take Peter over to Elsie's house, the street looked much the same as usual. Maybe, I thought, Jonas was just making sure I knew what to do if anything happened; maybe it wasn't that an attack was imminent more that the Japanese were playing a game of cat and mouse.

Two days later Lorna-May arrived at the house and said she and Conrad were moving back to America. 'We only planned to be here for a few years,' she said, 'and now it's time to go back.'

Normally this wouldn't have worried me, but because of the heightened tension and the departure of Jonas, I suddenly felt afraid. 'Does Conrad know anything about the Japanese attack on Peking, Lorna-May?'

'Why would Conrad know about the Japanese's intentions, Lizzie?'

Quite honestly I didn't know, so I said lamely, 'Well, he's the head of the American Bank here in Shanghai and maybe the FBI has warned him to leave.'

She laughed. 'You've been watching too many films with your friend Elsie. Conrad doesn't know anyone in the FBI or in any other government agencies. No, we planned this move a while back, but can I give you some advice?'

When I nodded, she went on. 'Get Jonas to go back home with you and leave Shanghai, and please tell your friend Elsie to do the same.'

'Jonas and Alex have gone to Peking to write about the battle between the Japanese and Chiang Kai-shek's army.'

She went quite pale under her Max Factor medium-beige foundation and her red lips clamped together. 'I can't believe Jonas would leave his wife and son alone to go off filming and writing about an incident a thousand miles away.' She took her little notebook from her elegant handbag. 'I must phone Conrad at the bank and get him to arrange two tickets for Peter and you on our ship.'

I was so surprised that for a moment I was speechless. As she thumbed through her book, I finally found my voice. 'I'm not. leaving, Lorna-May. Jonas will be back and if anything does develop then we'll make plans, but not at the moment.'

She gave me a sorrowful glance. 'I wish you would change your mind, Lizzie, and leave with us. But if you've made up your mind, I'll have to say goodbye.'

She was at the door when I ran after her and gave her a hug. 'Thank you for the thought, Lorna-May. You've been a very good friend to us and I won't forget it. I hope you both have a happy trip back home and, who knows, we may meet up again one day.'

Lorna-May wiped her eyes with a tiny handkerchief and she hurried down the veranda steps. 'Say goodbye to Jonas and Peter for us, and I hope you all stay safe.'

I was touched by her concern for our safety and tried to tell myself that their leaving Shanghai had been planned beforehand, but that didn't ring true. If that had been the case, then she would have put on a grand leaving party at the Racecourse club. No, something or someone had warned them of danger. Was it the presence of the Japanese naval ships or some other danger I couldn't even begin to imagine?

I went back inside but was suddenly bent over with pain in my side. It made me feel sick, but after a while it subsided. I made a mental note to go and see the doctor at the hospital, but first I had to make Peter's breakfast.

I was washing the dishes when Elsie hurried in. She was out of breath and I thought she was ill.

'What's wrong, Elsie?'

She sat down and began to cry.

'Is it Ronnie who's causing more grief?' I asked, feeling really angry with him for his offhand treatment of his wife.

She nodded, but it took two cups of tea before she felt well enough to tell me what was wrong. Peter was playing on the rug with his toy wooden train that he'd got for his birthday, and I kept giving him fond glances as he made train noises while pushing it around the wooden tracks.

I sat beside Elsie. 'Do you want to tell me what's happened now?'

She looked so miserable and tearful, but she nodded. 'I haven't seen Ronnie for four nights now, so last night I was determined to have it out with him. I went and hung around the American Café and he came out at midnight. He was with that dark-haired woman we saw that day on the Bund. They went to a house a few streets away and I followed them. A light went on in the window, so I went up to the apartment door and knocked.' She stopped and swept her hair back from her wet, tearful face. There was an expression of grim defiance on her face that I hadn't seen since the day on the ship when she'd told her mother off. 'The woman answered the door and I saw Ronnie lying on the bed. When he saw me, he jumped up and almost pushed me down the stair. He said I was never to embarrass him again and that I should go home to my mother. I told him I loved him, and he laughed. It was a terrible, sneering laugh and he said he was in love with Ivanka, that's the woman's name, and he was going to divorce me and marry her.'

I was shocked. 'That's terrible, Elsie. You must get a solicitor or write to his father and tell him how awful his son is.'

'I did that this morning,' she said. 'I wrote to his father and asked for the money for a ticket back to Scotland. I mentioned the divorce and Ivanka so that he knows it isn't just me wanting to leave his son on a whim.'

I made another cup of tea and thought bitterly of the young girl I had met on the outward journey here.

'Last night I was so unhappy that I wandered around these narrow streets and I got lost in the alleyways. I began to panic, but out of the blue this policeman appeared. He's with the Municipal Police and he originally comes from Edinburgh. I realised we had been at the same school. His name is Robert Macdonald. At first he didn't recognise me, but when he did he asked me why I was wandering around in the early hours of the morning.' Elsie sat in silence, a deep-red flush spreading up from her neck. 'I told him I had lost my way after being out for the evening with my husband. He offered to see me back to the house. We got chatting and he asked my husband's name and what his job was in here in Shanghai. I told him I was Mrs Lomax and my husband was in charge of his father's cotton mills. He gave me such a concerned look, Lizzie, when he said, "Ronnie Lomax: is that your husband?" When I nodded, he never said another word but wished me goodnight at my front door.'

'Well, that was courteous of him to see you safely home, Elsie.'

Her voice rose until it was almost a scream. 'But don't you realise he knows Ronnie and it looks like he's been in trouble with the law? When he writes home to his parents, who live just a few streets away from my mother, then all her neighbours will know my situation. I've been writing to tell her how happy and contented I am here and now she'll know I'm a liar.'

I didn't know what to say but told her she was welcome to stay with me until her ticket arrived. She was obviously concerned about her image of a happy marriage and that overcame her unhappiness. She knew her mother would be the target of gossips back in Edinburgh and she was ashamed at the thought of being the cause.

Betsy and Jeannie were overwhelmed by the numbers arriving from Peking. Elsie and I went to help, but there wasn't enough food to go round. 'We're hearing terrible stories from the refugees about Peking now being occupied by the Japanese and all the killing and fires and the utter devastation.'

I was really worried about Jonas, as I hadn't heard anything from him since he'd left. I now realised this was what my mother would have experienced when my father had gone to France. I hoped history wasn't repeating itself, and I tried to feel confident. I managed it fine during the day, but in bed at night all my fears and worries emerged and stopped me from sleeping, which meant I was tired in the mornings.

Ping Li came round every morning to help with Peter, as Elsie had gone back to her own house. I could see my Chinese friend was also worried about the future.

'Zheng Yan says the Japanese naval ships have fired on some of the boats coming into Shanghai. A Chinese houseboat with a family on board was sunk and they all died. The Japanese captain said it was a spy ship and they were within their rights to fire on it. Zheng Yan said it was clear it was a local boat and the family could all be clearly seen from the riverbank.'

I was now getting twinges in my side, but I didn't want to go and see about it until Jonas came home. However, by the middle of August I couldn't put up with the pain any longer. I decided to go to the doctor after Peter went to bed and thought maybe Elsie or Ping Li could look after him.

By teatime I was doubled up with pain, and luckily Ping Li called round. She took one look at me and called for her husband.

'Lizzie needs to go to hospital, Ping Li,' he said. 'Try to get a taxi for her, as I don't think she'll be able to walk.'

I knew I couldn't walk, as the pain came in waves and made me feel nauseous. I managed to ask Zheng Yan if he could ask Elsie to come and look after Peter, and he nodded. Thankfully a taxi arrived at the door and Ping Li helped me into it. I held on to her hand.

'Can you come with me?'

'Yes, I am going to come with you, Lizzie.'

I don't remember much after I was examined by the doctor, except that I heard him tell the nurse I had a perforated appendix and he was afraid peritonitis had set in.

'How long have you had the pain?' he asked.

I only managed to gasp out a few words. 'For a couple of weeks.'

He looked concerned, and I was whisked away along the corridor on a trolley.

The next thing I recalled was the sun shining in through the window of my little room in the hospital. For a moment or two, I couldn't think where I was; then the pain struck me again and I called out loud. A small Chinese nurse came hurrying in, followed by the doctor, who sat in the chair by my bedside.

'I've had to take your appendix out, Mrs O'Neill, but because it burst, you will still be in pain. I'll give you something to dull the pain, but you must lie quiet and rest, with no sudden movements.'

If I had had the strength to laugh, I would have, but every movement felt like my body was on fire, so I just nodded.

The doctor went on. 'I believe your husband is away on a job to Peking?'

I nodded again but became alarmed when he turned to the nurse and shook his head.

'Have you had any word from him?' I asked, and my voice sounded deep and gravelly.

He said he hadn't, but when he did manage to contact him he would let him know I was recovering.

I managed to fall asleep but was awakened by the sound of voices in the corridor. It had turned dark and I realised I must have slept all day. The voices became agitated, but I still didn't think anything about it, as my pain had returned.

The door opened, and I expected to see the nurse, but it was the doctor and Elsie. She was agitated as she came to my bedside.

'Lizzie, you must listen to me. The Japanese have attacked Shanghai and there are dead bodies and fires all over the city.'

I suddenly grew cold. I felt my heart hammering in my chest. 'Is it Peter? Or Jonas?'

The doctor tried to get her to leave, but she was adamant. 'There's a British ship leaving tomorrow to evacuate the women and children. I have to go on it and I want to take Peter with me, as I can't leave him behind while you're ill. Betsy and Jeannie say they aren't going, but David has made them promise they will.'

'Will Zheng Yan and Ping Li be going as well?'

She shook her head. 'It's just the expatriates and their families. The doctor tells me you will be in hospital for ten days or more and this will be the last chance to get Peter to safety.'

I looked at the doctor. 'Can I be discharged right now?'

'No, I'm sorry.'

I grabbed Elsie's hand. 'Please look after Peter. Take him to my aunt's house in Carnoustie, and Jonas and I will join him when we can.'

She gave me a kiss on the cheek. 'Of course I'll look after Peter, and we'll see you sometime when you leave and return to Scotland.'

She was almost out of the door when I said, 'Can you pack his wooden train, Elsie? It's his birthday present.'

She gave a backward glance and a tiny wave before disappearing. I cried silently into my pillow. I knew I had made the right decision, as I wouldn't want Peter to be in any danger, but why wasn't Jonas back home? Surely he had written up his story and Alex had taken his photos, so they should be coming home soon. Then, in the grey light of dawn when worries seem to magnify, I had the terrible thought that they were both either injured or dead. I knew history was repeating itself and I was now in the same position as my mother had been away back in 1917, with my husband missing in action like my father.

Ping Li came to visit me every afternoon and she said there was no word of Jonas or Alex. 'Zheng Yan has gone to see the editor of the *China Times*, but he hasn't heard anything except that the Japanese army has occupied Peking and is attacking Shanghai and Nanking.'

My wound was still painful, but I wanted to go home. I kept asking the doctor when I could leave the hospital, but he said only after my stitches were removed and that would take another day or two.

On her next visit I asked Ping Li to try to contact Sue Lin. 'If anyone knows the whereabouts of Jonas and Alex, it'll be her.'

Ping Li seemed evasive as she answered me. 'We can't find Sue Lin.'

I was vexed at her disappearance, but it was typical of her to be away when I badly needed some answers. Hopefully I would catch up with her when I got home. The doctor removed my stitches the following day and he said the wound had healed satisfactorily, so I could return to my house provided I rested as much as possible.

Ping Li brought my clothes around and we set off for Bubbling Well Road, with Ping Li carrying my suitcase. As we walked along the main road I was shocked by the devastation. People were still thronging the streets, but a good many of the houses had been destroyed in the shelling.

Ping Li said the railway station had been badly damaged and there had been lots of casualties, with children left crying by the side of their dead parents. She said that a British ship, the *Rajputana*, had evacuated the women and children, and that the houses on Bubbling Well Road were now empty.

'Your friend Elsie has taken Peter away with her and the two ladies from the Mission have gone with her, so there are hardly any of our neighbours left.'

I was glad to be home and pleased that there wasn't any damage to the house. It seemed odd not having Peter running around, and when I went into his bedroom I saw some of his toys neatly put away in his toy box. The train set was missing and I was glad that Elsie had managed to pack it. Our bedroom was as I had left it apart from a vase of flowers that had wilted, so I threw them out along with the brackish water.

Ping Li made some tea and we sat on the veranda. Everything was so peaceful that it was difficult to reconcile the bombed streets and deaths with our little corner, and I prayed that Jonas would return soon.

After Ping Li left, I wandered around the house because I had nothing better to do. Picking up Mr Wang's box, I tried once again to find a way to open it, as I had done ever since I had received it. The sun was setting as I sat with it on my lap and I fiddled about with it. Suddenly, and much to my surprise, the lid sprang open and I found a lovely jade pendant on a fine silver chain nestled inside.

I gasped in wonder as I drew it out of its recess in the box. It seemed to shimmer in the fading light and I fastened it around my neck. For a brief moment I wondered if I should return it to his niece, who now ran the shop, but then I remembered he told me that I would find the secret of the box when the time was right. It now seemed as if that time had come.

Ping Li came in to make sure I was fine before going to bed and her eyes opened wide when she saw the pendant. I told her about the box and she said, 'Your pendant is a lucky symbol and it will protect you if you are in danger.'

I thought it was just a very pretty piece of jewellery and not a potent symbol of protection. But for some reason this comforted me, and I put the pendant under my pillow when I went to bed. It was strange not having Elsie or Lorna-May popping in and out, but when Jonas came back then we would both leave Shanghai to be reunited with Peter.

I still found walking a bit hard and had to take my time, so I was sitting having my breakfast when Zheng Yan and Ping Li came in. I went to pour them a bowl of tea, but Zheng Yan held up his hand.

'We have very bad news for you, Lizzie,' he said, his face serious.

I held my breath. Was it news about Jonas?

'We haven't been able to get in touch with Jonas or Alex, but I have to tell you that Sue Lin is dead.'

I was stunned. 'Dead?'

'Yes, I'm afraid so. She was covering a story about the

amusement park, but Chinese planes dropped bombs on it and a thousand people have been killed, including Sue Lin. The plane's pilots were meant to bomb the naval ships in the river, but they dropped them too early. About two thousand people have been injured, some very badly.'

The amusement park was a very popular place to visit and a great attraction for the Chinese people, with its theatres, halls, menageries and refreshment room, and now it was a scene of devastation, with a thousand men, women and children killed and thousands injured.

I couldn't take in this terrible news. Young, vibrant, career-minded Sue Lin had had so much to live for. It was hard to imagine her dead. Then I remembered Alex. 'Alex is going to be devastated.' It then struck me that he was also dead, along with Jonas, and I prayed so hard for it not to be true.

Zheng Yan sat beside me. 'Now you must listen to me very carefully, Lizzie. I must get Ping Li out of Shanghai and go to Hong Kong with her. The Japanese are targeting the Chinese people and killing them, and the stories coming out of the other cities are of slaughter and atrocities. I've managed to get a passage on a ship leaving the harbour tonight that will take us to Hong Kong. Now you must come with us, as we can't leave you behind, so I want you to pack a small bag and gather as much money as you have in the house and we'll leave when it gets dark.'

I began to protest. 'I must wait on Jonas . . .'

Zheng Yan stopped me. 'Jonas said we were to look after you and Peter. We couldn't do anything for Peter, but you have to come with us. Remember what Jonas made you promise if there was danger?'

I nodded but couldn't speak because I was so choked up with worry over the future.

Zheng Yan smiled. 'You can pack a bag right away and we'll pick you up later. You'll have to make your luggage light, so just one bag or suitcase. Also you must wear something warm, as it will be cold on the water.'

After they left, I wandered around the house in a daze. Peter's room was just as I had left it to go into hospital. His colourful blanket from his bed was gone, but everything else was still in place. It was the same in our room, and I remembered the last time Jonas and I had been in it. It was the morning he left to go to Peking, and now the Japanese army had occupied it and Jonas was missing, as was Alex.

I didn't know what to take with me, but Zheng Yan had said one case, so I had to choose carefully. I packed Mum's carriage clock and Mr Wang's box, in which I put the pendant for safekeeping. I took what clothes I thought I would need in Hong Kong and looked out all my photographs and Peter's calligraphy chart. If we were going by sea then I had to make sure they wouldn't get wet so I looked out a waterproof coat and wrapped them carefully in it before tying it up with string.

I took what money was in the house, telling myself that Jonas would maybe get to the bank to withdraw the rest. Finally I took my money belt from the wardrobe and placed my two gold bangles and Mum's wristlet watch inside, along with my passport. As I put it round my waist I had a sudden image of the first time I had worn it on that long-ago cycling holiday with Laura and Pat. It seemed a lifetime away, being young and longing for adventure. Now that adventure had come knocking at my door I realised all I wanted was a life with Jonas and Peter. But my life now seemed fraught with danger and loss.

I was also worried about paying my young paper boy and the old lady from the laundry, so I left their money in two envelopes under a stone on the veranda and hoped they were still alive to pick them up. I sat on the veranda in my thick woollen coat and looked for the last time at my garden. The birds were still chirping in the trees and everything looked so normal that it was hard to believe that fires were raging all over the city and thousands of lives had been lost.

As soon as darkness fell, Zheng Yan and Ping Li came to collect me. They were well wrapped up and they each carried a large bag. We made our way down the road towards the waterfront. The Bund seemed to be untouched, but fires were burning in the Chinese old town and we had to avert our eyes from dead bodies lying in the gutter. Ping Li said the British government had sent a battalion of soldiers to protect the international community, but who was protecting the Chinese population?

I couldn't understand the clandestine way we were leaving and I asked Ping Li why this was.

'It is because I have no passport. Zheng Yan has his from his work in Hong Kong, but I have never had one, so he thinks I might not be able to leave Shanghai.'

We could smell the river before we reached it, and dark shadows made the jetties and wharves seem deserted. But we heard voices, as ships were docked in the harbour. I saw lights on these ships and dim figures walking about.

Zheng Yan knew where he was going and he led us to a dark shape that turned out to be a Portuguese cargo vessel. The captain was tall, fat and had a dark beard, and he looked as fearsome as my childish pictures of a pirate. I saw Zheng Yan hand over money to him and he quickly ushered us up the gangplank.

'Hurry now,' he said in broken English. 'The naval ships are watching all the shipping going in and out.'

He took us to a small compartment beside the cargo hold and told us to stay quiet until we had cleared the naval blockade. Ping Li huddled close to me, while Zheng Yan arranged the three bags against the wall.

We heard the sound of the ship's engines and the movement of the ship as it slipped out of its moorings. Shortly afterwards we heard voices, but we couldn't make out the words. After an hour the captain, whose name was Rodrigues, came and told us to come up to the galley.

'One of the Japanese ships called out to us, but I told them I was a Portuguese cargo ship, so they let me through. There is a storm forecast tonight, but hopefully we will miss it.'

Ping Li looked frightened. 'Did he say if it was a typhoon, Zheng Yan?'

Her husband said he didn't know. 'We have to face what's ahead of us with courage.'

To begin with the water was a bit choppy but nothing out of the ordinary. However, by the time we were out in the open sea, the wind had grown stronger and the boat rocked from side to side.

Ping Li's eyes were wide with terror. 'It is a typhoon. I know the sound of that wind, as I was caught up in one when I was young. It was a miracle we survived it.'

I didn't realise I was clutching my St Christopher medallion, as my hands had grown numb with the cold. The wind grew even stronger and the sea looked as if it was boiling. The cargo shifted in the hold and the ship's bow seemed to rise right up out of the water with each huge wave.

I closed my eyes as if it would all go away if I didn't look at it, but I knew we were going to drown on this ship and that I would never see Jonas or Peter ever again. I heard myself quietly muttering a prayer as the captain's voice shouted at the deckhands to make manoeuvres, but the ship twisted and groaned as it hit every wave. The deck was awash as the waves crashed over it and spray splashed against the small windows of the galley. We had to sit where we were, as there was no other place to go.

The captain appeared and was soaking wet. 'We've hit a typhoon and you may have to get into the lifeboat,' he said before hurrying out.

We all looked at one another. We would have no chance of surviving in a small lifeboat, not in these mountainous seas. Zheng Yan put his arm around his wife and I huddled next to her. If we were to drown, then we would all go together, that was for sure.

A crashing sound made us all sit up. It was as if part of the ship had broken. The captain didn't reappear and I silently thought the crew had abandoned us and gone off in the lifeboat. It was a sobering thought. I tried to take my mind off this terrible voyage by recalling in my head all the books I had read about pirates and seafarers and how I had envied them their swashbuckling lives full of adventure and buried treasure.

'Yes, Lizzie,' I scolded myself mentally. 'Be very careful what you wish for, as it has indeed come true now.'

Then, much to our relief, the captain made another appearance. 'Part of the ship's hold has been flooded, but we are bailing it out now.' He made the sign of the cross. 'With God's grace, we'll make it.'

The three of us were too traumatised to answer, and he turned on his heel and went out, no doubt to help bail out the flooded cargo hold.

I can't remember how long we sat in that little galley, but when the first light of dawn appeared in the window I thought the wind had dropped a bit, although the sea looked just as rough. Then a deckhand appeared with a pot of coffee and we gratefully took an enamel mug each. We had to hold the mugs because the small table in the galley kept moving to and fro, but the coffee warmed us up.

Zheng Yan suggested that Ping Li and I should have a sleep, so we put our feet up on the bench and much to my surprise I fell sound asleep.

When I woke up, Ping Li was still sleeping, but her husband had good news.

'Captain Rodrigues has said the typhoon has moved further east and we should be all right. He said we were lucky, as we only caught the edge of the storm and things could have been worse if we had met it head on.' He seemed to be worried. 'The only thing is we've been blown off course, so we won't be landing at Hong Kong. We should manage to get to Macao, though, where he hopes to repair his ship.'

I said, 'Macao? That's the Portuguese territory, isn't it?'

He said it was. 'We can get another ferry to Hong Kong from there. It may take a bit longer, but we seem to be over the worst.'

I almost said amen to that.

When Ping Li woke up, we said were heading for Macao, and she gave her husband a terrified look. The sun was going down when we docked. When we saw the damage to the ship, we were grateful that it hadn't broken apart, but Captain Rodrigues was in a good mood.

'I can't turn back to Hong Kong till my boat is repaired, but you can stay here in Macao till you get another passage. Here is the address of an old woman who has rooms to let. She will put you up for a couple of nights.'

Zheng Yan said, 'A couple of nights? Can we not get a passage tonight or tomorrow?'

The captain shook his head. 'The storm is moving towards Hong Kong, so I think you should stay here till it passes.' He shook Zheng Yan's hand. 'Goodbye my friend, and safe journey.'

We looked a sorry trio as we trudged up from the docks, which were busy with ships' cargoes, and we made our way towards the tavern that the captain said the rooming house was next to. We soon found the bar, as the noise coming from it was deafening: sailors of every nationality were drinking, singing and fighting. A few women were screeching at two men to stop fighting, but their screams went unheeded.

We found the rooming house, and the dark-skinned old woman who opened the door said to come in. 'I only have one room,' she said, eyeing the three bedraggled customers standing on her threadbare mat inside the front door.

Zheng Yan said that would be sufficient, as we were only staying for a couple of days. The room was grubby-looking and very basic. It held two beds with thin blankets spread over them. There was a tiny brown-stained toilet next door and a jug of water on the marble washstand.

We were too tired to argue over the price and Zheng Yan paid in Shanghai dollars.

'So you've come from Shanghai, have you?' she said.

We said we had. And as we hadn't eaten for almost twenty-four hours, I asked her where we could have a meal.

'They do food in the tavern,' she said, but on seeing my expression she muttered, 'Maybe not. There are some shops that sell food in the town so you can go there.'

Zheng Yan said he would go to see what was available, and he came back with three cartons of rice with sweet and sour sauce. The three of us ate our meal quickly, as we were starving, and then we went to bed. I shared one bed with Ping Li and Zheng Yan had the other. Because we were exhausted, we soon fell fast asleep.

The sun rising on the horizon woke us up, and we found a cold-water tap in the courtyard. After we had had a quick wash, we drank some water in place of breakfast. We sat in the courtyard and basked in the warm sunshine, which we had thought we would never see again after our trauma at sea. Ping Li and I were fascinated by the banyan trees, with their exposed, weird-shaped roots, and I found myself unconsciously clasping my St Christopher – something I had done a lot of since we'd left Shanghai.

Later we made our way up the cobbled street to see if we could get some more food. In a dark corner of the square we found a small café and enjoyed coffee and little baked rolls.

Zheng Yan said he would go to book three tickets on the ferry to Hong Kong later that afternoon. I tried hard not to worry about Jonas, but he was on my mind all the time. I knew we had to get to Hong Kong immediately because he might be looking for me there, but, as Zheng Yan said, he was going to get the tickets today.

Back at the rooming house, which incidentally looked more derelict and squalid in the sunshine, I gave Zheng Yan all the money I had taken from the house. At first he said I should keep it, but I said I wanted him to look after it as I was afraid I might lose it.

Then Ping Li and I changed our clothes and washed what we had worn on the trip. We found an old bucket and filled it with cold water from the tap before hanging the clothes out to dry on a small washing line hanging limply from two tree trunks. They soon dried in the heat of the sun and we folded them back into our bags.

46

MACAO

Zheng Yan had set off for the docks and the shipping office in the afternoon. He asked the woman at the rooming house if there was an office where he could buy tickets for a ferry to Hong Kong, and she said there was. When he'd asked for directions, she'd said it was a building at the far end of the loading jetty.

Ping Li and I went back into the town, mainly to get away from the house, as the woman had scowled at us after Zheng Yan left. The streets were cobbled and quaint and not unlike the narrow alleyways in Shanghai. Small shops were open and the warm sun was pleasant on our tired bodies. I still felt twinges of pain where my wound had been stitched, but I hoped it would soon settle down. The doctor at the hospital had said to rest, but the tossing of the boat the previous night hadn't helped.

We sat down on a stone bench and watched as people went by, but after an hour Ping Li said her husband should be back with the tickets, so we made our way to our room.

'I hope my husband has managed to buy tickets for a sailing later today, but if we have to wait until tomorrow we'll just have to put up with our landlady,' said Ping Li.

This was a sentiment I heartily agreed with. We admitted that we were grateful to have survived the typhoon, although we realised we were in a strange country and had no one to turn to for help. As Macao was a Portuguese territory, we didn't understand the language, so I suppose we were lucky that the owner of the house had a small English vocabulary, which I reckoned she had gleaned from British seamen who had stayed in her house over the years.

There was an ancient-looking clock in the room. It was now five o'clock and we were growing uneasy about Zheng Yan's search for the shipping office, then when darkness set in we became really worried.

Ping Li said she would go and look for him. 'Maybe there is a queue of people booking the ferry,' she said.

I didn't say that if that was the case it must be a very long queue. I was unhappy about her going out alone in the dark, so I said I would go with her.

'You will look out of place here, Lizzie. The docks will be full of seamen and they won't give an old Chinese woman a second glance.'

'I'm not letting you go alone, Ping Li. If I wear my thick coat and tuck my hair into a cap, then neither of us will attract attention.'

She wasn't convinced, but I had made my mind up, so we set off for the harbour looking like two old women, which wasn't hard, as I was limping because of the pain in my side. By the time we got there it was scary, with shadows everywhere and not many lights. Luckily the place seemed deserted, as no doubt most of the ships would have had their cargoes loaded or unloaded during the day.

Ping Li whispered, 'We must find the ticket office. That old crone said it was at the far end of the jetty.' So we made our way gingerly past dark warehouses, but the place was a warren of narrow alleys that stretched into the darkness. We reached the end of the jetty, but there was no sign of Zheng Yan, so we retraced our steps, carefully watching we didn't trip over any obstacles on the ground.

Ping Li was in despair. 'Something has happened to him, Lizzie. Someone has murdered him and thrown him in the water. I just know it.'

I was thinking the same thing, but I couldn't let Ping Li panic, otherwise there was a risk that we would also be murdered and thrown into the sea. I had an idea. 'Let's go back to the house and get the local police force to look for him.'

Ping Li looked wildly around. 'Is there a police force in Macao?'

I was just about to say I didn't know when a dark shadow emerged from the shadows and walked towards us. I almost screamed, while Ping Li gasped in fear.

'Can I help you lassies?' the voice said.

I couldn't believe it. He was Scottish! I almost threw myself into his arms.

'We're looking for this woman's husband. He came here to buy tickets for the Hong Kong ferry and he hasn't come home.'

By now I could see his face, as he held a torch. He was tall and bearded, and was dressed in a dark seaman's trousers and jersey. He said, 'How marvellous to hear another Scottish accent. I'm working on a ship where everyone, including the captain, is Portuguese.' He shone his torch on the ground. 'Now, let's look for this missing man.'

We were able to enter the alleys now, as we had a light, but it was a good half an hour before we found Zheng Yan lying behind a large crate. Our Scots friend knelt down and shone the torch on his face. There was a dark patch of blood behind his head.

'It looks like he's been robbed and they've clubbed him. Did he have money on him?'

I said he had.

'Well, it looks like there's nothing left.'

Ping Li began to cry. 'We must get him back to the house, Lizzie.'

The three of us picked him up, but as he was unconscious we had to carry him.

'At least he doesn't weigh a ton,' said the man.

We made slow progress, but we soon reached the house and put Zheng Yan on the bed. He groaned and I knew he was still alive.

The man went to the door. 'I have to go, as my ship is sailing in a couple of hours, but I hope you manage to get some help for your husband. My name is Ian Murdoch and I come from Glasgow.'

'I'm Lizzie O'Neill, and this is Ping Li, wife of Zheng Yan. Because of the typhoon we landed here last night instead of Hong Kong.'

He whistled. 'God, you were all very lucky, as it's killed hundreds. Look, I'm sorry, but my ship is going on to Singapore, so I can't help you any more.'

I saw him to the front door. 'Thank you so much, Ian,' I said. 'We would never have found Zheng Yan if you hadn't come along.'

He waved as he went back down the road to the harbour.

Back in the room, Ping Li was trying to examine her husband's head. 'It's a deep wound, Lizzie, and Zheng Yan seems to be dizzy.'

'He needs a doctor, as he probably has concussion as well as a head wound. I'm going to ask the landlady where we can get a doctor.'

The woman answered her door with a scowl. There was a strong smell of alcohol on her breath. 'What do you want now?'

'We need a doctor for my friend's husband. He's been attacked and robbed at the docks.'

She gave me a sly look. 'It will cost money for a doctor.'

I had a few Shanghai dollars in my purse and gave them to her. 'I want him now, you understand?'

She scowled again, but an hour later an old man appeared with a medical bag. He looked at Zheng Yan and shook his head. 'I can do nothing for this man. He just needs to rest.'

I was angry. 'But you're a doctor. Can't you do something for his head wound?'

He said it needed stitches and that they would have to be done at the hospital.

'Where is this hospital?'

'You will have to pay for his treatment there,' he said before picking up his bag and leaving.

'I gave my last Shanghai dollars to the landlady to get the doctor and a lot of good he's done,' I said angrily.

Ping Li said if we wrapped Zheng Yan's head up maybe things would look better in the morning. Quite honestly I doubted it, but I took my underskirt out to the tap in the courtyard and then wrapped the wet cloth around Zheng Yan's head. There was still blood oozing out of it, but Ping Li tried to bring the edges of the wound together. He was still feeling dizzy and disorientated.

We took it in turns to sit up with him all night, but in the morning he wasn't any better. We had no money for food and we hadn't eaten in twenty-four hours. Then the landlady arrived at the door.

'You will all go now, you only paid for two days.' She saw the pillow that had been marked with blood from the cut. She almost screeched at us. 'That will cost you more money.' She held her hand out.

'We've no money left, as we've been robbed.' I told her. I went to my money belt and took out Mum's wristlet watch. 'You can have this as payment until my friend gets better.'

She turned the watch over in her hands.

'It's a gold watch,' I said.

'You can stay for two more days,' she snapped, eyeing up the gold bangles in my belt.

I was furious with myself for letting her see them, and I suddenly had a strong suspicion that she was behind Zheng Yan's robbery. After all, why pick on an innocent-looking Chinese man amongst loads of other nationalities? He didn't look like he was carrying money, so his attack could have been the result of a tip-off from this old crone to someone she knew.

I narrowed my eyes at her and was about to speak when she said, 'Two more days, that's all.' She held up two fingers as if to emphasise the point before turning away.

Ping Li was upset. 'Zheng Yan won't be better in two days, Lizzie. Not without a doctor to look at him.'

I put my money belt on. 'I'm going into the town to see if I can sell one of my gold bangles, but I want to go right now, as I think that woman had a hand in robbing us. I don't want her getting in touch with her accomplice.'

Ping Li was worried. 'Please watch out for yourself, as these people are bad.'

I went outside, but there was no sign of the owner, so I hurried into town to try to find a jeweller's shop or pawnshop. I retraced my steps from yesterday but went further along the street. Every so often I stopped and looked behind me, but although people were walking about I didn't see anyone who looked threatening. I was hoping that I had got out before the landlady had had time to tell her accomplice about my gold bangles. Then I thought that perhaps I was wrong, but I still wasn't taking any chances.

I didn't see any shop that was likely to buy jewellery and I was beginning to get worried. If I didn't sell a bangle, then I would have to take them back to the house, and I knew the chances of being robbed were then very high.

I almost passed one narrow lane but doubled back and walked quickly down the cobbled road. To my delight, I spotted a small shop that had gold chains and rings in the window. I opened the door and a bell tinkled. A very attractive dark-haired woman was looking in one of the cabinets.

An old man approached the counter. He spoke to me in Portuguese. I said I didn't speak the language, but I showed him the bangle. 'I want to sell this, please.'

He took it and had a good look at it, but he answered again in Portuguese. I started to say again I didn't understand, but the woman came over. 'Please excuse me, but can I help you?'

I turned to her in desperation. 'Oh, thank you. I'm trying to sell my gold bangle and I wondered if the jeweller was interested.'

She rattled off a stream of words and I wished I had been able to study Portuguese at school instead of French.

'Mr Ramirez says it is South American gold.'

'Yes, it is. It was a present from my aunt, who bought it when she lived in Rio de Janeiro.'

There was another round of conversation with the word 'Rio' as the only word I understood.

'He will give you a good price for it.' I had no idea what a good price was, but she said, 'This is a good price and Mr Ramirez will not cheat you.'

I said I would take it, and he went to the back of the shop and came back with a thick wad of Portuguese notes.

I thanked them both and went to go back to the house. The woman left with me and she walked down the lane by my side. I was a bit suspicious, but she said, 'You seem to be desperate for money. Has something happened to you?'

Before I knew it, I was telling her all about our misfortunes since leaving Shanghai and she said I should come back with her and have some tea. We walked further along until we came to a high wall with a bright-blue door set in it. She opened the door and I found myself in a beautiful cool courtyard with a small fountain in the centre.

We sat on a lovely sofa and she brought tea to a low table. 'My name is Senhora Alveres and this is my home.'

'I'm Lizzie O'Neill, and I've come from Shanghai with my friends Zheng Yan and his wife, Ping Li. My son, Peter, was evacuated along with my friend Elsie, as I was in hospital with appendicitis. My husband, Jonas, and his friend Alex were away on a trip to Peking to write a story about the Japanese bombing the city, but I've had no word since they left.'

'Your husband is Jonas O'Neill, the author of *Dragon Land*?'

I was surprised. 'Yes, he is.'

'My husband and I love this book. Now tell me where you are staying?'

I told her all about the robbery and how we needed to get to Hong Kong, as well as the fact that we had to get out of the boarding house in two days.

'I gave the landlady my mother's gold wristlet watch and I suspect her of being involved in the robbery, but I can't prove it.'

Senhora Alveres stood up. 'Let us go and see your friends and this fiendish woman.'

'Oh, it's all right now that I have the money to get us to Hong

Kong. Please don't trouble yourself, as you've been so helpful to me.'

'No, I want to go, as I don't like visitors to Macao to be robbed and cheated.'

When we reached the house, the landlady rushed out and began to demand more money for the pillow, but when she saw Senhora Alveres her demeanour changed dramatically. She didn't bow, but she began to whine how we had made a mess of her house. Senhora Alveres looked around in disdain.

'I believe you have a watch belonging to this lady? I want you to give it back.'

I almost collapsed in surprise.

'I only took it because I'm a poor old widow woman who has to make a living,' she said.

Senhora Alveres held out her hand and the old crone slunk away, but not before giving me a malicious, sly look. She came back and put the watch in my hand. Senhora Alveres said that a car would be calling to take the injured man to a doctor and that we wouldn't need our two extra days in her fragrant house.

Ping Li was speechless and so was I. I couldn't believe my good fortune in meeting up with this obviously important woman who had loved reading *Dragon Land*. We soon gathered up our belongings and a man came and helped to carry Zheng Yan to a smart-looking car that we all managed to get into.

I was last to go, and as I turned the landlady glared and spat at me. I had the urge to go and give her a slap, but resisted it because she was no longer in our lives. To my surprise, we went back to the Alveres house and Zheng Yan was put to bed in a small apartment by the side of the building.

'You can all stay here and I will call out my doctor,' said Senhora Alveres.

Ping Li sprang forward and gripped her hand. 'Thank you so much for all you kindness and may there be a blessing on your house.'

Senhora Alveres smiled and went away. Within an hour a very

professional doctor appeared who gave Zheng Yan a thorough examination.

'He has a bad cut to his head, which I will put stitches in, but he was lucky to be wearing a thick cap when he was hit because it cushioned the blow. He has wounds to his hands, legs and back, but they are not serious. He also has concussion, but hopefully in a few days he will get better. I will call in again tomorrow.'

I went to get some of the money I had received from the jeweller. 'How much do I owe you, doctor?' I asked.

He held up his hand. 'It is all right. There is no charge.'

When I told Ping Li, she was overwhelmed. 'How did you meet this good woman, Lizzie?'

I told her and also said, 'She's read *Dragon Land* and has heard of Jonas and Alex.'

With the money we were able to buy food, and Zheng Yan slowly got better. He still had difficulty remembering some things, but the doctor said it would all come back to him once his head had healed.

Senhora Alveres came every day to see us, and when she asked me where I came from I told her about Dundee and being a teacher before coming to Shanghai.

Her face lit up. 'You are a teacher?'

I said I was, although I hadn't taught since leaving Hong Kong.

'I have two children, Isabella and Frederick, who are taught here at home. Their tutor had to leave to go back to Portugal and I am waiting for another tutor to arrive. He will be here in three or four weeks, and I am wondering if you can teach my children until then?'

I was taken aback, but I wasn't sure if we could stay that long in Macao. 'We were hoping to go to Hong Kong as soon as possible. Once my friends are settled then I will get a ship home to my son. I will also try again to get in touch with my husband.'

'How long do you think the money you have will last if you go now, Lizzie? I will pay you well, and when my tutor arrives you will have enough to give to your friends and to get back home.'

I thought about it and told Ping Li.

'Well, Zheng Yan isn't back to good health yet, but I know you are desperate to get home to Peter.'

'Senhora Alveres said she would try to get news about Jonas, so I think I'll accept her proposal and it will give you both more money to get settled.'

I wrote to Margaret that night and told her what had happened. I said I would be coming home soon and asked if she could get in touch with Jonas's father in Ireland and give him the news that Jonas was missing but hopefully still alive.

I put my jade pendant around my neck, convinced it had been the source of our good luck in finding Senhora Alveres and Ian Murdoch.

47

THE KINDNESS OF
SENHORA ALVERES

I can't honestly say I was happy and contented in Macao, even though we were well treated by the family. This was because I had had no word about Jonas or Alex, and as the days went on it seemed likely they had either been injured or killed. I couldn't contemplate the fact that Jonas was no longer with us, so I kept trying to be positive about his disappearance. I also felt like my mother in 1917, and now I was in a similar situation I gained a deep understanding of how she must have felt about the news of my father's fate. What worried me was the fact my letter said we were heading for Hong Kong and that he could be looking for us there.

We hardly ever saw Senhor Alveres, but his wife explained he was with the Portuguese government in Macao. I met Isabella and Frederick, who were delightful children. Isabella, who was seven years old, had long black curly hair similar to mine and she had an impish smile. Frederick was five, and he was quieter than his sister and inclined to hide behind his book while his sister prodded him and told him to look at the tutor. They both said, 'Good morning, Senhora O'Neill,' and I was overcome with emotion at their childish faces.

The classroom was a large room in the house. It had a blackboard and book-lined shelves, and three desks and chairs, one of which was mine. Senhora Alveres had written out the last tutor's notes so I had an idea which subjects to teach them, and the days soon passed. The classes began early in the morning, at eight o'clock, and continued until one o'clock, but if their mother was out then Ping Li and I would look after them well into the afternoon.

Ping Li adored the children, and she often came into the classroom and sat down. They loved listening to our stories of living in other countries and Ping Li told them all about growing up in Shanghai. She also taught them how to write down some words in Mandarin.

Senhor Alveres and his wife also had a busy social life, which meant Ping Li and I would stay with the children until their parents came back home in the evening.

Zheng Yan was almost fully recovered and the doctor had stopped calling. He would get up every morning and go out to do some gardening for the family. He had asked if he could do this and Senhora Alveres had said she was so glad she had found us, as we were such a good help to her.

I had still had no word from Margaret, and enquiries about Jonas and Alex in Shanghai and Hong Kong had proved to be fruitless. There had been so many deaths due to the Japanese attacks and bombing that many bodies still had to be identified, and there had been no word of the two men in Hong Kong. Then there were the hundreds of deaths caused by the typhoon. It was a country in turmoil.

Despite how welcome Senhora Alveres made me feel, I was glad when the new tutor arrived. He was a young man with a thin face and rimless glasses. Isabella and Frederick looked at him in horror, and after he went to his room to freshen up, Isabella said, 'Please stay with us, Senhora O'Neill.'

I went over to her. 'I'm so sorry, Isabella, but I must go back home to look after my own little boy. You do understand, don't you?'

She nodded, but she was crying, and Frederick, picking up on her distress, began to cry as well. Their mother came in and asked what was wrong.

'We want Senhora O'Neill to stay with us, Mama, and Ping Li as well.'

She went over and dried their eyes. 'You will like your new tutor, but you've just got to get used to him.'

She asked me to come outside with her and I thought she was going to accuse me of starting this. 'I've made some tea,' she said.

When I was seated next to her, she said, 'I've been thinking about asking Zheng Yan and Ping Li to stay here with us instead of going to Hong Kong. My husband tells me the colony is overcrowded with refugees from Canton and other cities in China. He also says it's only a matter of time before the Japanese armies set their sights on the colony. I would have liked you to stay as well, but I know you have your son to get back to. Another problem is that in Europe the Nazi Party is threatening war. It is a terrible world, is it not? But perhaps Britain won't be dragged into another war.'

I said I had read about the Nazi Party and also hoped there wouldn't be another war, especially when the last one had been called the war to end all wars.

I was in the apartment when Zheng Yan and Ping Li came back from their meeting with Senhora Alveres.

'We've told her we would love to stay here, Lizzie. It's a Portuguese colony and because Portugal will be neutral in any war then we should be safe here. When the family goes back to Portugal a few years from now, then we can go on to Hong Kong if we want to.'

I was so happy for them. It saved me a lot of worry, knowing they were safe and happy with the family.

Ping Li said, 'I will teach the children Mandarin, and they are happy we are going to be here, although they say they'll miss you.'

'I'll miss them, Ping Li, and also you and Zheng Yan, but I must get back to Scotland and Peter.'

As it turned out, I didn't have to go to Hong Kong to catch my ship, as Senhora Alveres booked me a berth on a cargo ship that had room for six passengers on board and was leaving Macao for

London. Senhora Alveres had wanted me to travel by a P&O liner that was due to leave Hong Kong later that month, but I said I was happy to take the cargo boat, especially as it was heading straight for London

It was such an unhappy time when I finally said goodbye to my friends. Isabella and Frederick gave me a posy of flowers, while their mother said they would look after Zheng Yan and Ping Li and keep them safe.

I stood on the dock where that awful night we had found Zheng Yan injured. I hugged Ping Li and her husband, and we were all crying while Senhora Alveres stood in the background. I waved to her. I had given her all my thanks before leaving, and she said she hoped Jonas was alive and well. I went aboard, ready to leave Macao and the Orient for good. I knew I would never go back to Shanghai or Macao, but hopefully some time in the future I would see Hong Kong again.

'I'll write to you,' I called from the rail. 'Let me have your news as well.' I held up my jade pendant and Ping Li smiled.

'Keep it safe, Lizzie. It will bring you great luck, as it has done here.'

48

HOMEWARD BOUND

I was glad that the ship had called at Macao for some more cargo, otherwise I would have had to travel to Hong Kong and to find a ship there instead. I was also glad I had chosen this ship to travel back on, as all of the passengers were elderly people who had left Hong Kong to travel back to Britain. Together, we were three men and three women, and although we were pleasant to each other, at mealtimes there wasn't the same emphasis on social occasions, as most of us retired to our cabins after the evening meal.

It was such a contrast to my outboard journey, when I had met Elsie and her mother, and Ada and Hannah. I wondered how the two sisters were now and if they were still in Egypt.

My main worry was Peter and Jonas. I hoped that Elsie had managed to get Peter to Margaret's house, and I couldn't wait to see him again, as he was my baby. I tried hard not to think about Jonas, as I had no idea where he was or if indeed he was still alive. Personally I felt he was still alive, but then I remembered my mother having this same feeling about my father.

Some days on deck I would gaze at the vast expanse of water and think back to that horrific night of the typhoon. I could never have imagined how strong the wind was or the height of the waves, and even thinking about it made me feel ill. At the time I really thought we were all going to die and I would never see my child again.

Still, I had to look on the bright side. We had survived that sea voyage, and meeting Senhora Alveres had been like meeting a guardian angel. I knew Zheng Yan and Ping Li had done the right thing in staying in Macao.

Although the ship was going to London, most of the crew were Chinese. I didn't understand the language, however, the captain spoke English and the crew couldn't do enough for us. Even the male passengers, who had been a bit grumpy at the start, were now happy to be aboard, and I mentally counted the days until we reached London.

There were a couple of stops, but only to take on more provisions, and none of the passengers went ashore. It was as if we all wanted to get back home. The two other women, Anna and Barbara, were sisters and they had been on holiday with an aunt and uncle in Hong Kong, while the men were all retired from various jobs in the colony. My favourite man was old Mr Matthews, who had worked for many years in a bank in Hong Kong but was now travelling back to live with his sister in Brighton.

We spent many an afternoon chatting on deck. I said one day, 'I loved working in Hong Kong at the school. My favourite shop was Mr Wang's Wonderful World of Books.'

His face lit up. 'I went there all the time, but I never saw you there. I'm sure I would have remembered such a pretty woman.' He lowered his voice. 'You know that Mr Wang has died?'

I was shocked and said I hadn't known. I asked how he had died.

'It was all so sudden. One minute he was sitting at his table with his abacus by his side and the next he was dead. They say it was a heart attack, but I'm not so sure.'

'What do you mean, Mr Matthews? If it wasn't a heart attack, what did he die from?'

'Well, I know he refused to pay protection money to one of the local gangs and I wouldn't have put it past them to kill him.'

I was upset at hearing this and I hoped it wasn't true. Lovely old Mr Wang had deserved a dignified death.

Mr Matthews also knew about the school. 'Sandy was a real character, wasn't he? He loved his Chinese food and drink.'

I said he did. I couldn't understand why I had never met Mr Matthews before, but with the teeming population of the colony that was understandable.

That night in bed I wore my jade pendant and thought about Mr Wang. I had adored him from the first moment I had met him, and he'd seemed to like me. I just hoped and prayed that he had died from a heart attack and not at the hands of a sinister gang. Thinking about gangs, I wondered if our landlady in Macao was still setting her accomplices off to rob innocent travellers. But maybe that was just my vivid imagination running wild because I didn't like her.

We were now passing through the Suez Canal and I knew we were almost back home. I just hoped the Bay of Biscay wasn't as turbulent as the East China Sea.

As it turned out it was very choppy, and most of the passengers stayed in their cabins. I was the only one out and about, and I was just so pleased that my voyage was almost over.

49

MARGARET'S ACCIDENT

It was cold and foggy when we reached the docks at London, and it was almost impossible to see where the water ended and the dock began. I gathered up my bag and made my way to the deck. Mr Matthews was already waiting.

'Let me carry your bag,' he said, picking it up. 'Heavens, it's light, isn't it? I like a woman who travels light.'

I laughed. By now we had been joined by the other passengers as we made our way to the customs office. After we were through all the formalities, I said goodbye to Mr Matthews

'I'm going to get a taxi to take me to the railway station. Do you want to join me?'

I had actually thought of taking a bus, but I had forgotten how cold it was in Britain during the winter, so I said yes.

The railway station was full of passengers and the trains stood on the platforms belching out huge plumes of steam. Mr Matthews scrutinised the destination board and found that a train was already waiting to leave for Brighton.

He shook my hand. 'Goodbye, Lizzie, and I hope everything is fine back home.' He squinted up at the board. 'It looks like you will have a couple of hours before your train.'

I said I didn't mind. I waved at him as the train took off, and he saluted. I was amazed by all the colourful characters I had met over the past few years and I knew I would never forget them.

The cold fog was seeping into my thin coat, so I made my way to the buffet and sat down with a hot cup of tea. I was back home and I would soon meet up with Margaret and Peter.

Then my train was announced and I boarded it. I was lucky to get a window seat, as the compartments quickly filled up. I had bought a couple of sandwiches from the buffet to keep me going on the journey home, and as I watched the ghostly silhouettes of buildings flash past me I knew my journey was almost over.

I had fallen asleep by the time we reached York, but I had to stay awake after that because I had to change trains in Edinburgh. I had a notion of breaking my journey to go to see Elsie, but by the time we reached Edinburgh I had changed my mind. I would get in touch with her when I was back home.

I felt a pang of emotion when the train crossed the Forth Bridge and a feeling of joy when we crossed the Tay Bridge. I hurried to the East Station on my last leg of the journey and caught the teatime train to Carnoustie. It was dusk by the time I walked to the cottage, and the sea was grey and choppy.

I couldn't see any lights on when I walked up the garden path and a feeling of panic gripped me. I couldn't see why Margaret would be out so late with a toddler. When I reached the door, it was locked.

I looked in through the windows, but there was no sign of life. Thankfully I knew where Margaret kept her spare key – it was still hanging from the hook in the shed. I switched the lights on and everything looked neat and tidy, but there had been no fire lit, at least not that day. Margaret's bedroom was the same as I remembered it, and the other bedroom had some children's books and a few toys in it, so Peter had been here, but where were they now?

By now the cold had really made me shivery, so I lit the fire and put the kettle on. I missed the warmth of Macao, Shanghai and Hong Kong, but the fire soon heated the room up. I had no idea who to call, but because I was so weary from all the travelling I decided to make something to eat; then maybe Margaret and Peter would come through the door.

It was the paper boy next morning who woke me. I hurried to

the door, but he must have been running because he was away down the road. I told myself that everything must be all right if the paper boy was delivering the newspaper.

After a hurried breakfast, I made my way into town. I thought my best bet would be the post office, so I went inside. A young girl was behind the counter, but when I asked about Margaret she shook her head.

'I don't know any Mrs Cook, sorry.'

I was almost in tears when a woman came in.

'Do you know a Mrs Cook?' asked the young woman.

The woman said, 'Yes, I do. Why do you ask?'

I almost threw myself at her. 'I'm her niece, Lizzie, and I'm looking for her.'

The woman looked at me in surprise. 'Her niece from Shanghai?'

I said yes. 'I've just returned from Macao and I'm looking for my son, Peter.'

'Well, I knew she had a little boy living with her, but I don't know where he is now. Your aunt is in the Royal Infirmary, as she had an accident and banged her head against a rock.'

'Oh my God,' I said. 'Where has the little boy gone?'

'I think someone came and took him away, but I think that was before she had the accident.'

I was almost in tears. Who had taken Peter away and why had Margaret allowed it? I couldn't understand it. My mind was in a whirl. I had to go to the infirmary to see her and find out what on earth had happened.

I caught the train and hurried up to the infirmary. It wasn't the visiting time, so I had to wait another hour in the waiting room. As the visitors streamed into the wards, I found out which ward Margaret was in and hurried along the corridor.

She was in a large ward, but she was sleeping when I got to her bed.

'Margaret,' I said, gently nudging her. 'It's Lizzie, Margaret.'

She opened her eyes and said, 'I thought you were dead,' before going back to sleep.

I went to see the ward nurse, who said Margaret was recovering from a bad fall on the beach and was suffering from concussion. 'She may not know who you are, but she should get better soon.'

I explained about Peter, but the nurse said that no child had been in the house when she was brought in a week ago. Margaret was sitting up when I returned, but as I sat down she said, 'Thank you for coming, Beth.'

I held her hand. 'I'm not Beth; I'm Lizzie, Beth's daughter.'

Margaret looked at me, but I could see that she wasn't the woman I had left when I went off abroad. She must have had a bad knock to cause this confusion, but as I was leaving the nurse came and said the doctor wanted to see me.

I met him in his room and he came straight to the point. 'Mrs Cook can go home now, as she has recovered from her head wound.'

'I'm worried about her confused state of mind, doctor. She doesn't recognise me and I'm worried about my son.'

'I don't understand,' he said. I told him the entire story about Peter's evacuation back to my aunt's house and how he was missing.

The doctor was nonplussed. 'She didn't mention a little boy when she was brought in. Have you spoken to some of her friends?'

'I don't know all Margaret's friends or where they live, so I don't know who to ask.'

'Well, you can come and take your aunt home tomorrow, and her memory will come back, unless of course she was getting forgetful before her fall.'

Before going home, I decided to go to see Maisie Mulholland at Victoria Road. I felt a bit guilty because I hadn't written to her since I'd sent Peter's photo. It was strange being back where I used to live with Granny and Mum, but there were different curtains on our window and a new nameplate on the door. I lingered for a few moments as the memories came flooding back, then went next door to see Maisie.

When I got to her door, there was a young woman coming out pushing a toddler in a pushchair. For one moment I thought it was Peter, but when she turned I realised it was a stranger.

'I'm sorry to bother you,' I said, 'but I'm looking for Mrs Mulholland.'

The woman gave me a sympathetic glance. 'Oh, I'm sorry, but Mrs Mulholland died three months ago. Are you a relative?'

I was shocked. 'No, she was a neighbour of ours a few years ago.'

Why hadn't Margaret let me know? Then it struck me that her letter would have gone to Shanghai after we had left. I felt like I was living in a nightmare where everything had changed and I was no longer in control of my life. It was like being on another planet.

I got back to the house and there was a note from the newsagent apologising for sending the paper to the house on the day I arrived and saying there would be no charge as the shop owner knew Margaret had been taken to hospital.

The weather had turned colder and bleaker, and the sea was a dull grey against an even greyer sky. I had never been so miserable in my life, but I hoped to write to Jonas's father in Ireland and get his help, as he was my only hope.

I knew Margaret's friend had said someone had taken Peter away before Margaret's fall, but as I sat looking out the window I had terrible thoughts. Why had Margaret been on the beach when she fell? Had she taken Peter to play on the sands and had he run off into the water? Was that why she had fallen? Had she been running after him and had he been washed out to sea?

I stood up. I had to try to banish these awful thoughts from my mind. Was this how parents of missing children felt? Did they imagine terrible scenes until they could no longer contemplate living without their child and went slowly mad?

I asked myself if this is what my mother had gone through when Dad was missing, and I realised that she had. At the time I hadn't understood her obsession with maintaining he was still alive, but now that I was in the same situation it was tearing me apart. All through the journey to get back home I had thought that Peter and Margaret would be here and that we would be reunited, but instead I had these nightmarish visions and was wondering where he was and if he was safe.

The next morning I went to the hospital and Margaret was discharged. I was worried about my financial situation in addition to everything else, but I managed to get a taxi to take us back to Carnoustie.

Margaret looked normal as she sat looking out of the window, but when she saw the sea her eyes lit up. 'We're going home, Beth,' she said, turning to me, then frowning. 'You're not Beth.'

'No, Margaret. I'm Lizzie, your niece. Don't you remember me?'

She didn't answer, and I saw the driver give me a puzzled frown in his mirror.

Thankfully we soon arrived at the house and I ushered her in. I had put the fire on before leaving and the room was lovely and cosy. I put her in her chair and went to make some tea and toast. When I came back, she said, 'Yes, it's Lizzie. I thought you had died.'

My heart soared. Maybe she was getting her memory back.

'No, Margaret, I didn't die. I left Shanghai, but Jonas, my husband, is missing. Did he contact you?'

'Jonas, Jonas . . . No, I don't know anyone called Jonas.'

I let it pass, as it would take some time for her to remember everything. She enjoyed her snack and said she would have a lie-down, as she felt tired. It was so sad, because Margaret had never been tired in all the time I'd known her. She had been my rock, but now she was frail. I realised she was an old woman with a failing mind.

I was writing my letter to Jonas's father when she came through. She was holding a teddy bear that had belonged to Peter. It was threadbare now, but he had loved it as a baby.

'Peter's teddy, he forgot to take it with him.'

I leapt up. 'Yes, Margaret, where did Peter go when he left his teddy behind?'

She frowned, as if thinking hard. 'Jonas took him to his uncle's house. He told me Lizzie was dead and he needed his family to take care of Peter, but I don't think he wanted his teddy.'

I was almost delirious with joy. Jonas was here in Scotland and he had Peter. Although I knew the address of the farm, I didn't know the telephone number and so had to go out and find it.

Margaret had never put a telephone in the house, so I said to her, 'I have to go out to make a phone call. I won't be long.'

I knew there was a phone box in the main street and I made my way there. A large directory hung from a chain, but it only listed the numbers for Dundee and district, so I made my way to the post office in the hope they could help me.

Thankfully the postmistress was on duty behind the mesh screen and not the young woman who hadn't been any help previously and didn't seem to know anyone. I explained my problem and she kindly looked the number up for me.

'You can use my telephone, as I know your aunt very well.'

It seemed ages till I was connected, but after a few rings it was answered by a man. His was a voice I loved so much and thought I would never hear again. It was Jonas.

I was crying but just managed to blurt out, 'Jonas, it's Lizzie,' before I had to sit down.

The postmistress took over the call, and I heard her crisp, business-like voice tell him that I was phoning from Carnoustie and that I had turned up a few days ago and was now with my aunt.

She put the phone down. 'He's coming straight away with your son and will be here as soon as possible.'

I ran to her side and gave her a hug. 'Thank you so much,' I said with tears streaming down my face.

When I got back to Margaret, I said, 'Jonas and Peter are coming here, Margaret. Isn't that wonderful?'

She gave me a blank stare and said, 'Jonas: do I know him?'

I could only offer up a prayer of thanks to whatever god looks after us. Margaret had had a lucid moment prompted by the appearance of the teddy bear and my life was wonderful again.

It was as I stood up that I realised I had been clutching my jade pendant all the time from the ordeal of the telephone box up to now, when I was back in the house.

'Thank you, Mr Wang, wherever you are now,' I said.

Margaret said, 'Do I know a Mr Wang?'

'No, Margaret, but you would have loved him if you had.'

I was still waiting later that day and even went to stand outside in the street. I heard a train go past and I hoped Jonas and Peter would be on it. I had no idea how long it would take them to come from Dumfries, but I was counting the minutes.

I was on the verge of going back inside when I saw two figures walking up the road, and I ran down to meet them. Jonas took me in his arms and we both hugged Peter. We were crying and Peter joined in, but I kissed him and said Mummy was back and not to cry. He was clutching a toy car, and never in my life had I thought I would experience such joy.

As we walked back to the house, Jonas said he never thought I had died. 'You're a survivor, Lizzie, but I had to face the likelihood that you had drowned in the typhoon.'

I said we would talk about it later, after we put Peter to bed.

Margaret was waiting for us and she seemed to recognise Peter. He ran to her and wanted her to pick him up, which she did.

'Do you want me to read you a story, Peter? Well, go and get one of your books from your room and I'll read it to you.'

I was amazed how quirky memory could be, as one minute Margaret looked blank and the next she was holding a conversation. I suspected it was words and objects that triggered her memory and made her remember.

Jonas gave her a hug and she responded. He took a bottle of whisky from his bag and said, 'I think we all deserve a drink to celebrate Lizzie's return.'

Margaret said she wanted a gin and tonic. I found the bottle in the kitchen cupboard and we sat at the fire while she read Peter a story. Later we had a lovely meal and put Peter to bed.

Margaret said she was also tired, so she left the room. Jonas and I sat on the sofa with our drinks.

'I thought you were also dead, Jonas,' I said. 'I left you a letter when Zheng Yan, Ping Li and I left to go to Hong Kong. Did you get it?'

He said he had. 'Alex and I went to Peking as planned, but the Japanese air force was bombing it and it was a terrible sight: fires everywhere and dead bodies lying in the streets. We were both shocked by the brutality of the attacks, but after Alex filmed the carnage while I wrote my notes we decided to leave. The roads were blocked by thousands of refugees fleeing the city and we took ages to travel a few miles. It was when we stopped for a break that a Japanese aircraft flew overhead and dropped more bombs. The poor people on the road didn't have a chance and entire families were wiped out. The grandparents, parents, children and babies . . . It was terrible. I was hit by a piece of shrapnel and lost a lot of blood. Alex saved my life, Lizzie: he made a tourniquet from his scarf and tied it around my thigh. He drove for a few miles till someone said there was a Mission hospital in one of the villages that had escaped the bombing. The doctor was a man called Crawford who had come out to China from Aberdeen. Well, he managed to stem the flow of blood, but he said I couldn't travel on the pot-holed roads as I would start bleeding again. We stayed there for over two weeks and then set off. There were more air raids and we had to take our time. We gave a lift to one young girl and her baby and took them to Shanghai, but by then the Japanese were also bombing the city and there were lots of dead people lying about.'

He stopped and wiped his eyes.

'Then Alex found out about Sue Lin and he almost went out of his mind. He went looking for her, but the dead people at the amusement park had been buried and he couldn't find her grave. Then I saw your letter and was grateful that you had all got out alive. I told Alex I was going to Hong Kong to find you and he said he was leaving as well, as there was nothing left to keep him in Shanghai. I cleared out our bank account and packed a few things while Alex packed his photographic equipment and all his negatives, and then we set off.

'We arrived just after the typhoon and there were hundreds killed in it. I had no idea when you had left, but when there was no sign of any of you in the colony and when I found out the shipping office had no booking for you and neither had the British Consulate, I had to face the fact you had all perished at sea. The school was closed and Mr Wang was dead, so I had no one to ask about you. Alex and I decided to come back here.'

'How is Alex?' I asked.

'He's just the same. Consumed with grief. He went to see Sue Lin's parents in Glasgow, but he's now in London working as a freelance photographer. He works night and day, and he says it's the only way he can cope with losing Sue Lin. I said I was the same, but I had Peter to look after so I couldn't let myself go mad with grief. I came here, as I knew Elsie was bringing Peter here. Margaret couldn't believe you were probably dead and she was grief-stricken. I told her I would take Peter to my uncle's house in Dumfries, but told her I would be back with him after my uncle and his family leave to go back to Ireland.'

'Are they leaving the farm?'

'Yes, they are, and they leave this week. I didn't know about Margaret's accident, otherwise I would have come back sooner.' He turned and looked at me. 'Now what happened to you and Zheng Yan and Ping Li?'

I told him of the terrible voyage during the typhoon and how we ended up in Macao.

'You ended up in Macao?' he said incredulously.

I said we had and related the whole story before finally saying, 'Zheng Yan and Ping Li are staying there with the Alveres family and they are happy and settled, Jonas.'

He sighed. 'I'm so glad about that.' He lay back on the sofa.

I looked at the clock. It was three o'clock in the morning.

'Come on, Jonas, it's time for bed.'

We lay in each other's arms and said we were so happy that we were together again. Then Jonas, with his usual romantic streak, fell sound asleep while I gazed out of the window and listened to the sound of the sea.

The next morning Margaret looked much better and her memory seemed to be improving. After breakfast, Jonas, Peter and I went for a walk along the beach.

'I don't know what your plans are for where we will stay, Jonas, but I don't think I want to leave Margaret alone.'

He smiled. 'I was intending to stay here anyway, Lizzie, so this will be our home. That's if Margaret wants us to stay.'

'Oh, I think she does. She'll just love all your stories of adventure and she'll tell you all about her times in foreign countries.'

50

A VISIT TO CORK

I couldn't believe how easy it was to slip back into a normal life again. Jonas was in contact with Alex, as they were planning another book on their experiences in Peking. He would travel down to London every few months to stay with his friend in his flat in Holland Park. I missed him terribly, but I had Peter to look after and Margaret for company.

I hadn't realised that a lot of Margaret's friends had either died or were now living with their families, which meant she didn't have a great social life like she used to, but she said she was quite happy at home.

'When you get to my age, Lizzie, going out and about doesn't hold the same pleasure, and I've had a lot of memories to look back on from when I was married to Gerald.'

'I'm sorry I wasn't with you when he died, Margaret. It must have been a shock.'

'Yes, it was, but then I realised he had died doing what he enjoyed, and he did say should he die in another country he wanted laid to rest there, so I obeyed his wishes.'

If the weather was good, Margaret and I would take Peter in the pushchair to the shops, where she liked to browse, especially the chemist in the High Street, where she would buy scented soaps. 'It's always been my one luxury,' she said as the assistant handed over the fancy box in a paper bag.

I wrote letters to Milly and Elsie, and Elsie said she would be coming for a visit. I was dying to meet her again and to thank her for looking after Peter. One day I took Peter into Dundee to buy him new shoes, and after leaving Birrell's shoe shop in the Overgate we made our way to the Hawkhill to see Irene and Wullie. I hadn't seen them since coming home but had written to Laura, who had written back with the news that she was now married to her teacher boyfriend. She said her mother had sent on my letter.

Irene's close was still as I remembered it and the memories came flooding back of my many visits to the house. Irene opened the door and looked surprised. 'Lizzie, how wonderful to see you.' She bent down 'And this must be Peter.'

Peter responded by hiding behind my back, and she laughed. 'Are you normally a shy little boy?'

'Sometimes he is, Irene, but not all the time.'

I was sitting with a cup of tea when she went to get Laura's wedding photos. They had been taken in a photographic studio in Lindsay Street and Laura looked lovely in a pale-coloured suit, while Pat looked uncomfortable in high-heeled shoes. The groom was not much taller than Laura. He had dark hair and was wearing glasses. He also had a serious look on his face, while Laura was smiling, and Pat, dear Pat, was trying to look like she was wearing comfy old slippers instead of toe-pinching new shoes.

'Laura wrote to you in China, Lizzie, to tell you about the wedding, but there was no answer. John was a teacher at the Morgan Academy, but he got a deputy headmaster's post in a school in Newcastle. He asked Laura to marry him so they could both go, and she's also working in another school in the same town. When your letter arrived, I sent it on to her.'

'I did explain that I had to leave China in a hurry and I never got her letter. It's probably lying in my post box in Bubbling Well Road.'

Irene looked delighted by the name of the road. 'It sounds much better than the Hawkhill, doesn't it?'

I said no, it didn't. I hadn't gone into any detail about my life after leaving Shanghai and I didn't want to mention it now, so I said, 'It's so good to be back, Irene, and will you tell Laura to keep in touch and I'll send her a wedding present.'

Irene went to take the cups away and I looked at the photo again. John was an average-looking man, just like Jonas, and I couldn't help smiling at our younger selves when Laura and I used to swoon at the Hollywood film stars and tell each other they were going to be like the men we married. It was all fantasy, of course, and real life was nothing like it. Falling in love was all that mattered, and having a happy life.

When Irene returned, I asked, 'How is Pat?'

'She's still teaching in the same school in Kirriemuir and living with her parents. Between you and me, Lizzie, I don't think she'll ever get married – she's not interested in having a boyfriend.'

'I see you still have your piano, Irene. Do you still play it?'

'Yes, I do, but not so much now.'

I stood up, ready to go, and took Peter's hand. 'Please tell Wullie I'm asking after him, and I'll hopefully see you soon.'

She came to the street to see me off and waved while I walked to the station to catch my train.

Margaret was reading the paper when we got home. She was now wearing reading glasses, but it always amused me to see her with a large, round magnifying glass, which she used to read the small print.

She saw me looking and she laughed. 'It's a real burden when you get old, Lizzie.'

'You're not old, Margaret. Maybe a bit well preserved, but not old.'

She burst out laughing. 'You always had a way with words.'

Later that year, Jonas suggested going to see his father in Cork and I said it was a great idea. We had been writing to one another since we'd come back to Scotland, but this would be my first visit to Jonas's family home.

Margaret was also excited because she said she had never been to Ireland before. 'I've been all over the world, but I've never been there.' That made two of us.

We set off in the summer, but I had a moment of panic as I stepped aboard the ferry. I still had nightmares now and again about the typhoon, but they were getting better. Now it all came back to me. Jonas must have felt my body stiffen as we boarded, and he clutched my hand tightly.

'It'll be fine, Lizzie. The weather forecast is for light winds and the Irish Sea should be reasonably calm.'

I nodded and felt so embarrassed by my panic attack. As it turned out, the sea crossing was a pleasure, and when we reached Dublin we caught the train to Cork. My father-in-law's farm and horse stud lay a few miles from the city and I couldn't get over how everything was so green.

We were made so welcome, not only by Jonas's father but also by his uncle and aunt, Sean and Kathleen, who had a farm not far away. Kathleen was slightly younger than Margaret, but they got on famously with one another.

Jonas's father was the same height as his son and had the same colouring. He was very thin and wiry, with strong-looking arms, which he laughingly said came in handy when controlling the horses.

The farmhouse was just as I imagined it, with a big, cosy kitchen with a log fire, and tiny bedrooms under the eaves. Jonas, Peter and I were in his old bedroom, while Margaret's bedroom overlooked the garden.

On the first day there, Jonas said, 'Please don't let Peter near the horses, Lizzie.'

When I said his father might want to show them to us, he told me to make sure Peter wasn't near them, and I promised.

Kathleen had an old but very comfortable car, and she would take us into Cork for shopping. She would go off with Margaret and they'd end up in one of the many cafés while I'd look round the shops with Peter. We would take his pushchair, and I loved walking around the town with him before joining the two ladies as they sat chatting over their morning coffee.

One morning while Jonas was out for a walk, his father

said, 'Let me show you the stables, Lizzie. Peter will like them.'

I was in a quandary. I had made a promise to Jonas, but I didn't want to hurt his father's feelings. I hesitated and the old man gave me a keen look. 'Jonas doesn't want Peter to be near them, does he?'

'No, he doesn't. I'm sorry, but I did promise him I wouldn't let Peter near them.'

He sighed. 'I suppose it is all my fault, this phobia Jonas has about the horses. He's been frightened of them since he was a child.'

I was surprised. 'Frightened by horses?' All the time I had known my husband, he hadn't been frightened by anything.

'When he was small, he was playing near the stables and his ball went into one of the stalls. Jonas ran in after it, and we had this very skittish and frisky horse there and it reared up just where Jonas was standing. My late wife Mary managed to grab him and get him out, and she gave me such a telling off about it. She told Jonas that horses were dangerous and he should never go near them again, and he didn't.'

I felt sorry for him, and I understood how Jonas felt. It must have been a terrifying thing to happen to a little boy. In fact, it was a wonder he had been able to go and lead a life full of danger with his work in China.

When Jonas came back, I mentioned the conversation. 'Can I not hold on to Peter and let him look at the horses from a distance? It'll make his grandfather happy.'

I must have had my pleading face on, because he relented. 'Now don't go too close.'

The next morning, much to Jonas Snr's delight, we made our way to the stables. There were twelve stalls and everything was clean and fresh. I heard the noise from the stalls and the horses put their heads out of the doors. Peter gave a cry of pleasure when he saw them and stretched out his chubby arms towards them.

His grandfather said he could touch them if he liked, but I was full of misgivings. I edged a little bit further forward, and to my amazement the horse in the nearest stall let Peter clap him on the head, and it even nuzzled his little hand.

His grandfather stood beside him with a look of pleasure. 'Peter loves the horses, but more importantly they love him back. Horses pick up frightened thoughts, and because Jonas was always frightened around them they reacted to his fear.'

'But that's just one horse who likes Peter,' I said. 'Maybe the others will be different.' But they weren't, and I couldn't believe my eyes.

I told Jonas later how the visit had gone and he shook his head. When I mentioned about being frightened, he said, 'Well, that's true enough, I was frightened of them.'

Every day during our visit, Peter and his grandfather would be at the stables, where the horses would gently nuzzle Peter's outstretched hands as he helped to feed them. In the evening, after a huge meal and after Peter was in bed, we would sit around the fire. Sometimes Sean and Kathleen would be there, and we sat with a glass of Irish whiskey and chatted. The talk was usually about the farm or the stables, but it soon turned to the state of the world.

'There's going to be another war with Germany,' said Sean. 'Yon Hitler fellow and the Nazi Party are determined to march into the Rhineland.'

My husband agreed with him. 'It's the same in China. Japan is going to overrun the east coast port cities and it's only a matter of time before they attack other places. Then there's this civil war in Spain. My friend Alex has been there to document the fighting. He tells me it's terrible, with hundreds dead.'

I hated all this talk of war. What a terrible world we lived in when people couldn't live in peace with their neighbours and get on with living day after day without the fear of bombs and advancing armies.

Margaret said it was the fault of the Versailles Treaty. 'It left Germany on the brink of bankruptcy after the war, and now all this discontent and vast inflation has set it all alight again. Gerald and I saw lots of local skirmishes in the countries we lived in, but this war, if it does come to that, will be much more serious.'

Jonas agreed with her, and after we were in bed I asked him, 'Do you really think there's going to be another war?'

'I don't think it, Lizzie, I know it. The Japanese won't be content with what they have, because they plan to rule the entire Asian continent and the Pacific Ocean islands.'

It was difficult to think about war in this green and peaceful land, so I tried to put it out of my mind.

We stayed for two months in Cork, but soon it was time to go back home. Jonas was keen to get back to writing his book and I knew he would want to see Alex and discuss it with him.

It was difficult to say goodbye, but we boarded the train as Jonas's family stood on the platform and saw us off. 'Try to come back soon,' they said, as the train pulled out of the station.

The sea was a bit rougher on the homeward crossing, and I stayed in the salon with Peter and Margaret while Jonas went up on the deck.

I was glad to be home, even though we had had a wonderful time. I opened all the windows to let the fresh air into the house, as it was a bit musty, and the sea breeze soon dispersed the stale air.

There was a letter from Elsie waiting for me and I answered it immediately, telling her we had been away. She said she was planning to come and visit, and we made a date for that.

Autumn had come early and the weather turned more chilly, but the sun shone the day Elsie arrived. She looked better than the last time I had seen her, as she had put on some weight and was not as thin as she had been in Shanghai.

I thanked her for looking after Peter and asked her if there was news of Ronnie.

'He's dead,' she said simply. 'The manager of the mill has come back to England and he told Ronnie's father that he had been killed in a bombing raid. His father wanted to bring his body back home, but the Japanese said he had been buried in a cemetery in Shanghai.'

I was upset at this news, but Elsie had remained dry-eyed when she'd mentioned it.

'I should be sorry for him,' she said, 'but he told me the marriage was over, so although I never wanted him dead, I don't feel any emotion about him.'

'What about the woman he was living with?' I asked.

She shrugged her shoulders. 'The manager never mentioned Ivanka, so I don't know what's become of her. Maybe she died along with Ronnie. I don't know. I felt sorry for her, Lizzie. That day I confronted Ronnie, she came running after me and begged me to try to get her a passport, but I had to tell her I couldn't help. I still feel guilty, though there was nothing I could do.'

I walked her back to the station. 'Are you still living with your mother?'

She screwed up her mouth. 'Yes, I am, but I suppose I'm grateful she's given me a roof over my head.'

'What about Ronnie's father, could he not help out financially?'

'I told him I didn't want his money because I blame him for sending Ronnie out there in the first place. Maybe if we had stayed in Edinburgh and got our own little artist's studio we could still be happily married.'

I doubted that, although I didn't say so. I thought Ronnie would have been the way he was in Shanghai even if he had stayed in Edinburgh, or indeed in any place.

As Elsie was boarding the train, she said, 'Do you remember I told you about Robert Macdonald, that policeman in Shanghai? The one who had been at school with me? Well, guess what, he's back in Edinburgh and has joined the police force there. We met up quite by accident and we've become really good friends. We go out to the pictures and dances, and he's good company.'

'Aye aye,' I thought. 'Do I suspect a romantic involvement?' Well, I hoped for Elsie's sake it was, but time would tell.

51

A NEW ARRIVAL AND ANOTHER WAR

I suspected I was pregnant but hadn't said anything to Jonas. I felt nauseous in the mornings, but I wanted to make sure before mentioning it, so I made an appointment with the doctor and he confirmed it. We would have another addition to the family in September.

Although I was pleased to be having another baby, I was worried about the state of the world, with all these rumours of war. Peter was getting bigger every day and it would soon be his fourth birthday.

As we lay in bed that night, I told Jonas about the new baby and he sat up and held me tight. 'That's great news, Lizzie. Peter will have a new brother or sister.'

I told him of my fears about bringing a new baby into a world where another war could break out at any time, but he said that women had been having the same fears since the dawn of time and either you survived or you didn't. 'Don't worry, Lizzie. All will be well, because we are survivors.'

I said the baby was due in September, which meant Peter would be four and a half years old. We told Margaret the next morning as we sat down for breakfast, and like Jonas she was also delighted.

'It's lovely to have a family around you, Lizzie. Sadly Gerald and I couldn't have any children. Whether it was his fault or mine I don't know, but at the time we didn't mind, as Gerald loved his work. I would have liked a child, but it didn't happen.'

She sounded so sad that I went and gave her a hug.

'You were like a mother to me, Margaret, especially after Mum died, and I appreciate it.'

She took my hand. 'I also felt like I was a sister to Beth when my mother married your grandfather. She was like my baby sister, and then you came along and you took her place. I've been very lucky to have had two children to care for.'

I was planning on having a small family party for Peter and I had ordered a birthday cake from the local baker, Goodfellow & Steven. Then I had to smile when Jonas came back from the town with a train set. It had metal rails, an engine and carriages plus a station, signal box and even some houses and trees.

Jonas set it up the night before Peter's birthday so he could see it when he woke up. As I lay in bed that night, Jonas was still playing with it and it made me wonder if he had bought it for himself or his son. When he finally came to bed, I said, 'Well, is the train safely parked in the station?'

He grinned at me and said he had to make sure it was working, otherwise Peter would be disappointed if it wasn't.

Peter had birthday cards from Ireland and also from Elsie and Betsy and Jeannie Miller in Edinburgh. We gave him our cards when he woke up and he adored his train, but I was surprised when Jonas produced another present. It was a rocking horse, which along with Margaret they had secretly bought and hidden in the wood shed. When Peter saw it, his little eyes lit up. He called it Corkie after one of the horses at his grandfather's stables. His grandfather had sent him a couple of books about horses, and his great-uncle and -aunt included a furry toy in the shape of a pony, so it turned out to be a 'horsey' birthday.

We had a family tea, but this time Peter managed to blow out the candles in one go and was able to eat a slice of cake instead of sticking his fist into it like he had done in Shanghai.

I was so pleased Betsy and Jeannie had remembered his

birthday. Elsie had said they were now retired and living in a small bungalow in Edinburgh. Their brother David had stayed at the Mission in China and Elsie said that was a continual worry to them.

The summer arrived, with a heatwave in June, and Peter played on the beach most days with his bucket and spade. For some reason, he never liked the water to go over his feet and I was glad, because that meant he wasn't in danger of going out too far.

Margaret loved the sun, and she would sit in the old faded deckchair on the veranda doing her crossword or reading. The situation in Europe was getting worse, but I hoped it wouldn't come to anything. After all, the last war, which had killed so many people, was still fresh in people's minds.

In the evening we loved to sit on the veranda and watch the sun go down over the sea. At ten o'clock, Margaret would go and make cocoa and take it to her room, where she had a small wireless she liked to listen to. Meanwhile Jonas and I would sit until twilight.

One night I was so overcome by the beautiful sunset that I asked him, 'Jonas, do you miss living in China?'

He didn't answer straight away but sat looking out to sea. Then he said, 'Yes, I miss it sometimes. I miss the sounds from the streets and playing mah-jong with Zheng Yan. I miss the rickshaws and the people and the adventure of going to places and writing about them.'

I was sorry I had asked, because I thought it meant he was unhappy living in this tiny town and this small house by the sea.

'Although I said I miss things, Lizzie, it was when I thought I was going to die when that bomb exploded that I suddenly realised I might never see you or Peter again, and that made me realise the true value of life. It's not searching for adventure or living with danger that counts, it's the value of love and family and home. That's what life is all about.' He put his arm around me and I snuggled up to him. 'What do you miss?' he asked.

I had no hesitation. 'I miss our house on Bubbling Well Road, the little paper boy and the old lady from the laundry. I often think of them and hope they're still safe and well under the Japanese regime. I miss Zheng Yan and Ping Li and the friendship they gave me, and all the little shops in the old town where entire families served their customers almost twenty-four hours a day. The person I miss most of all is Mr Wang and his Wonderful World of Books. Did I ever tell you that a passenger on the cargo ship coming here told me he thought he was murdered by a criminal gang?'

Jonas laughed. 'I doubt it. Mr Wang was ninety-five when he died.'

I couldn't believe it. 'Ninety-five? I thought he was sixty or seventy.'

There was one thing I hadn't brought up with Margaret and I mentioned it to Jonas.

'I sent a letter from Macao to Margaret to tell her where I was and that I would soon be home, but she has never mentioned it and she seemed surprised when I arrived at the hospital that day. In fact, she said I had died. What do you think about that?'

Jonas said he had no idea. 'Perhaps it got mislaid or never arrived.' He stood up. 'Right then, little mother, it's time for bed.'

It was a month later when I was cleaning out one of the drawers in the kitchen that I found out what had happened to the letter. At the back was a hard lump that looked like papier mâché. I held it in my hand wondering what on earth it was when I noticed one small patch that looked like an air-mail envelope. I tried to pull the lump apart, but it disintegrated in my hands.

I went to see Margaret and showed it to her. 'What on earth is this, Margaret?'

She took it and frowned. 'I've no idea. Where did you find it?'

'It was in the kitchen drawer.'

'Oh yes, I remember now. The postman left the mail in the box. It had been raining and there was a huge pool of water on the path. I tripped over a stone and the letters went into the water, and when I fished them out they were all soggy and the handwriting was blurry. I tried to dry them out by wringing them, but they went all lumpy, so I shoved them in a drawer to dry out. Was it anything important, Lizzie?'

I looked at her dear sweet face and smiled. 'No, Margaret, it's nothing important. I just wondered what it was.'

I mentioned this to Jonas and he said, 'Just as well you weren't shipwrecked and desperately needing help, wasn't it?'

I almost told him that I had indeed needed help, but I didn't.

It was a Sunday morning when I went into labour. I was due to give birth in the infirmary in Dundee, and Margaret collected my case, which was already packed, and saw me and Jonas off in the local taxi. Peter stood beside her and waved, but I told him Mummy would soon be home with a new sister or brother. He was clutching his toy pony and seemed more interested in that than in the new sister or brother, and that amused his father.

'I think it's very naughty of you, Lizzie, to be having a child and not a pony,' he said laughingly.

The taxi driver looked back in amazement. 'Don't worry about my husband,' I said. 'It's just his sense of humour.'

The man looked relieved. When we got to the hospital, I was admitted to one of the large wards with rows of beds on each side. It was so unlike Peter's birth in the small hospital in Shanghai, but I was glad I was in capable hands.

By now the contractions were becoming stronger, but it wasn't until eight o'clock that evening that our daughter was born. By then I felt exhausted and was just glad it was all over. The midwife put her in my arms and once again I had that strong maternal feeling of overwhelming love for another small scrap of humanity.

Jonas was allowed in to see me briefly and he said our daughter was beautiful. 'Just like her mother.' He said he would be back with Margaret during the visiting hours next day. Before he left, I said to tell Peter about the baby, and he gave me an impish grin. 'He'll be very disappointed it's not a pony.' Thankfully no one was around to hear this, as they would have thought I had married a madman.

Margaret and Jonas came the next day to see me, and I panicked when I didn't see Peter. Margaret said, 'It's all right.

Elsie is looking after him, and she's downstairs in the waiting room with him. She says she'll only stay a short time, because you'll want Jonas to be here all the visiting hour.'

Elsie came in and she looked radiant. It was so good to see her, and she congratulated me on the birth of a daughter. I asked her how she was, and she smiled as she held out her left hand to show me her engagement ring.

'Oh, Elsie, how wonderful. I wondered why you looked so happy when you came into the ward.'

'We're planning on getting married next year, and Robert and I are looking for a house in Edinburgh.'

I admired her ring before she had to leave, but Jonas also wished her all the best when he came in.

After she was gone, I said, 'I'm so pleased for her, as she had a rotten marriage to Ronnie.'

Jonas said that was true, and although he hadn't said anything to me at the time, Ronnie Lomax was well known in Shanghai's illegal opium dens.

'Did Elsie know this?' I asked.

'No, she thought he was just a drinker and a womaniser, but it was much worse, as his drug habit was getting out of control.'

'Do you know that she met her fiancé when she was in Shanghai?'

Jonas said he hadn't, but that it had proved to be a fortunate meeting.

I was allowed home after a week, and Jonas came in a taxi with Margaret and Peter to pick us up. Peter looked at his sister, then began to point out the tramcars as the taxi made its way back to Carnoustie.

That night, I said, 'We must choose a name, Jonas. I got to choose Peter so maybe you should choose your daughter's name.'

'Well, my mother's name was Mary, so what do you think about that?'

'I think that's very suitable, as my granny was also called Mary, but if you don't mind I would like to add my mum's name and make it Mary-Beth.'

Jonas thought for a bit. 'Yes, that sounds good.'

I wasn't sure how he would take my next suggestion, but I voiced it anyway. 'I would also like Margaret. I know Mary-Beth Margaret O'Neill is a mouthful, but I would like all the important people in our lives to be included.'

Jonas said I could add the entire phone directory if it made me happy, and I gave him a playful nudge.

Margaret was delighted that her name was to be given to our daughter, but she was even better pleased that I had called her Mary-Beth. 'Your mother and grandmother would have been so proud of you, Lizzie, and of Peter and the new baby.'

'Yes, I know, and I wish they were still here with us, but I do have my memories, Margaret.'

The following Sunday, on the third of September, we listened to the wireless as Neville Chamberlain announced we were now at war with Germany.

I was so upset, but Jonas said that with God's grace we would all come through this new conflict, and as we watched our daughter lying asleep and Peter playing on the rug at our feet, I gently closed my hand around my jade pendant and said a prayer as well.

I think Jonas was trying to cheer me up. 'I've just remembered another thing I miss about China.'

'What's that?'

'We won't have Ping Li singing her lullabies to Mary-Beth.'

I couldn't help but laugh.

EPILOGUE

MARCH 1952: THE YEAR OF THE DRAGON

It had been a sad year. King George IV died in February and we now had lovely young Queen Elizabeth on the throne. She had to fly back from Kenya in February when the news of the king's death broke.

We were in Hong Kong when we heard the news. Jonas, Peter, Mary-Beth and I were there to visit our old friends Zheng Yan and Ping Li.

Zheng Yan and his wife were now back living in the colony, and they were waiting to welcome us on our arrival. It was so emotional when we saw them. Ping Li ran forward with a cry of delight. They didn't look a day older than the last time I saw them on the jetty in Macao.

Ping Li gave Peter a big hug, and as she only came up to his chest it was so comical to watch. I was so proud that Peter hugged her back, while Mary-Beth hopped from one foot to the next in order to get her attention.

Ping Li turned and said, 'Mary-Beth, we are so pleased to meet you.' She looked at Peter. 'I knew your brother well, and I used to sing lullabies to him when he was a baby.'

Peter looked bewildered, but he smiled at her.

Zheng Yan shook hands with us and said he never thought this day would come. 'Come, my friends, and we will show you our factory.'

It was a large space that had once been the offices of the British Bank, but was now the workplace for forty workers who sat at their sewing machines and turned out lovely clothes.

Ping Li was beaming. 'I do the designing and Zheng Yan is the manager. We are very prosperous now, Lizzie.'

They had a lovely apartment up on the Heights, and although it wasn't very large it had a wonderful view. When we were sitting with our evening meal I said I was so glad they had come through the Japanese war and had prospered.

Zheng Yan said it was mainly because of the Alveres family, who had treated them so well during the ten years they had lived with them.

'After the Japanese were defeated we came back here, and to start with it was tough, but slowly we have built up our business. The Alveres family left Macao in 1947 to go back to Portugal.'

Ping Li told the children, 'We lived next to your parents in Shanghai and we had many adventures.'

Mary-Beth said she knew. 'Mummy and Daddy have told us all about you, and I wish I had been born in China like Peter.'

Ping Li gave me a look that said it was fortunate that she hadn't. 'Did you enjoy the Chinese New Year, Mary-Beth? It's the Year of the Dragon.'

Mary-Beth said, 'Yes, Mummy and Daddy have told us all about the twelve animals that make up the Chinese calendar. I was born in the Year of the Rabbit, but I wish it had been the Dragon or the Tiger.'

Ping Li said the year of the rabbit was a very fortunate year to be born in and this pleased Mary-Beth.

'I'll tell my friend Sheila at school and she will be jealous because she hasn't heard about the Chinese calendar.'

Peter and Mary-Beth were wide-eyed as we went around the streets, and Peter couldn't get over how congested the harbour was with the sampans. I told him I had been the same when I first saw them.

At New Year they had been delighted with the celebrations. There were dragon parades and fireworks, and we had spent ages walking through the streets, stopping to eat prawns with sticky sauce and rice and other delicacies.

When we came to Mr Wang's shop, it was no longer a bookshop but had been divided into three shops. Peter and Mary-Beth spent ages looking at the goods on display, and Ping Li bought them what they wanted.

'You mustn't spend your money on us, Ping Li,' I said.

She gave me one of her wise looks. 'Who else can I spend it on if not my good friends' children?'

Mary-Beth was fascinated by everything she saw, and although Peter was interested, it wasn't with the same intensity. My daughter very much reminded me of myself when I had first come to the colony.

At Mr Wang's old shop, Jonas said, 'This was the shop where I first met your mother.'

Mary-Beth was hopping about in delight. 'What were you doing here, Daddy?'

'I came with your uncle Alex to sign our books and this girl kept staring at me, so I felt I had to marry her,' he said with a laugh.

Mary-Beth looked at me and I nodded.

'That's right, I did, but he also stared back at me, so I accepted his proposal.'

With the mention of Alex, Zheng Yan asked, 'How is he keeping now, Jonas?'

'He'll never get over Sue Lin's death, but he keeps busy with his work. We have a new book coming out and hopefully it'll be another bestseller.'

I said I had heard from Senhora Alveres. 'They are planning on coming to London next year to see Queen Elizabeth's coronation, and Jonas and I will meet them there. Isabella won't be there, as she is working in Paris, but Frederick will be with them. I'm really looking forward to seeing them again, Ping Li. Elsie has got married again to a policeman she met in Shanghai but who went back to Edinburgh before the Japanese invaded the city. She's now Mrs Macdonald, and he was an old school friend of hers when they were young.'

'What about Margaret, is she still well?'

I said she was. 'She's moved in with a friend until we get back, but she's remarkable for her age, although she gets a bit forgetful now and again. I also had a letter out of the blue from Lorna-May Hamilton. She must have seen Margaret's address when we lived in Bubbling Well Road and she wrote on the off-chance I would get it. Conrad is now in politics and he's hoping to get elected to the Senate in Washington.'

Ping Li wasn't impressed. 'I didn't like her, but I can imagine she will be revelling in her status as a senator's wife.'

I wasn't keen on her either, but I still recalled her worry over Peter and my safety when she offered to buy us our passage out of Shanghai, so for that small act of kindness I was able to think of her favourably – not that I said this to Ping Li.

We were out sightseeing one morning when I caught Zheng Yan gazing wistfully over the harbour to the new territories.

'Will you ever go back to China?' I asked him.

He gave it some thought but shook his head. 'No, Lizzie, I don't think so. China is different now that the Communists are in power with Mao Zedong as Chairman. Oh, I'm not saying it will be any worse than it was before, but Chiang Kai-shek was right when he said he was afraid they would take over. It's a true saying: never to go back, as it will be a disappointment.'

'What about Ping Li?'

He smiled. 'She's very happy here, being the boss of her own business. We try to be good employers to our workers, as we know what it was like for the Chinese population in Shanghai, and they are grateful for the work.'

We only had another couple of days before we left to go home, and I knew I would get emotional when we said goodbye. We had been through so much together, and no matter how far apart we lived, we would always think of one another.

Mary-Beth and Peter were sad at having to leave and Mary-Beth was crying as she said goodbye. Peter was more stoical, but he let Ping Li hug him again as we left to come home. Ping Li and I held one another tight and we were both crying. Jonas said they should come to Scotland to visit us. Zheng Yan said maybe they would when they retired.

Ping Li said, 'You still wear your jade pendant, Lizzie.'

I told her I was going to give it to Mary-Beth when she was older, and Ping Li smiled and patted my hand. 'That's good.'

Then we were on our way back home.

Margaret was pleased to see us and she had news from Marie McBeth and Sandy McFarlane, or Mr and Mrs McFarlane, as they were now married: they were coming to see us and at the end of the week.

Marie looked just the same. She was dressed in her woollen jumper, thick tweed skirt and furry boots, while Sandy wore an open-neck shirt and his straw hat. He looked like Somerset Maugham.

They were pleased to see Margaret looking so well and I asked them if they liked living in Oban.

'After we got married we went to Skye to begin with, but Sandy didn't like it, so we moved to Oban and he likes it there, don't you, Sandy?'

He rolled his eyes at me but said, 'Well, I didn't to start with; then I rediscovered the gourmet delights of the fish supper and the white puddings.' He winked at me and I smiled.

'Dear Sandy,' I thought. 'If his stomach is happy, then so is he.'

Marie said she was glad they retired from Hong Kong because they would still have been there when the Japanese invaded in 1941. Sandy shuddered at the thought and I was surprised he seemed frightened. Still, I need not have worried, because he said in all seriousness, 'They might have banned Chinese food and replaced it with their own cuisine, which I think revolves around raw fish.'

'When did you decide to get married, Sandy?' I asked.

'When we came back from Hong Kong, we decided two could live cheaper than one, so that was that. Anyway, I've always had a soft spot for Marie, in spite of her culinary tastes.'

I had to laugh, as he was incorrigible, but I was so pleased for them both.

Another visitor was Milly, who was doing so well. Her son Bertie was at the university in Glasgow and was hoping to become a doctor. I couldn't help but remember the day she left Dundee, but it was the best move she made in her life.

After she left I wrote to Laura and her husband. They still lived in Newcastle but now had two sons. Pat still taught in Kirriemuir and we met up now and again to catch up with the news. The far-off days of teaching college were just a pleasant memory, as our lives had taken us down different paths.

I was in the town one day when I was approached by a young man. 'It's Miss Flint, isn't it?'

'Yes, I am, although I'm married now and I'm Mrs O'Neill.'

The lad smiled. 'You probably don't remember me, but you were my teacher at Ann Street School. I'm Charlie, and you lent me your book.'

'Oh, Charlie, how lovely to see you again. How are you?'

'I'm working in the library. It was you who gave me a love of reading and I love my job.'

After he went off, I had a small glow of pride. But it seemed neither of us became pirates.

Peter left for Cork after our trip to Hong Kong. He was going to run the stables with his grandfather, who was delighted he loved horses as much as he did, much to Jonas's amazement. I gave Peter my St Christopher medallion to keep him safe.

Alex would be coming to see us, as the new book had been published. It was called *A World in Conflict from the Rising Sun to the Swastika*. It wasn't an easy book to read, as it portrayed the brutality of war on different continents, but Jonas's text was wonderful to read and the words complimented the photographs. It was full of the courage of ordinary men and women who lived through the Blitz and the destruction of lives and homes and somehow managed to come out at the other end. It was similar to the Great War, when my father was killed.

One book critic wrote, 'It is a book that should be read by every government, dictator and tyrant to tell them war isn't the answer.'

Jonas said it wouldn't make any difference to the world, as the Korean war was being fought with the Chinese Communists and the Western powers and nothing would ever change in the world. 'There will always be wars,' he said.

We were really lucky during the war in our house by the sea. We didn't see any conflict, not like the devastation of London, Coventry, Glasgow and Clydebank and other major cities. Jonas had travelled extensively during the war years to see Alex and document the carnage, while I stayed with Margaret, Peter and Mary-Beth.

We heard the door slam and Mary-Beth came rushing in from school. I had told her repeatedly not to slam the door, but she never remembered. When she came into the room, her eyes were accusing and her face red.

'Mummy, you've forgotten to wind up the grandfather clock. You know I like to hear it ticking, as it makes the house all cosy and friendly with the little clock people looking after us.'

Margaret popped her head around the door. 'Is that Mary-Beth? I thought I heard the door.'

Jonas sighed. 'Heavens, Margaret, you could hear her in China.'

He was standing lounging against the door frame and I felt a strong urge to go and kiss him.

'Isn't it strange the traits we pass on to our children,' he said. 'There's Peter, who loves horses like his grandfather, and Mary-Beth, who loves clocks like your mother.'

I gave him a kiss as I passed. 'Yes, and she has your imagination, Jonas O'Neill. Little clock people indeed,' I said as I went to wind up Granny's grandfather clock.

As I passed my dad's photograph in its frame, I thought back to my meeting with Andy Baxter a few months earlier. He looked so happy as he introduced me to his wife and two children. They had just received their keys for a new house in Kirkton and were looking forward to a new life.

I recalled his first visit to the house, and I remembered how my father had saved his life and how some good had come out of the carnage of the trenches and the Great War. My father died a hero, but then he had always been a hero to me.

I gave him a smile in passing.

Also by Maureen Reynolds

From the bestselling author of *Voices in the Street*

MAUREEN
REYNOLDS
McQUEEN'S
AGENCY

McQueen's Agency
RRP £9.99 – 978 1 84502 295 2

When Molly McQueen returns home after an unhappy time in Australia, she needs a new challenge. As the coronation of Queen Elizabeth II lifts the spirits of post-war Britain, Molly opens her brand new venture, McQueen's Agency. Hiring out temps to local businesses, Molly soon finds it tough going, until a lucrative job comes in which almost seems too good to be true. On her first day working for Lamont's Antiques, Molly senses that something isn't right. She's determined to get the job done, until she gets caught up in a web of intrigue and deceit that puts her life in grave danger.

A MOLLY McQUEEN MYSTERY

A mother's hope,
a daughter's secret...

Private Sorrow

MAUREEN
REYNOLDS

A Private Sorrow
RRP £9.99 – 978 1 84502 342 3

It is autumn 1954 and after the success of Molly McQueen's detective agency, she decides to add a new branch for domestic disputes. It is not long before one of the newly hired employees, Maisie, uncovers a riveting mystery by accident while visiting a client.

Vera Barton's husband Dave and young daughter Etta went missing in 1930. After Dave's body was found, everyone assumed the worst. But decades later, Molly reluctantly agrees to take up the search for the long-lost child and ends up unravelling a tale of misery and revenge, laced with family secrets and heartbreak.

www.blackandwhitepublishing.com

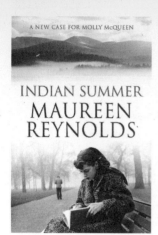

A NEW CASE FOR MOLLY McQUEEN

INDIAN SUMMER
MAUREEN
REYNOLDS

Indian Summer
RRP £9.99 – 978 1 84502 448 2

There are lots of changes happening at Molly McQueen's Agency. Biggest of all is that Molly herself must decide whether or not she should move to Australia to be with her family. If she does, it will mean the end of the Agency she has dreamed of and worked so hard to build.

Before she decides on her future, however, Molly enjoys a trip to Pitlochry Festival Theatre to see her old friend Deanna on stage. But when she goes for a walk through the hills at Killiecrankie she comes across a frightening scene. An elderly man has tumbled down a hill and has serious head injuries. As her friend goes for help, Molly stays with the man and tries to comfort him, convinced he does not have long to live. Then, unexpectedly, he hands her a pouch and tells her to 'warn them'.

Little does she know that those words and the pouch the man has given her will set in motion a chain of events leading to one of the most challenging cases of her career.

www.blackandwhitepublishing.com